Temper The Wind

by

MARY ELLEN BOYD

ISBN-10 : 1493763695
ISBN-13 : 978-1493763696

Cover design by Victoria Cooper Art

Many thanks to:

The members of the
Minneapolis Writers' Workshop,
for years of entertaining, moving, insightful books,
magazine articles, biographies, essays, homilies
and all the other bits of literature we shared. You taught me more about
the art and craft of writing than I can say,

My husband,
for listening to me moan and groan about computer problems
and being willing to shell out seemingly endless sums of money
to keep them running
even though computers are not his thing,

our son Christopher,
who was always proud of his mom
despite my almost never letting him read
what I wrote until he got older,

Julie,
for letting me bounce story plots off her whenever I had her bottled,
a captive audience, in her own car
and she couldn't get away,
and for all the years of auctions we enjoyed together,

and Ruthia,
who shares my passion for books,
and has done more to help me than I can count,
letting me use her computer when mine didn't work,
with programs I didn't have access to otherwise,
editing book after book after book for me
and not being afraid to be honest.

How many rough plot edges, typos, character glitches,
and other author mistakes
did you save me from airing to the world?

Deuteronomy 21: 10- 13

When you go out to battle against your enemies, and Yahweh your God delivers them into your hands and you carry them away captive, and see among the captives a beautiful woman, and you are attracted to her, and desire to take her as your wife, then you shall bring her home to your house. She shall shave her head and trim her nails. She shall take off the clothing of her captivity, and shall remain in your house, and bewail her father and her mother a full month. After that you shall go in to her and be her husband, and she shall be your wife.

World English Bible

PROLOGUE

Ammon, 1173 B.C.

The rock was not large enough, but there was no time to look for anything better. She was too far from the city already, almost at the midpoint of the armies, the small separation that kept them apart. They were still far away, though, the sea of men spread out before her, swordpoints catching the sunlight at the smallest movement. Leather shields mingled with the ones made of copper and iron, those held only by the mightiest of the warriors.

The very air seemed to hold its breath as the two armies faced each other, the men of Minnith on the hill, the men of Israel in the shallow valley. Not even the armor jangled.

She could not get close enough to make out faces.

Taleh's heart hung suspended, hardly beating in terror. Somewhere in that crowd of men at the top of the hill stood her father. He did not know she was here. She wondered for a moment if her mother had missed her yet. She could not explain what drew her, why she even cared, why she wanted just one more look at him.

If only she could find a better vantage point! But the stillness oppressive in the very air held her in place, afraid to breathe.

The air exhaled on a mighty shout, and the two armies swelled and surged. Taleh did not, could not, see who moved first.

A scream of pain cut through her, the first ugly sound from the battle. Taleh bit back her own cry of horror as one scream blended with another, piercing cries that should never come from a man. Dead and dying, the men dropped, to be stepped on as the battle swept past. The blades flashed, not so brightly, and stained in red.

Taleh kept her eyes on the men of her city, hoping, praying to any god that still cared enough for her to listen, that her father would appear, whole and strong. But the armies blended into a waving mass, and the sounds were terrible, ringing in her ears, filled with pain and the crunch of men falling, dead men, more and more.

She could not see him. The scene before her blurred, but she fought the sobs. This was not the time! She would miss seeing him if she could not stop.

With sudden shock, the men were there, fighting around her, swords swinging and arrows twanging and cutting as they hit. Taleh cried out, her voice shrill above the din.

A man, a big man with a sword to match, an Israelite from the beard, glanced down. Taleh saw his eyes widen. The sword behind him ripped downward, shaking the air. She screamed again, seeing his death coming, not knowing why she warned him. He whirled away, catching the oncoming blade with his own. A red line opened on the other man, his eyes widened, and he fell at her side, spilling gore.

She shoved with her feet, back, away, against the rock, away from the man whose eyes were dead and staring, and the red pool that crept across the dry ground toward her feet.

The big man flashed a startled, questioning look down at her, but whirled and met the next blade.

And the battle moved away again, like a wave on a lake.

She stumbled to her feet, and ran, hoping her secret entrance to the city was still open.

CHAPTER 1

TALEH HUDDLED CLOSER TO THE WALL, TRYING TO STILL HER TREMBLING AND shut out the screams that grew ever louder. Ever so much closer. Did her father still live? The battle was swinging over to the other side. She could think of no other explanation for its nearness to the city. If the men of Minnith had been winning, the fighting would never have come this close. She looked at her mother, and saw the same helpless worry mirrored in her eyes.

"Mother?" Taleh whispered, even though there was no chance anyone else could hear.

"Yes, child?"

"What will happen to us if the Hebrews take the city?"

Mara said nothing for a moment. Taleh held her breath, afraid of what her mother might say, but needing to know. If she knew, maybe she could think of something to do, some way to save herself.

"Mother, what will happen?" Taleh repeated the question. "Will they kill us all? Will they . . ." her voice trailed away. She could not put the terrible thought into words.

Mara stood. Life came back to her dark eyes.

Taleh pressed against the stone wall at her back, cringing from that measuring look. The rough stone was warming from the heat of the day. Not even its thickness kept those inside cool. A stray sunbeam crept between the slats of the lattice, locked against the inevitable advance of the enemy, and threw Mara's thin features into determined lines.

When had her mother's black hair turned gray?

Mara sighed. "Did you think you could rebel against Molech and escape punishment?"

No, she had not expected to escape. She knew she tempted the gods by staying away from the sacrifices made in ever-increasing numbers as the Hebrew army drew inexorably closer. The priests of Molech said they had to assure their gods that they, in this city of Minnith, still had faith and deserved protection.

For days, Taleh had hidden in her room, or on the flat roof, anywhere to avoid going to the altars where the firstborn babies were dying and their mothers' hearts were breaking.

"Daughter, we warned you about the judgment Molech saves up for those who show disrespect. We tried to make you listen."

A knife in her heart could not have hurt as much. "Mother, the whole city is doomed! This cannot be my fault! Why would the gods punish everyone?" But her mother only shook her head. It was easier, Taleh now knew, to be disrespectful of the power of Ammon's gods when punishment was not in sight. What awful torments did Molech have in mind for her?

Chelmai burst into the room. Her face was stark. "Mother! Mother! The line has given way! What are we to do?"

Mara grabbed her eldest daughter's hand. "Chelmai, we must be prepared to beg for our lives." She pulled Chelmai into the sleeping room the two girls shared.

Taleh followed slowly. Why did her mother not show grief? If the line had been broken through, what of the men who had fought there all day? She knew her parents held little affection for each other. Few married people did. People married for wealth or for children, after all. But why did Mara not shed a single tear for her husband? Despite the trouble her father had put her through, her own heart ached and tore to know he was surely dead.

Perhaps her mother could not accept it. Perhaps she had to believe he had survived.

Standing next to the simple wooden box with leather hinges, Mara flung garments out with little regard for where they fell. "Chelmai, find your purple robe. You look magnificent in it. I have heard they do not kill women."

"They only do not kill the pretty ones," Chelmai said bitterly. "Taleh is sure to be saved." She turned and glared at her sister. Taleh was past wincing, but not past being hurt. Chelmai hated her. Was it her own fault that the gods cursed her with a face so beautiful that men stopped in the market to stare? Her looks had kept her in danger in her own city, until she could barely stand seeing herself in the mirror.

And her sister hated her for it. Little did Chelmai know she would have traded faces in a heart's beat just to be safe, her sister would not have believed it anyway.

And now her family might depend on her pleadings – and her face.

Chelmai was already undressing as Mara turned her attention to the younger girl. "Taleh, my little lamb, you have no knowledge of men at all. Perhaps one of the soldiers will be eager to be the first. You must make sure they see your face." Standing next to her own simple wooden box with leather hinges, Taleh had no chance of escape from her mother's will. Mara flung garments out with little regard for where they fell, and then Taleh heard her sigh of relief. She knew without looking which robe had been chosen.

"I knew this was in here somewhere," Mara gloated in satisfaction. "This is what you will wear. How silly of you not to have worn it before. It is so beautiful. Your father would have had his price if you had worn this when men came to offer for you. But, no, you always refused. Such a silly, stubborn girl."

Taleh listened to her mother's scolding with disbelief. What did it matter now that she had not been sold to the highest bidder as wife? If they were to escape, it made more sense to bring their ordinary clothes, not these fancy robes. Surely they did not want to attract attention on their flight, and flee she would!

Mara fluttered about some more, handing over combs, brooches, and headbands before saying, "Fine, fine. You have everything you need. Now I have myself to prepare, although . . ."

As her voice trailed off, Taleh knew with sharp pain that her mother was still herself, that fear had not snapped her mind. She also knew what her mother was thinking. Mara had been beautiful once, but that was long ago, and the years showed in the faint lines and loose skin about her face, the drooping eyelids, her thickened waist.

Taleh fought back the fear that battered her, and looked at the garment her mother thrust into her hands before she left. Woven of finest linen, it dipped low in front to accent her breasts. A richly embroidered border ran along the edge. Her mother had tucked a large gold brooch with it, to hold it together over her left shoulder. The robe was of soft yellow, a color to attract the eye like sunshine. Taleh had never worn it simply because it was designed to flatter, and she had done her best to keep herself covered these past few years.

"So, little sister," Chelmai said, her voice thick with mockery, "you finally will have to get off your little pedestal of purity. You can put it off no longer. Just think, you will not even have the satisfaction of knowing Father is happy with the price." Laughing, Chelmai flipped the edge of her robe over her shoulder, tossed her dark hair back, and left the room.

Her mocking laughter lingered behind. Chelmai's footsteps moved toward the back of the house, where the stairs were. Taleh knew she should be past letting her sister hurt her, but her heart refused to listen. Not too many years ago, Chelmai would have been the one to comfort her, but as Taleh's body had begun to mature, her sister became distant. Chelmai had been spending time at the high places then, and Taleh thought at first that seeing the terrible sacrifices had changed her, for truly who could see what went on there and remain unchanged?

Then Taleh had seen the difference in the image looking back at her from the metal mirror. She had been pleased at first with her smooth skin, the soft line of her nose, and the fine cheekbones. But with the changes had come the looks, envious from the women, something else from the men, something that frightened her and stole the pleasure from her metamorphosis. Men began coming to their home, to look and to touch with their clammy hands that pinched and humiliated, more and more as she passed from gangly child into graceful maiden.

And they offered for her. Always for her, never her sister.

Chelmai became progressively colder, for she had nothing to compare with Taleh's remarkable beauty. Her eyes were lighter in color and had no shine, her hair was brown, not strikingly black. It did not even curl. Sometimes Taleh thought Chelmai actually hated her, but she could not forget the older sister who had doted on her as a child. Now, when she needed her most, Chelmai offered no support, no kindness, nothing.

Wild noises from the street distracted her. Peeking through the lattice, she saw disjointed figures running past her house. Shrill voices echoed in the narrow street and bounced off the stone walls. "The city is taken! The battle is lost! Run! Flee while you can!"

Mara's voice joined the confusion outside, but closer, clear even above the growing din. "Taleh? Are you ready? Taleh! Answer me!"

It was too late, there was no time to look for something else. The common robe she wore was too old to withstand the rigors of a flight. Taleh stripped off the plain garment, heedless of the tearing fabric, tossed it aside, and slid on the yellow robe. She clipped on the brooch, poking her finger in her haste, and flung the edge with its heavy embroidery over her shoulder. With shaking hands, she jerked the braided headband over her forehead.

She had no sooner finished than her mother appeared in the doorway, her terror as obvious as if it were a cape wrapped around her. Chelmai stood behind, dragged there only because of Mara's tight grip on her wrist, looking more sullen than scared. Mara held out her free hand to Taleh.

"There is no more time. The soldiers are everywhere. They are killing almost everyone, but some have been spared. I will go out and plead with them for our lives. Both of you must remain here. I will come for you if it is safe."

Taleh watched, horrified, as her strong mother began to weep. Mara released Chelmai's hand and moved across the room to her daughter as in a daze. "My beautiful child," she sobbed, "my baby girl. I would have spared you this fate if I could have."

Over her mother's shoulder, Taleh saw Chelmai still in the doorway, ignored, and the familiar guilt twisted through her again.

Heedless, Mara cradled Taleh's face in her hands, controlling herself with difficulty. "If I do not come back, you must find a way to hide until the soldiers have gone. Take your father's gold with you, and leave the city. Go at night. Go east, to the morning sun. There are cities that have not been touched."

One fierce hug and then Mara left her, crossing the room with a heavy tread, all light extinguished from her eyes. At the room's entrance, she wrapped Chelmai in her arms, kissing her cheeks and stroking her hair. Then she was gone, leaving behind only the sound of her footsteps on the stairs. Tears ran down Taleh's cheeks. When had she started to cry? The sound of her sobs surprised her, for surely all her feelings were gone, frozen with fear, lost in the creeping darkness.

"Weep all you like," Chelmai said, cutting through the misery with bitter words. "It will do you no good. I refuse to stay here and wait. Mother said that they were sparing some, or were you not listening? If you wish to leave, you will have to save yourself. Do not look to me for help. I owe you nothing." Her eyes were as bitter as her words.

Taleh was alone.

Terror goaded her into action. She knew that her mother would not be back for her. She looked frantically around the room. It sat toward the front of the house, closest to the sounds and smells of the battle. A small path ran along the back, away from the street, but the only way to get there was out the front door and along the house. That way would be certain suicide.

The sounds of many feet coming up the street told her she was too late. Heavy feet marching with purpose, male feet. Deep voices, saying, "Check every house, men!" "I have someone here!" "Stop them! Do not let them get away!" Terrible ripping sounds, dying screams. Metal on wood. More screams. And a sickening smell that slid heavily through the air coming in the lattice slats.

She looked frantically around the room, and saw the disarray, the clothes scattered carelessly about. It looked as though a mighty wind had swept through, or . . . or marauding soldiers.

There was only time to hide.

CHAPTER 2

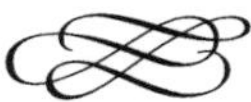

JAVAN LEANED ON HIS SPEAR AND CAUGHT HIS BREATH. HE HURT IN EVERY bone. The fighting had been fierce, but his men had acquitted themselves well. The field outside the city was littered with bodies, bodies and blood. God be praised, most of it was from the other side. He raised his head to look at the city that nestled on the hill in front of him. They still had to enter it.

He dreaded this part. It had to be done, he could see that, but it was much easier to kill a man who was armed than to devastate a city.

A tall outcropping of stone on the edge of the hill caught his eye. The hair on the back of his neck prickled as he recognized what it was.

A heavy hand clapped his shoulder, making him start.

"Do you see it, too?" a deep, familiar voice asked.

"Yes, Jephthah, I do," he replied, turning to his commander. The man was big, heavily muscled and imposing. Yet about him there was an odd warmth, an instinctive impression of trustworthiness. Jephthah had given him hope after his father's farm had been ruined by the Ammonites, the sheep and cattle stolen, the crops burned. Not even the fences had been left. He had been seventeen then, suddenly without home or family or work. There were so many of them, men without hope, men who had lost all that mattered. Until Jephthah. He had taken them with him, displaced himself because of the jealousy of his own brothers, and they had gone to Tob. More followed, as the attacks continued. There they trained, building an army and dreams of the future. When the men of Gilead, Javan's home territory, had called Jephthah to fight their battles, they had agreed, knowing that in return they would have their lands again, their homes. And there would be time when this was all over for wives and children.

Right now there was work to do.

Jephthah met his eyes evenly. "Will you do it?"

"Yes. I will. But I must tell you, Jephthah, I am so tired of seeing these little bones. I have always wanted a family, sons for my name. Every time I see one of those altars, I feel sick inside."

Jephthah's eyes softened into those of a father. "I know, Javan. I know. It tears at me, too. Just remember when you get into the city – these people are the ones who did that. Do not stay your hand."

Javan smiled grimly at his commander, and whistled for his men.

Javan puffed for air as he neared the top of the hill. Dread, not effort, sucked at his lungs. He had walked up one too many, seen the leering visages that watched over the sacrifices mock his attempts to wipe out what happened there.

He hated them, the carved stone, the altar filled with bones of murdered babies, the people who could do this.

He looked up at the ugly faces carved in the huge stones. The menace in the frozen expressions sent strange prickles down his spine. The sun stabbed at his eyes as he walked around the rock pillars. He winced at its brightness in a place so profane.

His men gathered around and Javan saw his own thoughts on their faces. He gave the orders tersely, turning away deliberately from the faces on the stones. His men could smash the stone pillars and crush those hideous countenances to dust. He wanted to destroy the altar himself.

Deep inside, he found the cold separateness that served him well at these times, that let him look into the face of such evil and remain untouched. He strode over to the altar, tightened his grip on the iron war club, and raised it for the first blow.

Something caught his eye.

He leaned in to look.

The little body had not fallen down the slope of the altar. The blow that killed it prior to being placed here for burning was clearly visible. But it was so tiny – barely newborn. A boy – someone's son. Javan whirled away. The coldness vanished before his grief and horror.

He vomited on the stone platform where he stood.

He lifted his head, wiping his mouth on the back of his hand. His men stopped their work to stare at him, even though he was not the first to give in like that in these abominations.

"We must dig a grave," he said simply, and picked up one of the metal implements that rested against the altar. The hard soil gave way reluctantly as he scraped a hole for the tiny body. Walking back to the altar, he used the improvised spade to carefully peel the infant from the altar. Out of the corner of his eye, he saw several of his men promptly vomit, just as he had done.

He lay the baby carefully into the hastily scratched grave and covered it. There should be words said, but he could not find them.

He turned back to the altar. His men stripped off their swords, shields and spears, and joined him with only their heavy war clubs. The metal heads caught the light as they all with one accord raised them. At Javan's nod, the clubs came down, and the altar shuddered, then crumbled under their rage.

Not long after, Javan and his men entered the city through the closest gate. Jephthah had already breached the primary entrance to the city, the large gate on the far side. This smaller one was used mainly to get out to the high place for sacrifice. Javan knew many would come this way, trusting in their gods to protect them as they fled the push of soldiers coming through the main gate.

For many blocks, Javan and his men cut down the panicked people of Minnith, spurred on by the memory of the terrible sight at the altar of death. As the city fell under Jephthah, there was less and less resistance, then none. He finally held up his arm and stopped his men.

"Enough! It is time to begin the search. Half of you will start from here and return to the gate. Check every house as you go. You may take plunder. Most of their wealth came at our expense, so it is ours. So says Jephthah. Remember the rules of the Law."

Javan divided his men into groups, and sent them off just as teams from Jephthah's main force turned the corner onto the street where he stood. Acknowledging their presence, Javan called out, "We will start here." The chieftain waved back, his voice caught up in the din around them. Javan stepped over to the nearest house.

The thick wooden door was closed. Javan tugged on the bolt by reflex.

It moved.

Why was it not locked against the invaders? Perhaps the owners had fled and locking it would be a perilous waste of time. He shrugged. He would probably never know.

The door swung inward, moving silently on its pivots. The large house was quiet, with no sign of an occupant. An open courtyard greeted him as he entered. Doorways stood agape in the walls on either side, and an opening directly opposite showed a stairway leading up to the second floor. Looking above, making no move toward the middle of the room, he continued his survey. A railing above ran the length of both sides of the house, guarding the edge of a balcony. From the railing one could look down upon the courtyard where he stood, but it was made of wooden slats, poor cover, and no one lay in wait. He could see more rooms on the second floor, presumably sleeping chambers, and the upper end of the stairs. The wall that hid the middle of the stairway could also hide an attacker, but the stillness was so complete, he believed it deserted.

He looked at the furniture, chairs of polished wood, low couches, richly embroidered pillows big enough to sit on, and fancifully shaped oil lamps. Through the open doorways on either side, he saw more evidence of wealth.

There was still no sign that anyone hid here. He motioned his men in, and crept cautiously across the room toward the concealed stairway. The floor, like the walls, was of stone, and his footsteps echoed back to him.

Still no one appeared, and he spared a thought for the rest of his men, moving cautiously through other houses, expecting death around every corner. He turned to the men who followed him in.

"We must not be careless." He kept his voice low. "Let us be sure the house is empty before we turn our attention to the spoils. We would not like to have a knife in our ribs because we were greedy. I will go upstairs. You search the rooms on this floor. If you find any foodstuffs, take them. We will need food for the march home."

The men nodded and moved slowly through the open doorways, weapons ready.

His shield in place and his sword in hand, Javan swung around the wall that hid the stairway. It was empty. He eased quietly up the stairs, swung around the opening at the top, and moved down the passage to the front part of the house, passing each doorway carefully. No one burst out to challenge him, and he relaxed slightly when he reached the far room. He spared a quick glance at his men below, their caution mimicking his own.

The room before him was obviously a woman's. A hint of myrrh floated lightly on the air. Combs and hair ornaments lay on small tables alongside two highly polished copper mirrors. Women's robes of all colors were tossed about, silent testimony to the speed with which the dwellers fled. In one corner, pallets had been rolled up and shoved out of the way. But it was strange, he realized as his war-sharpened eyes went back to the pile. How many pallets would it take to make a pile that size?

He tightened his grip on the sword as he crept noiselessly across the wooden floor. Using the tip of the sword, he gently lifted the coverings.

A scream of terror echoed through the room and down to his men. Javan's sword swung up to strike.

THE YOUNG WOMAN huddled under the pile saw only the blade. She did not even realize she was screaming as her death was poised above her.

CHAPTER 3

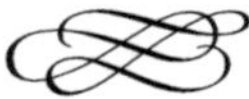

THE VISION OF HER BLOOD STAINING THE WALLS SMOTHERED HIM. THAT HE had been able to check his swing in time amazed him. He could not move. He could not lower his sword. His lungs hurt from the breath stopped up in them.

The young woman before him was the most beautiful creature he had ever seen. Every feature of her face was delicate. Her cheekbones were high, giving definition to the fine bones. Her nose was straight, her skin golden, her hair black as night and long, falling around her shoulders and down her back in gentle waves. Her eyes were as dark as her hair, and large in her fragile face.

After her first screams faded, she made no further sounds, no movement at all, just stared up at him in fear.

Javan's men burst into the room, and he whirled to face them, his sword still poised to strike. For an instant, uneasy silence prevailed. Javan lowered the sword but did not move away, blocking her from their sight. Possessiveness gripped him like a fever as he said fiercely, "She is mine."

The Law said he could, even permitted marriage, so long as the woman was untouched.

The men slowly left the room, casting odd glances as they went. Alone with her again, Javan sheathed his sword and knelt beside her. A sudden image of her rose in his mind, frail and tired in slave's garb, hair cut short to announce her status as she served at his table, and he felt uneasy. Something was wrong, but he did not know what it could be.

"Are you a virgin?"

WHATEVER ANSWER SHE GAVE, it could hardly matter now. Afraid to look at him, and yet too frightened to look away, Taleh nodded.

"What is your name?" She noticed the suggestion of an accent, a little shift at the end of his words.

"Taleh."

"Well, Taleh, my name is Javan. I claim you as my prisoner. You will be put with the other captives and taken to Gilead, where my home is . . . where it will be. When we get there, we will see what will become of you. Until then, if anyone – anyone at all – asks, you must tell them that you belong to Javan. Do you understand?"

She nodded, hoping he did not see her surprise. During those few moments she had stolen to hide herself, she had prayed fervently to all the gods of Ammon to protect her, to let her end be quick and painless, but had not placed any hope on having those prayers answered. The gods of Ammon did not deal well with the women who believed in them under the best of conditions, and she had not been obedient recently.

This was not how it was done. She had heard the Ammonite men tell their stories. She tried not to listen to such tales, for she did not want to know of all the different ways to make people die.

Would he get angry if she returned his survey? She lifted her eyes to his and saw a smile in them. He was still on one knee in front of her, so she could not tell his height, but he seemed to take up a lot of space. His eyes were a warm brown, and his hair, too, was dark, and curly with sweat.

He had a strong, masculine face. Thick eyebrows, slightly darker than his hair, emphasized the power in his unblinking gaze. A beard that must have once been neatly trimmed did little to hide his well-formed jaw. His forehead was high, shiny with sweat and dotted with splashes of blood. More brown dotted his straight, thin nose.

Although the beard could have hidden them, Taleh saw no smile lines, nothing to soften his face. Had he come to her dressed as a common man, Taleh would have known just by looking at his face that he was in disguise. There was too much *living* in it, a concentration of power held in check, to ever be ordinary.

She pulled her gaze away from his face, and some undisciplined part of her wondered how old he was. His hair had no gray, but his expression held too much sadness and experience for him to be young. His body was not the slender, rangy one of a young man. He had broad shoulders, well-muscled. His arms were massive, and a brief vision of what they could have done to her with that sword made her shudder. His coat of mail she avoided, for she could not bear to wonder whose blood coated the metal-encrusted strips of leather that so thoroughly covered his chest.

The soldier – Javan, he said his name was – suddenly stood up, and towered over her as he did so. He held out his hand to her. She looked at it, and back up at his hard face, and after a long hesitation she tentatively put her own in his. His big hand dwarfed hers, and she had to stifle a shudder. He pulled her to her feet. She found herself a mere handsbreadth from his chest and the leather breastplate. The smell of the blood assaulted her, heavy and sweet. It combined with the pungent scent of his drying sweat to overwhelm her, burning her nose. Taleh felt herself sway.

The man noticed, for her arms were grabbed even as she stiffened, willing herself not to faint. She would preserve that much of her dignity at least. Pulling herself out of his gentle grasp, she stepped back until the heavy smell of blood faded.

The soldier turned his attention to the clothes strewn about the room. He picked up a cloak of fine wool out of the pile. Despite the heat of the day, he walked over to her and slipped it around her shoulders.

"Keep this on until you are with the other women." His voice was the voice of an army commander as he gave the order, and Taleh knew that she must not disobey, despite the sweat that already trickled down her back.

He moved toward the doorway of her room, and then stopped. "Is there anything in here that you need for the journey? When we go we will burn your city, so if you need a blanket, or sandals for the walk, you must take them now."

Need? She *needed* her family. She *needed* the world that his army had invaded.

A pillow peeked out from the mess, the one stuffed with goat's hair. Her mother spent hours embroidering the covering. Taleh picked it up and held it close, hoping he would not see her tears. Her cloak would have to serve as a blanket. Who besides herself would carry whatever she took? She looked down at her bare feet. He had mentioned sandals. She found her most comfortable pair, sensing his eyes upon her while she put them on. His unrelenting gaze made her feel awkward. He must be expecting her to try to escape, she thought. In a macabre sort of way, it was almost funny. There was no place for her to go.

She would have liked to wear a different robe, but she did not want to anger this man, and she certainly was not going to change clothes in front of him. The one she wore would have to do. At least she had the cloak. She was not naïve, she knew why he had covered her, and she was not sorry to obey his wishes on the matter, despite the heat.

"I am ready." Taleh made herself walk toward him. She did not want him to have to come get her.

He nodded and drew his sword. A flash of panic gripped her before she realized it was not pointed at her. He again became a soldier, expecting the enemy to jump out from each opening. She followed him along the passage and down the stairs. The time for escape was long past. The city had been taken.

Her soldier hurried her across the courtyard. She did not know the reason for his haste until they neared the doorway and the emptiness of the room finally caught her attention. She knew when he saw the awareness on her face. He refused to allow her to look back, but shoved her ahead of him into the street and pulled the door shut with unnecessary force.

As her eyes adjusted to the glare of the lowering sun, she saw the street was filled with activity, except the people moving about were not Ammonites, and they were loading up their plundered goods on her neighbor's carts. Taleh turned her eyes away, unable to watch, but not before she recognized much of her family's own possessions.

Anger rose in her with shocking speed, burning off the numbness, and it took all her strength to control it. She focused instead on her sandaled feet, and on the angry tears that sparkled like jewels as they fell.

How long she stood silently she did not know, but finally a tall figure stopped before her. A familiar voice said gently, "You will not find living with us to be oppressive. Be grateful you still have your life."

Grateful. She could not bring herself to acknowledge his words, or even to look up at him.

JAVAN WAITED a moment for her to react. He did not like her silence or her tears. He liked the way the other men looked at her even less. She seemed fragile, as though she were about to shatter, and all of the soldiers were aware of it. He knew that, at the first sign her unnatural composure was breaking, he would be trampled by men trying to reach her first, despite his claim on her. She was worth any risk.

Looking at her more closely, Javan noticed the moisture glistening on her forehead. More tiny beads shone above her lip. The heat had to be intense under the cloak, and it concerned him. He had chosen that one because it looked to be the lightest one there, but he knew that it put additional stress on her to suffer its warmth. He considered for a fleeting moment letting her take it off, but decided against it. His men watched her too closely already, and the garment it covered was much too revealing.

A sudden thought disturbed him. What would he say if one of his men offered for her? Such a thing was only too possible. He forced down the thought, and turned deliberately to the work at hand.

TALEH HEARD NO ORDER GIVEN, but the soldiers stirring about her started down the street, surrounded by donkeys laden with goods hastily strapped upon them. More donkeys and oxen pulled carts and wagons piled with the possessions of Minnith, her family's among them. She knew the city had wealth, her own house had been filled with its share, and her anger grew at seeing it appropriated so freely.

She forced her lips to shut against the livid words that wanted to spill out of her mouth. If she said what she wanted to say, they would kill her where she stood. She did not know why, but she did not really want to die yet.

The procession of soldiers, carts and a few prisoners wound its way down the sloping streets of the city toward the valley outside the walls.

Everywhere Taleh saw the painful evidence of defeat. Their way was littered with the rejects of the soldiers' spoils. Chairs sat in perfect condition in the hard-packed street next to remnants of doors splintered with iron clubs. Cooking pots lay in heaps alongside the houses from which they evidently had been taken. Clay shards added to the clutter, remains of water jars and vessels for flour and grains.

Clothing lay scattered about the street. Some had already been piled out of the way, but more draped from windows, or peeped between still-closed lattices. She told herself the gaily colored fabrics were simply discarded, tossed aside during the search. The dust irritating her nose did not hide the scent she now knew was blood, too pungent to ignore, its stench heavy on the air.

Taleh looked, and saw the bodies of the dead.

She tore her eyes away from the houses, and the windows with their terrible sights. She kept her gaze on the ground, seeing only what lay before her feet. She felt sick, torn between anger and relief. It could be her body lying in a tangled mass. Her robe could lend grotesque gaiety to the blood-stained dirt. How could she be glad to be alive, walking meekly among the victors, when her city lay dead?

As from nowhere, Chelmai's arm appeared in Taleh's sight. She stopped, barely in time to avoid stepping on her sister. She knew, somehow she knew with absolute certainty, that she was totally alone. The pain in her heart came out in a keening cry, tearing at her throat, searing her with despair.

Falling to her knees, Taleh wept terrible sobs. She ached to take Chelmai in her arms and forgive her for the cruelty of the past years, but she could not bring herself to touch the mutilated body, all that was left of her sister. Instead, she caressed Chelmai's hair where it lay spread upon the street, rocking over the corpse as grief swallowed her up.

Strong arms came around her waist and lifted her away, letting her dangle. How dare they intrude in her personal sorrow? She screamed with rage, kicking back before the ground met her feet and skinned her heels. Angered beyond comprehension, she whirled around with both hands clenched into fists, ready, eager to inflict whatever damage she could. Before she could hit anyone, her hands were caught and held fast, and then blackness engulfed her.

CHAPTER 4

The smell of smoke greeted her, tickling her nose. Someone held a skin of water to her mouth, and she swallowed without opening her eyes. Heaviness lay around her heart and she could not remember why. She heard the sound of a multitude of people. From somewhere close by there was much weeping. She opened her eyes, only to see the face of the Hebrew soldier who had spared her life.

Her grief washed back over her, cruel in its force, and she rolled away from him, curling tightly into herself as the tears began again. She knew they were out of the city now, and wondered how she got here. Could someone have carried her? Why would the victors bother? Why not kill her beside her sister?

The wind shifted and the smoke became thicker. She recognized the difference in the smell of this smoke. It carried the stench of death, burning her nose and eyes, and she began to cough.

Apparently Javan was satisfied with her recovery, for he lifted her gently from behind, and set her onto her feet. He walked around to face her. She knew the tears had stained her face, for she could feel their drying tracks. She refused to look at him, and pointedly turned away. That was a mistake, she found, for before her lay her city, slowly surrendering to the fury of the flames that burned high into the sky. She gave in to her anger, and whirled around, striking his face with the flat of her hand.

It made a very nice sound, a solid crack that eased her pain a little.

To her surprise, he did not move toward any of the weapons hanging from his belt. In fact, she suspected the look on his face was satisfaction, but that was hardly credible. He smiled, not a taunting smile. It was gentle, almost as if he understood what she felt.

She refused to accept that, until he put her thoughts into words.

"Let your anger out. You are too small to hurt me, but I know you want to try." He turned and walked away from her, leaving her alone and aching with sadness that felt too big to fit inside her body.

She took her first good look at the people around her. She stood in a small group of young women and girls, all captives. A few of them, mostly the younger ones, carried their grief as heavily as she, but the rest were blatantly angry. Most of them had cloaks covering them, and she wrapped her arms around her reaching for her own.

It was gone! She looked down in alarm, only to see it carefully folded in a neat pile at her feet. Had the soldier done that? Had he seen how hot it made her?

Why was he being so kind to her?

Only a handful of guards stood around the frightened girls, although these were well-armed. No tents had been set up for the guards, nor any for the women. That did not surprise her, for she did not expect her captors to care about her comfort.

Except, perhaps, for Javan.

A slight distance away, she saw a group of young men. They, too, were under guard. More captives from Minnith? Why keep them separate from the women?

Unless they feared a revolt. Very wise of them.

Dusk was settling in, frustrating her survey, but she could see enough to know they would go no further this night.

Taleh turned her attention back to the women. She recognized several of them. It gave her a flash of pleasure. She did not know their names, but just to see a familiar face, even if only from the marketplace, was soothing.

Firelight flickered in the growing dark, away from the glow of the burning city. In the dim light of the faraway flames she saw forms passing to and fro. So *that* was the camp of the army!

No one could accuse them of becoming too familiar with their captives, she thought bitterly. The fickle breeze changed again, this time bringing the scent of cooking food, vague whiffs against the darker scents from the city. Taleh realized for the first time that she had not eaten all day. Would *he*, that soldier, think of bringing her food? It was one thing to spare someone from death, but quite another to treat her as an ally. No, she decided, she had better prepare herself for a hungry night.

When she picked up her cloak, her pillow tumbled out. Her sandals were there as well. She could not remember having them in her hands after she had seen Chelmai – she stifled a flinch. She would not think about that now. She could not. Perhaps tomorrow she would be able to see hope where none existed tonight.

She smiled grimly. How could tomorrow be any worse?

Still, someone had carried her pillow for her – in fact, must have carried her as well. Might they want her for a slave? She was young and healthy in spite of her frail appearance, doubtless good for many years of work.

With a sigh, she arranged herself on the ground gingerly and laid her head on the pillow. It seemed to hold her mother's scent. Wrapping her cloak tightly around her against the first chill of the coming night, she closed her eyes and waited for sleep to take her.

JAVAN STRODE THROUGH THE CAMP, trying not to let his fatigue show. This was the last city, Jephthah had promised. Tomorrow they would start for home.

Home. He wondered if there still was such a place. What waited for him? No family, no house. He did not know who still lived from so long ago. He looked around him at the sea of men, an army of the dispossessed. How many of them felt the same?

At least they would not go back empty-handed, the way they had left. In all directions, men stood around campfires, bathing their robes and armor in the water from the cisterns outside the city. The Law required purification for the taking of life. It seemed especially appropriate here in Ammon. The defilement of the land seemed to seep into every pore, polluting them with too many ugly sights, too much grief.

Blankets and robes taken as spoil lay about unused. Until they had time to wash these things, too, they would not use them. The goods felt heavy with the uncleanness that was Ammon.

Pots scrubbed earlier now bubbled with food. Rich smells of cooking meat, vegetables and garlic drifted on the air. While the men waited, they chewed on dried fruit and fresh bread, nuts and grain, and new wine. The larders of Minnith had been generous. If they were careful, the food should last them some time.

A tall man with a purposeful stride caught his attention. He walked toward the largest of the few tents set up, the same one toward which Javan headed. Javan watched the man with affection. Soldiers stood up to greet the man respectfully, and from time to time he would pause to exchange a few words.

Where would he have been without Jephthah?

Several of the men followed the commander, and Javan picked up his stride, joining them at the doorway of the tent. He looked back quickly. Jephthah had picked a spot far enough away from the rest of the camp so they could speak freely. Their words would not be overheard. He smiled at his friend as the big man ducked under the flap, and followed him inside, letting the tent flap drop behind them.

JAVAN SAT cross-legged on a rich rug, looking across at Jephthah. Between them lay a wineskin, still full, and a bowl of fruit, almost empty.

The rest of the men had gone. Javan felt safe in teasing his friend. "You have resorted to a tent now, Jephthah? Who would think it? Can it be that you have finally become as tired as the rest of us? Or are you getting old?"

"Old? Never! I just could not pass it by, even though it is much too heavy to carry any further. I will have to leave it here. It is far too large for one donkey, as I see you have already noticed. We have more than enough animals loaded down with plunder already. But it does not hurt to give our slaves something to look at, does it?"

"Perhaps not."

Jephthah's levity dropped away, and he looked at Javan with somber eyes. "So, Javan, our war is over. Do you have any questions on the route I have chosen back to Gilead? Have you wondered how our people will receive us?"

Javan's lips thinned. "We have fought their war. After releasing them from eighteen years of unrelenting attacks, I hope they will receive us well." He paused, his thoughts far away. "I have asked about my home from time to time. Every traveler, every caravan of traders that came near . . . When the Ammonites came, the whole city was destroyed. I have heard it was rebuilt. I hope there will be some in the city who will remember me." Again he hesitated, but the older man did not rush him. He waited patiently for Javan's next words. "I have learned something, Jephthah. I have learned not to underestimate this people's capacity for cruelty."

For a moment both men were silent. Javan, for his part, knew that no matter how far away he got from this land, he would never be able to forget the altars he had seen. Child sacrifice. He was not sorry to be leaving. Neither was he sorry for his part in this war.

The tent was quiet for several moments. Javan's thoughts went out to the camp of the women. *She* sat there, Ammonite, angry and beautiful. What had possessed him to spare her?

Jephthah finally spoke. "So, tell me, Javan. What other thoughts are troubling you?"

Javan looked at his commander with narrowed eyes. He had not expected him to be so quick to notice his preoccupation. Had he not hidden it well?

Jephthah grinned. "We have known each other too long. Your face gives you away." At Javan's look of chagrin, he hastened to add, "Only to me, of course."

"I want to marry a captive." Javan heard himself say the words and knew they were true. He did not know who was the more surprised.

Jephthah burst into a roar of laughter. "The truth, Javan," he finally managed to say.

Javan sat silently while his chief laughed, stunned himself at the decision his mind had made, shocked at how right it sounded. "I mean it. I know it is difficult to believe. I surprise even myself." He wondered if he dared even pray for wisdom on this decision, the pull of his heart was so strong and he knew what he wanted

Now he said, with no trace of humor, "It is true, Jephthah. I want to take a captive as wife."

Disbelief replaced the smile on Jephthah's face, and for a long breath he could not speak. At last he said, "Do you mean what you have said?"

Javan stood up, unable to sit still with the force of his thoughts. At the tent entrance, he pulled back the flap and gazed out over the camp. "I swore vengeance against this people for what they had done to me. I am all that is left of my family. I learned to hate them when I saw all the altars . . ." his voice trailed off, but he recovered himself and continued. "She was hiding under the bedrolls. I knew someone was there – it was so obvious. I cannot say what made me look first. I could have killed her." Pain and delayed fear crept past his defenses into his voice. He did not mention the moments on the battlefield. Her reasons were her own and Javan wanted to allow her that. She had lost too much already, and would lose more in the days ahead. Everything familiar.

Jephthah did not speak. Javan went on, "We passed someone she knew, probably a relative, on the way out of the city. Before that happened she was mostly afraid, but I am sure she hates all of us now, myself included. In spite of that, I find I cannot give her up."

He stopped, surprised at himself, the open flap clenched in his hand. As chief, Jephthah *had* to understand. They were friends, and Jephthah knew how much he had against the Ammonites, and how strange it was that he wanted to take one as wife. Jephthah had not wanted the men to take captives at all, much less as brides, but the Law said it could be done and Jephthah would never go against the Law.

How grateful he was for that Law.

The camp of the women was too far away, and he could not see her, but the guards were still there, their clothes light patches against the darkness, the city's fading glow casting sparkles off their armor, and so she was there, too. He wanted to look at her again, to ensure himself that she was real, to see if she still drew him. With a sigh, he dropped the tent flap and turned back to face Jephthah. "Well?"

"It is the Law. If she is pure, you are free to marry her. She must be beautiful to have this effect on you." Jephthah's voice was devoid of emotion. Javan knew the struggle his friend had not to argue with him. Somberly, Jephthah went on, "Javan, you do know the rules for captive brides, do you not?"

"Yes, I know. I cannot know how she will react, though. Shaving her head, her hair . . . I never gave it a thought before. She will fight that, I am sure."

"There is more to it than that, Javan." Impatience crept past Jephthah's control. "The hair will grow back. It is you I worry about. She is a worshipper of the Baals. Who can know what beliefs she will want to keep? Can you prevent that from corrupting your household? Those very altars you hate so much, she is a part of that. Can you keep your faith when you want to please her? If the fields go dry and she wants to beg Baal for rain, what will you do?"

"I will tell her the rains come from God."

"She will no doubt agree with you." Jephthah leaned forward. "But which god, yours or hers?" He took a breath, not long enough for Javan to reply. "Also, you do know that for a lunar month, you cannot claim your rights. You know that? You accept that?"

"Yes."

"You say that as if it was easy. I can only make you aware of your responsibility." Jephthah's eyebrows came down in a scowl. "As long as you know and abide by the rules of the Law, you may have her. But I am surprised."

Javan watched Jephthah struggle not to change his mind. He could almost feel the 'no' hovering on his friend's lips. When nothing more came, he sat down, limp with relief. "Thank you, my lord."

"Know this, Javan. I do not like this. You know my reasons as well as I do. Do not make me regret this."

CHAPTER 5

TALEH WOKE TO THE SUN SHINING IN HER FACE. HER BODY WAS STIFF AND sore, which surprised her. She felt disoriented, as if something was not quite right. It had all been a bad dream, had it not?

A shadow fell across her still-closed eyes, and then she knew. No, this was no dream. The grief that had haunted her sleep washed over her, and she rolled onto her belly, moaning with the pain of her sobs. The shadow never moved. She could feel it beside her, a patch of coolness in the early glare, and knew without looking who it was. That made it even worse. What did he expect, gratitude for leaving her alive to live with her loss? Today there was no room for appreciation, not even for her life.

Agony threatened to tear her heart in two.

JAVAN STOOD without moving for a long time, as the young woman sobbed. Even though he expected a reaction like that, it did not make it easier to watch. He did not know what to say, how to begin working around her grief and rage. Right now he had to get her up and fed. The army was preparing to leave. They were done here, and they were going home – to his home – but the captives would be leaving their own land behind.

He knelt beside his captive, and gently put a hand on her shoulder. Her reaction was immediate and furious, her hand aimed to catch him full across the face. All his soldier instincts came into play, a quick twist, a pull, and she tumbled onto her back, staring wide-eyed and livid into his face.

"I am a soldier. You should have known better than that," he said. "I intend you no further harm, but you must cooperate. If you insist on being difficult, I will have to restrain you. I would rather not have to do so. Make no mistake – if I must, I will." He motioned to a small bag laying on the ground. "I have brought you some food. You must be hungry by now. You had nothing to eat yesterday. Whatever you may think of us, we do not intend to starve you."

TO HER SHOCK, he smiled at her, a warm smile, full of some secret humor.

She wanted to refuse, to throw the food back into his face, but her hunger got the better of her. She pushed herself into a sitting position, and picked up the bag, ignoring him. He, however, seemed to have no intention of being ignored and took the bag from her hands gently.

"It opens like so," he said, and the bag lay flat on the ground, full of dried fruit, bread, and some well-cooked meat. A flask lay on its side, and when she opened it, she smelled sweet wine. The soldier spread himself on the ground, propped his head on one hand, and watched her. Refusing to be cowed, she began to eat. The soldier watched her a little longer, and then spoke.

"Do you remember my name?"

She nodded.

He persisted. "What is it?"

"Javan," she ground out. She did not particularly want to be manipulated into polite conversation.

"You are Taleh. I remembered as well." He looked smug and Taleh's hand itched to take another swing. He was quiet for another moment. She ate silently, refusing to look at him. Gentle fingers lifted her chin, and she met his eyes reluctantly.

They were filled with concern. He took a deep breath, as though to brace himself, and then asked, "The woman on the street – who was she to you?"

Taleh went cold inside, the memory came too quickly, borne on waves of grief and desolation. The fingers on her chin tightened and held her fast. She spat the answer at him. "She was my sister."

Everything about him changed, his eyes, the feel of his hands, even his posture, as though the wounding was done to him and not to her at all. He said softly, "I am sorry."

"That will not give her back!"

"No," he agreed. His voice was kind again, his eyes sad as he watched her. She blinked in surprise. Surely a soldier did not care who he killed. He let go of her then, and she looked down at the food on the cloth. She was no longer hungry. He seemed to understand, for he reached over and tied the bag again.

He got to his feet. In spite of herself she marveled at the grace and power he exuded. In the early morning light, his skin glowed gold. Thick veins lined his hands and forearms, springing to life and subsiding as he moved. His eyes were not as dark as she had thought. Lighter tones flecked the brown. He had bathed recently. All the blood was gone, even off his armor. His hair looked soft, the brown shimmering and shifting with each movement of his head.

What a handsome man he was.

The thought appalled her. How dare she think such a thing?

He reached down to help her rise, but some spark of perversity flared within her and she turned away. He would have none of that, though, and grasped her around her waist, lifting her easily to her feet. "Are you testing me? Have you no care for the value of your life? We are moving out now, and you will go with the rest of the women. Do not give us any trouble, and I will not have you bound."

There was more than a threat in his voice. Taleh did not want to test him further. "I understand," she said with a meekness that was more real than feigned.

"Good. Get with them, then," was all he said, and he moved away. She looked down at her feet, and saw the foodbag still there. He had left the food with her. She stared at it, then picked it up, along with the rest of her belongings.

Armed soldiers again surrounded the women, who made a sorry group. None had more than the clothes on her back, a small bag of food if she was lucky, and something to cover them from the night's chill, even if only a blanket. The women looked lost and quite afraid. Did they see the same when they looked at her?

She could not see the group of captured boys.

An order was shouted from somewhere ahead, and the army began to move, an ungainly procession. Along with the large army of men, she saw vast herds of cattle, as well as sheep and goats, being prodded into reluctant movement. Their deep lowing blended with the higher bleats of the flocks in a chorus of protest, one with which Taleh felt a strange sympathy. They did not want to leave either.

Here and there, a camel plodded, its hump bobbing in a sea of animals and men. The whole valley looked as though it had suddenly come to life. Her gaze passed over the city, the last of the flames burning among piles of rubble, all that was left of the place of her birth. She felt beaten and alone as she trudged along with the others, and the soft sounds of weeping from the other women mingled with her own tears.

THE ARMY MOVED SLOWLY through the gently rolling plateau. Taleh sweated under the hot sun. She removed her cloak, tying it awkwardly around her waist, risking burn rather than continue smothering under it. She saw the other women doing the same. The bright colors of the gowns they had worn in hopes of saving their lives made an odd contrast to their drawn, grief-stricken faces. The soldiers seemed oblivious to their plight. Taleh's feet kept moving, step after step, until she felt she had been walking forever. Everything was sore, not just her feet. Her back felt as if it would break in half.

Midday came, and the army halted, covering a vast area of the Ammonite countryside. The men settled down on the ground for a meal. Some of them stretched out, catching a few minutes of rest while they were able, for someone had to stand guard during the night.

It was so hot, and she was so hungry. What little food she had had was gone, in stolen bites as they walked. She sank onto the ground, her misused muscles hampering her movements.

Javan, she wished his name would vanish from her mind but it was stuck like a burr, moved through the captives. She saw him coming and pretended he was not there, but he would not leave. Without care whether or not she even wanted his company, he knelt on the hard ground. She did her best to ignore him, but he reached out and touched her face. She jerked away, nearly toppling over onto the ground but he held her arm with one giant hand, his grip without pain but without give, and turned her head with his other until there was no choice but to look at him.

"There is plenty of time later to tell me what you think of me and my people." He reached into his own food pouch, pulled out a bit of the circular puffy leavened bread, clearly stolen from someone's table, tore off a piece and held it out to her. "I suggest you enjoy it while we have it. We will be eating unleavened bread soon enough."

Reaching for the bread gave her a chance to look at something other than him. She took the piece and ate awkwardly, feeling his gaze on her. The look in his eyes made her slightly uncomfortable, as though he knew something she did not but should. She stole glances at him while he fed her. His face had faint lines in it, traces his life had left. Few came from smiles. He was so big, so strong, the kind of man that had always frightened her, yet, in spite of his size and profession, he had been nothing but gentle with her. When would that change?

What kind of man was he? Her anger did not impress him, she stood no chance of hurting him physically, there was nothing left for her if she were to try to escape back to her city, every step brought her closer to his own land, and worst of all, he showed no signs of letting up in his pursuit.

Javan pulled back the food pouch and tied it. "Perhaps eventually you will see I am no threat to you."

She could not let that pass. "You killed my family."

Was it her imagination, or did he stiffen slightly? "The war is over."

"Not for me. It will never be over for me!" Tears began again, unbidden, harsh, gasping sobs that barely dented her anguish and fury. The soldier pulled her to her feet, and to her horror, wrapped her in his arms. Frantic, she wrenched herself away.

He let her go. She lost her balance and fell heavily onto the hard ground, wincing as she landed. She ignored his outstretched hand, getting to her feet without assistance despite the screaming of her abused muscles.

He watched her silently, then scooped up his food pouch and wineskin, now severely depleted. "Very well. I concede this bout, but be warned you have not seen the last of me."

TALEH WAS ready to give up any pretense of dignity. She had never been in such pain. The other captives echoed her distress. Grumbling grew about her. Irritation at the soldiers increased with every step. How dare they act as though this was a pleasant stroll? Did the Israelite soldiers think everyone was equal to a journey on foot without a rest? If not for the wariness she caught in their sharp eyes whenever one would chance to look her way, and the heavy weapons none put aside, Taleh would have thought they had no cares. Laughter drifted on the air from time to time, and the sound hit her like a blow.

The heat was frightening, making the baked ground shimmer and waver in the distance. The soil was hard from the force of the summer sun. Few trees broke the monotony of the landscape, and the grasses were brown and dry. They poked their sharp edges through the gaps in Taleh's sandals, adding their own discomfort to the grit and sand trapped under her feet. The leather soles abraded her sore skin.

The land rolled in seemingly endless waves. The shallow hills and valleys were misleading, she thought bitterly. The first few had been easy enough, but as the journey continued, it became harder and harder to pace herself going down the depressions. Her legs trembled with the effort to drag her up the other side.

Only the fact that there was no evidence of a flatter route kept her from accusing the soldiers of torturing them deliberately.

Taleh's eyes joined the rest of her body in its rebellion, for it looked like they were nearing a city. Colors fluttered against the horizon, and she blinked to clear her vision. When she opened her eyes, the colors were still there.

Was it a city? Sudden excitement flared within her. Perhaps there would be a way of escape. Her feet felt lighter, and eagerness lifted her spirits.

As they neared the swelling mass of humanity, Taleh's hopes dashed to the ground. Hebrew soldiers stood firmly, watching over a huddled group of more Ammonite captives. The army of soldiers divided, and flowed around the waiting assemblage. Taleh's own group merged with the seated captives. Only then did she see the ropes binding them one to another, wrists tied tightly behind them. Was this to be her fate?

Soldiers took up positions around the captives, as several well-armed men entered their little enclave. Taleh watched them approach, and fought panic. If they came for her, she resolved she would not die quietly. She had not come all this way, enduring heat, heartache and pain, to be dispatched in the wilderness!

The men with the terrifying weapons merely went about releasing the bonds of the restrained captives. *Please,* Taleh thought, *make no foolish moves.* As though they heard her, the newly loosed prisoners sat quietly.

One of the men raised his voice. "Do not take this sign of our compassion as weakness. We will tolerate no revolt. Any attempts to escape will be met with death. Accept your fate, and you will be well-treated. Do you understand?"

His powerful voice reached to the outer edges of the camp of captives and beyond, to the soldiers milling about. Taleh looked around her, seeing her own emotions mirrored on the faces on all sides. Anger, sorrow, acceptance. Defeat. She was hot, thirsty, hungry, tired and dirty. She had nothing to eat or drink, no way to take a bath, but she still had her pillow, wrapped in the cloak tied around her waist. Even if she met none of her other needs, she could sleep, and for the moment that was enough.

She untied her cloak, and the sudden touch of air on the sweaty fabric at her waist felt cool. The pillow was safely inside, making a lump in the folds to announce its precious presence. Sinking stiffly onto the baked earth, Taleh unrolled the bundle and pulled the pillow out. She spread open her cloak and improvised a bed. Lying down, her head cushioned on her mother's pillow, she idly watched her fellow captives through half-closed eyes.

Something shiny caught the sun.

Even as her mind registered what it was, some inner sense told her to lie still, to pretend to sleep. Had she flinched in the first shock of awareness? Her breathing was too fast, her heart beat too loudly. Frightened, she counted each breath in her head, measuring them, hoping no one would see her effort.

They were so close! Surely they would look down and *know*!

"You have it?" a voice asked in a hushed whisper. "How did you manage?"

There was a short silence, or if the question was answered she did not hear it. Taleh remained motionless. The dust drifted onto her cloak, tickling her nose, but she could not allow herself to give in to the urge to sneeze. She opened her mouth a crack, breathing through it instead, and the urge passed. As she expected, the conversation resumed. She soon lost track of who was speaking.

"What good will one dagger serve?"

"What makes you think this is all we have?"

"How many *do* you have?"

"Enough. We do not yet know who we can trust. When we are sure of those who are for us, we will make plans."

"We cannot wait too long. We still have to make our way back. If we hesitate, we will find ourselves out of Ammon. Who will there be to help us then?"

"It is too soon." This was said with authority. The owner of the voice must be the leader of the revolt. Taleh kept her eyes shut. She did not want to know who it was. The voice went on, "We must wait until they let down their guard. While we wait, try to determine who might be willing to join us – but carefully! And do not approach any of the women who are visited by soldiers. We know we cannot trust them."

A sick feeling held Taleh immobile while the group moved away. She was one of the women being visited by a soldier. What did they plan for those like her? How had they managed to conceal daggers? Did they think to take on the whole army? Or just those foolish or daring enough to venture into the camp of women?

She concentrated on holding her body loosely, mimicking sleep, while her mind whirled. Would Javan's presence cost his life, or her own?

Which danger was the worst, having her fellow captives, whom she now knew to be armed to some degree, think her a traitor? Or saying nothing and letting Javan and the others walk into a trap? Would she be killed with the rebels? For they would be killed, of that she had no doubt. She wanted no part of such folly.

She hoped Javan would stay away.

Someone stopped at her side, and she flinched before she could stop herself. At the touch of a hand on her shoulder, she reluctantly opened her eyes, pretending they pulled her from sleep.

A young woman about her own age knelt beside her. Taleh looked at her and waited. Unlike her own heavy waves, this one had hair as straight as an arrow, and warm brown to Taleh's black. Her eyes were not dark as midnight like Taleh's own, but light, green and gold blended together. Her face was oddly free of the ravages of grief. The sun had left its red trace across her tilted nose and the smooth skin of her forehead. She was very pretty, with the kind of inner sparkle that attracted men.

At the sight of her vivacious face, Taleh's fear lifted a little.

She smiled guilelessly and handed Taleh a waterskin. Water still dripped off the bulging sides.

"We are near a well," the young woman said. "You had better drink your fill now, for we will be moving on soon."

Taleh smiled back. "Thank you. This is very kind." She took a few swallows and took a risk. "My name is Taleh. You are the first person to talk to me. Other than the soldiers, of course."

"Of course." The other woman smiled a knowing smile. "My name is Merab. You have a soldier who has chosen you. I, too, have been chosen." Merab's face glowed with pleasure. She certainly was not suffering the same torn loyalties as Taleh. Taleh wanted to be ignored by her captors. Merab obviously found the attention exciting.

"I will not be a slave," Merab continued, openly boastful. "I will be married. Is it not wonderful?"

Taleh choked on the water she was swallowing. When her throat was clear, she asked frantically, "Who told you this?"

"The soldier who chose me. Some will be slaves, naturally, but the women the soldiers come to, I assure you, they are all to be wives."

Taleh could not think. "That is not true! It cannot be true."

"You do not believe me?" Merab drew up in offended pride.

"No! No, that is not what I meant." Taleh did not know how to explain. "I believe your soldier told you that. It is just that . . . I think . . . you see, I am to be a slave. I know the soldier will not stay away, but he has not mentioned marriage."

Merab smiled the superior smile Chelmai had used when she wanted to gloat. "You will know soon enough that I am right. I will come back, and we can talk more later." With a conspiratorial wink, she walked off into the milling crowd.

Had Merab told the truth, or was she lying? However unlikely it seemed, was she part of the revolt? Were they trying to search out her loyalties? Or was Merab no more than what she appeared, a young woman pretty enough to catch the eye of a soldier, and clever enough to see the advantages in it?

CHAPTER 6

JAVAN STOOD OVER HIS WOMAN, COMPASSION WARRING WITH DUTY. Moonlight outlined her slender form in its blue glow, giving her the ethereal appearance of a night's dream. Her dark hair spilled over the pillow and onto the dusty ground, but it made little difference in the amount of dirt coating the long strands. Her face was drawn with exhaustion, and caked with sweat and grime. She had fallen asleep without eating, he knew, for he was the one with the food.

They had encamped near a large cistern, cut deep into the rock. Steps led down to the water so well protected beneath the ground. The waterskins had been refilled before the soldiers had gone below to bathe in shifts.

Now the captives got their turn. It was several days' march until the next cistern this size, where the women would again be able to bathe in private. Javan knew if Taleh were to miss out on the chance to be clean, her feminine vanity would be injured, and he had a compulsion to show her he would be kind to her. Perhaps it would make things easier when they got to Gilead. He had no desire to sleep with one eye open in his own house.

He knelt beside her, and gently shook her shoulder, holding it longer than he needed to. "Taleh? Taleh, wake up."

Someone kept saying her name. Taleh struggled awake. She opened her eyes and looked up into the face of her soldier. Alarmed, she sat up abruptly, heart pounding, looking about her in fright. He should not have come! He was placing both of them in danger. Even the darkness could not shield them.

Javan gave her an odd look. Too late, she knew she had made her fear all too visible, but he asked no questions. "I did not mean to frighten you. I only brought food. When you are done, there is a cistern near here in which you can bathe. It is deep enough and no one will disturb you."

Taleh willed her heart to slow. The trap grew tighter, pinning her between her loyalty to her people and her fear of the repercussions waiting for the rebels. Her life now was not much, but it was life. She had seen too much death, she did not want to give it up easily.

He was offering her a bath. She had never been this dirty in her life. Her face felt stiff with dirt and sweat, her ankles and feet were brown with dust and sand, and as a final embarrassment, she could smell herself. If this was her only chance to wash, she would gladly miss out on sleep for it.

She moved to rise and every muscle screamed with pain, bursting out between her lips. "Ohhh!" Even the thought of effort hurt.

"Come with me." His voice was quiet and calming. He handed her a piece of bread. "The cistern is not far. I will return to watch your things."

She nodded, and took a bite. Taking the lead, he guided her through the vast camp. His leather belt creaked against the weight of the weapons it held.

Taleh did not see the cistern until they were nearly upon it. Only the swell in the ground gave away its location. Javan stopped to get a pottery hand lamp, absurdly delicate in his large hand, the flame dancing at the end of the tip, from one of the soldiers standing guard nearby, and handed it to her. She brushed the crumbs off her hands and took it. Oil splashed in the bottom, oil no doubt stolen from someone's house. The lamp, as well, and she felt her face wrinkle in an angry scowl.

"Do not worry about the men. No one will disturb you." She turned her scowl on him and Javan grinned. Grinned! What was it about this man –

aside from being one of the victors – that made him so quick to smile? "You are almost the last one to bathe. Have you heard any screams?"

Still provoked, she retorted, "I have been sleeping."

He gave an impatient shake of the head. "You will see. Go down there. Take your bath. I promise, you will be safe. Can you find your way back, or shall I come for you? It is dark."

"I can find my way," Taleh responded a little sharply. "All I need to do is look for the guards."

Javan nodded, refusing to be baited. "The camp of the women is well marked. Very well. I will stay by your supplies."

By her tiny pile of things, hardly worth such a guard. And he was taking a risk at that, but she could not tell him so.

"I will watch for you, in case you become lost. I will not allow harm to come to you."

Taleh looked at him in surprise. She could not honestly fault him for his care of her until now, but these words carried the weight of a vow. Was Merab right? Were more of the soldiers taking women as wives? No one would make such a promise to a slave, would they?

Confusion seemed to be her normal state in the last day, that and grief. Taleh turned away, carefully picking her way down the rocky embankment. Steps had been cut into the walls of a natural cave, leading down to an underground pool. The rock stairs were wet from the bathers who had gone before, and she went down slowly, holding the lamp aloft to make the most of its light. Sounds echoed up to her, bouncing off the curved walls, women enjoying themselves. Laughter rippled through their voices. For this brief time, they could forget.

Torches had been placed in holders to light the way down. In the heavy dark of night and the oppressive dark of the cavern, they provided eerie patches of flickering brightness that the blackness quickly swallowed up until the next glow appeared. When she got to the bottom, she saw that the water level in the cistern was low enough to permit her to walk out onto the cave floor. The rainy season would be coming soon, and this cistern would fill up along with the others scattered throughout her land, but there would be no one to use them. The thought depressed her, so she resolutely thrust it aside.

The other women saw her when she stripped off her robe and walked out into the water. Silence descended.

One by one, the others left the water, taking care not to look her way. Taleh watched them go, too hurt to find the words to ask them to stay. Did Javan know what his presence had done to her? She was now an outcast among her own people, being forced – by *Him*, and them – to make a choice for which she was not ready. Could they not see that she was just as much a victim as they were?

She moved further into the pool, and wallowed in water and misery. How long she would have remained there she did not know, but she heard muffled footfalls coming down the steps. She hastily scrubbed the tears from her face before anyone could see her weakness.

The steps ceased.

She waited, but no one came. Taleh could feel someone watching her. Keeping very still to make no sounds in the water, she held her breath and listened. Despite the silence that greeted her, she knew she was not alone.

Javan would have come boldly down. If not him, then who was it?

She had managed to get the worst of it off, and her hair had been rinsed. That would have to be sufficient. She wanted to get out of this dark cavern where evil could hide. Trying to keep away from the puddles of light, away from the watcher, she eased through the water over to where she had left her robe.

It was gone.

Taleh covered her mouth to muffle the whimpers of terror that bubbled up, and forced her mind to work.

The watcher?

She rejected that possibility, for surely no one had made it all the way down to where her robe had been. She would certainly have seen them, even in the dim light from her small oil lamp.

The women?

Would they have been so cruel as to take her robe with them? A fresh ache started around her heart. Yes, the women might have done this thing to her.

She took a chance, and lifted the lamp, looking about frantically for something – anything – to cover herself. A flash of yellow caught her eye.

Along the shadow cast by the steps, against the wall of the cistern, her robe was floating in a sodden mass. When she picked it up, she knew it was no accident. It had been tied in a tight ball to ensure it would fall straight down, that no trailing edges would give it away. With shaking fingers, she untied it, struggling with her emotions as much as with the wet robe. She pricked her hand on something sharp, and unrolled the tight wad more carefully. Inside, her brooch had been pinned as added weight to make the bundle sink faster.

How very fortunate the water level was low.

Anger boiled inside her as she struggled with the dripping fabric to get dressed. It was a good thing the dress was light in weight, it would dry enough to walk into the camp but it would take time, too much time.

Javan sat in the midst of a rebellion. What would he think, if the women chose tonight to attack and she was not there?

What reason had she given him to believe in her now?

NIGHT MOTHS FLIRTED DANGEROUSLY with the smoky campfires. Taleh had been gone much too long. Javan turned the gift he had for her around and around in his hand – a comb, beautifully carved from rich dark wood. When he had first seen it, several cities back, something moved him to set it aside. He saw it sliding through her hair, and smiled. He had better enjoy her hair while he could, for after it was shaved off, it would take a long time to grow to this length again.

There was still no sign of her.

All was not well. He shoved the comb into his belt and stood, walking quickly back toward the cistern. The guards were all in place, the same ones as when he brought her. He knew two of them by name, Hanoch and Enan, and approached them.

"Do you remember a young woman I brought over here earlier this evening?"

"Oh, yes," Hanoch nodded eagerly. "I remember her." He stopped speaking abruptly after a look at Javan's face.

"Has she come out yet?"

"No, my lord. One group left just after she came, but she was not among them."

"Thank you." Javan whirled away and hurried down to the entrance. Another guard stood before the opening. Javan knew him well, and was surprised. A chief of the army assigned to guard duty? He felt a vague stirring of unease. Pelet was an impressive soldier and a stern commander, but Javan had never been able to find anything else about the man to respect. He was harsh and haughty, rude to those beneath him. To his leaders, he was a man of two faces, fawning to those over him to their face, yet disrespectful and slanderous behind them. Still, if Jephthah had seen fit to keep the guards over the bathing women under guard themselves and if he had chosen Pelet to do so, Javan would not fault the decision.

"Greetings, Pelet," he said, trying to keep the stiffness from his voice. "How have the men been conducting themselves?"

Pelet did not answer for a moment. It was an ugly silence, an unexplained silence. Javan forced himself to remain composed. Caution let the other man make the first move.

"There have been no incidents, Javan. What brings you here? Did you miss your opportunity to bathe earlier?"

Javan knew he looked and smelled clean. "No. I am here to check on a young woman I have claimed. Is she still bathing?"

Pelet snapped, "How should I know? Do you think I would go down and look? Is that what you are saying, Javan?"

Javan held his sudden anger in check. "I made no accusations, Pelet. There is no need to take offense, for I meant none. The young woman belongs to me, and has been gone too long. I was simply checking on her."

Grim and unspeaking, Pelet looked at Javan. Tension made the air thick enough to touch. Javan said nothing and waited. With a harsh laugh, Pelet yielded.

"Forgive me, Javan. It has been a long day. If your slave went down to bathe, she will still be there. No one has attempted an escape. You are free to go down and get her." He stepped aside stiffly and motioned Javan below.

As Javan neared the bottom, the smoky air played tricks. The little lamp was out. He thought it had enough oil. He did not see Taleh, and fought alarm. Three men would not lie in collusion as they stood guard in the middle of camp, would they?

Then, in the shadows, there she was, sitting very still, almost a statue. Before he could speak, she leapt to her feet, whirling to face him.

"You!" If he had never claimed her, if he had only left her to herself, she would not be in this position. She would be able to find friends among the women. She would not have to worry about being stabbed to death in the night.

She would not have to feel responsible for his fate.

But she could not tell him any of that.

"Yes. Me." He stood there, arms folded. "I waited for you. You did not come."

She seized on a convenient excuse. Her hair had soaked through the back of her dress. "I was still wet."

Did color rise on his cheeks? "I had not thought of that." He paused. "Wait here, I will go back and get your cloak." And he left her alone.

Again. Only she was not certain she was alone. Where was the watcher? Undoubtedly whoever it was had vanished when Javan came. But how far away had they gone? Was it one of the women? Or a soldier? Threat loomed on all sides.

She waited, wondering how fast he would move. Water lapped against the sides of the cistern. One of the torches sputtered out and Taleh shuddered in the increasing gloom. She was dry now. She could walk out and across the vast camp . . . past the huge army of soldiers . . . toward the camp of women . . . alone . . .

No. That would be utterly stupid.

Heavy footsteps came down the stairs. "Taleh?" One of the torches was pulled out of a holder, Taleh heard it scrape, and the light bobbed closer. "I have your cloak. Put it on, and let us go back."

The guards were still in their place outside the cistern entrance, and bid Javan goodnight with respect. They showed no guilt.

Was either of them the watcher? Both? She did not look back as they walked away. For the moment, odd as it was, she was protected. By the enemy. Javan.

He showed no tension as they neared the camp of the women captives, but then, he had no way of knowing the danger, and he had a belt of weapons and a sword swinging in its scabbard by his leg.

How could the women think they stood a chance against such an army?

When they reached the spot that was hers, he pulled something out from his tunic and held it out. A beautifully carved comb for her wet and tangling hair. From which city had it come, and how long had he been keeping it?

When she hesitated, he looked up and smiled again, a different smile, warm and appealing, inviting her to appreciate his gift. She did not want him to smile. She did not want him to do anything to tie them together, to make him matter, to let her forget he was the enemy. It would be so much easier if he kept his distance. It ruined everything when the enemy had a face, and a smile, and compassion.

Just being here could very well cost him his life. Too many years of watching death on the high places, too much death in the destruction of her own city, now even one more death, no matter whose it was, was one death too many. She had forgotten, or perhaps she no longer knew, on which side she belonged.

She sat down and looked at the comb still waiting in his hand, not wanting to presume on his generosity, not wanting any watchers to see her accept his gift. Not everyone was asleep.

It was better if she took nothing for granted.

Heaving a frustrated sigh, Javan sat down an arm's length away, reached for her own hand, ignoring her resistance, placed the comb in it and wrapped her fingers around the smooth wood, holding her gift and her hand in his.

"You will accept this." He made it a command, not a question. "Your hair needs combing. Either you will do it, or I will. Choose."

Taleh cringed inwardly. How intimate this must look, how friendly, how treasonous to any open eyes! "I will do it myself."

Javan released her hand, leaving her the comb.

Wet, her hair hung down almost to the ground on which she sat. It had been a long time since she had combed her hair without the help of an ointment. Despite her care, the long strands tangled. Javan did not take his eyes off her, and his unwavering gaze added to her nerves. She was certain there must be alabaster cases of myrrh, or calamus, perhaps even nard, among the spoil that she could use to smooth the way of the comb, but she dared not ask.

The longer Javan watched, the more her hair tangled. And the worse her frustration grew. She knew that the scattered campfires gave off enough light to make them the object of many eyes. How could he not feel it?

JAVAN COULD NOT TAKE his eyes off her hair. He saw himself cutting away the wonderful lustrous bounty, and he had to clench his fists into the ground. *I will obey*, he repeated in his mind. *I will obey*. But it was so beautiful. How long would it take to grow back? He wanted to grab it, and bury his face in it, smell its fresh-water-clean scent, twist it around his hands and hold on tight. How could he follow that command? How could he shave it off?

Finally, he could bear it no longer. She was losing control, tugging the comb through her thick hair and tearing strands out. He let go of the soil, brushed off his hands and rose, to walk the few steps to her side. Slowly lowering himself behind her, he watched her go absolutely still. He took the comb from her fingers, working it free of her grasp, and set it to her hair. He saw his hand tremble and subdued it, then drew the comb down, watching the dark curls part as the wooden teeth slid past.

With all the gentleness he had, Javan worked the tangles from her hair. The damp strands were cold. He was close enough to catch the freshly washed scent drifting from the silken glory. He captured more of her hair, guiding the comb through the shimmering thickness, working the snarls from the ends, and tried not to think of the razor that waited it back in his village.

Just a few more days to watch it move in the sunlight, see it kissed by the gentle moonlight. Just a few more days, and he would have to slice it all off himself. And she would have another reason to hate him.

I will obey, he chanted in his mind, and reached for the next section of uncombed hair.

And all the while, Taleh never moved.

With hundreds of people surrounding them, how was it possible the night was so quiet?

That thought was like a dash of cold water upon him, startling him back to reality. The weight of his responsibilities settled back upon his shoulders, among them the necessity of telling her what her future was to be.

Reaching over her shoulder, he dropped the comb into her lap. "I am finished," he said with a lightness he was far from feeling, and heard a soft sigh. Was it relief, or regret? There would never be the right time for what he had to say to her. It would never be easy, delay would not help.

He stretched himself out on the ground, feigning relaxation, lying so he could see her face.

"It is time for us to talk," he said simply.

Taleh flinched. Javan did not wait for her to respond. "I do not want to be your enemy, Taleh. I am not the one who killed your sister, but it would make little difference if I were. I am sorry she died. Being a soldier is not easy. I do not like killing people." He looked closely at her in the poor light, hoping for some reaction. She gave him none, looking back with black eyes devoid of expression. He continued, "I do not know what you were told about this war, or the reasons for it. I can guess. Now I think you should hear our side."

"I know your side," she said.

He forced back a smile. She was listening. It was a start. "Oh?"

"I know that you are on our land. I know we have tried to get it back for many years. I also know that the herds you are taking back with you are your own."

He was surprised to hear such an admission, even if all she would grant him was the right to animals.

"Why does that surprise you?" she asked. "I know we took your flocks. Everyone does. Why should we not have taken them? They were on our lands."

Their land? Javan let the claim go. "They were our animals."

"I will not argue with you. Yes, they were your animals," she said, a resigned tone in her voice. "I can see why you would want them back." Her sudden anger crackled in the air. "Take your animals! Take your herds! Take our clothes, our food! Take whatever you want. But there was no need to wipe out our cities!"

Javan saw her sister's body as clearly as if it were reflected in her eyes. "Taleh, we were not the ones who started this war."

"Of course you would say that. I expected nothing less."

He frowned. Convincing her would not be easy. Very well, he had chosen her, this was the first challenge of their life together he would face. He would tell her the whole story, the parts her people would never admit. "This war began as most do, as you say – over land, a piece of land that has not belonged to your people for more than three hundred years." She gave him a look of disbelief. "What I say is true. I would hardly expect your people to admit that they lost a war to the Amorites." He lost his own battle with sarcasm. "Of course, no one would ever admit that. That would take honesty, and we cannot have honesty in Ammon, can we?"

"How dare you?" she hissed. "What do you know about us that gives you the right to speak so?"

"More than I ever wanted to know," he replied just as sharply. "I have seen your altars. I have buried the bones of your babies, slaughtered in payment to your gods!" At her gasp, he knew he had touched a sensitive point with her. Had he committed blasphemy in her eyes, or did the sacrifice of infants hurt her, too?

He took a calming breath. "Please, let us begin this over. Yes, your people owned the land of Gilead once. The Amorites won it from you in battle, whether anyone has bothered to tell you about it before now or not." He caught himself as the sharp edge came back into his voice, and took another breath. "When we entered the land, we won it from them, again in battle. It became ours. If your kings had wanted it back, they should have done something about it when it was first taken by the Amorites.

"Eighteen years ago, your armies started raiding our lands. At first, we did not know what was happening, why we were suffering so. Then your king accused us of taking your land. We sent our messengers, but your king refused to accept Jephthah's explanation." He smiled sourly at her look of surprise. "Yes, Jephthah tried first to settle this without war. Your king chose to ignore the truths of history. We were provoked beyond enduring. We have been the legitimate owners of this land for three hundred years. Why question our right now? The land of Gilead is ours."

"Why should I believe you?"

"Little one, we did not just charge into your land like your people have been doing to us these past eighteen years. We tried reason first. Why do you suppose I joined with Jephthah? I have nothing left of my family. I survived because I was out in the hills looking for sheep that had wandered off. When I came back, it was too late. There was nothing left. I found our crops burning, all the cattle and flocks driven off except the few I had gone to find. Our house had been put to the torch. I left because I could not stay and do nothing. Jephthah offered me hope, and a chance to find out what had happened to my mother and sister. I found the bodies of the others . . ."

He was lost, locked back years before when he was first transfixed with horror at what he had found one sunny afternoon. If it had not been for some silly sheep . . . He speared her with eyes that burned with old grief and hatred, not seeing her, seeing instead that awful day. "What you saw of your sister was nothing! Nothing, do you hear me?"

A movement from his young woman pulled him back to reality. She was sidling further away, frightened by what he had let slip past the defenses of fifteen years. He shook his head, clearing the old image from his mind, and fought down the old rage as he tried to pick up the thread of what he had been saying.

"There was nothing to show me what had happened to the women of my family. I still have no answers." Bitterness, well aged and refined, tainted his words. "I have seen your country. I know what you do to your prisoners. I must assume the same thing happened to them."

TALEH COULD NO LONGER MEET his gaze and see the haunting echoes of his pain. She had seen long lines of prisoners being taken off to be killed. She had heard the tales. For the first time, she saw Javan as a victim like herself. They both had grief to carry.

Javan was not done. "Taleh, Jephthah offered me the chance to get some vengeance. I am sorry that my vengeance cost you so much."

Knowing that he had endured some of what she had just gone through gave her the courage to ask the one question that tormented her. "When we get to your land, what will become of me?"

It was tempting to tell him that someone had been watching her bathe at the cistern, that it might possibly have been a soldier, but it would gain her nothing. How could she prove it? He wanted to blame her country for all the evils. No matter his answer, she was still a slave, just a slave.

THIS WAS NOT THE TIME, Javan decided. He would tell her only enough to ease her mind, but they were both too raw tonight. "What do you want to know?"

"Will I become a slave?"

"No."

"If I am not to be a slave, why did you spare me?"

"What have you heard?"

"Merab – she is one of the other captives – she has said she will be married to a soldier."

She made it sound like an accusation, Javan thought. Aloud, he asked, "Has she? And how does she feel about that?"

"She is delighted. She spends all her time gloating over the rest of us."

"Does she indeed?" Javan started to grin. So Obed's woman was delighted with her fate, was she? How fortunate for Obed. "And you? How do you feel about her future?"

"I do not understand it. Why bother to wed a slave?"

"But she is not a slave."

"She was *taken*. You *captured* her. You can do whatever you wish with her – with all of us."

"First of all, little one, *I* did not capture her, Obed did. Second, we can *not* do whatever we wish. This may sound strange to you, but we have laws in our land that protect even slaves. You have not been harmed, have you?"

Taleh had to admit it was true.

Javan continued, "If you obey, you will not be. Your lot will be much better among us than it ever would have been with your own people. You will have the protection of our Law. Does that sound intolerable?"

WAS he telling her the truth? While his attentions had been unwelcome, they had not been unkind, and certainly not cruel. Quite the opposite. A ray of hope appeared in the darkness that was her future.

Javan took both her hands, holding them firmly. "That is better. Now you need to sleep. We have another hard day tomorrow. You have nothing to fear from us as long as you obey. I promise you."

Nothing to fear – until the revolt was discovered. And then what?

LATER THAT NIGHT, Javan lay awake, struggling with his decision to hold back from telling Taleh her fate. Perhaps she would have been ready. No, he was sure he had done the right thing in waiting. With a groan, he rolled over, trying to find a comfortable position. It was not the hard ground that kept him awake, he knew. No, the real problem was trying to figure out what was so difficult about telling a woman that she would become his wife.

CHAPTER 7

THE FIRST FEW DAYS WERE A BURDEN. THE HEAT NEVER LET UP, AND THE army did not slow its pace. Soldiers were accustomed to the rigors of travel. In sharp contrast to their endurance, the women's faces became drawn with exhaustion, thirst and pain, but the army dared not linger.

Javan was sorry when the fancy food confiscated from the larders of Minnith ran out and they were forced to make do with plain fare. Many of the cattle had to be slaughtered to provide meat for the journey. Sacks full of grains were carried into the women's camp each night to be ground into flour for the flat, unleavened bread more appropriate for the trip. Tempers frayed. Each evening Javan felt stretched thin, assigning chores for his men, watching the women, trying to find time to visit Taleh between his responsibilities. He waited and prayed to see her first real smile. When would she bend?

He had seen nothing during his passage through Ammon to make him think anyone would willingly stay in that land. Did she not know that her firstborn could have been sacrificed on one of those profane altars to Molech, asking the gods for rain which would come or not regardless? Was it possible she knew and did not care? How could anyone not care?

His fellow chiefs struggled as well to maintain discipline. For the most part, they succeeded. Javan was proud of his men, proud of the part he played in their training.

Things were not going as well among the captives. Javan heard several of the soldiers guarding the prisoners had picked up signs of trouble. He was not surprised to see Jephthah walk past, and motion him to follow.

Jephthah did not break his stride. "I have heard disturbing reports. A soldier standing guard thought he saw one of the captives with a dagger."

"Which one?" Javan's heart lurched. Please, not Taleh!

"It was one of the young men."

Javan released his breath with an audible sigh.

Jephthah fixed him with a close look. "I believe we have a rebellion brewing, Javan. We have to stop it, and we have very little time. We will be out of Ammon within a few days. Those who wish to escape will have to do it soon. If one dagger has been seen, we would be stupid to think there are no more. They cannot hope to overpower us, but even one injury is too much to bear this close to our home. We would not like to be made fools of by our captives. If the young boys we took are strong enough to work our fields, they are strong enough to kill."

"I agree." Javan hated to ask the next question, but he knew where his loyalties belonged. "Is it just the boys? What about the women?"

There was no doubting the look in Jephthah's eyes. Javan felt guilty just trying to meet the iron gaze of his leader. "What about the women, Javan?"

"Is my woman under suspicion?" Javan's chest tightened and burned.

"What if she is? Javan, if your woman is found among the rebels, what will you do?"

Javan marveled that his legs could still move normally. Taleh, a rebel? Taleh, gone from his life? Taleh, dead?

He owed his commander the truth, but the words came hard. "I cannot be the one to cut her down, if that is so. May God forgive me, but I cannot do it. I will not stop another, but I have made the decision in my heart. She is my wife. Could you have raised a sword against your wife?"

Jephthah's face showed heart-deep sadness. "To lose a wife, whatever the cause, is a great grief. Very well, I will not ask that of you. It would be best, Javan, that you do not hope for too much. We will attack the camp at our last stop of the day. Prepare your men, but do not let word spread. We cannot give the captives any warning."

The cold distance that had served him well for killing slipped back into place, but this time he felt a hole around his heart. "Jephthah, will you grant me one favor? If she is found to be among the rebels, may I see the evidence against her before her sentence is carried out?"

"My friend." Jephthah scowled at him. Javan felt his impatience, but he would not take back his question. "How many favors will you ask? You wish to see evidence? What if it is not sufficient to convince you? Will you then plead for her life? Will all of the claimed women be set free because my men think with their hearts instead of their heads? Do you imagine you are the only man among my men who fears for his choice this day?"

"I cannot give up hope. I do not believe my woman will be found among the rebels. I have noticed she is shunned by the others. Her beauty may well be her protection."

"We shall see." Jephthah would commit to nothing more. "Send me Obed. We will eat together for the noon meal and plan our strategy. Until then, you must tell your men and begin moving them into position."

"It will be done."

Javan had gone just a few steps before Jephthah's voice reached him, only loud enough for his ears. "There will be no visits to the camp of the women."

As Javan moved his men into position, gradually, like the wind across the sand, his thoughts kept turning to Taleh. He could see her from time to time, moving within the group of women, her yellow robe reflecting the sunlight. He was torn between a frantic need to imprint every part of her onto his memory and the foretaste of bitter grief in case today would be her last. Endless years of discipline made his face a mask, he knew, for his men reflected his standards and he could see no weakness in any of them.

How many weapons would they find this evening? No matter how quickly they accomplished their task, warning would be given like lightening. It would take less time than that to slip a blade between the leather strips of a coat of mail.

When the vast company stopped at midday, all was in place. The plan was set. There was no turning back.

TALEH THOUGHT they stopped earlier than usual. She was grateful. The soldiers would be coming soon with grain to grind into flour. It had never been her favorite chore, not even in the comfort of her home. Here, in the heat of the plateau, after the day's journey, it took on all the traits of deliberate punishment. With an entire army to feed the next day, when the soldiers appeared with the small mortars and pestles each evening, they were met with groans of displeasure and bitter mumbling.

Taleh had never eaten such bad bread as her fellow captors had produced these last days, full of husks and sand. She knew the soldiers were well aware that it was deliberate. How much longer they would tolerate the subtle retaliation she could only wonder.

Tonight the soldiers were not as prompt as usual. Taleh took advantage of their delay to make herself comfortable. They would be coming soon enough and then there would be no time to rest until after the next day's supply of bread was done.

Stretched out on the ground, her eyes closed to the glare of the lowering sun, Taleh heard a shout. It was cut off almost immediately. Bolting upright, she barely registered an unusually large number of soldiers in their camp before she was grabbed from behind.

A scream tore at her throat, muffled by the hand crushing her mouth. The arm around her was so tight her ribs hurt. The air in her lungs burned, trapped between the cruel tightness binding her and the equally cruel hand over her face. She was being smothered. She could not move her hands, could not claw, could not fight, could not get the hand away. In desperation, Taleh kicked her legs, trying to inflict pain, to make her tormenter let her go. Her heels connected with something. He only gripped tighter, making more pain. She was too afraid to think, too occupied with trying to breathe around the huge hand.

She only knew this was not Javan.

JAVAN SWIFTLY GRABBED the woman in front of him, covering her mouth while he captured her arms in the iron restraint of his own. The women all over the camp responded with totally unexpected fury. Weapons appeared from nowhere. Out of the corner of his eye, he saw two soldiers struggle to subdue a single woman. Silver caught the light, but he could only hope the men were alert.

The woman pinned in his arms suddenly bit his hand. Let her scream, Javan thought, dropping his hand from her mouth. She immediately let loose an ear-splitting shriek, fighting to free her arms, and lifted her feet off the ground without warning. Had she been larger, the weight shift might almost have caught him off guard, but this one was too small.

Her fury increasing, she continued to scream and kick, making Javan's ears ring with her noise. Thick leather protected his legs from the worst of her blows. All the other men were as busy as himself. Where was Pelet? He had been in sight but a moment ago.

"Pelet!" Javan roared, drowning out his prisoner's shrieking for an instant. The woman renewed her struggles. She must know he acted alone. Her wrists were within his grasp and Javan wrenched them behind her back. Pinning them both in one hard hand, he whipped the length of rope from his belt, wrapped it tightly around her wrists and tied it. Only then did he let go, but just to grab an arm and keep her in place. With his free hand, he did a quick search, dodging her kicking feet. He found nothing resembling a weapon hiding in the folds of her robe.

He frowned at the small sack holding her belongings. Someone had to search it. *Where was Pelet?*

Something smashed into Javan from behind, throwing him and his prisoner into the dirt. She was still conscious, gasping for breath beneath him.

He rolled off her and came to his feet, sword drawn, in one smooth movement.

The woman who had run into them was already caught, the soldiers tying her up with angry jerks. A dagger bounced off the hard-packed dirt. That woman would not be alive at the end of the day.

Something stirred at his side, capturing his attention, and he turned to see his own prisoner awkwardly easing herself into a sitting position. Pelet stood beside her, looking very official with his weapon in his hand. If one had not been watching closely, Javan knew it would appear that Pelet had been busy the entire time.

"Where have you been?" Javan snapped. "I saw you nowhere. What kept you from your duty? How could a woman get free?" His anger slapped at Pelet's pride. He did not care.

"Do you think you were the only one with troubles?" Pelet asked with a cruel edge. "When have I ever shirked my duty?"

"Your *duty,*" Javan said, keeping his voice too quiet, "was here, among the captives, searching for weapons. Each one had his own assignment, and yours was here."

The two men glared at each other, the air thick with tension. The woman at their feet picked up her screaming where she left off when she fell. Javan looked down at her with disgust, and hoped any man who thought to choose her was watching – and listening. It would give him something to think about.

Pelet flinched, and then began to laugh. "My apologies, Javan," he said cheerfully over the din. "I had not realized that your need was so very great."

Javan's anger eased as the situation, finally under some semblance of control, struck him. His laughter joined Pelet's.

"She is not yours, is she?" he asked with wicked delight.

"Praise God, no!" Pelet answered, and both men were off again, their raucous laughter an odd contrast to the harshness around them.

They resumed their search, the woman still screaming, her voice shrill even in the wild noises.

Pelet looked over at Javan once, remarking, "A pity we did not think to bring some extra cloth."

"A pity, indeed."

THE SOLDIER suddenly let Taleh go.

Falling limply to the ground, gasping for air, Taleh was only dimly aware that similar struggles were taking place on all sides. She was jerked to her feet by the hair, shrieking at this new and sudden violence. Her head was pulled back sharply, sending a flash of agony along her neck. The face above her twisted with anger.

"Shut your mouth, woman!" her tormentor snarled. "You are among the fortunate. You will still be alive tonight. Look around you!"

Still held by the hair, he grabbed her arm, twisting her about to face the camp with punishing strength.

Taleh took her first good look at what was happening. The camp that had been only women swarmed with soldiers, swords flashing. Nearby, she saw a woman flung to the ground, her hands quickly tied behind her. One of the soldiers clutched his arm, where a vicious slash bled freely. A red-stained dagger lay on the ground at his feet, while the woman screamed curses at the man.

Another burst of movement caught her attention, as the scene was replayed further away. As Taleh tried to absorb what was happening, she saw many women laying bound, soldiers standing over them with swords at the ready.

In the distance, skirmishes could be seen in the camp of the boys as shouts and screams pierced the air.

Unable to tear her eyes away, Taleh watched soldiers pull the struggling prisoners out, past the boundaries of the captives' camps, past the vast sprawling mass of soldiers, moving beyond even the animals on the fringe. Only when the last of the prisoners was out of sight did the soldier release her, moving off with the others. There was no mercy in any of their faces. She did not need to be told what was happening. The cries of death carried on the air, and only fear of the guards placed so liberally around them kept the remaining captives from releasing their grief and anger.

As though nothing was out of the ordinary, more soldiers came with the small hand mortars and grain. Taleh reached mindlessly for her stone, kneeling to grind her flour, too occupied with her inner turmoil to pay attention to her work. Grain spilled to the ground unheeded. Her thoughts whirled: Javan and his kindnesses, the watcher at the cistern who had to be a soldier, Merab and her delight at being chosen for marriage. And now this unexpected display of savagery.

Which was real, and which feigned?

Would life be this way from now on? Would there be periods of calm, shattered by executions designed to keep the rest subdued?

She did not want to see any more death. Who had given the revolt away? Why had Javan sent someone else to terrorize her? Why had he not come himself? Surely he knew his presence would have helped calm her, saved her those moments of paralyzing fear.

The fragile trust she was finding for him trembled under this latest assault.

Javan watched Taleh from several cubits away. He could see that she knew little of what she was doing to the grains under her stone. Added to her pallor, he could guess how badly she had been frightened. Had the soldiers thrown her to the ground? Tied her up? Should he approach her or would she turn on him?

The flour accumulating on the dirt decided his course. They could not afford to waste food. The more she spilled on the ground in her blind absorption, the more she would have to grind later.

He walked over and knelt on one knee beside her. "Do you understand why we did what we did?"

She rubbed an arm across eyes that he knew were moist, even if he could not see them. "Yes. I do not like it, but I assure you I do understand."

Her answer surprised – no, amazed – him. "Did you know any of them?"

"No."

"I am glad of that." He wanted to be glad, to rejoice that she had survived, that she sat before him spared the fate of so many, too many. And with such calm. She did not seem angry, had not even raised her voice. But he could not find a smile when sadness hung heavy over her, a bone-deep sorrow.

Her time of sweet ignorance had reached its end. Later this night, or perhaps tomorrow, she would begin to think, to brood, perhaps even to hate. He had to prevent that, to get her while her defenses were down. "I think it is time that I tell you what your fate will be when you arrive in Gilead." Taleh did not take her eyes from him, but he could feel the tension rising in her, like a gazelle waiting for the lion to blink.

"What did the men of Ammon do with their captives?" He would make her admit his nation's way was better.

"Many were killed, just as you have done. The rest were enslaved."

"So you see no difference between your people and mine?"

"It was wrong of me to say the captives in Ammon were killed as you have done. Our – well, not me, you understand, but I saw . . . " Taleh floundered, then continued with determination. "It was not the practice in Ammon to let captives die quickly." She glanced up at him, then looked away quickly. "I would try to get out of watching, but I could not always manage . . . " Her voice trailed off. "I know you did not do so," she finally said.

"Tell me, Taleh, except for being a captive, have you been threatened at all?"

She hesitated. "No, except for that."

Javan waited until she looked up again. "I understand how much you despise being a captive." He ignored the skeptical lift of her eyebrow. "But surely you have seen that we do not torture our captives. In fact, when we arrive in Gilead, I intend to make you my wife."

TALEH FELT as though she had just been kicked in her middle. The air coming into her lungs tangled with that going out, and went nowhere. She could not speak as the news seeped into her brain. Merab had told her this. Why did it come as such a shock?

"How do you feel about that?" Javan asked, sounding almost . . . hesitant.

"Why?" was all she could think to say. Her voice came out as a strangled gurgle.

"Why what?"

"Why would you take me to be your wife?" Wife. The rebels were gone. She should be safe from reprisals from her own people.

What about from his? Since the night at the cistern and the watcher on the wall, she had noticed nothing amiss from the Israelite men.

The soldiers watched her, but men had always watched her. There was one, a soldier who . . . but surely that was nothing. He had made no move even to speak to her, nor tried to approach her. It made her uneasy, having him meet her gaze every time she turned around, having him stare. He had only watched from the edge of the camp. She could bring no accusations against him for looking.

Wife.

THE FACES of his parents rose before Javan's mind, suddenly clear. Their marriage had been a good one, full of love and happiness. He wanted the same for himself. Could he have such a blessing with an Ammonite wife?

"I have never married," he began. "I was just reaching the age when we were attacked. When it was all over, I had no family, no crops to sell for money, and only a handful of sheep. The village near our home was leveled to the ground. I stayed only long enough to register my claim to my hereditary possession – my land – and then I left to join Jephthah. I have not been back since. This will be the first time in fifteen years that I will have seen my birthplace. I am the sole heir to a large farm. I must secure it for my name, and so I must have children. Therefore, I must marry."

She was not drawing away. He took heart. "You know that you are beautiful. I have eyes. Yes, I desire you. I have since I first saw you. But do not think your beauty alone appeals to me. I need a woman who can work, and I have watched you do so. I also need a woman with courage. You will need to be brave if my people will accept you. Remember, they have good reason to hate Ammon."

Did he hope to frighten her off? Why was he telling her this? Taleh tried to imagine him as a farmer. The image did not come. Her mind refused to let him hold a sickle, or grasp a plow handle.

"Did you know of the revolt?" Javan's question came from nowhere.

If she said yes, what would he do? "What difference does it make now?" she asked him.

"None, perhaps. I believe you did know. Yet you said nothing. Why? Do you want to know what I think?" Javan allowed no time for her to answer. "The rebels are your people. To turn them in, to tell even me, whom I hope you are learning to trust just a little, would be to reject your past. This you are not ready to do. That must change."

She flinched. He did not know, and had not guessed, how much she had worried about his safety. She would not tell him, he would not believe it anyway. "What makes you think I will ever reject my people?"

Javan leaned toward her intently. "You will because you must. You will be living among *my* people, in *my* country, under *my* laws. You will be giving birth to children that will be Israelite, not Ammonite. You will come to accept your new life because to do otherwise would be to condemn both of us to a life of misery. We are too sensible to allow that to happen, I believe." He paused, watching her face. She did not know what it showed. "You will never be asked to sacrifice any of our children to any god. We do not allow such abominations in our worship."

Did he mean it? She met his eyes, dark, steady and clear. He spoke truth? She could hardly believe it. She would never have to watch the priests tear her child from her arms and feed him to the flames? Her mother had endured losing her only son that way, long before either Chelmai or Taleh had been born. She knew the story well. The gods punished her mother for her reluctance when the priest took the babe from her arms by denying her another son.

Taleh had known, down through all the years watching it happen again and again to others, that if such a thing were to happen to her, she would never survive it.

Now the fear was gone, banished by Javan's promise. All she had to do was marry him.

He had been part of the army that killed her family and burned her city. She looked down at her hands and said softly, "But we are enemies."

"No." Javan sounded very angry. "You and I are *not* enemies. I do not hate you, and I hope you will learn not to hate me. The war is over, Taleh. For both of us. It is time to look ahead. And I want you to be my wife." He paused, and aching worry filled his next question. "Would I make you such a bad husband?"

No, thought Taleh to herself as she looked back up into his eyes, so intent, *you would not make a bad husband. But I do not know if I can get used to the idea of being with you when your people killed my family. I do not know if I can let the war die – yet.*

JAVAN COULD ALMOST FEEL the battle going on inside her. He did not want her to have too much time alone with her thoughts. "Taleh, I would not have caused you pain. I know that you blame me for the death of your family, but I want the war to end. It is too hard to carry hate inside you. I know what I speak. You will be given time when we get to Gilead to mourn for your family. It is part of our Law." Suddenly grim, he added, "Life will be much better with us."

Javan looked at the young beauty before him, illuminated by moonlight and campfire, watching her thoughts run across her expressive face. Too many losses, too much pain too quickly, to absorb. Would she believe his story, accept that he knew what she felt, trust her future to him?

Leave her old gods behind? More, would she take his God?

TALEH THOUGHT back to what her life had held, only a few days before. Could it have been such a short time? It seemed an eternity ago. Her father had threatened to pick a man for her, and soon. What would he have been like? Would he have been old and wealthy to appeal to her father's greed, with many other wives to torment her? Would he have beaten her? She shivered.

Maybe it would not be so bad with Javan. He had been kind to her, in his own way. He was not so old. And he was wonderful to look at, with his strong-boned face, his broad shoulders, and the muscles that rippled and flowed when he moved.

He promised she could keep all her children.

The words stuck in her throat when she tried to say them. She coughed and tried again. "Very well." Was that her voice? It sounded so strange. "I will be your wife."

CHAPTER 8

PELET WANTED TO SMASH SOMETHING. HE NEEDED AN OUTLET FOR HIS RAGE. A pity he had not been chosen for the execution squads.

How could his plan have failed? Javan should by rights be dead now, and his slave woman would be free. She was indeed a beauty, but he knew the depth of Javan's hatred for this land. The man would never choose a wife from Ammon. So what was he doing with her?

It was so simple, leaving Javan unprotected. When he saw the woman with the weapon break free of the soldiers, he was certain the job would be done. Why even bother to have a weapon if one had not the wits to use it? Javan's back was even turned to her!

This time he would not leave it in the hands of others. He was not a fool who did not learn from his mistakes. And a mistake it had been, to leave Javan's death to chance. It was too late now to count on removing Javan. That opportunity was gone. But that would not prevent him from finding another solution to the problem. If he did it tonight, it just might work.

Taleh did not move for a long time after Javan left. He had not touched her, not kissed her. A smile, and he was gone. Was she supposed to feel gratitude, say "thank you?" Her family was still dead. And yet . . . she would not be a slave. He was going to *marry* her.

That should not feel so strange. She had heard of it happening before, even in Ammon.

But this time it was happening to *her*. The man was her *enemy*. He said he already put it behind him, that the war was over. It could not be that simple, not for her.

Could it?

Anger and hatred were very tiring emotions, she discovered. She wanted to let go of them, but her grief kept getting in the way.

Javan had been very kind to her, too kind. She was not ready to feel these things for him. She had already betrayed her people by agreeing to marry him. Would she compound that by foolish yearnings?

She was embarrassed to remember her childhood dreams for a husband strong, handsome, who adored her completely. Such things were impossible. How unfair that Javan fit the first two requirements perfectly.

They were no longer the important ones.

She suspected her only guarantee of stability was if Javan could somehow come to care for her. The idea was laughable, but she was learning the hard way. She would not be young forever. Childbearing would alter her figure, age and work line her face. There would always be younger, prettier women to draw his eye.

If he could only love her . . . then she would be safe.

Her head hurt from the force of her thoughts.

The soldiers came to collect the flour, and she welcomed the distraction.

Then they saw the small amount of grain she had completed. Taleh watched them, trying not to tremble, while they glared at her, and muttered fiercely among themselves. She could not hear what they said.

What a fool she had been to ignore her work!

They reached a verdict quickly. "You will go short of food tomorrow," one of the men snapped at her. "If you do not see fit to do your share of the work, neither will you get your share of the food. Perhaps tomorrow night you will find your way to doing the tasks you are given!"

With that, they left, and she lay down with a moan. She stared at nothing, thought of nothing, until a little smile started. The soldiers, for all their threats, had reckoned without Javan. She doubted very much that he would let her go hungry.

Footsteps came up beside her and stopped. She winced inside. Her submission had taken too much from her. She was not ready to face him so soon. She waited for him to make the first move, not even opening her eyes.

A voice she did not recognize, harsh and deep, ordered, "On your feet, slave!"

Her eyes flew open and she looked into the cold, unfeeling face of the soldier who had been watching her from the edge of the camp, the same one she had not thought significant enough to mention to Javan. His eyes were slits in the dark. She scrambled to her feet, feeling awkward in her haste.

"I have work for you to do," he continued. This time, she saw the look in his eyes, and her mouth went dry with fear. He grasped her arm fiercely, and she bit her lip to catch the cry of pain his tight fingers caused her.

Taleh's heart pounded in her ears. Where was Javan?

She stumbled as he pushed her ahead of him through the group of captives. Most of them were asleep. No one so much as looked up as they passed. None of the guards made a move to stop them, or questioned where they were going. She tried to look back, hoping to catch someone's attention – it made no difference who – and received a vicious shake for the attempt.

She continued to move ahead, guided from behind by the pressure on her arm. Bruises were forming under his ruthless grip. They made their way further into the camp of the soldiers unchallenged. Taleh scanned the darkness frantically for Javan.

They neared the furthest edge of the soldiers' camp and still her captor showed no sign of slowing. Cold panic spread through her body, squeezing the air from her lungs. She recognized the path they were taking, even in the dark. He was bringing her out to the place where the rebels had been executed.

She pulled back, frightened enough to struggle. He slapped her across the head in a shocking blow. Taleh fell to her knees from the force of it, but the soldier never lost his hold on her arm and jerked her to her feet.

"Stop this!" he hissed in a voice as cold as death, and grabbed her other arm, hauling her close to him.

Panicked beyond reason, Taleh at last screamed.

Soldiers jumped to their feet, swords in hand.

Her captor let go, his face flushed with rage. Taleh quailed before the swords surrounding her. She could not decide which danger was worse, the danger in front or the one behind. The soldiers looked confused. From the group, several voices asked, "What is the problem?" "What is she doing here?" "Did we overlook a rebel?"

Her captor spoke quickly. "I do not know what is the matter with her. I told her I needed her to work, but she fought me. I did not think it necessary to search her for a weapon after this evening. She may have thought to kill me with my own."

The soldiers turned as a body to look at her. Taleh warily stepped back. They moved forward. They would kill her first and ask questions afterward, if at all. It would be too late for Javan to help her then. A rush of anger cleared her mind, and she looked at her captor with disdain. She was not going to cower before him now and let him spin his lies.

A big man with dark hair and an air of command came up behind the cluster of soldiers. "Let her speak."

Taleh watched in amazement as the soldiers lowered their weapons and stepped aside to let the dark-haired man through.

He fixed pale, piercing eyes on her and asked, "Why did you fight him?"

She met his gaze without faltering, willing him to see the truth. "I have done nothing. I am not one of the rebels, and I will not go meekly to be killed!"

The cruel soldier at her side did not look at her. Taleh could feel the waves of his anger lap at her, threatening to pull her back from the brink of freedom.

Her questioner asked, "Why did you think you would be killed? Did he not tell you he needed you to work?"

"I saw where you took the rebels. I tell you again, I am guilty of nothing! I could not allow myself to be killed for no reason."

At that, the cruel soldier turned to her. He stood so that only she could see the murderous intent in his eyes, and she knew he did it deliberately. His voice did not give him away to the others as he said calmly, as though to a stubborn child, "I was not going to kill you. I *told* you I needed you to work."

The soldiers stood quietly, weighing the evidence of their eyes and ears. Taleh did not know how to convince them. But there was one who could. "I want to speak to Javan."

Several of the soldiers looked startled, but not the dark-haired commander. "How do you know Javan?"

"He was the one who spared me back at Minnith," Taleh answered. She began to let herself hope. Javan's words that first day came back to her. "He told me I was to tell anyone who asked that I belong to him."

At last she had their full attention! The dark-haired man asked, "Has he claimed you? Are you to be his wife?"

"Yes," she answered quickly, thanking the gods Javan had made his intentions clear at last.

The soldiers eased away, leaving only the three: Taleh, her captor, and the one who had done the questioning. He turned to her captor, whose face was still a mask. "So, Pelet," the soldier asked, "did you know this?"

The dangerous man's name is Pelet, Taleh thought. She would have to remember that.

Pelet met the other's eyes fairly. "No, Obed, I did not."

He lies well, Taleh said to herself, wishing she dared say it aloud.

"Good," Obed responded. He spoke quietly, but his voice was rich with menace. "I think it would be best if you took her back and chose someone else to do your . . . *work*." He put a small stress on the last word. Taleh wondered if he believed her, if he thought as she did, that Pelet had been intent on doing her harm.

An angry noise rumbled in Pelet's throat. Obed was not done with him. "You might do well to choose a woman who has not been claimed next time, Pelet. Remember, I, too, have chosen a wife from among the captives. I would protect her with my life. Perhaps your *work*" – again he stressed the word – "would do well to wait until morning."

Pelet did not look at Obed, as though the comment did not deserve a reply. He took Taleh's arm and turned her back toward the camp of captives. His hand was not so tight on her arm this time. Taleh looked back and forced herself to smile at the soldier named Obed. He surprised her by smiling back.

What a strange army this is, she thought. They slaughter city after city and then come to the defense of a captive.

Pelet's grip tightened. He pulled her roughly along behind him as he stalked back toward her camp. The moon slipped behind a stray cloud, leaving complete dark. Taleh could see nothing of his face. How was it there were no campfires near their path?

Where was Javan in this vast crowd of men? How could she see him in the dark? If by some chance she were to find him, would he see her?

Pelet abruptly turned off in another direction. Before she had a chance to protest, he pulled her close, whispering in her ear, "If you do anything, I will kill you and tell them whatever I want. It will be too late for Javan to save you then."

Taleh believed him. Her skin crawled at his nearness. She thought she would be sick. He took a single step back, but it gave her no relief. The edges of his knife gleamed in the dark, cold and deadly.

"Walk," his voice came, as murderous as his knife.

THE DARKNESS THREATENED to swallow her. Pelet stayed close, the dagger never wavering from her side. They had not gone far when he spoke. "You think yourself clever for that lie you told?"

What was he referring to? When had she lied?

"You are not betrothed," Pelet accused her. "Javan hates your people. He would never lower himself to take a wife from the people of *Ammon*." He spat the word out like a curse. His words, his voice, hit Taleh like shots of poisoned arrows, replete with hatred and disdain, shivering with threat. "I fight for the glory of it. I have no need of revenge. He has. He lost his entire family to your people, but you would not know that."

She knew as much of the story as he did, but if she were to tell him so, he would not believe her.

The dagger poked her sharply as they both stepped heavily into a shallow hole, and Taleh gasped in pain and surprise. Her nose and lungs filled with the smell of him. As they moved on, she sifted through her impressions of him to find out what was wrong.

And then it came to her. He repelled her so completely that part of her mind expected him to smell evil, to exude it like a rancid odor. Instead, he was freshly washed. Had he done that to overcome her resistance with an appealing scent?

Perhaps evil had no smell. Perhaps it had texture instead, cloying and tight, and a taste, of sickness and bile.

Taleh stumbled on in the darkness. She no longer paid attention to their course, for it would make no difference. Fear played tricks on her mind, for she thought she saw Javan. She blinked to clear the cruel fantasy from before her eyes.

He was still there, standing next to a lone campfire, illuminated in the dark, and wonder of wonders, he was facing her direction. Just a few more steps and she would be in his line of sight.

There was no sign from him. It was just too dark.

Despair filled her. She would walk past him, her sole hope of rescue, and he would never even know. Where would she be tomorrow? How far into the night would Pelet take her before he stopped to have his way? Would Javan try to look for her? Or would he simply think she had run away, the prospect of being his wife too much for her to endure?

She stole a glance at Pelet, wondering if he had seen Javan. His face was as before, cold and unfeeling. No, he had seen nothing. But then, neither had Javan.

From across the camp, Javan saw Taleh, walking with another man, leaving the camp. His heart went cold, filling his chest with burning ice. She was taking this drastic step just to avoid him? Was she so frightened of him that she could not say to his face that she did not wish to marry him? She would sneak out under cover of darkness? She would enlist another man's aid?

Beneath his hurt pride, another sense began to work, some soldier's instinct, and he forced himself to look again. Something was wrong. She knew no other soldier than him. Who could she ask for escape?

His woman was being frightened into silence. He had seen her walk, seen her angry, hurt, sad, and afraid. She was too rigid, the man with her too close, her arm held in a strange manner for one who was helping her flee.

He would have sacrificed his pride and let her go if she wished, but he would die rather than let her be stolen away against her will.

Taleh tripped. The man with her jerked her back to his side, a harsh, unfeeling lurch.

Javan abandoned courtesy, shoving past men. "Get out of my way!"

Despite the men and the space still between them, he could see her face, despairing and frightened. Anger beyond anything he had ever known filled him, starting at the soles of his feet, pounding against his skull. For a brief instant he could not even see, his rage was so intense. Whoever had her would die.

He would do it himself.

He had to save her first.

He saw the man's face clearly at last, and something else as well. Pelet had a knife!

Gathering all his hard-learned control, holding himself rigid under the strain, Javan stepped into their path.

Fear weighted Taleh's steps. Her legs felt heavy, like an old woman's.

To think, she actually *wanted* to stay within the embrace of the army, wanted to have soldiers surround her! She almost giggled at the thought. She felt lightheaded, giddy with dread. She even thought she saw Javan again, still as a statue, one with the night, standing directly in their path.

Out of the darkness, like the visions of her mind come to life, it *was* him!

Her knees gave way, and only the hard strength of Pelet's grasp kept her on her feet.

And then Pelet saw him, too.

For a brief flash, Taleh thought Pelet was going to draw his sword. Javan's eyes held him in check, and she felt him shudder. He let go of her arm as though it were on fire. Somehow her legs kept her up.

"Javan," he said in uneasy greeting.

"Pelet." Javan returned the greeting, and Taleh had never heard a single word hold so much danger. Neither man spoke. Taleh could not move.

Javan broke the silence. "I see you have noticed my woman."

Javan's hands caught Taleh's attention. They were clenched into massive fists. He reminded her of a rope stretched too tightly, humming with the tension.

"Your woman?" Taleh saw the surprise on Pelet's face. It looked genuine. She had told him, and he had not believed. He had to, now. "I would be happy to give you your price for her."

"She is not for sale," Javan snapped, his too-rigid control cracking. He took a quick breath, his nostrils flaring. Taleh watched him fixedly, afraid to hope. In the voice that held the quiet menace, Javan went on, "I might ask why she is with you, but I am certain you are ready for my question. If I find that any harm has come to her, I do not think I need warn you of the penalty." He reached out and took Taleh's hand.

Taleh held on as if it were her lifeline, and used his strength to make her legs move again. She took the steps over to his side awkwardly, wondering at the slight tremor in his hand.

Javan seemed to have dismissed Pelet from his thoughts if not from his presence. His whole attention was focused on her. He turned his back on Pelet and started in the direction of the women's camp. The first few steps, Taleh expected an attack from behind. When Javan's hand let go of hers, she tried to walk on her own, but her legs were rooted to the ground. Her body's refusal to obey alarmed her. She trembled violently. A buzzing noise filled her ears. Through the haze, she felt Javan pick her up. The warmth of his body, his arms, slowly seeped into her, but she could not stop the trembling, or the weakness that still left her limp.

Javan kept walking. The noise in Taleh's ears faded with every step he took, and she became aware of how closely he held her, how strong his arms were around her, and how very safe she felt. His breath tickled her face. His broad chest pressed against her with each inhale. The steady beat of his heart even through his leather armor drummed in her ear. She liked this – very much. These strange new feelings collided with her embarrassment. She faltered, "I do not know what is . . . nothing like this has ever . . ."

Javan looked down at her and their eyes met in the darkness. "Do not feel you have to apologize."

"Please, I can walk," she said firmly. It might even have been true. "Put me down."

Javan said absently, as though his mind was far away, "There is no need."

"I am too heavy for you to carry." The words came out like sharp pebbles.

"No, you are not." He did not even bother to look at her.

"I *can* walk."

"I know you can walk. I have seen you do it. Right now, I want to carry you." Javan withdrew again into his thoughts.

They reached her little pile of belongings. He lowered her feet to the ground, and turned her to face him. "I will now give you an opportunity to explain."

"Explain?" Taleh stared at him. What did he think he had seen? He could not seriously believe she had gone with Pelet of her free will, could he? She wanted to – wished she dared – slap him. Hard. Instead, she turned her words on him. "Explain what? Explain how? What did you think you saw? If I tell you he held a knife at my side, will you believe me?"

"Woman," Javan returned with strained calm, "you test my patience. I have made no accusations. I merely asked what put you in Pelet's company leaving camp in the dark. Surely you know I have something at stake in this. Do you think I did not see the fear in your face? Please assume I have a little intelligence! Now, tell me how this came about."

The story tumbled out, the night of fear, her words spilling over each other as she tried to remember everything, every mad step they had taken.

JAVAN LISTENED to her with growing horror. He forced himself to remain in place while she told her tale, when every instinct told him to find Pelet and slit his throat. The anger mounted inside him as he thought about what might have happened, what Pelet wanted to happen.

Pelet would pay the penalty for this night.

He caught her arms, holding her firmly in place. He wanted to crush her against him, wrap her in his arms and keep her safe. He could have lost her this night . . . "I think you should know that under our Law, if he had violated you, he could claim you as his wife. It sounds like a bad law, but at least such women have someone to provide for them. The girl's father has the right to refuse for her, but you have no father to protect you. If he had succeeded, there is nothing I could have done to keep him from marrying you."

Her eyes opened wider, overwhelming her face even in the dark. "I thought he would kill me afterward. He said he would kill me if I tried to scream."

Javan pressed his lips together, holding in his angry words. When he could speak calmly, he said, "Yes, I heard you say so. I do not believe that would have happened. He merely wanted to keep you quiet. I should kill him for what he did to you tonight."

He caught himself before he said more. The border was still several days' march away. He was proud of the army he helped command, and would not air its faults, even to her.

What would Jephthah think when he heard word of tonight's events? Jephthah would be fair, it was not in him to be otherwise, but his opinions on the Ammonites were well known. The revolt was barely over. Unknown tensions still seethed beneath the surface of the seemingly subdued captives.

Too, Pelet had been stopped in time, before he was able to carry out his wickedness. He could simply plead ignorance of Taleh's status as an engaged woman. He had looked honestly surprised. How could it be proved otherwise?

He still held Taleh's arms. He was truly afraid now, afraid to have her out of his sight for even a moment. He pulled her against him, wrapping her in his arms.

Her softness was much too tempting, her eyes wide and startled but warming with desire, her lips parted on a gasp as she tilted her head back to look up at him. He lowered his head, losing his struggle as his lips met hers. At the moment of contact, she made a tiny movement, but his arms held her in place. She stood stiffly at first, and he could hardly blame her. They were still strangers, truly . . .

She tasted like he thought, hoped, she would, warm and sweet. She shifted against him, the stiffness easing away in silent surrender, and slipped her arms around his waist, just above his belt of weapons.

Weapons.

The thought nipped at the edges of his mind. He thrust it away, but he had been a soldier too long. The instant of suspicion broke offensively into his pleasure. Caution intruded.

He ended the kiss, hoping she had not noticed the change in his mood. He could not stop his smile at what he saw, for the startled delight of a virgin's first kiss was on her face. Her eyes were unfocused, her lips, glistening with his moisture, trembled with the unfamiliar emotion.

"I must find a way to protect you better," he whispered into her hair. He knew she heard him, because she nodded, her fine hair sliding softly against his arms.

Her hair. He caught a handful that danced too near his fingers and lifted it slowly to his lips. It would take a long time to grow back after he shaved it. He had never doubted the Law before, but this one would be hard to obey, very hard.

Taleh stood within the circle of his arms, too astounded to move. She could not see what he was doing to her hair, for his other arm still held her firmly against his chest, her face pressing heedlessly into his coat of mail. He had not left off wearing it, for they were still within the boundaries of Ammon. The metal was cold with the chill of night. She felt the bumps where the metal bits had been stitched to the leather underneath her fingertips, and caressed them. The leather, warmed by his body, smelled musky and male, and very much like Javan.

The battle inside her raged, and was lost. Or was it won? She no longer knew. The only thing she was certain of was that somewhere during the kiss the last of her resentment of him burned away. In the never-ending nightmare in which she found herself, he was the one secure point she had to cling to.

CHAPTER 9

He would waste no more time, Javan decided. How could he protect her? So many other duties kept him away. She needed a guard, but who could he trust?

He had to talk to Jephthah. Now. As commander of this army, Jephthah was in charge of enforcing the Law. The responsibility for deciding Pelet's fate lay with him.

Javan looked down at her, still wrapped in his arms, seemingly content. There had to be a way to keep her safe. He wondered what she was thinking. Did it matter? He had her, and he would not give her up.

He looked out over the camp, firelight flickering here and there across the vast throng, wisps of smoke bringing the smell of burning wood. Somewhere in the darkness, Pelet waited, alert for another opportunity. Javan remembered the look in his eyes: humiliation, wild frustration, rage. Pelet was angry now, angry enough, he knew, to try again, to try anything.

He pulled back enough to see her face, but he kept his arms around her waist. He did not want to lose even that contact. "You will have to come with me. It is not safe to leave you here." He gave her a quick hug, then reluctantly let go. "Bring what you have." Taking her hand, he led her back toward the camp of the soldiers.

As they walked, Taleh saw men watching them with interest despite the poor light from the scattered fires. A few of them grinned at Javan as they passed, and Javan nodded in return. The farther into the group they got, the more embarrassed he appeared. Chuckles and pointing fingers spread the word of their approach. Uncomfortable as she was by all the attention, Taleh had to smile at Javan's reaction. She knew without his saying a word that these were his men.

They were not following the path Pelet had chosen, to Taleh's relief. No wonder he had gone the other direction, she thought. It must have been merest chance Javan had not been among his own command.

Javan let her hand go, to slide his arm around her side, moving her close. His hand caught in the folds of her robe, pulling it. A sudden sharp pain made Taleh gasp.

The small sound stopped him instantly. "What is it? What is wrong?"

Taleh raised her eyes to his. "It hurts."

"What hurts?"

"I do not know. My side . . ." she turned to look, and her words choked.

Javan stepped around her to see for himself. Blood had soaked through part of the right side of her robe. Taleh gaped at it, horrified by the size of the stain, baffled at how she could have missed it before now. The pain settled into a dull ache. She could feel the faint trickle of more blood as it oozed out of the wound and down her leg.

Javan crouched down, and turned her carefully to get more light on it. His voice bit at the air. "How did this happen? Did he hurt you anywhere else?"

"It must have happened when we stepped into the hole." Javan's barely restrained ferocity reminded her sharply of what he was, a soldier, a man of war, capable of killing at a moment's notice.

"He has sealed his fate."

Taleh said nothing. Fate? What fate awaited Pelet, a man of war among his own army?

"Can you walk a little farther?" He lifted her chin with a finger. His voice was surprisingly mild.

"Of course." Taleh blinked at his sudden transformation. The soldier in him was gone, the gentle man back in his place, that mighty strength under careful control.

She plucked at the robe, the drying blood stiff under her fingers. The fabric must have stuck to her wound and dried. When Javan accidentally caught her robe, he pulled it away and started up the bleeding again. She could not imagine how so much blood had escaped her notice. She wished she could take a look, see how deep the cut went.

Javan stood. "Come along, then. We have much to settle this night, and it grows late."

Left with no choice again, Taleh followed. "What do we have to settle?"

"Pelet's punishment," he said. "I will not permit this offense to pass."

"But Pelet went the other way." She looked vaguely out across the camp. Where was he now?

"I am taking you before Jephthah. He will make the decision."

Taleh stopped in her tracks. Jephthah? The leader of this army, the man who had made whole cities cower at his approach? She would not do it. He could not make her. She turned around. The camp of the women was nowhere in sight. How far had they gone?

Javan stopped several paces ahead of her. "What do you think you are doing?"

His harsh tone brought her chin up. She knew her wishes would not matter, but some small spark of perversity made her try. "I wish to wait here. These are your men, are they not?"

"Yes, they are, but you will not."

"Why do I need to see this Jephthah?"

"He is the only one who has the authority to punish Pelet, and under our law the one wronged must bring the complaint." He reached for her hand, catching it firmly. "Now come with me. We have no time to delay."

He walked on again, and she had to step quickly to keep up with his long strides.

Ahead in the darkness, a campfire sat off to one side. She knew instinctively that was where they were headed. She slowed her steps, her weight pulling at Javan's arm. It made no difference. Javan did not slow, but moved stubbornly forward.

The lone man sitting beside the fire rose as they drew near him, dark hair beginning to gray, eyes reflecting gold from the fire, tired and careworn. A big man. whose sword would be nothing in his hands. This one was a soldier through and through. He greeted Javan warmly, and then turned a frowning face on Taleh. She quailed under his stern gaze. A slow smile lit his face, and unnerved her with its unexpectedness. It only deepened as he turned to Javan.

"I understand now," he said.

The two men prepared to sit down, and Javan tugged gently on her hand so she sat with them, distinctly uncomfortable. Their customs were so unlike what she was used to. She had never felt as odd as she did now, sitting on the ground with two Hebrew soldiers at the edge of a vast encampment, with no other women in sight.

She folded her hands in her lap. She wanted them to finish their talk so she could be taken to Jephthah, and get this ordeal finished. How many times would they repeat this scene, how many more men would have to approve her, before she met Javan's commander?

"Taleh." Javan said her name. "Taleh, meet Jephthah, leader of this army. Jephthah, may I present Taleh of Minnith?"

This was Jephthah? *This* man had terrorized her country, burning cities one after another, wiping out their whole populations? He was the oldest man she had seen in the army, as befitted his rank. Despite the evidence of age manifest in his gray hair, he still looked strong. He did not have four arms and four legs and fangs, as the stories had said, but he was certainly big, massive arms, broad-chested, and shoulders even wider than Javan's.

He seemed not to mind her scrutiny. His eyes drew her own, and she was reminded of her initial impression. He *was* tired, his responsibilities sitting heavily on his shoulders. His face became surprisingly kind as he looked back at her. Then he smiled again and his face creased easily in comfortable lines.

"I understand your fear," he said. "The stories I heard about myself frightened me, too." He chuckled, deep and rich, the sound warm in the cold night air.

His laughter hurt. Did this man, who had terrorized her whole country, possess a sense of humor, or was he laughing at her people? She looked over at Javan for assistance and saw his answering smile. She relaxed slightly, but she would not join in. Her people were the tellers of those stories Jephthah found so funny, and they had been left with nothing to laugh about.

Jephthah's laughter tapered away. He made no apologies. He slapped his hands down on his bare thighs, leaned toward Javan and said abruptly, "Tell me why you brought her into my presence."

"There is a problem," Javan returned quietly. "My wife . . . my woman was abducted this night. She was being removed from the camp by force, against her will."

The older man's eyes widened. He quickly masked his reaction, but Taleh saw it. Then Jephthah turned his attention back to her, and his eyes pinned her as surely as a stake. Whatever she said, she knew it had better be the truth.

Women had just died today for attempting to conceal their actions.

"You have agreed to become his wife."

Now that it was time to speak, Taleh felt, not fear, but shyness. Jephthah arched a thick eyebrow and waited. "Yes." The word sounded too plain, and she added quickly, "Yes, I have agreed."

"The soldier who was taking you away, did he know you were to be wed? Think carefully before you answer. Much depends upon it."

She hardly needed his cautionary words. Did he really think she had forgotten her place, who and what she was? She turned her mind back. They had almost reached the edge of the camp, she remembered, before she had said a word. The soldier named . . . Obed, he was there. "He did not know at first," she answered honestly. "But even after I told him, he would not be stopped."

Jephthah absorbed her answer in silence, his gaze never wavering from her. After a moment, he sighed. "Tell me the story as it happened."

Taleh looked over at Javan. At his nod, she began. "Tonight, I was lying down in the camp of the captives and I felt someone walk up next to me. I thought it was Javan coming back. But it was not." She went on, slowly and carefully, watching the faces of the two men and leaving out nothing, how she learned Pelet's name, and tried to point out the direction he first took her. The darkness made it difficult. When she repeated the words Pelet had used to threaten her just before Javan arrived, something she only then realized she had not told him before, she could feel his anger building. His jaw clenched, his hands tightened into white-knuckled fists, and a small twitch started by his eye.

Jephthah turned to Javan. Something passed between the two men, something she did not understand. Neither spoke.

Worries danced through her brain and coiled in her stomach. Was a woman allowed to bring an accusation against a man? She was not even of their people. Did that matter? Her side ached again. Javan caught her hand. At his touch, she realized she had been rubbing at her wound without thinking.

Jephthah finally spoke. "Taleh, I must have words with Javan alone. I will send one of my own guards to watch over you. You may sleep safely. No one will be able to disturb you."

Taleh nodded obediently, although she did not want to leave Javan's side. A short, over-muscled man came in response to Jephthah's signal.

"Go with him."

She stood, giving Javan one last look before being led away. The firelight gave a warm glow to his brown hair and softened the strong bones of his face. She wanted to believe that more than the fire was responsible for the brightness of his eyes as he looked back at her.

"He thought she lied, Javan." Jephthah waited until she was barely out of hearing before he spoke.

"It is he who lied."

"Indeed? And who told you this?"

"I need no one to tell me. Look at his actions! He was taking her out under cover of darkness. Is that the action of an innocent man? I should have killed him where he stood!"

"You would take the Law into your own hands? And then who would be punished?"

Javan refused to answer. Jephthah tried again. "Who knew you two were to wed? I knew only because you wished to get my blessing. Did you announce it to your men?"

Reluctantly, Javan answered. "We had told no one."

"Ah. Yet you would kill him for what he did to your woman. On what charges would you claim your right to do so?"

"Abuse of women captives is forbidden."

"True. But he did not get that far, did he? I know he has chosen his own woman. What would he need with yours?"

He had? "And who is she?"

"I have not seen her." Jephthah held up a hand. "But until tonight, I had not seen yours."

Javan *knew* he had justification for his anger, yet his chief would not act in his behalf. He glared at his commander. "My lord, under what grounds do you defend him?"

"Javan, I was not given an army to control simply for my strong arm, nor for my skills at war. I was given an army because I could think when it was difficult, and know when not to act. You are letting your emotions guide you. You must learn to be calm in the face of provocation, and to direct your anger to have the most effect."

He leaned back and watched Javan. "Believe me, Javan, I do understand your desire to get revenge against him, but there is little I can do. I saw the blood on her robe, so I know she was hurt, but I also saw the wound did not cause much harm. However angry it makes you, I must act with care. He believed she lied about her betrothal to you. Now he knows she did not."

Javan saw Jephthah grow serious. "Javan, I do not take Pelet's actions lightly. Pelet is dangerous. I have never liked him, but he is a good soldier. I needed good soldiers. Your woman is in the most serious danger as long as Pelet is around. Perhaps he thought to take two wives for himself. I could hardly forbid it when the Law permits it. But now he knows he must content himself with just the one."

Javan listened solemnly. "Tell me how I can protect her. Tell me how I can keep her safe!"

Jephthah regarded Javan with compassion. How like a son he was, the son never had. "There are no answers to your questions, Javan. I have said I will speak to Pelet. I will do so. There is one thing I would have you remember. You are in this situation by your own choice. Did you think, when you first spared her life, that no one else would see what you saw in her?"

Javan did not have time to find an answer, Jephthah was not finished. "My friend," he said softly, "you will always have men take a second look at your wife. You will never get used to it, so you will have to win her heart. It may not be so hard a job as you think. I believe she is already learning to trust you." He gave a laugh. "She would not like to hear me say that. She is a stubborn one, your woman. Still, I think it is true. Trust is a very good first step." With a great yawn, he sat back. "It is very late. I must speak with Pelet, and you must get rest. Go. I will send for you if I need you."

Javan nodded and stood. However badly he wished to be there when Jephthah confronted Pelet, it would not happen. He left. His steps took him past his own men, asleep by their fading campfires, and into the group of sleeping women.

Jephthah's man stood in the darkness, watchful and imposing. Nearby, on the hard ground, he saw Taleh's yellow dress peeking out from under her cloak. Was she asleep already?

He stepped closer, his sandals nearly soundless on the dusty ground, but Jephthah's guard whirled to confront him. Beyond the guard, he saw Taleh cringe. He would not leave her like this. He wanted her to know he had not left her completely in the care of others.

At the sentry's nod, he walked over to her side and knelt on one knee, ready to rise at the first threat. Her eyes were open and frightened. When she saw it was him, she gave a soft sigh of relief. "Javan," she whispered. "I thought it might be . . . him."

"I wanted to tell you it is safe for you to sleep. Jephthah has assigned his best man to watch you, and will soon speak to Pelet." He hoped he convinced her. The dark hid her expression, leaving only the glistening of her eyes, but he thought she relaxed a little.

"Will you be here during the night?" She asked the question shyly.

"No. I have my own place, my own responsibilities." He did not want to leave her yet, and searched for something else to say to prolong his visit. "I will come to see you tomorrow when my duties permit." Was it wishful thinking, or did her eyes beg him not to leave? "Perhaps there will be some time to tell you about my home."

"I would like that." She did not take her eyes off him, glowing against the darkness.

"Yes, well, I bid good night." She was safe and he could think of nothing else to day. "I will see you tomorrow. I promise that." He rose to his feet.

"Tomorrow, then. And, Javan?"

"Yes?"

"Thank you – for everything."

He knelt again. "Taleh, you are to be my wife. It is my obligation to protect you. I owe you an apology for failing that duty to you."

"No, you must not blame yourself." Taleh sat up abruptly. "I should have told you before this happened that he had been . . . watching me. For several days. I did not think it would turn into this. I had been afraid of him – a little. If I had told you earlier – "

"We both made mistakes," Javan interrupted. "We will take extra care that nothing like this happens again."

"Yes."

Javan smiled at her in the dark, touched her hand gently, stood and walked briskly away.

THE GUARD REMAINED in his place, a silent sentinel, and under his watchful eye Taleh felt comforted, and drifted into sleep.

CHAPTER 10

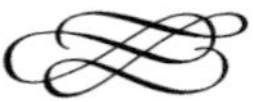

PELET STOOD BEFORE HIS COMMANDER. ANGER SPARKED BEHIND HIS EYES.

"I have received a report about an event this night. I would like to give you a chance to tell me your side of it." How easy it was, Jephthah thought, to show favoritism. It was common knowledge that Javan and he were old friends. They had been together since the early days of training in Tob. Jephthah had a marriageable daughter of his own. He had held dreams . . . A daughter was a good thing, but ah! to have had a son.

"Can I be told the nature of the report? It would help to know what I stand accused of. Much happened this day." Yes, anger's edge was in Pelet's voice.

"I have been informed you were stopped with another man's woman this night on your way out of the camp."

"Why do you take his side before hearing mine?" Pelet demanded.

"Did I take Javan's side? I will gladly hear yours."

Pelet glared at Jephthah, anger and betrayal pouring off him. "You told me I could take a wife! That woman, the one you so easily turned over the Javan's care, is the one I chose! You let him have her! How else was I to get her? You gave me your word!"

Jephthah looked at him, startled. "I did not know." He caught his tongue before he said more. This needed thought. After a pause, he asked, "Why did you not come to me with this before? He has informed her, she has agreed."

"Did she know I also had appealed for her?"

"Do you think she will change her mind after this night?" Jephthah snapped back at him. "I cannot believe you thought to win her over by your actions. There are plenty of other women, if you must have one from Ammon."

"I acted rashly. Perhaps, if I could explain . . ."

"No! I have made my decision. There are plenty of other women, if you must have one from Ammon. Choose one of them."

"There are no others I want." Pelet sounded like a sulky child.

"You do not even know her. It is true, she is exceptionally beautiful, but no one can know what kind of wife she will be. She might not want to obey our Law. Javan may wish he never saw her."

But Pelet only stared stubbornly ahead, not meeting his eyes. A pity Pelet had not revealed this rebellious side of his nature before now, Jephthah thought. He could only hope a warning would suffice. "Javan spoke for her first, in front of his men. His is the better claim. I am sorry, Pelet, I know this grieves you, but I say again, if you want a wife from Ammon, you still have many to choose from. I do not recommend that path to anyone, but it is permitted. That is all I have to say."

Pelet did not stay to argue. Jephthah watched him go uneasily.

JEPHTHAH'S GUARD did not have to awaken Javan, for he had not yet slept. His eyes, when he arrived at Jephthah's fire, were red with dust and exhaustion.

"You sent for me, my lord. I am here."

Jephthah motioned Javan to sit. When they were both settled comfortably, Jephthah said, "My friend, I have seen your woman and heard her story. While I have enough evidence to believe it, I will not take action against Pelet." Even Pelet deserved to keep his pride, he thought. It would do no one any good to air his humiliation. If Pelet had told any of his close associates of his woman, he would have to find his own way out of the embarrassment. Jephthah would not add to his burden by sowing any more seeds of enmity. If Javan were to find out about the claim, nothing good would come of it.

Indeed, Javan glared, disbelieving. "Do you think he will stop? Or will he bide his time until he sees a better opportunity?"

"I can no more see into his thoughts than I can keep the sun from rising. But *neither can you*." Jephthah paused, giving Javan time to let it settle past the still-simmering anger. "He has been warned. He knows we will be watching. I do not think he will attempt another abduction."

"I have another fear, Jephthah." Javan's voice was tense with an inner struggle. Jephthah imagined he wanted badly to rail at the decision. "You know the army will disband soon. What will stop him from waylaying my party on our way home?"

Jephthah shook his head. "You are the best soldier I have. Do you have less trust in your skill than I have?"

Javan had to smile, although it looked reluctant.

"I will not send you on your way alone. Obed, too, comes from your village. If your party travels with his, surely no one, not even Pelet, would attempt to attack. Are we agreed?"

"Yes. There is no one I would rather have at my side than him." Javan's smiled more easily this time. "Other than yourself, of course."

Jephthah laughed, and the sound lightened the darkness. "Of course. When you say it like that, I might even be able to forget it is flattery."

Javan's smile stretched into a grin. "I would never attempt to flatter you, Jephthah. I said it because it is true."

THE NIGHT DID NOT BRING Javan peaceful rest. Repeatedly, noises jerked him from sleep into full wakefulness, his dagger already in his hand. Each time, he found nothing amiss. The early light of morning brought an end to the attempts to coax his body into relaxing.

The activity of breaking camp that morning kept Javan from attacking Pelet. He had hoped the light of day would cool his temper, but it did not.

Somehow their paths, while coming close, never crossed. He strongly suspected Jephthah had a hand in that.

Javan watched Pelet during the day's journey for signs of danger, but found nothing. The other man kept himself very busy and out of Javan's way. As a precaution, Javan spent what little time he had free with Taleh.

He worried about Taleh's growing friendship with Obed's woman. Merab made him nervous. She stared at him with undisguised longing and slow, measuring looks when she thought no one else watched. When he saw her cast the same hungry looks at another soldier, and then another, he feared for his friend.

Her eagerness to please must have charmed Obed away from his good sense, and her care never to play her games when either Obed or Taleh were around. Perhaps his friend would catch her at her ploys, and finally see beyond her pretty face. Failing that, he hoped when Obed was free finally to take her to wife, *if* he did, that she would keep her eyes to herself.

But the uneasy feeling that the woman would only bring misery persisted, growing like an unreachable itch.

He wanted the journey to be over. They were back within the boundaries of Israel again, and he wanted to be home. He wanted to be on the land of his father, to see the village of his youth.

Most of all, he wanted the time of waiting for his bride to be over.

CHAPTER 11

THE SCENERY CHANGED SO GRADUALLY THAT TALEH WAS SURPRISED WHEN she first realized it. She knew for a certainty, without having to ask, that they had left Ammon. The hard-packed ground looked the same, but there were more plants underfoot, dried and stubbly from the summer heat but enough to add a cushion to each step. The grasses beneath her sandals were longer, thicker, and even in the prickly brown stalks she could see the promise of lush growth after the rains came. In the darker shadows of the deepening valleys ahead of them, she thought she saw trees growing tall and thick. The air held more humidity, mixing with the heat of the day to cover her with a sheen of moisture.

They had been going uphill all day, and her legs knew it. When they reached a stretch of land that was flatter than anything they had crossed, Jephthah called a halt. Taleh sat down for a few moments to rest while the camp took a semblance of order. It was too early in the day to stop. What was ahead?

She struggled back to her feet, looking from their camp out at the horizon. At the very edge of her sight, beyond the rolling hills ahead that rose ever higher, she saw a faint ridge. Were they heading toward mountains?

After the relatively flat land of Ammon, the steep hills came as a surprise, as did the green haze that tipped the shadows. It was almost . . . pretty.

She heard footsteps coming up behind her. Whirling around, she sagged with relief. Javan smiled down at her. "I did not mean to surprise you. I am sorry." He stretched a hand toward the view. "What do you think of my land?"

"It is so very green. There are lots of trees. I did not expect that." She turned back to the horizon and pointed to the faint blue ridge. "What are those mountains called?"

"They are not mountains," Javan answered. He smiled. "Those mountains, as you call them, are the edge of a deep valley. At the bottom, the river Jordan runs."

"Oh." His smile pleased her. She was tired of being guarded by strangers. "Will we go that way? Will I get to see it?"

He shook his head. "Not this time. Another time, perhaps. We are going that way," and he turned her slightly, facing toward the hills of green. A happy smile lit her face as she drank it in.

Javan wrapped his arms around her and held her close. His coat of mail was not uncomfortable against her, or else she had grown used to its feel, the cool circles of metal and the thick strips of leather. He rested his chin on the softness of her hair, and that, too, was familiar. They both stared out at his homeland, waiting in the distance for them.

"Tomorrow we will be leaving," he said into her hair, and tightened his hold at the sudden spasm that shook her. "No, do not try to get away. Let me tell you what will happen. Everyone will leave for their own villages. We are within our own land now, and there is no longer a need to travel as an army. After tonight, I will no longer be a soldier. I will be a farmer again."

Panic and relief pulled at Taleh. Eight days had passed since she took her first step away from her burning city, eight days that had taken her far into a new land and a new life.

There it lay, stretched out before her. Was she ready?

Javan slowly turned her to face him. She kept her eyes lowered, afraid her thoughts and fears showed on her face. Javan must have seen something, a thought she had not the skill to hide. A strong finger tipped her chin up in that way he had. At last she looked into his eyes.

A deep sound rumbled in Javan's throat. "Taleh, Taleh, when will you trust me?" His lips came down on hers, giving her comfort. Surprise became pleasure, breaths melded and merged into something of both of them.

HE PULLED AWAY. The noise of camp penetrated with annoying persistence. In his arms, Taleh trembled. Guilt consumed him. He had swept her along with him, loosing newborn passion, and neither of them had an outlet for the raging desires he had stirred up.

"I am sorry, Taleh. I am sorry. I had no right to do this to you," he murmured in her ear. His hand rubbed her back, up and down the slender spine, hoping to soothe her ragged breathing.

"Do what to me?" Her eyes were unfocused pools of dark. "Why do you apologize?"

He stroked a tumble of hair off her forehead and kissed the smooth skin, puzzled and uncomfortable at the odd clenching in his chest, a quick sensation of lightness, of disconnectedness. He forced his mind back to the question she asked.

"The kind of kissing we were doing has its ultimate end in the marriage bed. Without satisfaction, it leads to . . . frustration." More for him than for her at this early time, he suspected. "Do you understand?"

"Of course I understand. I merely asked why you felt pressed to apologize." Her midnight eyes met his own, and then embarrassment colored her cheeks. "You did nothing that . . . I, well, I do not think you need ask forgiveness." She said the last words to the ground.

He grinned down at the top of her head. "You are very kind." He struggled to cover the amusement in his voice. She looked up at him, waiting, but he had age and experience on his side and kept his face under control. "I think we should get rest. We will be on our way early tomorrow, and we have given everyone enough to look at for one night."

Taleh seemed to suddenly remember that they stood within the middle of the camp. Heat flooded her cheeks with red. She covered her face in embarrassment.

Javan laughed out loud. "There is no need for that, lamb." He tugged lightly on her hands. "Everyone knows we will be husband and wife soon. No one will mock you. I happen to know I am the envy of every man here."

Her head lifted, confused eyes peeking from behind her fingers. "How do you know?"

"They told me," he answered, waiting for her reaction with something very like delight. The flush that had barely faded bloomed again, up past her eyebrows. They had spoken often, but never with such enjoyment, such intimate freedom, and he was pleased.

She dropped her gaze at his answer. In a small voice, she said, "Oh. I did not know. I wish people would not watch me like they do. I hate it."

So do I, Javan thought. Aloud, he said, "You handle it with grace."

"I try not to handle it at all," she returned sharply. "For as long as I can remember, I have tried to ignore the looks and comments. I could not even go out of my house without having people whisper and stare. I thought, if I acted as though I did not notice, it would no longer bother me. I was wrong."

Javan listened to her in surprise. He had never thought of what it was like to be so beautiful, so out of the ordinary. He himself had chosen her for her beauty. And naturally she knew that. He found that realization uncomfortable.

He resented the looks the soldiers cast in her direction when they thought he was not watching. If it bothered her so as a young woman, what had her childhood been like?

How did a child cope when strangers suddenly began to stare? He would love daughters that looked like her, but now he knew how vigorously he would have to guard them. Even in Israel.

THE CAMP STIRRED into life early again. After so many days of sameness, from the beginning this day was very different. Taleh watched as the soldiers claimed what was theirs and said farewells. Men were paid in gold and jewelry, seed and donkeys, cloth and cattle. Javan had brought over several bundles when he woke her, and she sat on the sturdiest one while she waited for him to come back for her. A number of women wept quietly, clinging to each other. Taleh tried to ignore the pangs of longing. She had no friends other than Merab, whose interest in her she suspected was only on the surface. Taleh felt no need to seek her out, for Merab and her soldier were continuing the journey with them.

She knew she should be pleased that Merab was coming. Another woman, another Ammonite woman bound for the same fate, could mean companionship and commiseration. Taleh did not think it would work out that way. Merab's initial happy acceptance of her circumstances showed signs of souring. No longer notable for being picked as a wife, unhappy that she was not exempt from the daily chores, she complained whenever Obed was out of hearing. Poor Obed, Taleh thought. Eventually the scales would fall from his eyes. What would he think then?

She lost track of Javan. Men milled about, and animals complained noisily. Hooves churned up dust, men chased wily creatures as they tried to escape, and shouts and laughter rose from the din. Javan had told her he needed seed, sheep and goats and slaves as well. She did not know when he would be back, so she sat and watched and tried to be content.

Groups of soldiers and slaves began to separate from the main body, pulling donkeys laden with goods and driving flocks ahead of them. The air rang with the bleating and lowing of the protesting animals. Good-natured shouts and laughing clung to the breeze, lifting above the other sounds as the soldiers took their partings with a joyous spirit notably missing from the women and slaves. Taleh looked on, her emotions a tangle. Her own turn would come shortly; she, too, would leave the meager support of her fellow captives.

One of the soldiers stopped, a stillness in a sea of movement. The contrast caught her attention. Pelet, with his leering face and evil grin. Regardless of the distance between them, she jumped to her feet, tripping over the bundles as she backed away.

Pelet winked at her, and her skin crawled.

A group of men passed between them, cutting off her view. When they moved on, Pelet was gone.

She turned around in a frantic circle, wondering which direction he would choose to come at her. She was safest when he was in plain sight.

Through the throngs of men and animals, she found Javan, at last coming back.

Her mouth went dry. He no longer wore his armor. Knots of muscles once concealed by his mail rippled under the lightweight linen tunic stretched tightly across his chest. His legs covered the ground in a vigorous stride, the muscles flexing with every movement.

A purely feminine thrill tingled down her spine. For a heartbeat, her mind went blank.

Her hands itched with the desire to touch him. She rubbed her palms quickly against her robe.

Javan reached her side before she pulled her breathing under control. He smiled at her and she saw home-coming delight shining in his eyes. She could not look away, unable to break the link with him, as real as a touch.

Her hands tingled again, the wishes of her mind come to life. At the laughter in his eyes, she looked down and saw a thick rough-fibered rope. Her fingers had closed over it without thought, carried away by her fancies.

Javan chuckled. "We have four donkeys to lead home."

Taleh looked down the rope to its end, a crude harness around the head of a lazy-eyed, gray-haired donkey heavily laden with sacks. She felt her cheeks warm, and knew with embarrassed certainty that her face was as red as it felt. Perhaps Javan had not noticed her silly reaction. Maybe he was so happy to be going home that her unguarded response escaped him.

And maybe the donkey at the end of her rope could fly.

JAVAN SETTLED down for his turn at nighttime watch feeling contentment seep through his bones.

His woman was indeed falling in love with him. Jephthah had been right.

He smiled into the darkness, reliving again the moment when he had seen Taleh devouring him with her eyes as he crossed the camp toward her. Such a look made a man feel invincible, powerful, and very wanted. It had also been very unexpected, despite Jephthah's confidence.

He chuckled to himself, quietly.

They were at most two days from his family's lands. The beauty of Gilead spread out around him, even in the dark. The air was soft, warmer than on the plains of Ammon, and rich with the familiar smells of freshly turned earth and ripening fruit. They had purchased some fresh figs from a farmer near midday, and old memories had nearly overwhelmed him. The man had a young son playing at helping, so like Javan himself had done at that age.

But tonight was not a night to waste on grief. This was a night for the future, for looking ahead.

The Law gave him one year free of obligations, free of the call to war, in which to make his wife pregnant and ensure his name's survival. What would the end of that year bring? Would he find himself a father? Would his wife be quick to conceive a child? Perhaps his first would be a son. How many nights had he wondered if he would ever live to see a child of his own?

The time was within his grasp – almost. He still had the month to fulfill.

A month. It was a long time not to take her. Eight days had gone by since he first saw her, eight days to be grateful for duties and hard work and the constraints of many people. How else could he have endured?

Would the villagers make him wait the full time, or would they only impose the month less these days gone past?

His mind whirled with arguments to use on the older men of the village. When his watch ended, he presented them to Obed, barely awake, but his friend merely laughed.

"Go to sleep, Javan," Obed said. "You always get what you want in your dreams, and I believe that is where your arguments belong. Subtract days from the waiting period and miss seeing us suffer? Why would they want to do that?"

Taleh woke with a start. Something brushed against her. Her heart raced in fright, her breath stuffed tight in her throat.

"Do not panic."

Javan's voice. Whispering close to her ear. Right beside her.

He was sitting next to her, his hand resting lightly on her hip. "Just watch." He spoke softly, so none would overhear.

Taleh strained to look over her shoulder at him. He was so close. She saw only his shape, large and male, and the firelight's pale reflection in his brown eyes.

"No, do not look at me. Look that way." He gently turned her head away from himself. She lay stiff until the first rays of the rising sun caught the underside of puffy clouds.

She sighed in awe. She wanted to tell him how beautiful it was, but her throat was too tight. Her strong soldier woke her to watch a sunrise. She did not know which moved her to tears.

In the first glow of morning, the valley below them took shape, tiers of olive trees standing in graduated rows down the hill, late summer flowers glowing at their base when the light touched their dew-covered petals. Birds hiding in leafy branches called greetings to each other. Fences made of white limestone rocks marked paths through the base of the small valley, and at the bottom, a white-washed house stood, its half-opened window shutters like sleepy eyes.

"Is your land like this?" Taleh asked, reluctant to spoil either scene or mood but curious enough to take the risk. She rolled over, to see him smiling down at her.

"It was, except it is not in a valley. It is flatter, but there are olive and fig trees like these. Even some date palms. My father had grapevines and we made our own wine. We also had flocks of sheep and goats, and two stubborn bulls for plowing. I have no bulls, so I will have to use my donkeys." He paused and Taleh saw the memories come to his eyes, but they did not chase his smile away. "It was a good place to live. I hope it will be again."

The small camp began to stir with the rising of the sun, and Javan stood. Taleh stretched, and the small movement seemed pregnant with intimacy. He reached over and held out his hand.

Without hesitation she put her hand in his, and let him pull her to her feet. The closeness of the moments they had shared was with her as she smiled up at him. He leaned over and gave her a quick kiss on the lips. She laughed.

"Good morning," she said.

"Yes, it is," he returned, and then he went over to help pack up the camp.

JAVAN WATCHED the slaves carefully as the journey reached its end. Since he and Obed worked right along with them and took pains to treat them well, he saw no signs of revolt. It would have done them little good, for they were well inside the boundaries of Israel now and everyone knew it.

Javan kept a surreptitious watch on Merab also, but her coy behavior seemed a thing of the past. Perhaps she and Obed had been having a fight, perhaps she had become settled in her mind regarding the man who would be her husband, perhaps it was a reaction to the lovely area through which they walked. Javan did not know, but the change relieved him. He did not want trouble between himself and either his wife or his friend.

Had Taleh noticed Merab's flirting of before? She gave no sign. The two women got along well with each other. Javan felt with pride that it was more Taleh's good nature and kindness than any effort on Merab's part.

He had chosen well.

CHAPTER 12

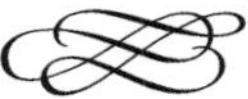

Taleh felt the tension in Javan. It cracked around him like a whip as they walked up to the top of another hill, steeper than the ones they had climbed so far. He stopped abruptly. She almost bumped into him.

Motionless, he looked out over the broad valley stretching before them, beautiful despite being brown from the last of the summer heat. Sheep grazed on what was left of the grasses, and goats, dark furred spots, gamboled about on the far side of the valley. At its bottom a walled village sat, not large, but clean-looking, as though none of the buildings had yet had a chance to age.

Taleh noticed as she surveyed the scene before her that the hillside was covered with the ruins of what must be the original town. Javan had not lied when he told her what the Ammonites had done in his land. No wonder they had wreaked such vengeance on hers. Very little had been left to rebuild, if the sad remains below could be believed. At one time, this had been a large city, for chunks of it lay halfway up the hillside. Only the sheep and goats paid any attention.

She looked over at Javan, but his face gave nothing away. Then she saw his eyes, and knew. This had been his village.

Nothing else could account for his coldness, for the hollow look there.

Obed stepped over to Javan's side. Their expressions matched, bleak and pained.

Merab came up behind Taleh and whispered, just loudly enough to catch the attentions of the somber men, "This is not where we are going to live, is it?"

Taleh had been wrapped up in the waves of sadness that washed over her from the men, and Merab's lack of perception dismayed her. "Merab, watch your tongue," she whispered fiercely. "We must show respect for these people, else they make it harder for us."

Her glare did little to stifle Merab. "Really, Taleh! Surely you expected better than this! I thought I was going to a place with some grace, some refinement. Had I known, I never would have accepted Obed's offer of marriage. He cannot expect me to agree to stay here, in this pitiful excuse for a city. I come from a family of power."

Obed turned toward them. Taleh was glad that look was not aimed at her. She hissed quickly, "What difference does your family make now? They are all dead." Obed stopped in front of Merab, his expression fierce.

"Do you remember what your precious city looked like when we finished with it?" His eyes flashed with anger. "This one looked the same. How long would it take your people to rebuild? Very few people here survived to do even this much." Grasping her shoulders, he growled, "If you wish to join your fellows in their slavery, it can be arranged. Just remember, this is *my* land. These are *my* people. If you persist in this course of foolish pride, you will find your life here a hard and lonely one."

Letting go, he turned his back on her and walked over to check the ropes holding his plundered goods to the donkeys. His every movement was stiff with rage.

Taleh took Merab's hand. "He is right, you know. We cannot expect the people to welcome us. Most of them would rather see us dead. We will have to earn their respect. Let us not make it harder on ourselves than it has to be."

Merab pulled away, still sulky, but Taleh saw worry and perhaps a bit of fear in her green-flecked eyes.

A sudden puff of wind blew dust at Taleh. The flocks had arrived. The sheep and goats had long ago tired of the march. Keeping them with the rest of the group was a frustrating task, requiring all the efforts of the slave boys who drove them along.

After days of holding back, the sheep finally showed an interest in what was up ahead, and began to bleat with enthusiasm. Taleh watched Javan. The noise and flurry pulled him from his thoughts. Taleh was relieved when she saw him come back to the present. Javan nodded at his slaves, struggling to hold the eager animals back, and the group moved down the hill.

As they neared the bottom, Taleh saw what attracted the animals. A huge trough had been carved from one of the stones left among the ruins. Water filled it. Sitting in the meager shade on the other side of the well conveniently located next to the trough, a little boy with tousled brown hair drew pictures in the dirt. At the sound of their arrival, he jumped to his feet, his eyes wide with surprise.

Taleh could imagine what he thought. They were a mixed group, the hardened men with their tired women and slaves, and the thirsty flock that eagerly pushed toward him and the scent of water. At the fear in his wide dark eyes, Taleh knew he recognized them as Ammonites. He turned to run, giving a shriek as he did so, but Javan caught him in a few steps, swinging him off his feet and clapping a hand over the little boy's mouth.

"Do not be afraid. I am an Israelite, just like you. I have been fighting with Jephthah. The war is over." He repeated it over again, until the boy's eyes calmed. Javan removed his hand from the child's mouth as he set him back on his feet.

The little boy's fear had transformed into excitement. "Were you really with Jephthah? Did you fight lots of wars? Are they all killed? Did you kill them yourself? Will you come and tell my father? What is your name?"

Javan laughed, and the little boy laughed with him, pleased to have a new friend. "One question at a time, young man. Yes, I really did fight with Jephthah. I was even one of his chiefs."

The boy's eyes got bigger, and Taleh covered her mouth to hide her smile. "Really and truly?"

"Really and truly," Javan answered, grinning at the child. Then he knelt, and Taleh felt a curious pain in her heart as she watched. Javan said firmly, "I killed a lot of people, but I did not like doing it."

"Why not?" the boy asked, the concept plainly confusing his dreams of vengeance.

Javan held his hand out to Taleh. She hesitated, but walked to his side. Clasping her hand, Javan said, glancing up at her, "This is my wife, or she will be today. Her mother, father and sister are all dead." He looked firmly at the boy. "That is what war is, losing your family. I hope you will never see a war in your whole life."

"Oh," the boy responded, "but I want to go fight. I want to have a sword and bows and arrows. I would be a good shot, I just know I would."

"Yes, you would, I am certain," was Javan's only reply to such childish eagerness for blood. He rose, still holding Taleh's hand. "Now I would like to see if I can find a place to stay while I rebuild my own house. Can you tell me where I can find lodging for all of us?"

"My father can help you. He makes things out of leather. His name is Jesse, and he works in the village sometimes. The rest of the time he has to work away from it, he tells me. He'll probably take you to Old Sarah."

An odd sound from Obed caught Javan's attention, and he turned to look. Obed was staring fixedly at the little boy, his face pale and his eyes wide. "Obed? Are you all right? What is it?"

Obed blinked, and looked back at Javan. "It is nothing. Truly. For a moment, I thought . . . but I must be mistaken."

Javan regarded his friend closely for a moment, but Obed shook his head. "Pay it no mind." Obed's voice was very definite.

It would be a waste of time to pry, Taleh could see from the finality in Obed's voice. Javan seemed to realize it as well. The little boy tugged at his arm, and he knelt again.

Taleh did not hear any more of the conversation. She had stopped listening after he said she would be his wife that day.

That day.

During the past week and more, she had come to know Javan, and was beginning to accept her fate, perhaps even welcome it. He was kind and protective. He was strong enough to carry her burdens as well as his own, and he was faithful to his word. It would not be hard to be his wife, but she felt a thrill of fear.

That day.

Part of her wanted to get the joining over with. Part of her wanted to put if off as long as she could.

She needed to sit down. Javan let go of her hand, and she sank to the ground.

THE BOY busily pointed parts of the city out to Javan, who nodded his agreement, even though a city wall blocked the way of the little finger. He would never be able to find anything if he followed the child's explanations and gestures, but the child was trying so hard to help that Javan could only agree and try not to laugh. Or cry. Finally, he pressed a piece of silver into the boy's palm, successfully stopping the endless prattle. While the boy was distracted, he pulled Obed aside a few paces.

"I think I remember this 'Old Sarah' he spoke of, Obed. There may be others with rooms to share, but we should start with her."

Obed still seemed pale, but maybe it was just the sun glaring down on them, washing everything in its glare. "I agree. We also have claims to make. If there are people here who remember us, it will help. What about your land? Do you foresee problems?"

Javan rubbed a hand over the back of his sore neck. "I made it clear before I left that I was not abandoning my ancestral lands. If there are any records here, my claim will be among them. There should be little trouble proving who I am, at any rate."

Obed nodded. "It is getting late. We have too much to arrange to stand about in the sun. Shall we go?"

"Both of us?" Javan nodded behind him at the slaves watching the flocks. "We may be deep in Israel, but do you think they will stay here because we tell them to?"

Obed looked at the worn, dirty faces of the young men. "Yes, Javan, I think they will. I think they could fall asleep where they stand. Running back to Ammon is the farthest thing from their minds."

Javan studied the people he now owned and decided Obed was right. Jumping on a nearby rock, he called the group to attention. "Obed and I will arrange lodgings and food. You may take your ease. Satisfy your thirst and rest, but do not let the flocks wander. Our journey is done."

Despite their fatigue, the slaves gave a tired cheer and flopped as one onto the hard ground. Obed grinned at Javan. "No rebellion today, my friend. Shall we go?"

Javan looked at Taleh, sitting on the ground. He wanted . . . no, needed to remind her that she was his. She did not know what awaited her. What would it take before she would welcome his attentions after this night passed?

"One moment," he said to Obed, and he walked to her side. He reached down and grasped her arms, lifting her to her feet. Her lips were chapped and dusty, but he did not care. It was enough to feel their fullness under his own. He slid his fingers into the richness of her hair, easing her head back. He claimed her mouth as his, rejoicing in her acceptance, something to remember after she hated him.

He forced himself to pull back. He still held her hair, and as it slipped through his fingers, he felt an embarrassing lump in his throat. Tonight it would all be gone, and he would have to shave it off himself. It was hard to think of cutting off this beautiful bounty. He had grown attached to it, watching it slide over her cheeks as she bent to her work, seeing it shimmer in the sun while it dried, feeling it drift across his fingers whenever he found an excuse to touch her. It draped her like an exquisite black garment.

Would he still find her beautiful without it? Yes, he thought so.

But what would she think of him?

Taleh touched her fingers to her lips, a dazed look on her face. Javan smiled. Before he had a chance to try again, Obed jerked on his arm.

"We will be late," he snapped. Obed hurried down the path to the city gate, his anger obvious. The little boy who led them tried valiantly to catch their attention as he skipped along at their side.

"My name is Micah. I forgot your name." He tugged on Javan's sleeve. "I forgot your name."

"Javan." He looked at Obed, the back down to Micah. "Would you like to run ahead and tell the village elders we come?" Micah nodded with little boy importance, and scurried off, giving Obed a wide birth. Javan felt vaguely guilty for setting the boy an impossible task. Who would listen to the wild stories of such a young child? But it was necessary. Obed wanted to speak his mind, something he could not do in front of Micah.

Obed stopped and whirled on Javan. "What a foolish thing to do! Have you taken leave of your senses?"

Javan did not have to ask what he meant. "Have you not wanted to do the same to Merab?"

"Of course, but I have no wish to violate the Law. We still have a month to go, in case you have forgotten. A *month*!" His voice raised until it was nearly a shriek. "Or is your control so complete that you can take liberties and not pay for them? Do you think you can ignore the parts of the Law that chafe? We are to leave the women alone!"

"I have not forgotten the words of the Law, Obed." He kept his voice quiet, hoping to moderate his friend's temper with his own calm, thin as it was. "I wanted her to remember that, even though she is without guard, she is still mine. It was a reminder, that is all."

A reluctant smile softened Obed's face. "It was quite a reminder. But how to you intend to explain to her that she will have to wait a month for what your kiss promised?"

Javan muttered, "I never told her about the month. I only told her she would be given time to mourn. And adjust."

After a shocked moment, Obed burst out, "She does not know?" He fixed Javan a piercing look and then he laughed, loud and raucous. Javan glared at him, but he refused to give in.

"You think it funny?"

Obed nodded. "Oh, yes. To have the upper hand for once on this journey is a pleasure, one I intend to savor. Javan, afraid of a young woman? Indeed, yes. I think it funny."

It was pointless to argue.

As they passed through the posts, they noticed signs of the fire, blackened stone that no amount of scrubbing could clean. The original gates still stood. Javan paused only a moment to examine the repair work, new pieces carefully placed and mortared in with the old. The gates seemed to be not as high as he remembered, but then, he had been younger and a bit shorter.

Just inside the city, long benches ran beside the walls, enjoying the coolness the protective shade provided. Men sat there, as they had all the years of Javan's memories, engaging in friendly debate. Talking stopped when they noticed Javan and Obed. The oldest man among them, white-haired and long-bearded, was the first to speak. "Welcome to our city. Do you come in peace?"

"We come in peace," Javan answered for them both. "We come from the war with Ammon, and from the armies of Jephthah. We were soldiers and now that the war is done, we have come to reclaim our hereditary possessions."

The men along the wall exchanged surprised glances. Again, the oldest one spoke. "What are your names, that you should have hereditary possessions among those of us who have survived?"

"I am Javan, son of Gideon. You must remember my father, who grazed his flocks on the other side of this valley. He sat among you on your council when the need arose. His wisdom was well spoken of in this city." Javan watched the faces before him closely, trying to find their names hiding in his memory, hoping they would remember him.

He saw the remembrance come, saw their eyes widen in wonder. His throat clogged. Their faces blurred.

"Can it really be you?" "Is this Javan?" "You did come back! We were afraid to hope." One by one, the men rose to embrace him, kissing his cheeks in welcome.

The tears, finally loosed, ran down his face. He was home, and they remembered him. The terrible loss of his family, so sharply repressed these many years, rose to overwhelm him with horrible pain. These knew his story, they knew what he had endured, for they shared it with him. Who would he find still alive besides these men at the gates? What further grief awaited him today?

The men at the gate gave their own names. Javan struggled to connect these old men with the much younger images he had carried inside all this time. The difficult years showed on all of them. Faces once smooth and unlined were now creased by worry and hardship. Hair that had been brown or black was streaked with gray, and thin on top.

He was pleased to see one sign of better times. The men wore new robes of fine wool and linen. The Ammonites had not been here recently. There had been time to shear sheep, to harvest flax and spin and weave. The endless months he spent at war gave his people a time of rest.

The old men next turned their attention to Obed, weeping openly himself. "I am Obed," he managed to say. "Son of Nathan, the leather-worker. I, too, have returned."

One of the men turned to Micah, standing wide-eyed nearby, and ordered, "Go to your father's shop and tell him that Obed son of Nathan has returned."

This time, no one wept. The men at the gate just smiled.

Javan looked at him and shrugged, then turned back to the older men. "I have other business to attend to this day. I have brought back a wife from Ammon, and I wish to have my marriage registered."

The smiles disappeared in that instant. He knew what was coming. He could not blame them, but what did they expect? Where else could he have found a wife?

The spokesman, Eli by name, was the first to scold. "You would bring our enemies into our village? What happened to you while you were gone? Did you forget what they did to us? You would defile the memories of your parents by bringing one of their murderers into their home?"

Javan struggled to speak respectfully. Eli, however cutting his words, was still an elder in the village, entitled to courtesy. "My *wife* had nothing to do with the deaths in my family. And when last I saw it, there was no home left standing. The house into which I bring my wife will be my own. And I ask you, would you have me live alone? Have I not done enough of that? What honor would I bring to my family if I let my name die off the land? Who would inherit, who would get all that was mine? How should I get heirs to carry my name?"

Eli was not impressed, Javan could see. "There are plenty of widows left after their last attack."

Javan held his temper with effort. "How was I to know that? I left before I had reached an age to marry. Even if I were to have stayed, how could I have rebuilt my home without crops to sell? Where would I have lived while I tried to begin again? How could I have brought a wife into that?"

"How did any of us?" Amos spoke sharply from the wall where he stood, listening until now without speaking. "We had no more than you did when you left."

"You tell me I should have stayed? Is that what you would have had me do? Twenty cities of Ammon are gone, the area is uninhabited, the flocks have been brought back as repayment. I had to do what I did. If none had gone with Jephthah, who would have fought this war, who would have put an end to their persecution for you? For that, I have brought home a bride captured from them. The Law states that I may do so, I have obeyed all the rules. I have taken enough lives, spilled enough blood, for all of you! I will be responsible for my wife before all, just as the Law requires. Obed will do likewise for his wife. Two Ammonite women will hardly be more than you can endure, will they?"

Javan's tirade was cut short with a sudden cry from Obed, a shout of surprise and joy. He turned to see Obed hurl himself, arms outstretched, into the disbelieving embrace of a man so like him they could only be brothers. The two men wept loud sobs, of pain and gladness, of sorrow so deep and abiding the scars would never fade. Little Micah of the well, big-eyed, startled at so much emotion flowing so wildly, stood fascinated.

Pangs of jealousy ripped through Javan, searing his heart. Why could that not be him, welcoming flesh and blood? Why did he stand alone while Obed had so much given back to him? Holding himself rigid against the rage sweeping through his body, he cursed himself for his selfishness.

Someone must have seen something on his face, for an arm came around his shoulder. Turning, he saw Eli, putting their disagreements aside, offering what consolation he could. But Javan could not summon a smile to thank him, even while he appreciated the kind gesture. The hurt was too deep.

Obed finally pulled himself away, looking at his brother now full grown. "You lived. You still live," he said, his voice warm with wonder.

"Yes, I lived. I wondered, all through the years, what became of you. No one could find you. We thought you dead, even though some swore they had seen you leaving the city. Who could believe it?" Obed's brother smiled, and smiled again. "There is even better news than me, older brother. Can you bear it?"

"You are alive. I can bear anything," Obed assured him with a laugh.

"This boy who brought you into the city is your nephew. Micah is my own son, my firstborn."

Obed looked down at little Micah, then knelt. "I am your uncle," he said after a silent moment. "What do you think of that?"

"What is an uncle?" Micah asked.

"Your father is my brother, that is what an uncle is. We are family."

That pleased Micah. His face glowed. "We are? Good!"

The villagers gathering to witness the event laughed at Micah's innocent pleasure. Javan had to get away from the happy crowd. Why would not his legs walk away? Why was he standing here, putting himself through this torture? He had no brothers living. He knew that, for he had buried their bodies. He would have no nephews, no nieces. No family would come out of the crowd to surprise him, no one would laugh at his pleasure. His chest grew tighter and tighter. His heart was desolate, emptied of anything but grief. It tore at his insides with bitter claws until each breath was a burden. Vengeance was over, the war that had given his life purpose, and what did he have now? His heart felt emptied of everything he had believed in, abandoned by the God he had trusted.

From the dark recesses of his mind, Taleh's face formed. The weight crushing him lifted just enough to allow a pain-free heartbeat. He had a wife, waiting outside the city walls in the hot sun. Whatever family he would have in the years to come, she would provide him. He would never have nieces or nephews, but he would have children. It would have to be enough.

A tiny light burned inside him, trust trembling to live again. He accepted what comfort his thoughts could give, grateful that the doubt had been so brief.

Then Obed's brother spoke. "That is not my only surprise, Obed," he said. "I have an even greater one." He paused for effect, and Javan braced himself instinctively for more pain. Obed's brother's next words were a sword, piercing straight to Javan's heart. "Our father still lives."

Bitter anger rose, and his faith trembled. Javan could no longer bear to witness all that he had lost. He pushed his way through the crowd and walked like one mortally wounded out of the city.

CHAPTER 13

THE SUN BEAT HOT FROM THE CLOUDLESS SKY. TALEH DID NOT KNOW HOW long they had been waiting. Sweat trickled down her back, just out of reach. Her long hair stuck to her neck, and the tendrils that escaped her braid slid along her skin, joining the drops of sweat in their itchy torment. The slave boys lay stretched out on the ground, even though the sun had long since baked heat into it. The grass was brown after the long summer, waiting like the people for the cool wetness of the rainy season to come.

"I am tired of waiting," Merab sulked. "I do not see why we have to stay out here. I am going in."

"You cannot do that!" Taleh had to protest, to provide the voice of reason, even though part of her agreed with Merab. "They said they would come back for us, and they will."

"I wonder what is going on in there."

Taleh echoed her feelings. Since it was really too hot to talk, she and Merab resumed their watch of the gate, as if they could make someone appear just by willing it. From time to time, they heard empty stomachs complaining in the heavy stillness.

Something finally shifted by the gate. Taleh blinked, half afraid it would disappear.

Javan stood, open palms pressed against the pillars, his shoulders bowed under some unseen weight. He made no move to come toward them, did not even seem to see them. As she watched, he slowly lowered his head to the stone, as if appealing to some unhearing god.

Taleh's welcoming smile wavered. Even at a distance the pain and anger reached her. Whatever had happened behind the walls of his city, it had hurt him deeply. She wished she knew what to do. Did she go to meet him, or would it be better to leave him alone, to come to terms with his burden in his own way?

Would he even accept comfort from his enemy wife?

Without warning, Javan began to pound his fist against the stone. The stone absorbed his blows, not even a whisper reaching her ears. Nothing else moved, only his fist, beating an irregular pattern on the gate of his city. He stopped as abruptly as he began, and slumped against the pillar as though his mighty strength failed him. Taleh watched in horror as he wiped his eyes. Did he weep? She felt sick with worry. What had done this to him?

Shoving himself away from the pillar, he turned and walked with eerie calm toward the group at the well. Taleh averted her eyes, not wanting him to know she had seen.

No one else had noticed, Taleh saw with relief as she glanced around. Merab still sat as before, head resting on her bent knees, shielding her eyes from the glare of the sun.

When Javan reached them, his normal compassion had vanished. The stern army leader was back. "Keep watch on the flocks! They are straggling all over the valley!" The slave boys sat up, surprised at this new Javan. "Taleh, Merab, gather your things and come with me. The elders of the city wait for us inside. The rest of you will have to stay here. Do try not to lose everything before I come back for you."

There was no patience in his tone. Taleh and Merab hurried to obey, collecting their small store of possessions. Taleh watched him warily. This callous sarcasm was not what she expected after his display of grief.

The boys scurried to gather the sheep and goats into a semblance of a flock, stealing anxious glances. Javan must have realized what he had done. He took a deep breath, pulling his control together, and continued more calmly, "I will have food brought out to you if we are going to be gone longer than I expect. I know it is hot. I must make arrangements to pasture the animals and find lodgings for all of us. I will be back soon."

Herding the women ahead of him, very much like he expected them to flee without his watchful eye to guard them, the trio walked toward the gates. Taleh tried to see everything of her new home, and slowed her steps as they passed the gates. The signs of the Ammonite attacks were very clear. The white stone was scarred with black, the mark of fire. Someone must have tried to scrub the burns off, but it had only rubbed away some of the detail in the carved limestone. The pomegranates and palms were still visible even through the charring, with lilies winding up the corners of the heavy stone pillars. It looked to her like pillars and gates had been knocked down at one time and reset. Here and there chunks had broken off, interrupting the flowing pattern that should have extended the entire length. Near the ground, where a base should have been, carvings sprouted out of the dirt. How tall had the gates been before the attack?

She tried to get a closer look, but Javan took her arm and moved her through the wall's opening. On the other side of the thick stone barrier, benches pressed against the coolness. With a flurry of robes, a small group of men standing around seated themselves on the dark worn wood. Unsure of the rules, painfully aware of the hostile eyes on every side, Taleh dropped her gaze to the ground. She was grateful for Javan's solid presence behind her. The crowd parted to let them through, backing away as though they were lepers. Javan placed his hand against her back, marking her as his and urging her along at the same time. Despite that, her steps lagged as they neared the benches and the men seated there.

The eyes across from her were angry. Forcing herself to look beyond that, she saw older men, gray-haired and heavily bearded. Nothing about their robes indicated their right to sit in authority, but she knew the authority was there.

One of them spoke. "Did you bring two wives for yourself, or can we assume one of them belongs to Obed?" His voice was abrupt and harsh.

"Only one is mine," Javan responded with surprising courtesy. Taleh stared at him. Why did he permit the man to speak so? He was a commander! Was it simply the other man's age? What power did the old man wield over Javan to command such respect?

Obed appeared without warning, his face tear-streaked and blotched with red. Taleh's mouth dropped open. What had gone on here?

When Obed reached for Merab's hand, Taleh held her breath, hoping her friend would feel, as she did, how precarious their position and behave accordingly. Merab, after a shocked look at Obed's damp face, stood in submission, or at least in silence. Something of the tension surrounding her must have penetrated.

The old men nodded, then turned aside, whispering together, ignoring the group before them. Taleh tried not to frown.

Surely there was a better way to be greeted. However much their nation was hated, how much of a threat could they be, two tired, dusty, hungry young women?

JAVAN RUBBED the back of his neck and tried not to let his frustration grow. If he had been alone with the elders, he would not have hesitated to speak up. But he had to impress Taleh and Merab with the position of authority these men held, and for that reason he would stand quietly.

Finally the council was done. "We will register your marriages. Old Sarah, widow of Geber, lives alone. Her house can provide you with lodging while you build your own houses."

"I have slaves who will need lodging." Javan knew this would not go over well. Wives, and now slaves from Ammon. "Is there a place near Sarah's where they can stay?"

Thunderous silence followed. Anger lapped at Javan in waves. "There are more?" Eli asked. "How many of our enemies have you brought back with you into our land?"

Obed spoke up. "We left with nothing. We bring back gold, and flocks, and slave boys to work our land. We took them as repayment for our losses, and we take full responsibility for them."

Eli sagged, as if under a heavy burden. "We will record that in the registers as well. Sarah has sheds behind her house. They have not been used since her husband died many years ago, but they should serve your purposes."

Javan nodded. "Your worries are for nothing. We saw horrors you can only imagine in our trek through Ammon. We want only to live in peace on our own soil. Thank you for protecting our family lands. It is good to be home."

Eli smiled then. "Despite our words earlier, it is good to have you back. Are you willing to obey all the Law's requirements for brides taken from captives? Allow me to recite that passage."

"No!" It was going to be difficult enough to explain everything to Taleh in privacy. To have her find out in front of everyone in the village was unthinkable. "I mean, I do know what my obligations are. Jephthah made them very clear when I first claimed her." To hear that she would have her head shaved, to have her shocked reaction exposed before the mocking eyes of hostile strangers, no, he would not permit that.

A long, thoughtful pause followed. Javan held his breath.

"Very well. But we will be watching you." Eli pointed at a man in the crowd. "Bring them to Sarah's."

The streets had been much narrower in his youth. After finding the gates shorter, the city smaller, the village elders less imposing than he remembered, this change pleased him. He refused to think why the alteration had been necessary, refused to dwell on homes and families gone forever that left even the smaller city with the extra space.

He found other marks from the war. Most of the houses were smaller, too. All the houses had been forever marked by the fire that burned inescapably into stone and brick. No materials were left unscathed.

TALEH WALKED BEHIND JAVAN, waiting for him to turn and look at her. He had not reached for her when they had been dismissed from the men on the benches, had not even looked at her, had just assumed she would follow obediently. Of course, she was, but his indifference hurt.

Taleh had not expected that anyone here would be pleased to see them. She was not that big a fool. She thought she had been prepared for this long walk, being ushered into an unwelcoming city. But every time she had imagined herself coming into Javan's home town, he had been beside her. Not even her worst nightmares had forced her to walk past angry faces alone. She believed they had been recognized as husband and wife. Had they not been called "brides?" She certainly did not feel much like a wife, and Javan did not act like a husband.

His bitter words had hurt, still hurt. He had said in front of everyone, *'We learned to hate more about the Ammonites than any of you.'*

Was he having regrets? Could he change his mind now?

Why would he not even acknowledge her, turn his head and ensure she was still there?

THE GUIDE FINALLY STARTED TALKING. Javan wondered sourly if he was prompted by the sparkle of gold glinting through the donkeys' heavy sacks. Although Eli had already mentioned it, the man made a special point of Sarah's widowhood. Javan wondered if her husband had died by the hand of the Ammonites. Was this another dart aimed at his wife? At least it had found him as target instead of her.

Sarah's house was large, with a main floor and an upstairs, oddly reminiscent of the house in which he found Taleh, Javan thought as he looked at it. It was much too large for one old woman, a constant reminder of children who never were born. Sarah had already been too old for childbearing when Javan fled the devastated city, and childless, long past hope of providing heirs for her husband's wealth.

The stone house was oddly unmarked by fire, a beacon in a scarred city. Geber must have bought new stone rather than rebuild with what had been left. Javan wondered idly if that had bothered the villagers. The house had plenty of windows, for lattices appeared with regularity all along the walls.

Behind the house neat sheds stood, the only sign of their abandonment the height of the brown grasses growing wild around them. He wondered if it would be necessary to lock the young men in at night with bars over the lattices, and fashion locks on the outside of the doors as well. It was strange to think like a slaveowner. He looked back at the small sheds. Some lime whitewash remained, and although it was faded, Javan judged it would be enough to keep them dry, should they still be here for the first rains. He could only hope the roofs were in good shape.

Their guide called out a greeting. His voice had scarcely faded when the heavy wooden door of the big house opened, and Sarah stepped out.

Javan's memory suffered yet another painful blow. He remembered her dark-haired, plump, her skin unlined. The woman before him was none of those things. Her hair was white, her skin wrinkled and spotted with age, her body thin and bent.

Only her eyes remained the same, and they snapped fire at Javan. She gave no greeting.

"I thank you for your kindness in providing us with lodging," Javan said quietly.

Sarah nodded shortly, but still said nothing. Her lips compressed into a tight line, her eyebrows drew into a gray scowl.

"Did they tell you who we are? We are not strangers to you, Sarah, wife of Geber. I remember you well from my childhood. I am . . ."

"I know who you are, Javan." She interrupted with the permission of age. "You have no need to introduce yourself to me. I knew your mother and father well. They are not here to tell you what they think, but I will! You bring your wife into my house like she is a prize, and I am expected to make my enemy welcome! I did not think I would live to see a day so black as this one. They tell me, into whose house you bring this woman, that I must let a worshipper of Molech take rest beneath my roof. I will do it, but only because I have been given no other choice."

She stepped forward, her movements no less threatening because of her age and awkwardness. "Hear me well, Javan, and you, too, Obed. I will watch these women whom you have brought into our land. I will watch them ever so closely."

With that, she turned away, and walked back into her house. The only sign she left for them was the open door.

Javan met Obed's gaze and shrugged. "There is no place else for us to go," he said, and stepped inside.

Obed motioned for Taleh to enter ahead of him. She hesitated, but Javan was vanishing into the dark interior. The only thing worse than going into the house of a woman who hated her was going in without his help, so she followed.

The light from outside was blocked briefly when Merab and Obed followed. The lattices had been closed against the heat of the day. The room's coolness came as a welcome relief. She saw the room had chairs set about, and a bench piled with cushions. Javan had followed their hostess farther into the house, and Taleh stood alone and uncertain. Obed held Merab's hand.

Javan peered around the doorway on the opposite side of the room. He seemed to bring the enticing smell of boiling meat, and vegetables. Taleh identified spices, dill and sage, and warm bread. The air itself smelled good enough to eat.

"Come." Javan beckoned to her, and smiled. She felt herself smile back. "Sarah has food. We must honor her by eating it while it is still warm."

As Taleh stepped past him into the next room, his arm went around her waist, guiding her. Did it mean anything?

A table stood in the middle of the room, spread with all the wonderful food that had scented the air. It was long, big enough for many more than their small party. Benches ran along each side. No oil lamps hindered the fragrant air with their sputtering smoke. Instead, the windows were open, and the warm sunlight danced along with the dust playing in the golden beams.

Sarah entered, carrying two heavy pitchers, glistening with water, straining her wrinkled arms, pulling her frown tighter with their weight. "Sit. Sit. I did not carry all this food in for you to look at it."

Taleh had a difficult time swallowing her food under the scornful eye of the old woman. Javan and Obed insisted on speaking words before anyone was allowed to eat. Taleh had become accustomed to their habit the last few days of the trip, and saved herself another scowl by waiting, knowing it would more particularly be done here.

After the meal, Sarah gruffly complained about the clean-up, and Taleh felt Javan's steady gaze. She fought off the quick irritation. Did he not know by this time that she was willing to work? She never shirked any of the tasks he gave her. She caught her return glare in time.

JAVAN LOOKED around what would be his home for the next month. After sleeping under the stars for so long, he was not disposed to complain. The room was medium-sized, with a latticed window set up high off the floor. When he had opened it earlier, he noticed it overlooked the small courtyard behind Sarah's house. The sheds sat further back, easily visible from the rooms on the upper floor.

Behind him, Taleh said nothing.

The room's only furnishings were rolled-up sleeping pallets of woven wool stuffed with goat's fur. The doorway was covered by a thick leather curtain of carefully tanned and beautifully pieced goatskins, likely the work of Obed's brother Jesse. Javan had avoided looking too closely at it, his envy of Obed's life too bitter to permit that.

No one had stopped by to welcome him. A few had paused to watch while he and Obed untied sack after sack from the donkeys, gold glinting through the weave, clinking as each was set on the ground. He had expected more to come, to renew old friendships. Had he already met those who remembered him? Were the ones missing all dead? Or was it more likely that this was their way of expressing disapproval?

As they had walked through the village, the people had stared at Taleh, and frowned at him. They saw only her nation and her beauty, and despised him for his weakness. He wondered if anyone would bother to find out just how much Taleh had endured already, belying her fragile appearance.

Taleh moved around the room quietly, peeking inside the large sacks, seeing his treasures at last. He smiled. "Do you want anything there?"

She jumped at the sound of his voice, and turned startled eyes at him. "What?"

Had his people completely undone the days of trust he had tried to build? He tried again. "Do you see anything you like?"

"I was merely looking."

"So I see. Do you find anything to your taste?"

"It is all very nice."

"These possessions belong to you now, as well. Do not be shy with them." Would they bring bad memories for her, seeing her people's possessions in this foreign land? She would have to come to terms with it. She would have to come to terms with much, and soon.

Taleh unpacked carefully, as though trying to arrange her new lodgings the way a woman would like, but she did not fool him. She was using the tasks as a distraction, busy work while she waited for him to start . . . something. He knew, because his nerves, too, were stretched to the breaking point, but not by her nearness. No, the task he had dreaded was at hand, and he had told her nothing, relishing the time of peace. The leather curtain might shut out prying eyes, but not the ears that monitored his every move.

He would not let them down. He was determined to follow the Law, however difficult it might be, to show everyone he had not been corrupted by the practices of Ammon. Especially after bringing home, not just an Ammonite wife, which was bad enough, but Ammonite slaves as well.

He was delaying. He knew it. Taleh's presence surrounded him, her fluttery movements betraying her nervousness. To tell her she had nothing to fear from this night would not be the truth. This night she would lose, not her virginity, but her hair. He was not sure which was the greater loss.

He had put it off far too long. How hard could it be just to tell her? She was on her knees by the bundles. His hands were damp. He wiped them on his tunic.

"Taleh, sit down. There is no need for all this work. I will have someone help you unload the sacks tomorrow. We have things to talk about now."

She turned large, wary eyes on him, and cautiously eased herself upright, the brightly painted jar she had been unpacking clenched tightly in her arms. Javan marveled it did not break. He walked over. It was strange to see her like this, for she had begun to relax in his presence. He gently pried her fingers off the jar.

"I want only to explain some things to you." Javan captured her hands in his. "There are things I should have told you before, but the time did not seem right. Now you have to know." How did he go from here? Did he simply say, *I cannot take you for a month? Furthermore, this night I must shave off all your beautiful hair?*

Did he say, *I like this no more than you? If it were not required, I would not?* Would that help?

Now that the time was here, he felt completely at a loss, unqualified for the task.

He sat down on the stone floor first, and pulled gently until she had to join him. She gave him a tentative smile, and guilt stabbed again. "We are now wed. It has been registered, and witnessed by the village. I fear you are in for a difficult time. I did not expect you to be welcomed, but I did hope for less anger." He looked at her closely, holding her gaze as well as her hands. "I hope you will remember how much responsibility you bear, carrying my name."

CHAPTER 14

Taleh straightened her back, stiff with hurt. He may not have meant it to be an insult, but it felt very much like one. "I shall endeavor not to disgrace you," she said with as much dignity as she could. She tried to pull her hands away, but he did not let go.

"I know." His eyes were kind, and he smiled at her. To Taleh's dismay, her anger slipped, and she could not bring it back. What power did he hold over her, that he could melt her anger with a smile?

"I have learned you always do your best at whatever you attempt. You also do not complain. You may find both these qualities tested in the days to come." Unexpectedly he dropped her hands and bolted erect, striding over to the window as though something drove him on. He stood looking at the closed lattice, not moving to open it.

Unease prickled at Taleh's spine. He turned to face her, and this time his eyes held pity. She wrapped her arms around her middle, trying to keep her fear at bay, her fingers cold where they touched her skin.

"I know you think I will take you tonight. I have been remiss in acquainting you with the rules of our Law. You cannot learn it all at once. In the future, I will make time to teach you when each day's work is done. But you must know what will and will not happen this night. This is not the night I will claim your body. Our Law requires I give you a month to mourn your family. Do you understand?"

"Yes," Taleh could not stop the words flooding out of her. "I repel you now that you are back on your own land! Your leaders have shamed you, and you now realize what a mistake you have made. Do I have to pass more trials before I qualify to be your wife? What will the men at your gates do if I fail one of them? Will they banish me to the desert? Or will they make it a merciful end and kill me where I stand?"

She was horrified after the words were out, but there was no way to take them back. Even if she could have, she needed to hear his answer.

Her tirade startled Javan, she could tell by his raised brows, but when he spoke, his voice was mild. "That is not true. I cannot regret what I said to the elders, nor will I apologize for my words. I might hate your country, what I saw there, but I know that was not your belief. I saw your face on the journey here when I mentioned the altars. There was much of your land you hated, also."

She wanted to turn her head away, but he caught her chin. "No, do not deny it. I saw it in your eyes, then and now." He sobered. He had been serious, but the ominous weight of moments ago was back, and knots reformed in her stomach. "We are not done with tonight. This month of waiting is the Law, if we wish to wed a captive. It applies to Obed and Merab as well. You will not be waiting alone. I, too, must endure this test. Do you think it easier for me? It will be torment for me."

He would be *tormented*? Relief slipped through her. Perhaps he did desire her, enough to overcome his hatred of her Ammonite-ness.

He kept speaking. "This time can help us if we use it the right way. You will be able to learn about us. I will go out to my land and rebuild my family's home."

She went suddenly cold all over, not just her hands. "You will leave me here alone?"

"I will be here each evening. I must fix us a house. I will have the house completed before this month is over. You will not be here alone. You have Merab, and Sarah."

Taleh raised a skeptical eyebrow. It was as much as she could do just then. She was going to be left alone all day with people who hated her.

"Do not let her gruffness frighten you. Win her over. Help her with her chores. She has much to do with so many staying here. She is too old to do everything herself. Besides, how else can we get through this? If we spend too much time together, we will surely fail this test."

He had used the wrong word. Before she could throw that word back at him, he added, "Yes, it is a test. A trial. You are right in that. But it is not just for you. It is a test for both of us. We both have much to prove."

She was no longer a child, Taleh told herself as she held his gaze. She had survived Chelmai's vicious words. She had endured the harassments of the men of Minnith. She had lived through the long journey across the desert, been unharmed during the destruction of the rebels. She could do this.

They thought she was not as good as they, that she, by her very presence, contaminated them. She may not know their law yet, but she could learn. She would show them what she was made of.

It would be easier if she had Javan's presence when she went among them, but possibly she had something to prove to him as well. As long as he was not going to abandon her, as long as he was willing to keep her, she would make it through this time.

She could be as good as them.

"Very well," she said aloud. "I will obey this law. I would not give them cause to speak out further against me."

"Good!" Javan's smile eased the coldness that had built from her first steps into his village.

As she watched, the smile disappeared. There was a menacing purpose about him that suddenly frightened her. He had the advantage as he came back across the room, for she still sat on the stone floor, and by the time she scrambled to her feet, he had reached her side.

"Do not be afraid. I am not going to hurt you." He caught her hands that she held up as though they would stop him. Despite his reassuring words, his face was grim. "I have one thing I must do tonight. It is something neither of us wants. If it were not the Law, I would not, but I have no choice. Neither do you." Javan sighed, a deep, heavy sound. "I must shave off your hair," he said bluntly.

"No."

"It is not a choice, Taleh. I must shave off your hair." He actually looked sad.

What a liar his face was. "I will not let you." But she did not know how she could stop him.

"It is my law, my covenant. I have not broken faith with it before, I will not do so now. And neither will you. It will be part of your life from now on."

"My hair is part of my life. It is part of *me*. I do not care what your precious law says. I will not let you shave my head!"

He did not answer, just looked at her with that implacable face. The force of his will lapped at her.

She could only stare at him. He was *serious*. This was not a trick. He meant every word. "I will hide it. I will wear a veil, a headdress, whatever you say. No one will know."

Javan made no move toward her. "Everyone will know. Even if they did not, my God will know, and he is the only one who matters. What kind of start is deceit?"

"I will cut a little." She even sounded like she was pleading, but she did not think demands would get her anywhere.

He was still, too still. "No. It must be shaved. All of it." Even his voice was hushed. "It is the sign of mourning. Surely you want to mourn your family."

Anger tore through her. "That is a despicable thing to say. I have been mourning them every day since you killed them. How dare you use that as an excuse to humiliate me in front of your entire village!" She took a step backward, hoping he would not notice. He must not catch her. She dared not look behind her, dared not take her eyes from him.

He simply walked over to the only opening in the room and stood, cutting off what her mind knew had been her destination. The hopelessness of her situation finally became clear to her. "I will hate you if you do this," she said.

"I know. I wish I did not have to do it. Surely you know it will grow back. I will never ask you to cut your hair again. I know that is no comfort now, but I make you that promise."

He blurred as tears filled her eyes. She did not care if she had to plead. "Please, please do not do this. I will never disobey you, I will be the perfect wife, I will never deny you anything, but please leave me my hair."

"I cannot. I cannot break my faith, or betray my God. It will grow back. You will gain the respect of the village. Did you not just say you would do what was necessary?" He finally took a step toward her. "*This* is necessary." He stopped right in front of her and gently set his hands on her shoulders. "Taleh, I do not ask you for your permission. This is *my* land, *my* law, and *my* home. You are my wife. I will make sure we obey this law, with or without your cooperation. Please make this easy for both of us."

She wanted to pull away, to lash out. Shave. He had said *shave*, as in nothing left. And he was not going to back down.

"I hate you for this," she said. Her words, so inadequate for her hurt, held no emotion. She would not let him hear her fear, and she had already bared too much with her tears.

"I know."

His eyes looked down at her, barely recognizable through the tears that spilled over their bounds. She remembered her own guilt when the armies swept over her village, remembered wondering if it had been her heresy that had brought such destruction on them all. She had betrayed her gods.

Would she actually ask him to betray his?

What punishment did his god have for them if Javan disobeyed? Would it be worse for her, the unbeliever? Maybe his god's retribution would come from the angry men at the gate. Maybe they would cut her down, her last sight their satisfied faces.

Did she really want to chance it?

An aching sob burst out of her, as the grief of weeks finally let loose. She shoved her fist against her mouth, bowed her head so she could not see his triumph, and nodded.

How long would it take her to forgive him for this night? The tears in her eyes were like a knife through him.

He turned her around so he could begin. Her hair was in its customary braid, and now that would serve to help him, for it would be a simple thing to cut through it with his sharp knife.

Simple. It was the wrong word.

He ached to get it over with. He pulled his knife out of its familiar place in his belt with one hand and took her braid with the other. It was so thick, so heavy. And so very long. He remembered combing it, how the ends draped nearly into the sand where she sat. His knife was so sharp a few hairs separated when he set it against its target. Fast, to get it over with? Or slow? But the knife made up his mind for him as more hairs sheared away. One swipe, another through the heavy mass that gave its own protest, a gasp of realization from his wife, and the braid came away in his hand.

He looked at it, dangling from his fist, and some quixotic impulse made him turn her around. The straggled ends tumbled around her white face, what he could see of it as she turned her head away. He slid his knife back into his belt, picked up her hand, and folded her fingers around it.

Her hand closed tightly, and she pulled the braid against her heart, folding her arms over herself to hold it in place. He saw a silver tear fall onto it.

Javan turned her away again, and reached for the razor he had hidden out of her sight earlier. His hand paused, and he looked over at the sacks of plunder. Somewhere in them was oil and ointment, something to protect her skin from the razor and to soothe it after. She stood where he left her, head bowed, clutching the braid as silent tears slipped down her face.

He rummaged quickly, afraid she would suddenly bolt. There it was, this one would be perfect, a rich lotion that he could pour easily. She had not moved. Taking the stopper out, he dribbled the lotion over her with one firm hand while the other tilted her head far enough back so the thick liquid did not run into her eyes. She flinched when the moisture hit her scalp, but stayed quiet.

He felt her shudder, and realized how hard she fought to keep her weeping inside. For a moment, he almost stopped.

When the jar was empty, he dropped it on the floor, hearing it crack when it hit. He picked up the razor and set the sharp edge against her skull.

His hand shook. He steadied it. It took an astonishing amount of willpower to slide the blade along the soft skin hiding under her black tresses, even more not to stop as the first strands came free.

The razor cut another dark swath, and another. Oil scented the air with oppressive sweetness, mocking the tears that ran down her face and mingled with the slippery liquid. A small silky curl slid free over her shoulder, and Javan saw her hand slowly reach out as it washed down her robe, and close over it. A braid and a curl were all she had left, and she held them both with poignant tenderness.

The last black curls lost to his blade, and it was over.

Dark, oil-covered hair littered his legs as liberally as it did her robe, sliding off onto the slippery stone beneath his feet. She must have known it was all gone, because Taleh burst into loud, agonizing sobs that shook her entire body as she slowly sank onto the floor. Javan flung the razor aside as he felt her go down, knelt beside her and pulled her into his arms, holding tight, trying not to think, to feel.

She continued to wail like a grieving mother over a lost child for long moments, soaking his tunic with her tears. He felt wetness on his own face, and knew with surprise that he wept with her.

Taleh suddenly went limp, her anguish burned out like a sputtering lamp. Javan's relief sapped his own strength. He looked down at her tear-streaked face, to discover she had fallen asleep. As he watched, her body grew heavy. He shifted her into his arms, and rocked himself onto his feet.

The sleeping pallets lay where they had been unrolled, and Javan kicked one into position. Kneeling with Taleh in his arms was more difficult than standing up had been, but he did it without waking her. She looked breakable, fragile and hurt. The scraped skin of her scalp made him wince. He had tried so hard to be careful. Her beautiful hair was gone, all of it, leaving her dark brows startling slashes across her skin. Oddly, the effect highlighted her features, their perfection all the more apparent without the distraction her hair had provided.

Still, he thought, if only there had been another way! But the Law was everything, his whole life, the contract with Moses and Israel, and obedience to his God was not negotiable.

Muffled sounds and thumping caught his attention. Despite his own problems, Javan stifled a tired smile. He was not the only one in for a difficult night.

Too tired to do anything more, Javan slipped off his outer tunic and threw it into a corner. It would have to be burned – tomorrow. He pulled the other pallet alongside hers. He would keep her warm during the night, and he would keep her *there*. He opened a blanket, laid himself down heavily, and covered them both with it. Warmth spread through him, easing the last bits of tension. He closed his eyes, and was asleep.

CHAPTER 15

THE SUN PEEPED THROUGH A SMALL GAP IN THE CLOSED LATTICE, TEASING Javan with the morning. Years of training had taught him to know instantly where he was. Without opening his eyes, he knew Taleh lay where she had been all night. He could hear her soft breathing, and turned his head to see her body relaxed in the sweet release of sleep. He took advantage of her unconscious state to look his fill.

Her lips were slightly parted, and dry. Tear tracks had left their silver trails overnight. The visual reminder of her restless night sat uncomfortably, of lying next to her, knowing she was not even aware of her soft sobs.

In the mellow light of the early day, he could see the damage the razor had done to her scalp despite his care. Her scalp was dotted with spots of dried blood where the razor had cut too closely. Other areas were abraded, leaving behind patches of tender skin, like an active child's knee.

He had done his best to make it as comfortable an ordeal as possible. He would not apologize for carry out the law.

He could, however, protect what was left of her dignity.

Among his spoil, the sacks hid beautiful swatches of linen specially woven for headdresses, and bands to keep them in place. It would take time for her hair to grow back, but there was no need for her to feel any more exposed than necessary. She was a stranger to the land, the customs and laws. She would have enough of a struggle finding a place for herself. Whatever he could do to smooth her way, was it not his responsibility to do those things for her?

He eased himself away from her side, hearing the slight change in her breathing that signaled her own return to wakefulness. For some strange reason, he found himself hurrying. Was he sparing her modesty, or his own? The thought that he might be uncomfortable with her eyes on him was almost funny. True, for many years it had been only men around when he dressed or bathed. There was little room for false modesty in an army of men, nor the time or inclination to pander to such foolishness.

He paused briefly to consider himself unclothed. He was not disappointed in his body. It was tall, and strong. It did what he wanted it to do. It had always been *there,* bigger than most, stronger than many. He had given it little thought, save on the rare occasions when he had been wounded. Now he wondered how she would see it, what she would think.

This was not the day to test her reactions.

He washed quickly, using what water he found in the pitcher. He looked at the robe he had worn yesterday, and many yesterdays before that. It needed burning, he had not changed his mind overnight. Somewhere in his soldier's pack, he had another robe. It would be dusty but whole, and untainted by the heavy oil he had used last night.

While Taleh slept, he searched through the spoils for things that might find favor with an aggrieved wife. What a lovely word that was – wife. Despite the long wait ahead of them, she was his wife now, and he was her husband. He liked the connection, the acknowledgement of possession, both his – and hers.

Robes of rich colors were pulled out. They felt gritty to the touch, thick with dust and sand. He could not give these to her! They had to be washed before anyone could wear them.

Taleh needed a new robe. Even if it had not been a part of the Law, necessary for him to obey in order to marry her, he would have done so anyway. Women in Israel did not wear such garments as she had.

He would have to get something from Sarah. She would not be happy but he would find something to serve as compensation.

"You never thought the robes would get dirty? How like a man," Sarah muttered under her breath, but she gave him a robe. It was too large and colorless, undyed, but it was linen and had a sash and headdress. In its place, Javan gave her a small golden bowl of the size women liked and men thought too little to serve any purpose.

Sarah smiled when she held it in her wrinkled hands. "I guess I can forgive you your foolishness."

Javan returned to his room, laid out his gifts and waited. The warming air released the heady scent of the oil he had used on her last night. He wished he could rid the room of the odor.

What would she think today?

A deep sigh heralded her awakening, followed by restless stretches. He braced himself. She yawned loudly, and he smiled at such a solid sound coming from such a frail creature. Her actions were so normal, so usual.

Until she reached up to brush her hair from her eyes in long habit.

Javan held his breath.

She froze for an endless moment.

When her eyes opened, he was surprised by the anger in them. He expected tears, but not anger.

"You did this to me," she hissed.

"I obeyed the rules of our Law," he quickly corrected her. "You agreed last night. I can give you my word that you will never be asked to do anything like this again, but I do not think you feel like accepting any promises. There is no reason for you to hide in here. I have a robe and headdress for you. It is not necessary for others to see your head. I think you will be more . . . comfortable with it covered. Go help Sarah with whatever she needs to do. You are healthy and young, Sarah is old." Javan wished he knew what Taleh was thinking. She gave no indications, just that mutinous stare. He continued, "Try to win Sarah's good favor. Word will spread of your kindness. Consider this a challenge, not punishment."

He ignored her glare. "They *are* willing to let you prove yourself, you will see. Now wash the oil from your skin and put on the robe. There is much to do today."

TALEH LOOKED at the small pile of gifts he had waiting for her. If only he would leave!

He sat where he was and waited. What did he want of her now? Her temper, pushed to its limits by the shock of her baldness, vibrated through her like a live thing.

Javan said firmly, "Taleh, Sarah is already up and working. Surely you do not want to give her reason to complain."

Lifting her chin, Taleh snapped, "I will help her, if she will let me. Please leave now, so I can get dressed."

Javan rose and went over to pick up a small pile of soiled clothes from the floor, then went to the curtain that covered the door. "I will get you water to bathe. Perhaps you would wash the oil off the floor. I find I grow tired of the smell of it. I will be back as quickly as I can."

Taleh sagged with relief when he was gone. Mourning and vanity and humiliation swirled around inside her. She wanted her hair. The pain of its loss surprised her.

Over on one of the many sacks of plunder from her city, something pulled her attention. It almost looked like another gift, long and silky-looking, ripples that reflected the morning light in shades of black and blue. Taleh took one step, another. She knew that color, that shape. She moved in slow steps until she reached the pile, then stopped, looking down at her braid, left out on top with the rest of Javan's spoils. Next to it she saw a simple curl.

She remembered him placing the braid in her hand, remembered rescuing that lone curl as it slipped away down her robe, remembered holding both tightly. Sometime during the night she must have let go, though she could not imagine ever releasing either, even in sleep.

They sat, both, on top of Javan's plunder from Minnith. Was that how he saw them, another bit of Ammon's wealth? Dare she take them back? But if she did – she had nothing in this room of her own, no place to hide them. Everything belonged to Javan.

He had kept her hair.

She reached out a finger, and ran it along the braid. "Just hair," she whispered into the air. "It will grow back." But how long would it take?

She had wasted too much time. He could just walk in. She was his now, regardless of this month he spoke so much of. As quickly as she was able, she stripped her robe off, tattered, stiff with dried oil, thick with scent.

The pitcher of water was empty. Wash yourself, he had said, but he had left her nothing.

Javan's gifts to her lay in obvious display on the floor. She glared at the pile as though Javan himself were there.

JAVAN WALKED QUIETLY UP the stairs with the heavy water jar in his arms, hearing no sounds from the room that served as Obed's dwelling. Sarah had grumbled, and he worried about leaving Taleh in her company. If he were not so constrained by the amount of work he had to do preparing his old home and fields, he would stay with Taleh on this first day. She needed to begin making her way among his people. She could not make a place simply by being his wife.

Somehow his justifications did not still his conscience.

He eased open the leather curtain. Taleh had not heard him enter. She knelt on the floor, wrapped in the blanket. His gifts, Sarah's gifts through him, still sat in a pile on the floor. She clutched her old yellow robe.

She could not mean to still wear it. Would she reject his gift out of spite?

"Give your old robe to me." Javan spoke without preamble. Taleh gave a sharp gasp and went completely still. "I must burn our clothes."

Still she did not move.

"Taleh, you know you cannot wear your robe again. It is worn and dirty, and nothing like what our women wear. It was not . . . appropriate even when new. I am burning my own robe as well. I can provide you with new garments. I do not want you to save it for the memories." Javan set down the water jar, walked slowly over to her and knelt at her side. He cautiously rested his hand on her shoulder and rubbed lightly. She stayed motionless under his touch.

She did not lash out at him. He took it as a good sign. Taleh slowly let go of the yellow robe. Javan reached behind him for the nearest sack and put it in her hand, tucking it around her clenched fingers. Without once raising her eyes, she hesitated, and then, as though getting a distasteful task over with, thrust the robe in the sack and shoved the ragged lump at Javan.

"Thank you. I have brought you water to wash yourself. Sarah waits by the table. She will need your help."

He rose to his feet, feeling as though he should say something more but not knowing what it could be. At the doorway he stopped, struggling to find words to extend as peace offering. "Taleh . . . I have not eaten this morning. I shall wait for you."

Her nod was a tiny one, but it was an agreement.

TALEH TREMBLED with a fury so powerful it was almost physical pain. The small area she had wiped clean on the copper pot was an unsparing mirror. Her head, once covered with lush hair, was bald. He had shaved it down to the skin, beyond in some spots that showed dark and raw. Her eyebrows stood out like freakish slashes. Her eyes, with their shocking darkness, took up most of her face. The pot pulled her face wide, the expanse of skin a cooper-tinted orange. The tip of her nose glowed back at her, betraying her tears.

She dabbed again at her swollen eyes, and set the pot down. She would never forgive Javan for this, never! And he sat at the table, waiting for her to come politely down the stairs and join him at his meal.

If she did not go soon, he would come back for her. She could not cower here in the room they had to share. Had she not told him, just the night before, that she would prove herself?

Last night, she had not known what a task she had been set.

She tightened her sash, pulled the too-large neckline of the plain, undyed robe back into place, and reached for the headdress. She placed it awkwardly on her head. The linen caught on the raw spots and she winced. The only times she had ever worn one before, her mother had put it on, adjusting it for her own purpose. It was much more difficult trying to do it alone. Her father had wanted men to see her hair, and did not permit her to cover it except rarely.

Tying the multi-colored woven headband around her forehead to anchor it, she braced herself and walked out.

Javan looked up when she entered. His only acknowledgement was a brief nod. Taleh cringed inside. She must have done something wrong. No wonder, with a pot for a mirror. The headdress must be crooked, or too low over her eyes. Or not low enough.

Was she violating some custom? He could – should have – come back and looked at her before she had to come down in front of everyone else. Unless this was another test.

Javan turned back to Obed and asked, "Will you be moving into your father's house?"

She stood in the doorway, her feet suddenly stubborn. He had said nothing to her. Not a word. Were women not to be recognized during the meal? Another thing it would have been nice for Javan to have told her, but he had invited, no, *ordered* her to come down. Why so insistent, if he could not speak to her once she got there? Merab sat, quiet and withdrawn, beneath her own headdress. Sarah was there also, sitting just far enough from Merab to show her opinion. Neither spoke.

Obed swallowed his mouthful of food and replied, "I do not think that would be wise. The house is too small already, and a mother-in-law is not the right person to instruct Merab on our customs. I would rather she know more of what will be expected of her before she spends too much time with my family."

Merab flinched from Obed's unthinking words, obviously hurt. Taleh waited for Obed to notice. Something uncomfortable hung in the air.

Obed sopped up another bite of soft curded cheese on a bit of bread and looked over at Javan. "And you? Will you rebuild your family's home?"

"The land is mine," Javan said with firmness. "I will go out today and see how much is left."

No one paid attention to Taleh. She felt awkward standing in the doorway waiting for an invitation that was not likely to come. Her feet came unstuck with sheer will. She walked over to the table and seated herself next to Merab on the long bench.

The bread was still warm, its freshness scenting the table. A pitcher sat there as well, and a large bowl of the soft cheese curds Obed was eating. More bowls held fresh apples, and dried pressed cakes of figs, dates and pomegranates. The fruit harvests were not long over, and Taleh worried that they were eating Sarah's winter store.

She suspected the old woman of going to so much effort so early in the day expressly to impress them with the burden they were for her.

A cup and bowl had been left in front of her place, directly across from Javan. She broke off a piece of bread and put it in her bowl, then reached for the dish of soft cheese curds. Javan glanced over as she lifted the heavy pottery, and apparently decided she needed no help, for he continued to discuss the orchards with Obed.

Everything smelled wonderful, fresh-baked bread and pungent cheese, sweet fruits and the sharp tang of goat's milk, but tension soured the feast. The men were preoccupied with their conversation, Sarah glowered, and Merab sulked. The table vibrated with resentment. Taleh felt choked by every bite she took.

How could the men eat so freely?

Merab handed her the pitcher, and Taleh poured the warm goat's milk into her cup.

The two men had almost finished eating. Obed asked idly, "What do you expect to find?"

"I do not know. There was fire everywhere. I remember the smoke. Even if the trees burned, I hope they might have grown back. It has been fifteen years. We had so much." His voice sounded far away, soft and lost in memory. "We grew dates and figs and pomegranates, olives and apples, some nuts, even apricot trees that were my father's pride. I remember climbing the trees and throwing the fruit down to my brother when I was small."

Taleh heard the pain in his voice, felt how tightly he held it in check.

"My mother had a garden. She grew watermelon and cucumbers, leeks and garlic, and celery." Javan's voice cracked, and Taleh's heart clenched around the hurt that started within her, his hurt and her own loss that could not be voiced here.

Obed coughed as though to clear his throat. "My father said he has some skins he thinks are done curing. I plan to go with Jesse to the pit and help dig them out. This is not the part I enjoy. Have you ever smelled skins when they are first dug up?"

Javan forced a laugh. "I did once."

"I much prefer designing. I like to look at the skin and try to see what it can become. I had forgotten how much I missed the challenge."

So Obed was a leather-worker, Taleh thought. Javan had been a farmer. She still found it hard to imagine Javan behind a plow. A warrior following donkeys? The picture would not come.

Javan stood up, and finally deigned to speak to Taleh. "I have much to do before the month is up. The land must be cleared, then the house must be built, the fences repaired, and the fields plowed and planted. The orchard must be trimmed, I am sure. If there is any fruit," he gave a harsh laugh as if the mere idea was ludicrous, "it must be picked and dried."

Obed stood as well, and turned to his own wife. "I, too, have much to do. We need a house. I must discuss sites and find craftsmen. The materials must be chosen and brought in. I hope to plant several olive trees for my own use, and perhaps a fig tree or two. My father also wants to teach me the things I have forgotten."

The two men left to begin the impressive list of chores. Taleh thought the list would have been more convincing if they had not been in quite so big a hurry to leave.

Sarah still glared. Perhaps she had no other expression.

An oppressive silence settled over the table after the men were gone. Merab picked at the piece of bread she held, absently dropping the small bits on the table in a crumbly pile. Taleh did not realize she was dipping her own bread into the cheese curds until a soggy piece fell off with a soft plop.

Unable to sit and pretend any longer, she mumbled an excuse, pushed herself away and fled up the stairs to her room.

It took her a little time to unload all of Javan's sacks. Sitting on the cool stone floor surveying the treasures he had received from the plunder of Minnith and the other cities, Taleh wavered between pain and relief. Nothing was familiar. None of his goods had come from her house. Had she really thought to find something that once belonged to her?

The pot Taleh held was covered in dust. She picked up another, and it was the same. The fabric and robes piled on the floor were gritty, the oil lamps clogged with sand. Everything Javan had taken from her city had parts of the long journey wrapped around them.

She looked at the piles around the room and groaned aloud. Until now, she had not given any thought to what had been happening to the things they carried.

She picked up one of the sacks and shoved the copper pots into it, staggering under the weight as she got to her feet.

Sarah had not moved from the table, where the remnants of the early meal curdled in the beginning warmth of the day. For the first time, Taleh saw the dark circles under the old woman's eyes. Guilt pierced her.

She had foolishly hidden behind walls of fear and ignorance, and missed Sarah's gesture of apology, of welcome.

"I am sorry," Taleh said hesitantly. How did one begin to apologize for running out on a meal, leaving the giver of all that hospitality sitting alone among the remains? "I have many things to wash. I thought, perhaps . . . we could wash everything at one time." She lifted the heavy sack slightly, and waited.

Sarah nodded. She cleared her throat, and Taleh could hear the tightness of her tears in the sound.

A shadow filled the doorway, and Merab stood there. She glared at Taleh, and the table.

Sarah turned around, following the direction of Taleh's eyes. Had she seen Merab's first expression, the anger she wiped away so quickly? Taleh hoped not. The venom there left her shaken.

"We will need more water," Sarah said calmly. "This is a good time to go. It is not so warm yet. Many of the women from the village go at this time."

Taleh and Merab exchanged horrified glances.

Sarah ignored their reactions. "Of course, you cannot use any of your things without washing them. I have some water jars. They are too large for me to carry, but you are both young and strong, and we will need plenty of water."

Taleh fingered her headdress. A single tug could dislodge it. Sarah was going to take both of them through the city, where everyone would see their headdresses and know what they were trying to hide.

She did not know quite how Sarah got them out of the house, but they soon found themselves swept up in the activity that started the day. People of all ages filled the wide streets. Doors stood open in the well-spaced houses and latticed windows were flung wide to catch the coolness of the morning. The shadows stretched long, the sun still low enough to provide welcome shade. Taleh saw olive trees at every house. Birds flitted from one to another as though unable to decide which tree was best.

Men walked past with purposeful strides, carrying the tools that marked their trades. Leather skins, hammers, baskets, wooden ladders, and carts laden with goods of all kinds moved in every direction. Children dashed with enviable skill between their elders, and their shrieks of laughter rose above the other noises.

Here and there a water jar bobbed among the crowd, as mothers led their daughters in the daily procession toward the village gates.

Sarah knew her way through the confusion, and Merab and Taleh had no choice but to follow. Taleh tried to avoid looking anyone directly in the face, but it was difficult, especially as the city was filled with curiosity about these 'enemy brides.' No one wanted to ask questions of them, no one wanted the truth, but plenty of them wanted a close look.

As she stepped outside the gate, the bright light of the morning sun caught Taleh in the eyes. She stopped abruptly, only to have someone behind her bump solidly into her back. She clenched the large water jar's handles as she stumbled forward.

"I am so sorry," a voice said. Taleh turned around.

The speaker was a young woman, perhaps a few years older than herself, with the ripeness of figure that comes from motherhood. Her hair was much lighter than Taleh was used to seeing, glowing wheat-like in the sun. Her eyes were the color of the first leaves of spring.

But the strangest thing of all was the lack of anger or distaste or dislike of any kind in her face. She smiled, an apologetic, half-embarrassed smile.

"I think the fault was mine," Taleh ventured, wondering without expectation if this sweet-faced woman might be a friend.

"I know how bright the sun is this time of the morning." The other woman had a kind voice. "There have been days when I wondered if my eyes would ever be the same."

Conversation died. Taleh looked across the gulf that separated the two women, despite how close together they stood.

"My name is Leah," the woman said, breaking the awkward silence.

"My name is Taleh."

"I knew your husband when he was younger," Leah went on. "He was always pleasant to me, polite and well-mannered."

Out of nowhere, jealousy burned through Taleh. It came as a surprise. How could she feel this way about the man who shaved her head just the past night? The man who had left her alone today, with no support, to face hostile strangers?

She could not respond.

"I married three years ago," Leah continued, as though unaware of Taleh's tension. "I have only been back a short while. My husband took me with him to his village, not too far from here. I came back after he died."

A widow.

With no husband. And very likely children.

An Israelite, with a long friendship with Javan, and already familiar with the customs of the land.

A rival? Or a friend?

Sharp fingernails suddenly dug into Taleh's arm, tugging at her sleeve. She turned to find Sarah scowling at her once again. "We have much to do today. There is no time to stand about." She stalked off, muttering about ingratitude.

"I did not mean to get you into trouble," Leah said. "Perhaps another day I can come to visit you."

Perhaps. Taleh nodded.

Most of the women were done filling their jars. The dirt around the well, dry yesterday afternoon, was muddy and bore the imprints of many sandaled feet, both large and small. Even little girls carried water in small jars as they learned their role. Merab stood to one side, out of the way of the village women. Taleh felt very much the outsider, interloper, not excluded but not welcome, and Merab looked like she felt the same.

Sarah pushed them ahead. Taleh resented her callousness even as she acknowledged that, without encouragement, she would have waited until everyone else was gone before stepping forward.

The women parted to let them through. Taleh felt much like an odd creature from a distant land. Perhaps here she really was.

Merab's hiss was barely audible. "I wonder what they expect us to do."

"Nothing good," Taleh whispered back.

When she was hauling up the full jar, a voice, taunting and carefully raised to ensure it would carry, asked, "How long do you think our newly arrived soldiers will wait before they take another wife? There are so many widows and virgins here. What a relief to see even two new men in the village."

The rope slipped through Taleh's fingers. The jar landed back in the water with a muffled splash. She could not remember quite what to do to bring it back up, and fumbled ineptly before a hand reached over her shoulder for the rope.

"Think nothing of their unkind words," Leah said softly. "They do not know you. It is unworthy of them to behave so cruelly."

Taleh blinked back tears, but not in time. She brushed one off her cheek with shaky fingers. *Please,* she thought quickly, *let no one see, let them not know they made me cry.*

"Javan is under no obligation to take another wife." Leah's eyes held compassion and perhaps some understanding.

"But he can?" Taleh already knew the answer. She wondered why it should hurt so.

"He can, but not all men do. Even if he does, you are his first wife. Nothing can change that."

"Can it not?" Taleh whispered bitterly, more to herself than to Leah. What place would she have if Javan took someone from his own people? What incentive would there be to help her fit in if he had another in his house who already had a place with his nation? How would he explain his Ammonite wife then?

"It is pointless to borrow trouble," Leah went on, as though Taleh had not spoken. "I doubt anyone in this village has any understanding of what Javan has endured since he left us. Yes, most of us had friends or family killed by your armies, but we were still on our land. Javan has been gone a long time, fighting. I suspect he feels a little lost himself." Then she smiled, a happy smile, full of unexpected humor. "Besides, after seeing you, why would Javan stop to look at another woman?"

In spite of herself, Taleh smiled back, although it trembled slightly. Perhaps there was something to be said for being beautiful.

It gave her a place to start.

CHAPTER 16

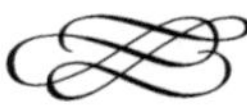

JAVAN WAS NOT PREPARED FOR THE SIGHT THAT MET HIS EYES. IT WAS NOT so much the tumbled stones, still blackened from the fire of fifteen years ago, that hurt, as it was the total devastation of the place. Weeds, grown tall over so many years, poked their stubborn way through the charred wood, remnants of doors and roof. The stone floor his father so lovingly laid in place had been torn apart by the walls' collapse and now lay tilted pieces.

Wild goats, perhaps descendants of the ones he had herded and milked as a boy, ran off at his approach, his feet whispering through the tall grass. Had he not known this place, had he come upon it as a traveler unaware, he would not have given it a second glance. It could have been abandoned five hundred years ago as easily as fifteen. The fences he had built with his father and brothers were blurred lines of rock, hiding among the vegetation. Wheat and barley stalks waved sparsely, lost in the encroaching wilderness. Olive trees, scraggly volunteers, had popped up from seeds fallen and left untended. Neat rows were long lost to neglect.

Javan hardly knew where to start.

He needed a house, but he also needed to get his seeds into the ground. There had to be crops for next year, to eat and to sell. The slave boys with him were full of the energy of youth. Perhaps it would not be impossible to do both.

He had no intention of taking his wife for the first time under someone else's roof.

The piles of stone that marked what had been his home beckoned with an ominous pull. His feet moved him forward while his heart pounded in his ears. The interior, if this exposed shell could be said to have such, showed no sign of the people who had lived here, nothing of his family. Was that better, or worse? Looking in and around the jumbled mess, Javan saw only simple blocks of charred stone.

A strange detachment settled over him. If not for the almond tree so close to the wreckage, he could believe this place had belonged to another family.

Twisted landmarks, shadows of the past, taunted him with echoes of memories, but he shoved them back with the skill of long years of practice. He examined the stone, counting blocks, measuring the ground, feeling safe nothingness. How many blocks were still intact? What would it take to lay a new foundation? Do not think, do not remember. He moved around the ruin, trying to turn his soldier's mind to more mundane pursuits, pacing off the steps, pulling deep into his mind to remember long-unused skills.

Here was where he found his father's body.

He stumbled, losing his footing at the tearing shock of the memory, turning away to see the slaves waiting silently for his signal, watching him with expressionless faces.

In that instant, he hated them, every one of them, hated them despite their quiet acquiescence, their seeming obedience and resignation to their own fate. It mattered not at all that they had not been the ones who killed his family. He knew, from somewhere deep inside, that their behavior was compliant because they were unsure of their place. There were too few of them and too many of his own people. Their land was far away, its very direction lost in the twists of the long journey. If they could be assured of success, they would find a way to strike back and flee to their homeland. He had no doubts about that.

He motioned them to come, reveling in their subservience, enjoying his power over them. It was fitting that they be the ones to undo what their people had done.

He pointed at one of the boys. What was his name? He could not remember, his mind too caught up in pain, bound to the past.

The boy came quickly, nervous at being singled out.

"You . . ." Javan's pointing finger trembled, and he lowered it quickly.

"Hadron," the boy gave his name.

"Yes, Hadron, you and . . . you," he gestured to another, "you two will pile the wood. *All* of the wood."

"Pile it where?" Hadron asked audaciously.

"Find a place," Javan snapped. "What difference can it make where?"

The boys hurried to obey.

Javan walked over to the others. They each took a quick step back, leery before his fury, palpable in the air. "Move the rocks. One pile for broken pieces, one pile for whole pieces. And remember this, all of you." He raised his voice so each could hear. "We are here to work. I will be watching."

Watching, yes, he would be doing that. Watching for sluggards, watching for rebels, for warning signs that would tell of trouble ahead. These were his enemies, though only boys. Boys could kill. He had seen it.

They obeyed.

Javan made sure of it. He ignored the odd discomfort he felt, as though his skin no longer fit around his anger. It was right that they sweat, even bleed on the rough stones that resisted their efforts before giving in.

He walked around the side of the house, away from their too-attentive eyes. He wanted no witnesses to his pain. Even the waving grasses and wild lilies could no longer disguise the sights he still saw in his dreams.

Here he had found his youngest brother, a spear through his belly. He had been six years old.

The almond tree still stood where it always had, having suffered no ill effects despite being so close to the burning house. He wanted to go over to it, but his legs would not carry him. The almond tree had shielded him from the first sight of Phineas, his closest brother and playmate, pinned by an arrow to its trunk. For a few precious moments the tree had been kind, hiding its secret, giving Javan blessed ignorance.

This was his land, but how long would it take before he saw only what was in front of his eyes? How long before the images from his past faded?

He had to turn away. He could not face the tree, not yet. A small pile of oddments the slaves had set aside caught his attention. Grateful for the distraction, he walked over to it.

Javan had thought for many years there was nothing left of his heart to break. He was wrong. Hiding under the charred wood and leaning stones were broken bits of his life before, secreted away from his first look. A bowl that had burned and rotted in the rain and moisture of fifteen lonely years, part of a bench his father had built that pretended at first to be just another piece of fallen timber.

A silver brooch, melted from the fire but still identifiable. His mother had worn it many times to decorate her robes and cloaks. The metal circle that had once been a mirror of copper, somehow surviving the worst of it. Tarnished, charred, and bent, it seemed to hold his mother's face within. If he looked closely, he could almost see himself as a young child, peering over her shoulder to see his wavering face next to hers.

He wanted to scream at the slaves digging through the ruins to leave things alone, to get out of his sight. Their presence was a defilement, an unexpected torment. He was ripping apart inside, bleeding unseen in agony.

Everything he touched, everything *they* touched, held a memory, a fragment of pain. The memories were spoiled, twisted by the taunting satisfaction on the faces of his slaves, and the devastation that surrounded him. It was hard to meld the images, the faces of his family too clear again after so many years when it had seemed they were fading, the home where they had loved each other now only so much wreckage.

He drove the slave boys he owned with a vengeance, trying to work them hard enough to wipe the expressions from their faces, trying to purge himself of memories in their sweat and strain.

"Look out!"

A shout of fear ripped the air, and Javan had his dagger out of its sheath. Dust swirled and stones slid, scraping against each other. The boys jumped like gazelles away from the ruin, stopping in a ring around its edge.

"What happened?" Javan yelled.

"I think we moved a support," one of them answered, his voice shrill with unrelieved tension. He brushed a bruised hand over his bleeding leg.

From all sides, wide, frightened eyes turned to Javan for guidance. He counted quickly. None were missing.

The slaves were smeared with charcoal and ash from piling charred wood out of the way, their fingers raw and bruised from heavy stone. The sun was past its peak, heat beating down, sweat making trails through the grime on their flushed faces.

Errant drops of his own sweat dripped into his eyes and he blinked against the sting. He looked at the faces of his enemies and saw only boys, not even young men, scared, hot, hungry, bruised, and tired.

Had they really deserved such punishment?

His anger seeped out of him, draining away, leaching into the forgiving ground.

He ordered a halt, and went to collect the food Sarah had sent, plenty of bread and wine, an oversized bowl, its fitted cover protecting cold stew with meat and vegetables, heavily spiced and smelling like paradise should, even fruits, figs and dates, and an assortment of nuts. They settled down in the meager shade the midday sun allowed.

He watched them while he eased his own hunger. Had he eaten like that when he was their age?

He allowed them to take their time, giving them the rest they needed during the hottest part of the day.

When they were ready to go back to work, they labored hard over their tasks, but Javan found he could be compassionate. His hatred had been spent.

Giving up that hatred exhausted him. He had spent so many years steeped in it. He watched and helped the boys, and wondered what to do about the gaping hole its absence left. It had driven him onward, gave him a purpose.

He had no idea what to put in its place. He had Taleh, the land, the animals, the slaves. Somehow, he doubted that would be enough. Hatred and vengeance had been his all-consuming passion.

What was he going to do with the rest of his life?

TALEH REFUSED to acknowledge the thrill she felt when Javan and his slaves came through the courtyard. She told herself it was because she had been working hard all day, washing pots and dishes, that she was simply tired. She told herself his presence meant they all could eat.

She tried to make herself believe she had not really missed him. How could she miss him, after all he had done to her?

But he looked so tired, more than tired. He looked like a man who had faced his demons and nearly lost. A sack was flung over his shoulder, black seeping through the threads. His tunic was streaked with the same black substance, his legs scratched and bruised, his face smudged with ash, his hands scraped and bloody. The slaves with him looked the same.

Sarah had set a basin of water by the door earlier, next to a bench. Taleh knew, even before Obed came back, what it was for. There used to be one much like it in her own home . . . her parents' home, she corrected herself. This custom was familiar to her, the traditional welcome of washing the feet of honored guests.

Sarah had glared Merab into washing Obed's feet. Merab obeyed with gritted teeth while Sarah stood guard to ensure her submission.

Now Javan seated himself on the bench, and reached for the rag in the basin. Some irritating urge made Taleh go over to his side and kneel.

"I will do that," she heard herself say, and bit her tongue. Excuses tumbled through her brain, explanations and justifications: Sarah was too old, Merab had done it, how could she let Merab do something she would not? She herself had done the same thing a hundred times in her father's house for his guests.

This time was different. None of the men in her father's house had made her heart beat and her breath catch like Javan did.

He leaned back against the rough stone wall and closed his eyes, stretching his long legs out before him. Wet rag in hand, Taleh looked down at the display of male legs and swallowed hard.

Despite the scratches, the dirt, and smears of charcoal ash, his legs fascinated her. They were thick with muscle, liberally covered with dark hair. As she hesitantly touched the rag to the nearest leg, the hair tickled her fingers, softer than she had expected.

His legs were as hard as the stone behind his head. They spoke of power, of the endless days of walking. She wondered idly how far he would have to go before exhaustion made him stop.

Javan cleared his throat, and Taleh jumped. Her hands had slowed into stillness while she gazed at his legs. She glanced up quickly, only to find a pleased smile on his face. Humiliation burned up her face. Did he know what she had been thinking? She focused all her attentions on her chore, finishing as quickly as possible, trying to ignore the odd feeling in her stomach.

Javan offered her thanks when she was done, despite his fatigue. Had she missed the sound of his voice, or was it always that warm, wrapping around her like a soft blanket?

Before she could rise, Javan caught her shoulders and pulled her against him, clutching her close, unmoving and unmovable. He covered her lips with his own, and claimed her. The anger Taleh had nursed all day still simmered beneath the surface, but something deeper fed it, something only Javan could bring forth.

"I want you to remember," he said when at last he stopped for breath. "You belong to me. Get used to the feel of me, to the sound of me, to my presence. When I finally can claim your body, I do not want you to be frightened by the tales of women who know no better, or the whispers of virgins who know nothing and believe everything."

His eyes were so close to hers. Sitting, he seemed to surround her, above, in front and behind, his arms solid against her back. She felt swallowed up by him. She was supposed to be angry with him for something. What was it? She could no longer remember, her senses so controlled by his taste and touch, by his smell, heat and hard work and Javan.

And then his hands caught the edge of her headdress and it started to slip. She remembered, and started to struggle away, but he would not permit it.

"Do not fight me now," he voice growled, and his lips claimed her again.

All thought fled.

CHAPTER 17

Taleh stood cautiously in the shade, one hand anchoring her to the wall of Sarah's house, and looked out at the busy street. Children played noisily, tossing small rocks at a target, little girls held their carved wooden dolls, or chased each other with little girl shrieks. A cart went by, stirring up dust briefly before the light breeze caught it and carried it off. The laundryman left one house and made his heavily laden way to the next one. At the far end of the street where it joined with another, she caught a glimpse of Obed as he crossed behind a tall white stone fence, probably going back to his father's shop after delivering one of the leather pieces they made.

Taleh stepped out into the street with a courage she was far from feeling. She had tried to venture out before, but each time she found she was not ready to face the resentment that pressed in on her from all sides. No one had done anything overtly cruel after the incident at the well, but their reactions ranged from turning away to looking down their noses at her to pretending she was not even there. It was hard to accept, day after day. If this continued, Taleh feared she would become as lost to view as the villagers so obviously wished she were.

What a contrast to her other life! In Ammon, she had often wished to be hidden from sight, that she could walk down the streets and no one would see her, no man would stop and leer. Now she had her wish, and found it was not what she wanted after all.

Despite the fact that she dressed exactly as they did, everyone in the village could spot her in an instant. How did they do it? Her robes were as bland as theirs, her fringe on the bottom no longer or shorter, the ever-present blue thread just above the fringe on every garment was in its place on her own robes. She was not the only woman, either, to wear a headdress.

Of course, they had hair peeking out from under theirs.

True, her hair was coming back in, she had known it would, Javan had promised it would, but it was little more than a sheen of fluff. She carefully wrapped her headcovering each time she went out where she could be seen, no matter how close to the house she would be. It did not help.

Every day Taleh hurt, seeing the other women's hair sliding over their shoulders as they went about their business, to see them pull their own coverings off if a breeze came and let it cool them. They did it so often that she suspected it was deliberate. She tried not to watch the wind lift the strands, playing with them before setting them back down. She often felt phantom memories of her own hair, but reality was hard to ignore and impossible to forget.

So how had Leah managed to make her promise to visit – today – allowing no excuses, further delays, or other stalling?

If she were not so frighteningly lonely, not even Leah's kindnesses and persuasion would have gotten Taleh this far. Her days had developed a pattern, one she was not happy with but did not know how to change. Javan left each morning early, most of the time before she even awakened. Some days he came home covered in soil, some days in dust, and sometimes he had wood chips liberally coating his body. Whatever occupied him, it still left her alone with Merab's sulking and Sarah's frowns.

This was not how she had envisioned her life going. She knew only she could fix it. Javan certainly would not. She wondered if he even remembered he had a wife.

It was still cool, this early in the day. The sun had not moved high enough yet to eat away all the shade, but there was a brief lull in the activity, and at the moment only children were on the street.

Taleh did not find it so hard to walk down the street with just children about. Much to her surprise, she got plenty of shy smiles. As she reached the end of the street and started around the corner, several boys came racing straight at her, far too quickly to stop. With a startled shriek, Taleh jumped aside. The boys never stopped, just continued on their way.

Taleh frowned after them, but she had not gathered all her courage together to be stopped by children, however poorly behaved.

She had gone only a few steps when she saw the man. As he struggled to get to his feet, his hand groped into open air, trying to find a familiar support. Without stopping to think, Taleh hurried over to him.

"Are you hurt?" she asked.

"No, not hurt. Shaken and skinned a bit, but nothing serious." He found Taleh's hand, grasped it, and pulled himself to his feet. He was not much taller than she. The top of his balding head was dotted with small brown spots. What hair he had left was liberally blended with gray. He turned toward her, and she found herself strangely at ease. His face was full of character, cheerful, as though waiting for his smile. Taleh expected his eyes to twinkle, but they were blank and sightless.

"I seem to have gotten myself lost," he said. "Could you direct me? I was going to the street of the tradesmen."

Taleh braced herself. It was only a matter of time, now. He must have heard of her. He would figure out who she was, and he would reject her like all the others had. "I do not know where they are. I am new to the village."

He laughed. Not a mocking laugh, but a delighted laugh, as though he had been waiting for someone to say something funny.

"So you are one of them." His words were pleasant, and surprisingly free of venom. "I could not place your voice, and now I know why. Which one do you belong to, Obed or Javan?"

"I . . . Javan," Taleh answered, still waiting for him to turn away in disgust.

"And what is your name?"

"Taleh."

"And mine is Saul. So, Taleh, how are you finding life among us? Hard?"

Startled, Taleh blurted out, "Yes."

"Ah, I thought so. Well, if you will lead me to where I need to go, I would be happy for your company." He tucked his hand into the crook of Taleh's elbow, and started walking. "I believe, between the two of us, we will manage to find our way. Have you made no friends at all?"

"Leah. I was on my way to her house."

"Ah, yes, Leah. I am not surprised. Javan has not taken you through the village yet." He made it a statement, not a question.

"No. I have not asked him to."

"Why not?"

She hesitated to answer. There was too much between Javan and herself that she did not understand.

"Has it been that bad?"

Taleh blinked, and then realized he was referring to the villagers, not to Javan. "Yes. I have gone with Sarah to the marketplace and to the well each day, of course. No one will talk to me. I feel them staring at me, but when I turn around, they all look away. The marketplace is worse than the well. At least at the well I know they are looking, even if I cannot prove it. In the marketplace, I might as well not exist, for all the notice they give me."

"You know many have suffered much at the hands of your people."

"Yes, I know. Javan told me about his family. But I lost my own family, too! No one wants to know that. No one asks me how I got here, or if I had a choice."

"Did you have a choice?"

Taleh thought for a moment. It seemed so long ago. How *had* she made her decision?

Saul interrupted her thoughts to ask, "Is that the carpenter's shop?"

"Yes, it is." Taleh had not even been aware of the rich wood scent, or the sounds of chopping, sawing, and pounding.

"We must turn toward a group of trees. I am told they are scarred by fire. Ah, I feel the shade. So Javan gave you no choice."

"My choices were marriage or slavery. I did not think I would survive slavery."

Saul nodded. "Javan is a good man. You made the right decision."

"He was kind to me on the journey." Taleh could not stop her next words. "But since we got here, things have been so different."

"He is not kind to you now?"

"He is not there now."

"What do you mean?"

Something inside Taleh warned her not to say more, but loneliness and need overruled caution. "He works all the time. He comes in late to the evening meal, when he is there at all. He is either too tired to talk, or he talks to Obed. I never see him in the morning. He leaves before I am even awake." The ache that had been building inside choked her voice. She whispered, "He is ashamed of me, and it is too late now to change his mind."

They stood in silence for a moment. Saul said softly, "I do not usually give advice, but I will this time. You are young. Men are not often good at saying what they feel. It is a mistake to make assumptions."

Taleh said nothing, for how could he know the true extent of her alienation? She realized suddenly that they had been standing in place for some time.

Saul chuckled. "We should be outside a potter's shop. Am I right?"

A wooden sign hung above Taleh's head. The writing on it meant nothing to her, but the pot painted in vivid colors did. "Yes, we are," she answered.

"This is my shop. Please come in. I will have to direct you to Leah's house from here. I am certain you will not find your way alone."

"Thank you." Taleh smiled in relief.

Saul stepped over to the door with remarkable ease, and swung it open. "Follow me," he said, as though he was the one who knew his way. And Taleh realized he did. How long had he known where he was, but permitted her to be the guide? She propped her hands on her hips and shook her head at him. A little smile tilted her lips up. Her first lesson in finding her way around the town had come to her from a blind man who saw with his heart.

Did she now have two friends? she wondered. What a treasure if that was so.

His shop was dark. A small oil lamp sputtered on a shelf, a concession to those who could see.

“Please light another lamp if it is too dark. People often tell me they cannot see in here.”

“Thank you.” Taleh saw several lamps that had been set about, wicks waiting to be lit, their dark ends announcing their use. She carefully lit two from the burning lamp, and in their glow saw the remarkable beauty of Saul’s work. She caught her breath, delighting in the graceful simplicity. Vases, bowls, water jars, and lamps of all sizes seemed caught in one timeless moment. None were painted, but his gift was undeniable.

Saul’s voice startled her, caught away as she was in the soaring heights of his work. “I wish to give you a gift. Please, take whatever you want, with my thanks,”

Taleh gaped at him. “But I did nothing. You were the one who helped me. I complained and you listened. I am in your debt.”

“Nonsense!” Saul sounded angry. “I was pleased to have your company. I was turned around, it would have taken me some time to figure out where I was. You must allow me to do this thing. Unless, of course, you find nothing to your taste. If you do not like what you see, I will not force it on you. It must be your choice.” His face drew down in an expression of deep injury.

Taleh looked at him with a frown. He must know how very remarkable his work was. He was teasing her, was he not? It had been so long, so terribly long, since anyone had treated her in a lighthearted, playful way.

She looked closer in the poor light. A corner of his mouth twitched. He was trying not to laugh.

Some bereft place, deep inside her, opened up and soaked it in.

“Very well,” she said with a smile. “If you are so anxious to get rid of some of your work, I can see I will have to take one.”

He laughed happily and sat down, still smiling, at his bench. Clay lay mounded in front of him, its rich earthy smell clean and fresh. “You take whatever you wish. Pay no attention to me. I have to get to work.”

She watched, fascinated, as he stepped on a pedal and the clay began to spin. He pounded the clay, turning it this way and that, adding water from a small bowl at his side. His hands were sure and confident, his actions without wasted motion.

“Have you found something you want?” he asked. Taleh was surprised that she had been staring. She had never had a chance to just watch someone without being reproved before. She turned quickly to the shelves. A small oil lamp caught her attention, and she picked it up. It perched in her hand like a bird, its edges folded over the top like wings.

"I like this."

"Bring it here. I would like to see what you have chosen."

She did, and he held out his hand. Carefully setting her discovery in his clay-covered palm, she watched him touch it with confident fingers.

He smiled. "I am not surprised. You chose well. I am pleased you picked this one."

The door opened suddenly, letting in brilliant sunshine. Shadowed against the light, a big man stood. She could not see his face, but she knew.

"Someone told me they saw you heading this way. Leah awaits you."

"Javan," Taleh said stupidly. He had never come into town in the middle of the day before, at least not to see her. "How long have I been here?"

"Not that long," Saul said. He turned toward the doorway, immune to the glare. "Good day to you, Javan. I have met your wife, at last. She knows good pottery when she sees it. I had expected to meet her long before this. You have been remiss in your obligations to old friends." His voice took on a censorious note. "You have been remiss on a lot of duties. So tell me, how does the rebuilding go? That certainly has been taking up your time."

"I have been busy. It goes well, Saul. I am pleased with the progress. I have my orchards pruned, and the walls up for the house. There is still much more to do, though, and time is running out. The rainy season will soon be here."

"I understand. I remember how I felt when I first wed my wife. How hard I worked to make everything just so. And do you know what I discovered, Javan? I discovered she did not want the perfect house. She wanted *me*, a little of my time. Remember that, while you have the opportunity." A shadow passed over Saul's face, and Taleh knew his wife was dead. Did anyone die of anything in this place other than being murdered by Ammonites?

The wonder was not that so many hated her, the wonder was that any of them did not.

"I hear what you are saying, Saul. You always did speak your mind. Come, Taleh. Leah is waiting for you, and has prepared quite a meal. It would not do to have her go to all that work and have no one to appreciate it."

"Thank you for your help, Taleh." Saul reached for her hand, and put the oil lamp back into it. "I hope you will come again and visit me."

"I will." Taleh smiled at him, and turned back to Javan. They walked into the sunlight, blinking at its brightness.

Javan was covered with sawdust. He looked sad, and tired. His beard was unkempt, his hair shaggy and untended. His robe, in addition to the layer of sawdust, was torn in several places and he bled from a long cut on his leg.

"What happened?" Taleh burst out, shocked at the change in him. Had he really been away from her that long? When was the last night they had eaten together?

She could not remember.

"It is nothing, merely a scratch. Pay it no mind. Show me this gift Saul gave to you."

Taleh held up the lamp, smiling again at its perfection. "Is it not beautiful, Javan? I did not want to take it, but I could not let him think I did not like his work. I could not take anything larger, I have nothing to give him in exchange, and I think he would have refused, but this was so beautiful." She needed his reassurance, his approval, enough to ask for it. "Did I do the right thing? Should I have accepted this gift?"

"He would not have offered it to you if he did not want you to have it. You did well in not rejecting his hospitality. What was this service you did for him?"

Did she hear censure in Javan's voice? "Some boys were running and they knocked him down. He said he got his direction confused. At first I believed him, but now I am not so sure. He seems so very . . . competent. Anyway, I helped him up, and he told me how to get to his shop. We . . . talked along the way." Please, she thought quickly, do not let him ask me what was said. "He was very kind to me."

Javan just looked at her. She felt uncomfortable under his unwavering stare. "I am surprised to see you," she finally said, to end the awkward silence.

"Yes, I suppose you are."

"How did you know where to find me?"

"That was not hard at all," Javan answered. "I had to come to the carpenter's shop. The workers had seen you go past with Saul. It was very easy to trace your steps after that. Everyone was only too pleased to tell me which way you had gone."

"Oh." Had she broken some law? Saul would not have done that to her, would he? She dropped her gaze to the ground, only to see his hand held out for her own. She looked up at him. Did he mean to walk with her through the village hand in hand? She glanced around, surprised to see people in easy view. He would do this in public?

"I am sorry, Taleh." Javan spoke softly, for her ears only. "I did not realize how you must be feeling. I have had so much to think about, and I thought Sarah would be able to keep you busy. It is a poor excuse, I know. Sarah might be abrupt, but she is not cruel. I did not think the others would be. Clearly, I was wrong."

JAVAN GAZED down at her lovely face, so sad, so starved for the simplest sign of friendship. What had he done to her in leaving her to herself? What had she heard, what had she endured, while he was off building their house and avoiding her scent, her smile?

A shadow raced across the ground at their feet, cast by an early cloud. A harbinger of the rainy season to come, it was one more sign to Javan of his need to hurry. There were seeds to get in ground that had not even been tilled, a roof to make. Wood had to be cut for a door, lattices made to fit the windows. The fences were down in so many places, and his sheep needed to be moved to the better food in his fields. The pasturage outside the village walls had been overgrazed, and his flocks were not getting fat. When winter came, they would need shelters that had not been built. The work yet to be done pressed in on him.

There was little time for anything but work, little energy even to dream at night. So how was it that his dreams tormented him? He awoke each morning with the images vivid in his mind. It took all his waning control to leave the room before she opened her eyes. He fled each day hoping to lose his desire in work, trying to exhaust himself so he would not dream.

It did not work. No matter how tired he was, each night he closed his eyes and she was there. He did in his dreams what he ached to do awake, tormenting himself with what he could not have yet, fleeing each morning before he broke faith with the Law.

And Taleh grew lonelier. The walls were still there, between them, and he did not have the time to tear them down. She still saw herself as an Ammonite, as not belonging, and why not? From what he could gather, only two people in the whole village had made any attempt to even be kind to her.

Why should they? Had he given anyone reason to believe he cared for her, even in the slightest?

He could only answer, no.

It was too late to change the past two weeks, but he could do this for her. He took her hand gently, and tugged. She followed his lead.

They walked in silence through the village, neither knowing what to say.

"I SEE JAVAN FOUND YOU," Leah greeted Taleh. She nodded at him, standing next to Taleh. He let go of her hand, and walked away. Taleh watched him go, then dragged her attention back to Leah.

"Yes. I met the potter, Saul," Taleh replied. "He was very kind to me. He gave me a gift." She held it up for inspection.

"He does beautiful work," Leah said.

They looked at each other awkwardly, each waiting for the other to take charge of the conversation, and then Leah gave a laugh. "Please come in. I have a meal waiting for you. I would like you to meet my son. He is the joy of my life." She stepped back and motioned Taleh inside.

Leah's house was very small, so unlike what Taleh was used to at Sarah's.

Taleh was disappointed that the only woman friend she had in this place lived so poorly. Made of wood rather than the more solid limestone, the whole house was scarcely more than a single room. There was one window, facing the sunrise. The only other opening was the door, placed directly opposite.

The lattice over the window had been pulled shut. A half wall formed a barrier, shielding what must be the sleeping area from the rest of the house. A low table took up much of the precious space. Food had been laid out: warm bread looking so delicious, a vegetable soup of what looked like leeks, carrots, celery, parsley and grains, and fresh fruit sat to one side. Water in a large jar waited to be poured.

Taleh felt guilty about eating when Leah obviously had little to spare, but she could hardly refuse. She had never received such open-handed hospitality before and it warmed her heart. She followed Leah over to the little table and settled herself on the floor.

"Isaac is sleeping," Leah said, "but it is time for him to get up or I will never be able to get him down tonight. I do relish the times he sleeps. I never knew how little time I would have to myself with a child." She smiled at Taleh. "I advise you to enjoy yourself before you have children. After they come, they keep you busy. But he is a joy. He is growing too fast." A wistful tone crept into her voice. "It seems just yesterday he was a baby, and now I fear he will be weaned soon. I am not ready to give up my baby yet."

She walked around the half-wall, and Taleh heard her croon, soft reassuring sounds to ease her little one awake. When Leah stood up, she held an exquisite baby in her arms, blinking sleepily and scowling at leaving his bed. He had lots of soft brown curls, big green eyes, healthy round cheeks, and chubby arms and legs, and Taleh lost her heart the moment she saw him.

"Oh, Leah, he *is* beautiful!"

Leah smiled with all the joy of motherhood. "Yes, he is. And so untouched and new."

The bitterness in Leah's voice puzzled Taleh. So did the pain that briefly touched the other woman's face. Was this another tragedy to be laid at the door of her people?

"He is part of the reason I wanted you to come, other than the fact that I enjoy your company. Let me feed him something and set him down, and I will tell you the whole story."

Little Isaac brightened when he saw the table set with food, and let out a demanding call. "Ummy! Ummy!"

"I have tried not to spoil him," Leah said with a wince, "but it is hard. I think I try to make up for his not having a father by feeding him, and food seems to be the way to his heart. He is too young yet to know our family is different, but one day he will ask where his father is."

"And you will tell him the Ammonites killed him. Am I right?" Taleh thought she could come to hate her own people, if this kept happening in this village where she somehow had to find her way.

Leah gave her son a piece of bread and set him on the floor. He plopped down on his swaddled bottom, and concentrated his entire being on eating.

"Taleh, I know you have wondered why, out of the whole village, only I held no grudge against you. Yes, your soldiers killed my husband. I did not live here, we were living in his village." She seemed to brace herself, then continued. "I was very unhappy there. I could have stayed after he died, but I did not know I was pregnant. His family paid little attention to me when he was alive. The thought of staying after he died was intolerable. So I came here, to my own family."

"You have family here?" Taleh was surprised. Leah had never mentioned them before.

"Yes, I do. They are all well. Somehow they survived each attack. My parents live in the house next to mine. They wanted me to stay with them. I said no. I needed time to recover, and I discovered that I liked freedom. They adore my son, and it is a good arrangement. This was originally a slave's house, but it is just the right size for us now. When he gets older, I will have to decide what to do, but I will not worry about that yet.

"But we are off the subject. Taleh, my husband was a cruel man. He abused me constantly. He beat me. There was no pleasing him." Her voice grew fierce. "When he died, I was glad. The Ammonites did me a favor by killing him. I know the others suffered horrible things, but it was a blessing for me. I sometimes think I will never be able to remarry, for I can never live like that again. Taleh, I am no rival for you. Please believe me. I have no interest in your husband."

Her eyes met Taleh's without evasion. "I like my freedom. I glean our food from the leftovers of the harvest. I weave cloth and bake bread and am free to sell whatever goods I make. I have no one telling me what to do." She smiled suddenly. "That is not precisely true. My parents try to tell me what to do all the time, but I no longer am required to obey. I have never told them what went on in my marriage, but I think they suspect. They want more grandchildren, but they will have to look to my brothers and sisters for that."

Taleh struggled with her shock and surprise. She had not expected such a tale from Leah. How could any man do that to her? But then, what man spent time worrying about the happiness of his wife? "I am sorry. In Ammon, I feared all the time that my father would sell me into that kind of marriage. My father was not cruel, usually, but he wanted the money he could get for me more, I think, than he wanted me to be happy. Some of the men who came to look at me frightened me so. But I knew I would have no choice."

"It is not quite like that here," Leah protested. "If my father had known what my husband would turn out to be like, he would never have permitted the marriage. But my husband had everyone fooled."

"Thank you for telling me this." Taleh could only guess what it had cost Leah. Surely such honesty deserved honesty in return. "You were right. I did worry that you might supplant me. No, that is not quite right. I think I knew from the beginning that you would never force me away. It is more that I thought Javan might want someone other than me, someone who fit in here, who already had a place. I feel the danger constantly. I do not know if he still wants me."

She went on, more to herself, struggling to put her torment into words. "I am so confused and afraid. Nothing is right. Nothing *I* do is right. I no longer know what it feels like not to be afraid. Perhaps I never did."

"Do not let the people here intimidate you. It is hard for them, too, but they are good people. No one will poison you, or creep into your room at night and cut your throat. Once you learn our ways, you will be happy here."

Taleh managed a watery laugh. “I never thought of being killed in my sleep. I have spent most of my time waiting for Javan to send me back. I never see him any more. He is trying so hard to avoid me. He has no use for me at all.”

“Oh, Taleh, you are so young!” Leah grinned at her, then laughed merrily. “Do you truly not know why he stays away?”

“I have been afraid he has either forgotten me, or wishes he could. I know I do not fit in here. I know none of your laws, and your customs confuse me. I do not know whether I speak when I should be silent, or if I am silent when I should speak. People ignore me every time I leave Sarah’s house. I am afraid to go to the market. No one will talk to me. It is bad enough to be ignored by one or two at a time, but a whole marketplace? So I stay at Sarah’s and help her cook meals, and watch her watch Merab and me.” Her throat tightened again, and she whispered, “And I wait for Javan to decide he no longer wants me here.”

“Silly Taleh,” Leah said. She looked to be on the verge of another outburst of laughter.

Her humor hurt. How could she make light of something so painful?

“You really know very little of men, do you? You think he stays away because he does not want to see you? My husband was not much of a husband, but even I know what the problem is. Do you sleep near him?”

“Sarah has given us one of the rooms in her house. Javan and I have no choice but to sleep in the same room.” Taleh could feel her cheeks warm, as though confiding something most private.

This time Leah did laugh. “I could almost feel sorry for him. Taleh, he stays away, not because he no longer wants you, but because he still does.”

Taleh started to protest, but Leah motioned her to silence. “He did explain that he must wait a month before he can lay with you?”

Taleh nodded.

“Taleh, he wants to make you his wife in his own house. He is hurrying to finish so that the first time will happen under his own roof, not under another’s.” Leah still grinned, full of secret merriment. Then she grew serious. “Taleh, it is not so hard for you, because you do not know what you are missing. If he were around you constantly, his desire for you might become too strong, and he could abandon all his cherished principles."

Lean leaned forward. "Javan is who he is because he believes and respects our Law. If he were to break it, he would violate all he holds sacred. So to protect his conscience and keep his desire under control, he must stay away. He works himself into exhaustion. He avoids you as much as he can. But men dream about women, and he wakes, and finds it was only a dream, but he wants it. Do you understand?"

"A little, I think." No one had ever discussed men with her. Taleh wished she knew what questions to ask. She was consumed with curiosity. She looked at little Isaac, happily smashing bits of bread into the floor. She knew that laying with men produced children. But birthing children in Ammon often brought heartbreak. "Javan told me that I would never to be asked to sacrifice my child. He told me the truth?"

Leah looked shocked for a moment. "Sometimes I forget," she said under her breath. "Yes, Taleh, he told you the truth."

"Ask your question, Leah. I see it in your eyes."

"I am sorry, it is not my place to sit in judgment upon your traditions, but, Taleh, how could your people do such a thing? I see Isaac and I think if anything were to happen to him, I would not be able to bear it. I could never hurt him. Never!"

"I stopped going to the sacrifices." Taleh spoke quietly, feeling her way past the sense of betrayal that stabbed at her. "I could no longer endure it. At the end, the priests were taking so many children, I wondered if there would be any left." The words spilled out, after being trapped inside, eating away at her. "They marched the processions through the city, so everyone would see. I could tell which were the mothers. They looked so . . . broken."

She wondered, briefly, how long she had needed someone to confide in, a real friend. Her mother had not understood, despite her own loss. It was the way things were done and if the gods were happy and the rains came, that was all that mattered.

The words kept coming. "I think it is one thing to see it happen to others, but how can you survive when the priests come in and mark your child for death? How do you live through that night? How do you say goodbye? My parents told me if the Hebrews conquered the city, it would be my fault, because I defied the gods." She heard Leah gasp. "But I could not believe my actions made any difference. Why would the gods demand so many babies? And why punish a whole city because of me?"

"Your parents told you it was your fault?"

"Yes." Taleh reached out and covered Leah's hand with her own. "Do not feel bad for me. I did not blame them for feeling that way. They were only repeating what the priests had told everyone. We must support the gods and the sacrifices or we would block their protection. It was to be everyone or no one." She stopped to think. "It was no one, was it not?"

"You lived." Leah shook her head. "Such a life is inconceivable to me. But we can discuss this another time. Right now, we have a meal to eat."

CHAPTER 18

GLEAMING WHITE LIMESTONE WALLS ROSE IN A PERFECT SQUARE, EACH SIDE boasting a window opening. Javan swelled with pride as he looked at his handiwork. He had had help, to be sure, but so many skills learned at his father's side came back once he got started.

The door revolved smoothly on its solid pegs. The lattices could be opened wide to greet the day, or pulled shut to keep wet out and warmth in.

The flat roof was on, the parapet around its edge strong and sturdy. All around the top of the house's walls, the strong poles stuck out at precise distance from each other, providing support for the roof, announcing to all that the roof and walls were secure.

Even the sheep and the goats had homes. Javan had helped the slave boys build them, as well, two large three-sided sheds with sloping roofs to let the wet weather drain off. The fourth side of each shed faced a pen protected by a pole fence. Gates on either end of the pens led into the pasture, grasses brittle in the late summer heat but showing promise of lush growth with the first rains.

The orchards stood in neat-rowed, if a bit sparse, lines of trees marching to the unplowed fields that lay on the far end. Rock fences built up thigh-high marked the boundaries where house land met orchard, and orchard met field. The pasture ran along the west side of Javan's land, the pole fences placed to stop the animals before they reached the forest. Javan expected to have to enlarge the pasture in the years ahead, but for now, the space he had would suffice.

Even the slaves had neat houses, built along the rock wall that edged the orchard. They were of wood, with wooden floors, but white-washed with lime to keep the wet out. Each house had a window to let the smoke out in the winter. Warm woolen blankets waited on shelves for the cold nights to come, and more shelves held pots and bowls, clay water jars, and cups.

Yes, almost all was in readiness.

Javan found the easing of his workload these past days both a relief and a burden. He no longer had an excuse to keep himself away from Sarah's house – and Taleh. Lately, as he finished so early, he had been arriving at Sarah's in time to catch the preparations for the evening meal, and to be further tormented by what he could not yet have.

He liked to stand just far enough away to be unobserved, while his woman and Obed's helped Sarah cook. From his vantage point inside the house, he could watch Taleh, framed in sunlight, as she bent over the kettle. The heat from the fire and the warmth of the day gilded her face with a sheen of moisture. She did not complain, at least not that he heard.

He knew Sarah was aware of his presence, but she had not given him away.

He stood again in his spot. This day, Sarah caught his eye and motioned for him to follow her. They met by the stairs to the upper level, out of earshot.

"I need to apologize to you," she said in her abrupt way.

"For what?"

"I spoke some cruel words to you the first day you came. I wish to take them back. You chose well. Your wife – I could wish she had been born here, but she will bring you happiness, I think. She is trying to adapt to our ways, but she has much still to learn. As for the other, pooh! She is not for our land. She does not know how to make herself happy. How can she be good for anyone else?"

A deep unease filled Javan. Again. "What has Merab done?"

"Done? Nothing. It is not so easy to describe. She sows discontent wherever she goes."

"Perhaps she simply needs more of Obed's attention," Javan offered, knowing it was a pitiful explanation.

"Perhaps."

Javan could tell Sarah was unconvinced. *He* was unconvinced. He felt Obed's presence in the conversation, his reputation hovering above their heads. He did not want to discuss this with Obed not there to defend his choice.

"You must not be too hard on her," he tried again. The words were distasteful in his mouth, but he continued. "People adapt in different ways. It may be taking her longer to adjust."

"I do not believe she is trying to adjust at all." Sarah seemed to mind her tongue, for she shrugged. "Well, not many more days and it will no longer be my concern."

"You have been most kind to all of us. We are grateful for your hospitality."

"It has not been all burden." A faint blush rose up Sarah's wrinkled cheeks. "It is good to be needed sometimes."

Javan surprised them both by drawing the old woman into his arms for a gentle hug. She soaked it up before pushing him away.

"Well," she fluttered, "I have no time for foolishness. There is much to do for the meal. I am very busy."

Javan grinned after her as she scurried away, not fooled at all. She had needed that hug, more even than he needed to show his gratitude – and affection. He knew she worked Taleh and Merab hard, but it did them no harm, and probably much good. There was much more work with five people in the house than there had been with one, but he seriously doubted Sarah felt the brunt of it.

He followed Sarah's path to the doorway in the back of the house, and stood, watching. Again. That was all he did any more, he thought. He watched, and lusted.

A slight breeze toyed with Taleh's hair. The women no longer wore their all-concealing headdresses in Sarah's presence, perhaps because their hair now covered the scalp. Merab's hair was coming in faster than Taleh's, thick and straight. She often ran her fingers through it, and had developed the habit of pushing it back even though it was not long enough yet to hang in her eyes.

Taleh had no such reward. Her hair was coming in with tight black curls that tucked close to her head. He knew her hair was full of bends and waves when long, but these curls tugged at something deep inside him. They framed her face to perfection. While he missed the shiny black length, he was surprised anew each day at how much he enjoyed watching it come back.

He had not realized how much a woman's hair meant to her until he saw the reactions of these two.

Merab brushed at a lock of hair, just to feel it. He heard a soft chuckle behind him, and turned to see Obed at his side. But he had not missed the look of pure envy on Taleh's face just before Obed made his presence known, a look of feminine desire and need and pain.

He could not bear it that she felt hurt still.

He walked over to her. A startled look flashed up into her face. What had his selfish avoidance done to her these past weeks, that she would be so surprised with such a simple thing as seeking out her company?

Javan leaned over her and she tilted her head back, staring up at him with huge, uncertain eyes. He smiled and enjoyed the blush that crept up her cheeks. Unable to resist, he dropped a quick kiss on her lips, and heard her soft gasp of surprise.

He blew lightly on her hair, and watched it flutter with his breath. Reaching out slowly, he touched a curl, and it wrapped around his finger. It felt like a caress, as soft as a sigh. His hand trembled, and he looked at it in shock.

They had only three more days.

Her eyes were so expressive, so vulnerable. Did she think he had stayed away because he thought her no longer beautiful? Could it be she really did not know the perfection of her face, the allure of her body?

He took a chance, gritted his teeth, pulled her close and wrapped his arms around her. He cupped her head with his hand and drew it down to his shoulder. A fine sheen of sweat broke out, sending chills down his spine, but he did not let go, not this time. She needed this small moment. Saul had told him, and Leah.

Her head fit under his chin, then slid into the hollow of his shoulder, nestling there, the soft curls tickling the bare skin of his arm. Her heart beat a soft rhythm against his chest, thrumming in time to his own.

It was too much.

He let go of her and stepped back, too quickly. Taleh looked as if he had slapped her. Perhaps he had, but his breath was still too fast.

They were alone. The others had already taken the meal inside.

A tear trickled down his wife's cheek, and his heart cracked. "Taleh, I do not have enough control to touch you again," he said. "Please do not cry. I am not rejecting you. If I touch you again, I fear I will not be able to stop, and I cannot do that yet. Please be patient just for three more days. Will you help me on this?"

She nodded, and hiccupped with a soft inhale, but her face cleared and the emptiness left her eyes.

TALEH AWOKE EARLY to watch Javan leave, and felt a pain in her heart. It worried her, and worse even, it nearly terrified her. It was harder to see him leave now than it had been in the first days.

And she finally knew why.

Javan had held her yesterday, and she knew.

She had fallen in love with him. But had he, with her?

What did it feel like for a man when he fell in love? How did he act? *Did* men fall in love? She did not think her father really loved her mother, or perhaps their feelings for each other died that day when their son was put to death. She knew her mother had not loved her father all the years she was growing up. Oh, she had done her duty as a wife and mother, but Taleh had never seen any signs that resembled what she felt.

Maybe men did not fall in love. Maybe the best a woman could ever hope to have was a man who wanted to provide for her, and have her take care of his needs and give him children.

She did not think that would be enough, not here in his land with his people around and constant reminders of who – and what – she was. He could not even walk through the gates without the reminder in the scarred stone.

Did Javan think of her during the day while he toiled? Did he hope she thought of him? Did he care what she thought of him as a man, as a husband? Did he miss her when they were apart? Did he fear disappointing her?

Why did women always have to be the ones with so much to lose?

JAVAN SURVEYED HIS NEW HOME. It was not as large as it had been when his parents lived, and his perception had nothing to do with his having grown to manhood. The house was simply smaller.

But it was sound, and clean, and finished. And his.

Tomorrow he would bring his bride here. She was packing their belongings back into the sacks for the last leg of her journey. At least, he had told her to do so before he left this morning. There was nothing more for him to do here, but he could not stay in Sarah's house and sleep near Taleh. He intended to stay here this night, in his new house. He had told Taleh so. He would go back to eat the evening meal. When he returned to his own home for the night, he planned to bring a portion of their possessions with him. Taleh had reluctantly agreed that someone must watch over them.

Both of them knew why. His goal for this night was to keep temptation away, to keep faith with the Law, and to give the village elders nothing about which to reproach him. To succeed, he could not be around Taleh. His endurance was gone.

He closed the door, and started back to the village. If he walked there, ate quickly, collected some of the sacks and walked back, he might be able to tire himself out enough to sleep.

If that did not work, it was going to be a difficult night.

TALEH LOOKED around the small room that had been her house for a month. This would be her last night here, and she was surprised to discover that she would miss it. Perhaps not the room so much as Sarah. From the frightening stranger who would have called down evil upon them rather than permit them in her house, Sarah had become almost a friend. She was still stern, and intimidating, but she had also been more than patient as Taleh struggled to learn her new duties.

How odd, Taleh thought, that they shared so many memories after such a short time of knowing each other. Sarah had taught her the weights used to measure grain, the best way to weave the single-fiber cloth they used here, and where the different shops were. Taleh now knew how to separate the flax from the fine linen fibers, and how to braid flaxen wicks for the oil lamps. She knew all the names of the village elders and could match some of the faces to their names. She understood that even the women and children in this land knew how to read. The markings on the sheepskin and papyrus and the hanging wooden signs still meant nothing to her, but Sarah had assured her that Javan would teach her.

She had been startled to learn that women could sometimes inherit from their fathers.

And she knew that it truly was against the Law here to sacrifice children.

The leather curtain opened, and Javan walked in. Would she ever get used to what the sight of him did to her senses? For a moment, she forgot to breathe. Javan stood still, as though he did not remember what he was doing there, then he grabbed two of the closest sacks and stepped back to the doorway.

"Sarah said to tell you that the meal will be on the table soon. I will carry these down. If you can bring two more, I will come back for the rest."

"Thank you." Taleh hated how polite her voice sounded. "I will do that."

"Do not try to carry the heavy ones. I will carry those myself."

"Yes." Was it like this for everyone, she wondered. Did all new husbands and wives make awkward conversation just before . . ?

Javan's footsteps echoed back to her as he went down the stairs. She hefted a few sacks, decided which two were the lightest in obedience with his order, took them and followed Javan down to the main room.

Obed and Merab were ready to move out as well. Obed had built a home close to his parents' house. He and his father were working together in the leather shop. It seemed odd to Taleh, having seen the two men as soldiers with weapons strapped to their waists, that they had not been born to that role. Even though she had seen them longer without their weapons than with them, the impression they made upon her as soldiers was a lasting one. They seemed to be playing at their new roles, soldiers in disguise, pretending to be everyday men.

Some of the frantic energy Taleh had sensed in Merab seemed to have eased. The two women were so different that Taleh knew they would never be good friends, but she wanted them both to do well here. She believed the villagers saw them as a single unit, as if whatever one did fell upon the other, also. Somehow the slave boys were immune, perhaps by the very nature of their lack of status.

Merab looked up at her from where she sat on the floor and smiled happily. Moving out of Sarah's house would be good for her, Taleh saw. She had been unhappy with Sarah. The two did not get along well.

Taleh worried that Obed would not be able to keep as close an eye on Merab as Sarah had done. He was gone most of the day, working with his father and brother. What would Merab do, left to her own devices?

Sarah sat quietly while the others ate. Taleh thought Sarah would be glad they were going. Instead, the old woman acted as though she was sorry they were leaving. Surely that could not be. Having uninvited guests thrust upon one for a month, extra food to prepare, the constant bustle and lack of privacy, who would miss that?

But there were tears in Sarah's eyes.

The meal was, if anything, noisier and more jovial than usual. Obed and Javan discussed work, and houses, and the best, most efficient way to transport their belongings. Merab said little, but she paid close attention to her husband, which relieved Taleh. Merab's sulks often were about him, when he was not around.

It would be good for everyone to get into their own homes.

Javan carried down more sacks after he finished eating, loading most of them onto the donkeys. The sun hung low in the sky, and the nightbirds chirped to each other as they, too, settled into their nests. The moon glowed its first moments against the darkening sky.

There remained one last thing to do. His wife stood quietly in the doorway, watching with large, dark eyes. He came back to her.

"Think of me this night," he whispered into her ear, resting his big, work-worn hands on her slender shoulders.

"Yes." Just one word, a single breath.

He stepped quickly to the donkeys, waiting placidly under their heavy burdens.

The journey to his land stretched before him, restful solace to his strained nerves. The donkeys tugged on their leads, starting slow as always. He had come to know the silly beasts well over this last month. The sacks gave muffled thunks with the first steps, adding to the soft evening sounds. Gentle as the night was, Javan found it hard to get started. This was different from leaving her in the morning. There was nothing to keep him occupied during the coming hours, only the night and his thoughts.

Taleh watched Javan leave. How odd that, even though she was usually asleep before he came in, just knowing he would be there had been a comfort. She feared it would it be harder to go to sleep tonight, knowing he was not coming.

Not knowing what tomorrow would bring.

She turned away from the doorway only when he was out of sight. The night suddenly seemed barren. Her thoughts felt scattered, her movements aimless, activity pointless. All their belongings were packed, and most of them had gone with Javan. There was nothing for her to do, even if she had the concentration to do it.

For once, Sarah brushed her attempts to help aside. Perhaps she needed work herself to keep her own mind busy. So Taleh paced through the house, bewildered what else to do.

The evening dragged into night. The sky grew black, and stars joined the moon. The air was rich with the scents of night, fig trees, dry ground, and animal smells from the busy day that slowly settled into quietness. Obed left for his own solitary night, and Merab joined Taleh in restless motion. Her own work done, Sarah just sat, a knowing smile on her face.

At last Taleh could no longer avoid going into the room. Javan had taken more than she realized. Only three sacks remained, and one pallet. Without warning, her heart began beating faster. The enormity of tomorrow, of the step she would take, became real.

Tomorrow she would become Javan's wife in fact as well as name.

The night crept past on slow-moving feet while Taleh stared into darkness. Finally exhaustion claimed her, and she slid into sleep.

THE MORNING SUN sent its usual welcome through the lattice. When she opened her eyes, she saw Javan sitting on the floor beside her.

"It is time to go," he said.

Time to go. Yes, it was that and past, she supposed.

"How long have you been waiting?" she asked inanely.

Javan gave a muffled laugh. "I just arrived, but as for waiting . . . I think we have both waited long enough. Gather your things. I will take these last sacks downstairs, unless there is anything inside that you need."

"There is something," Taleh replied quickly. She felt oddly lighthearted. Javan looked younger, more carefree. He had bathed, his hair was still darkened with dampness in places, and she had never seen the robe he wore. She smothered a smile, for in one of the sacks was a new robe for herself. How funny, after seeing each other dirty, sweaty, and bloody, that they should still need to make this effort to please the other.

"I have brought you some water." Javan laughed again, a joyous sound for all he kept it quiet, and caught her head in his hands. He kissed her quickly, then, all soft lips and tickling mustache, fleeting like a bird on the wing. "I will wait for you downstairs. Please do not take too long." He rose in a rush and left, leaving the sacks behind.

Taleh scrabbled through the sacks, finding the new robe in the last one. She scrubbed her face and body until they glowed. Then she put on the robe, the blue of the morning sky, simple in design. She had added the required fringe, and the blue thread that bordered the bottoms of all the robes here. The linen felt smooth and cool.

Her short hair was already dry, and she pulled on a headdress quickly. Her sandals were worn, but they were all she had for her feet. With one last adjustment of the belt, a final tug and pull, she was ready. She lifted the lightest sack, pushed aside the leather curtain, and walked down the stairs.

Javan stood by the door, his posture tense, like an over-stretched rope. Very few people moved about. The air was still cool, and dew sparkled on the leaves of the trees. Sarah was not in sight, and Taleh wondered if she was still asleep.

Javan turned at the sound of her sandals scuffing on the floor, and looked at her like a starving man at a banquet.

"There are two sacks yet in our room." Taleh whispered in the quiet. If Sarah still slept, she decided she did not want to wake her. This leave-taking belonged to the two of them, Javan and herself.

TALEH WANTED to see what was along their journey to her new home, but could not take in much. Small hills rolled endlessly like impediments in their way. Trees grew along the hard-packed path, thin poplar, sweet-smelling cedar, wild fig and olive trees, the low-growing thorny lotus, and more. In the valleys, flowers danced in the wind, huge patches of color, pinks, yellows, blues, and whites. Birds circled overhead, and flitted between the trees, calling to each other by screech and song.

But, other than the vague outline, Taleh was blind and deaf to what was around her. She saw only Javan, heard only his voice and his breathing, smelled only his fresh-washed fragrance, warming into something uniquely his own, sun-touched skin, breeze-tossed hair.

The sun rose higher in the sky as they walked, coming up behind them, casting their shadows in front of them, Javan's longer and broader, Taleh's oddly thin in comparison. They walked toward themselves, always chasing, never catching. Like the past month, pursuing an elusive goal.

Unlike the shadows cast by the rising sun, their goal came suddenly into view. Around the grove of trees, the scene widened to show Taleh a house, white stone blinding in the sun. The lattices had been thrown open. A single story high, it had a flat roof with a parapet guarding the edge. A wooden door faced them, with a fire burning low a few steps outside.

Far off to one side, smaller houses stood. Unlike theirs, these were made of wood, slaves' quarters. Rock and timber fences crept away from sheds that held sheep and goats. Donkeys grazed happily farther back, where pasture met orchard. Trees, some heavy with fruit, marched in straight rows toward the sprawling forest, a blue-green shadow in the distance.

Javan let her look for the briefest moment, and then hurried her to the house. Despite the opened lattices, the room was dim, and Taleh stood still, waiting for her eyes to adapt. A table with low benches, shelving along the wall with clay jars lined up, covered, their contents hidden. The scent of olive oil in the lamps clung to the air. Rush baskets were piled haphazardly against another wall, in the middle of which hung a curtain.

Javan urged her toward it.

The lattices in this room were still shut, but Taleh had no trouble making out the bed. Long and wide, with a pallet stuffed full on top, it was made of planked wood standing a bare handwidth off the floor. No one had used it. No form had been pressed into the pristine surface. A white linen sheet lay across it, waiting to be spread open. Blankets lay rolled against the wall, for the day was already too hot for them.

He let go of her hand, and went over to the bed, picked up the sheet, and spread it across the pallet. Taleh heard the crackling of the rush filling as he fitted the sheet around the edges.

"I will give this sheet to you," he said as he worked. "It normally goes to the bride's parents as proof of her virginity, but you have no one left. Instead, I want you to have it."

When he was done, he held out his hand. "Come, Taleh."

Now that her time of adjustment was over, the nerves she had firmly held at bay came back with a vengeance.

"Surely you know what happens between a man and a woman? It is nothing to fear. I will do everything in my power to make this first time easy for you."

She watched him cross the room, their room, to her. She could not remember how to breathe.

This was right, she told herself.

This was frightening.

This was his due.

This was so very final.

He had been patient. She wished he would wait longer.

He was her husband. There was no turning back now.

The warmth of his mouth passed lightly over her eyebrows, and lingered on her forehead before moving again. He wrapped his arms around her, holding her close in tender embrace. His lips met her own, nibbling, teasing.

She relaxed in spite of herself. She did so like his kisses.

"I can promise you it is nothing to cause this much fear, but you will not believe me until it is over." His voice was mild, low and soothing. "Do you trust me?"

She looked up at him, so big and beautiful. Did she trust him? "Yes." The single word came out on a tiny breath of air.

"Good. Now let us begin."

CHAPTER 19

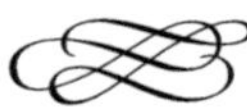

The feel of rain teased the air. Moisture hung heavily, oppressively, waiting for the signal to fall.

Javan lay in his bed, his wife wrapped in his arms. In the dimness, he feasted on her face. Her lips were red, still swollen from his attentions. Her lashes lay in dark crescents against her cheeks. Faint shadows left their tired color under her eyes.

He longed to soothe the exhaustion away. A finger moved of its own will toward her brow, where a small frown puckered the skin. He wanted her dreams to be happy ones, and worried about what she saw in her sleep that put it there. His finger stopped just short of touching her, fearful of waking her before she was ready.

He traced her features in the air, hovering just above the surface, comforting himself with the memory of touch. Her lashes had been soft as the softest feathers, her nose smooth and flawless. Her lips were kinder to his own than the first petals of spring.

The day called and, duty's faithful slave, he forced himself to rise. There was work to do, and it promised rain. It was early yet for the rainy season to being in earnest, but unless he misread the signs, they would be getting a warning shower.

He was grateful for the strong shoulders and backs of his slaves. They had done the work of men this past month. His neat orchards and careful fences attested to their efforts.

But the fields had yet to be plowed and planted. Some of the trees had not been relieved of their fruits. They would not wait much longer before the fruit spoiled.

He had the responsibility to set the example, both for his slaves and his wife. A farm was no place for sluggards. He looked down at the sleeping face of his wife, and saw again the dark circles under her eyes.

This one day she would sleep. Tomorrow would be soon enough to begin her duties.

TALEH WOKE WITH A START. Wakefulness was welcome. Something ugly from her dreams tainted her, then slipped away, leaving vague dread. She looked about, uneasy, searching for the ephemeral menace that had filled her dreams.

But no devils lurked in corners. She was in Javan's room, in Javan's house. She was safe here.

Taleh sat up slowly, wincing at the unfamiliar soreness and stiffness. She wondered how long she slept, and where her husband was. Her robe lay across the room where it had landed.

What kind of man had her parents in mind for her? It was an old question. They must have been waiting for something, or she would have been married off before, and she was fiercely glad it had not happened. Perhaps they had meant to marry her to someone incapable of making her happy, someone with much gold and no heart. "Oh, Father," she said aloud to the empty air, "who did you want for me?"

What would her parents think of Javan, if they had lived? If only she could believe they would be happy for her, glad she had surmounted, of a sort, the barriers between their two lands. She mockingly laughed into the quiet air. Her parents were too Ammonite. The setting aside of hatreds, it seemed, was only for the young.

If only she could see them one more time, try to explain. But they were dead, and furthermore, what would she say?

The house was empty. A bowl of pomegranates, grapes and figs sat warming on the table. A jug rested beside it, water beading on its sides.

A rumble of thunder interrupted her meal. She looked through the open door and saw heavy clouds hanging above the orchard. Where was Javan? The rumbles overhead sounded serious, and she worried if he would come home in time to escape the storm.

She walked outside, searching the horizon in all directions, her view broken by hills and trees. She wanted Javan here.

An odd fear filled her. The dream she had resolutely pushed aside surfaced, fed by the heavy air, the menace of the coming storm, darkness and dread.

Her family was gone, and she was alive. Their bodies, stiff and dead, crept into her dreams, all of them so clear even though in the war's aftermath she had only seen Chelmai. It was the first time she had dreamed of them in many days. Why now? Did she feel she had betrayed them by laying with her husband?

She saw again the dream, the pointing fingers, the accusations.

And remembered the horror that had driven her from sleep.

Two altars had stood before her. Javan was bound on one. Her family lay on the other. Everything was ready for the sacrifice, down to the burning torches poised above the wood.

Who would live, and who would die? The decision had been up to her.

She had not been able to choose, and the priests had made the decision she could not. Her husband had died, and she had wept with joy to hold her family again.

Had she betrayed them by living? She certainly had betrayed Javan in her dream.

Taleh climbed the small hill to the east of the house, and looked over the rolling land. The thin line of trees close to the house melted into the thicker forest, interrupting her view of the distance. If she figured correctly, somewhere out there lay Ammon.

"I am not going back." She said it out loud. She felt foolish, talking to nothing. The very lack of witnesses gave her the courage to continue, to expunge the guilt for being alive, and being happy. "I want to stay here, with my husband. I love him."

I love him, she thought. *I do.*

The road she set for herself was precarious, but it was the only one her heart could tolerate. As she stood alone before the growing storm, she wondered if she was up to the task.

JAVAN URGED the slaves to more speed as he kept one eye on the dark clouds. The sky had threatened all morning, but there was still too much to do in the fields. They had worked until the smell of coming rain blew in with the increasing wind. The first big drops fell as they reached the rock fence that edged the border of the field.

Javan closed the gate behind the last slave and latched it, looking back at the evidence of their day's efforts. The rain was just in time. The soil would begin to soften. His land needed the early rains more than the other farmers' land did, for his had grown only weeds for too many years. He needed soft soil before the roots would give way to the plow. He had taken the sickle to the stalks, but so much waited upon the rains.

Next year, Javan would have crops to harvest, seed to sell and to save to renew the cycle.

He turned and watched the slaves hurry into their dwelling, eager to get out of the worsening rain. He would be wet through by the time he got inside, but rain never bothered him.

A spot of blue on the opposite hill caught his eye, and he peered through the gray rain. What possessed her to come out in this weather? She was facing Ammon, and his heart gave a strange beat in his chest.

Before he could head after her, something in her stance held him in place. She was not moving, there was nothing to indicate any attempt to escape. He moved slowly toward her, not wishing to startle her, disturbed by her unnatural stillness.

When he was close enough to see her face, her expression stopped him.

Her shoulders were bowed as under a heavy load, her hands hanging limply at her sides. Her eyes looked out unseeing at the falling rain, her hair sticking to her scalp in tight, wet curls. Water ran off her face, but whether it was tears or rain, he could not tell.

No matter how many times he thought over his actions on that day, he would change nothing. He could not have taken her life. Nor could he have permitted her to become a slave. From the first time he saw her, he had known her life was in his hands. Making her his wife was the best of the ends she had faced.

Gusts of wind blew the rain in wild patterns, buffeting her frail figure as she stood, like she was in his land, separate and friendless. He could not let her stay out here or she would become ill. She did not have his strength or years of soldiering to protect her. He could not imagine what had drawn her out to face the storm. It made no sense.

The cold finally penetrated whatever pain she carried, and she wrapped her arms around herself for warmth, looking about as though she finally realized where she was.

Javan stood and waited for her to make the first move.

She saw him and smiled, holding out her hand.

An unfamiliar emotion wrapped around his chest. It was relief, he told himself. Relief and responsibility. The weight of the commitment he had undertaken grew both heavier and easier to carry. He was her family now, her protector and companion.

Battered as she had been by war and death, torn by loyalties that he knew still pulled at her, he alone stood to temper the wind.

CHAPTER 20

OBED POKED HIS HEAD AROUND THE CORNER OF THE THREE-SIDED SHEEPFOLD. "Have you heard yet?" he asked, his face alive with excitement.

"Heard what?" Javan scowled at the interruption. The sheep he bent over groaned as he pressed carefully at its belly. He suspected it had found some fermented grapes, probably from some vine hanging over a fence, or at least too near one.

"It is good to see you again, as well," Obed laughed.

Javan released a reluctant chuckle. "I apologize for my rudeness. My hospitality is lacking." He pressed once more, and the sheep swung back a hoof. He dodged just in time. It was a good sign. The animal might be unhappy, but it would survive. "It seems there is always too much to do. It has even been a while since I was free to take Taleh to the village."

Obed shook his head in mock reproach. "That is very cruel of you, to keep her penned here in the wilderness with only you and your flocks for company. For shame, Javan!"

Javan retorted, "If you came all this way to reproach me for my care of my wife, you are sadly misled. Each time I take my wife to the village, Saul gives her another gift. My home is overrun with pottery. I have jars, pots, oil lamps enough for ten houses, cups, bowls, and I do not know what else."

"My apologies, Javan. I have been too busy to keep up with local gossip. Perhaps soon you could send your wife for a visit. My wife would be only too happy to see her." Obed drew into himself for a moment, his thoughts far away, judging from the look in his eyes.

Javan felt the old familiar ripple of unease that tormented him whenever he thought of the things he should have told Obed about Merab, but had not.

Obed smiled, the shadow banished. "Have you no wish to ask what brings me here?"

"Very well. What brings you here?" Javan mimicked obediently.

"Traders are here from Midian. A big caravan, with many camels. I hope the well will hold out for their visit." Obed slapped Javan on the back, a bit harder than necessary. "Get Taleh, and come back with me. She will enjoy it. You might even find something to give her yourself, instead of relying on Saul. Women love presents."

"Very clever, Obed." But the idea had merit, he had to agree.

BY THE TIME they reached the village, Taleh was overwhelmed with Obed's oppressive good humor. Something was wrong with him.

Merab joined them near the impromptu marketplace quite happily, and clung to Obed's arm like a twining vine. Taleh would have doubted her earlier impression of Obed, had Merab's performance rung true. But she was almost giddy, and Obed's happy demeanor felt forced. His ever-present smile had a bitter edge and his laughter grated on the ear.

Merab was delighted, enchanted, effusive. The fabrics were too beautiful to be real, the gold blinded her with its glitter, the perfumes smelled sweeter than spring, the metal pans were the finest she had ever seen. And on it went. Taleh struggled with the urge to gag, and the equally strong desire to take Merab aside and slap her.

Merab flitted from one stall to the next, her movements frenetic. Taleh's worries grew. Obed guarded his expressions carefully, but Taleh could sense he was bemused by his wife's behavior.

Could it be she was merely lonely and heartsick, looking for something that reminded her of home? Obed must have thought so, for he finally bought her a gift of perfume. Her delight was painfully bright, her laughter too gay. Her eyes sparkled with something that felt much like desperation.

Taleh lost interest in the caravan. The brightly colored fabrics looked garish in their eye-catching display, the hastily-erected tents stifled her. The camels that rested behind each trader's stall smelled abominably. Everywhere the calls of the traders, and the raised voices of the buyers as they bargained, pounded at Taleh's ears. She wanted to leave, but no opportunity arose to ask. She caught Javan giving Obed worried glances, but he said nothing, so she kept her own silence and endured.

The strain made her head ache.

When Taleh noticed Saul on the edge of the bazaar, it was as a gift from heaven. She tugged at Javan's arm, heedless of the discourtesy. "Please, may I go and talk with Saul?" she asked, pointing.

Javan nodded. "I will come with you."

Obed waved them off, but there was regret in his eyes. What could be so wrong that he would need a guard to spend time with his wife, Taleh wondered.

As they took their leave, Javan said firmly, "No more gifts, Taleh. We have enough."

"I know," she agreed. It touched her each time she visited Saul to see her place in his life, to know he ignored her origins and sought to gift her with the best of his works. Each time, she accepted, knowing how rare this friendship was. Two friends and a husband seemed a small number. She would brave Javan's raised eyebrows and heavy sighs at the coming proffered gift, for there would be one, she knew. "I do not know how to refuse. Did you know he and his wife had no children?

"Yes, I know that."

"This may sound presumptuous, Javan, but I feel he may view me as a daughter." She looked apologetically at him. "That sounds arrogant of me. I am, after all, Ammonite."

"No," Javan said, surprised at his own lack of perception. "I think you may have it exactly right." They walked in silence, and then he spoke again. "You must still refuse him. We do not have enough room in our house for his gifts." He tugged at a blue-black curl, freed to the sun. She no longer wore a headdress, now that her hair had grown enough to cover her head and tickle the tops of her ears. Her new-born confidence pleased him.

Taleh giggled, whether at his touch or at his words, he could not say. "I am only too happy to let you try to refuse for me."

Javan smiled down at her, entering her lightened mood. "So you think I will not succeed, do you?"

Taleh laughed outright. "Not just think. I *know* you will not succeed. I wonder what he will make you take home."

Her mood charmed him. Javan retorted, caught up in her play, "I am stricken by your lack of faith."

"It is not that I lack faith in you, husband." She grinned up at him. "But Saul is older and very crafty. You will see."

Javan caught her hand, and held on tight as they made their way through the crowd.

Above the constant drumming of the late afternoon rain, the steady knock on the door pulled Taleh away from her cooking. The message must be urgent for anyone to make the trip in this weather. They had barely made it home dry.

She wished Javan was here. But he was out in some field with the slave boys, helping them round up the flock. Sheep were livelihood and needed care, and the storm had caught them unprepared.

Stepping around the over-sized water jar Saul had tricked Javan into accepting, the very sight of it making her smile again, Taleh cautiously pulled the door open. Merab stood outside, water dripping off her cloak, her short hair sticking to her head, and hanging limply over her ears. She was out of breath, and clung to the doorpost gasping for air.

"Merab! What is wrong?" Taleh pulled her inside, alarmed by the look on her face.

"Taleh, are you my friend?" Merab's voice was harsh.

"Of course I am," she responded, puzzled.

"You must promise you will not tell anyone what I am about to say. Do you promise?"

A warning went off inside Taleh. What reason could Merab have for such a request? "Why?"

"I have to leave here," Merab burst out. "I cannot stay. I must go home."

"To Obed?"

"Obed? By the gods, no! To Ammon!"

"You are leaving Obed?" Taleh could not think. He was a good man and she knew he was kind to Merab, whatever the problems that lay between them.

"You must promise to say nothing!" Merab gripped Taleh's shoulders like a wild woman. "Promise me!"

"Merab, do not do this thing," Taleh pleaded. "Whatever has happened, surely you can work it out with Obed. I know he would never hurt you. Talk to him. Please."

"I cannot. I will not. I have to get away."

"But *why*? Oh, Merab, please tell me what is wrong."

"I am pregnant."

Something dark, the color of despair, filled Taleh, choking off speech. A terrible premonition raised its ugly head. She stared numbly at Merab. "You are leaving Obed because you are pregnant."

"I am not like you, Taleh. I will not give up what I know. I have tried to remain faithful to Molech. Obed tried to stop me, but I found ways. I will not bring evil upon my head by failing my responsibility. If Obed knows I am carrying his child, he will never let me do the right thing for Molech, so I have to go before he finds out!"

"You are going to sacrifice your child?' Taleh's lips were stiff as she forced the words out.

"My uncle is a priest of the Baals, and he still lives. I found out today from the Midianites. I still fear the wrath of the gods, even if you do not. You think you are too far away for Molech to reach you? I know better. I will do my duty, and how better than to take vengeance on Israel? Leave with me."

If a cobra had appeared suddenly, Taleh could not have been more repulsed. "I can not! My life is here now. I will not go."

"I should have known! You have actually fallen in love with your husband, am I right?" Merab began to laugh, a cold mocking sound. "And I suppose you think he loves you in return? You, an Ammonite, an enemy? You silly fool!"

"How will you get away?" Taleh asked quietly, to turn Merab's pointed words away from her heart.

Merab laughed again. "And let you tell Javan, so he can tell Obed? I have it all planned, never fear. I know what I am doing. This is your best – your only – chance."

"But, Merab, if you leave now, he will know you have gone." Taleh willed her mind to work, hoping for an idea, an inspiration, anything to stop this from happening. "He will be after you before nightfall, and he will catch you, too. He was a soldier for many years. Have you thought of that?"

"He would never follow me. He will be glad to have me gone."

"You. Are. Wrong." Taleh spaced the words out for emphasis. "Because I *will* tell him you carry his child and plan to kill it. I have come to understand some of how these people think, and I promise you, he will come after you."

Terrifying rage disfigured Merab's face. For a moment, Taleh feared for her life, but she stood her ground. As though pinned before a poisonous viper, where a single movement could bring death, Taleh waited in stillness for the threat to break or pass by.

Merab blinked, and the spell was broken. "Very well. Perhaps you are right. He is watching me. I will wait."

For what, Taleh wanted to ask, but she contented herself with the small victory. "You are doing the right thing." She tried not to show her relief, tried to stiffen the knees that wanted to wobble. "It will get better. Give it time."

"I must go back. If he comes home early, he will wonder where I am. It would not do to make him suspicious." Merab's last words were bitter.

And she was gone. Taleh sank onto the bench, her hands shaking. Merab was not telling her the whole truth, she was sure. But she did not think Merab would leave in this weather.

THE NEXT DAY BROKE COOL. The sun was weak, and rather than endure a lonely meal in the autumn wind, Javan had come to eat with her. She cooked his favorite meal, trying to forget it had been a sheep she might have known not long before.

Sudden pounding on the door interrupted them. Obed's voice thundered through the heavy wood, "Javan, open up!"

For a startled instant, the raw fear in his voice froze them both. Javan reacted first, with the warrior's speed that still awed her. Obed stood in the doorway, a fist raised to give another blow. His face was reddened with exertion and the chill of the day, but sweat beaded on his forehead.

Taleh knew, before he said another word, the news he brought.

"Get in, before you let out what little warmth we have." Javan grabbed Obed's upraised arm, and tugged him inside.

Obed searched the room quickly, and the despair on his face tore at Taleh. What a fool she had been!

The two men exchanged a whole conversation with one glance. Javan turned to Taleh. "Please wait in our room," he said in a tone that allowed no reprieve.

Taleh was only too glad to go. How could she stay out there, knowing what she knew, carrying the burden of suspicion ignored, while Obed paid the price of her misjudgment? She pulled the curtain shut, but no amount of conscience could stop her from listening. The curtain was meager protection against voices.

"My wife is not here." Obed's voice held no expression, no surprise.

"No."

"She has not been here today?" Taleh ached with the plea, carefully hidden beneath the casual question.

"No." Javan added no comment. Taleh bit her finger to keep herself quiet. A curl tickled her ear, and she pushed it away impatiently, wondering what Obed's expression held. Did he weep?

A sigh trembled on the air. "I thought it might be so," she heard him say. He sounded utterly defeated, this man of irrepressible good spirits and unfailing optimism. Taleh did not know who she hated most in that moment, Merab with her lying poison, or herself, for her gullibility. "I should have known. I am the worst of fools. Would that I had cut her down the day I saw her."

JAVAN FINALLY ASKED the question that had plagued him. "What is the problem?"

"My wife," Obed spat the word out as though it sickened him, "told me that she and Leah were coming this morning to visit Taleh. She said they might stay through the midday meal. Except I saw Leah walking back from the market, and asked – out of politeness – how your wife was doing this day. She knew nothing about a visit to your home. Indeed, she was surprised when I asked. She wondered what difference one day might make, since our families had seen each other only yesterday at the caravan. But, fool that I am, I thought only that there might be things women like to discuss without their men around."

Javan needed no further explanation. "You did not really expect to find her here, did you?"

"I hoped. I prayed that I was wrong, that she would be sitting here, laughing with your wife and exchanging bits of gossip. But I did not expect it, no."

While Javan watched with open-mouthed surprise, Obed pounded his chest, clutching at his tunic with large, white-knuckled fists. "Merciful heavens, why can I not get her out of my heart?"

Witnessing Obed's pain was more than Javan's conscience could bear. To see his friend endure this, when he might have been able to prevent it! Which was better, to let him hold the memory and wonder, or to destroy what Obed knew of his wife? "Why did you choose her? What did you see of her?"

"She was lively, and made me smile. It sounds like such a silly reason, does it not?" He gave a strangled laugh, that caught near his throat and made him clear it viciously.

"Obed, I cannot stand to see you torment yourself so," Javan said, still not convinced he did the right thing either way. "Your wife was not what you thought."

Obed looked at him, bitterness in every line of his face. "You think I do not know that?"

"I say that, not for whatever made her leave you. She never was what you thought. She was a fickle woman, and never could have been content with one man. Had I told you what I saw before, I might have prevented this from happening?"

Obed became very still, watching Javan with a hawk's stare. "What do you mean?"

"On the journey from Ammon, she attempted to get close to any man who would look at her. It is to our credit that she did not succeed in seducing the entire army." Having committed himself, Javan could not hold back. "She even attempted it with me, but I refused to pay attention to her. It did not stop until the army disbanded. Perhaps she knew she could not keep her amorous intentions secret with all of us in such close proximity."

He could hardly stand to look at Obed's face, the pain was so clear. "I am so sorry, my friend. I said nothing before this because I thought she simply wanted some attention, and that she was trying to get back at you for the time your duties took you away from her. I did not know she would carry it this far."

"Do you think she has seduced any from the village?" Obed's voice had gone dead and flat. No surprise, no anger.

Javan was not certain. Still, he gave the best answer he could. "No, I do not think so. To be sure, I have been away from the city much of the time since we arrived, but you are held in too high a regard for anyone to dare. No, I think her favors belonged only to you."

"I wish I could believe that."

"You can, for it is true." He could only hope, for Obed's sake. His friend had enough to grapple with. What had their life together been like, that his friend made no objections, showed no anger, did not even raise a voice of protest. "Obed, it may be too soon to ask this, but what will you do?"

Eyes dark with hurt and disillusionment met his. "I will file a certificate of divorce with the older men at the gate." His face set in hard lines, brutal with determination. "She has made her choice. I will not force her to return." His voice lost its conviction as he added softly, "I do not want her now."

"You cannot let her go!"

Javan whirled in surprise. Taleh shoved aside the curtain and broke into the stillness that followed Obed's words. "You must go bring her back!" Her eyes were wild with fear and desperation.

He grabbed at his wife, stopping her as she tried to dart around him to reach Obed. "Taleh, we have asked that you leave us alone. This does not concern you."

She struggled in his arms, turning as though startled to see him. "It does! It does concern me!" She spoke with a firmness that surprised him, but he could feel tension vibrating in her, shaking her slender frame. "You see, she fooled me, too. Merab came to talk to me last night. She told me she was going to run away."

SILENCE thick enough to suffocate fell upon the room. Anger beat upon her, but it was too late to rephrase her words.

"You knew? Why did you keep silent?"

"Did you not think I should know?"

"How much of this plot were you involved in?"

The two men towered over her, thundering bitter words down upon her head. Javan's grip on her arm hurt, and Obed tugged at her other side. For a brief instant she feared what they might do to her. Was there a law for this, too, the keeping of one's counsel? She screeched at them, heedless of the consequences, trying to be heard and defend herself. "Please! Let me finish!"

Javan flung her arm away from himself as though it were diseased. "Yes, tell us your reasons for keeping this secret."

His voice pierced her with its coldness. The foundations of her world cracked. "I told her to stay! I did! I thought I had convinced her, she said she would stay. But she fears the wrath of Molech too much." She turned to face Obed. "Merab is pregnant, Obed. She carries your child."

Obed took a startled step back, but Taleh hurried on. "She means to offer it on the altars of Molech. Her uncle is a priest of the Baals. I did not know that until she told me yesterday. She could not leave the old life behind."

Obed's face was colorless, his lips pale and still. "Merab carries my child?"

"Yes."

"You are sure it is mine?"

"She told me so last night. I had hoped she would stay long enough for you to find out by yourself. I was wrong." Holding her tattered courage, Taleh glanced at Javan, but his face told her nothing. "I tried to talk her out of leaving. I thought I had succeeded. I cannot make you believe me. Why should you? I am only your Ammonite wife, and we all know what the Ammonites are like."

Her eyes burned. She looked at the condemning faces with as much dignity as she could manage. How could she convince them? "You would have to be born into Ammon to know what power the priests hold. She could never have adjusted to this life. Her roots are too deep. When you chose her in the camp of the women, I doubt she thought very far ahead."

She wanted to cling to Javan, throw herself into his arms and plead for understanding, weep out her regrets. His face was closed to her. Taleh turned and walked back to their bedroom, brushing the curtain aside as she went.

The dim rumble of the men's voices reached her as she lay curled into herself on the bed. She felt only pain. She was not worthy of him. Was that what he was saying to Obed as she lay alone and mourning? She was beneath him by accident of birth, by her country, a place of practices she abhorred, where happiness had been a fleeting thing squeezed between periods of fear and horror. She could no more change her origins than she could the color of her eyes. This new land had offered her a fresh start, some hope of peace and safety from the ever-vigilant priests of vengeful gods.

Now the man to whom she had given her heart felt only scorn for her. She had not become pregnant yet. There was no child to tie them together.

What would he do with her?

CHAPTER 21

Obed grabbed Javan's arm. "You are a fool, Javan. You made the better choice, and yet you stand, condemning her. There are worse things than being too trusting."

"We have only her word." Guilt lapped at Javan's conscience even as he spoke.

"Wake up, man!" Obed was stiff with anger. "I am the injured party, I am the one wronged, and yet you act as though the grievance was yours alone. I, more than anyone, know how convincing my wife can be. I am sure she saved her best performance for Taleh. Everyone in the village knows your wife would take an arrow meant for you, or throw herself before a spear if it would save you. Everyone knows, except you. Do you honestly believe she knew the full extent of Merab's treachery? I do not." Obed tossed Javan one final look of disgust and walked toward the door.

Before he stepped out into the weak sun and first cold of the coming winter, he turned back. "Have you ever told her you love her? That you are proud of her attempts to fit in? That you appreciate her courage? No? I can take care of matters with my wife. Your work lies here with your own."

Javan watched the door close behind Obed, and turned to look at the curtain to his room. Why had she not come to him with her worries? Why did her first loyalty still belong to her countrywoman? He may well have hurt her by his anger, but it was she who first found him lacking.

He would have to make what mends with his wife he could before he left, for he would go with Obed, he knew that. Part of the responsibility for Merab's escape lay with his household; he held equal responsibility for her return.

He found Taleh lying on the bed, staring at nothing. She looked very small.

She made no response when he cleared his throat. Was she trying to make this difficult for him? The apology stuck in his throat, but he forced it out. He was a man and men did not shirk even unpleasant duties. "Obed told me I was too hard on you."

Her eyes closed. He went on. "He was right." She still did not react. "I do not understand why you did not come to me with what you knew, but you did not. It is over. You did not leave with her, and I am grateful."

TALEH KEPT HER EYES CLOSED. She was not ready to look at him. If this was supposed to be an apology, she was not impressed. An admission caught between two scoldings, was that the best he could do?

He did not move from his position near the curtain, made no effort to come over and touch her at all. "I will be going with Obed to find her and bring her back."

Taleh sat upright. "How can you? I do not even know how she planned to get back to Ammon." Javan's eyes were hard and piercing, as though he was trying to see through to her very thoughts. Her anger rose another notch. "I speak the truth! I do not know how she meant to get away!"

"I might." His voice was mild. His gaze lost some of its force. "I think we will start with the Midianite traders. I believe Obed will find they are gone, when he starts to think clearly. What better way to leave than before dawn on camels? They can travel all day, their stride is nearly twice that of my donkeys, and Midian lies south of Ammon. They will have to go through Ammonite lands to reach their own. We will need to hire some camels of our own to catch up. Yes, I think we will find her with the caravan."

Taleh did not want to ask, but she had to know. "What will I do?"

"You will stay here." Javan spoke like the army chief he had been. "We will need food for several days, and a change of clothing, along with blankets for the night air. I will leave that to you, and I will make arrangements for the slaves. Someone will have to watch over them. I must find my sword, and sharpen it." His voice faded off when he looked at her. She must have done something, made some sound. "Taleh? What is it?"

"Why do you carry your sword? You do not mean to kill her, do you? She carries Obed's child!" Her questions rushed out, tinged with panic.

"Taleh, did it not occur to you that she might ask them to kill us? Do you think she will come back peaceably? She is with a caravan of traders. Do you think they are unarmed? We would be fools to go without our weapons, all of them."

Javan and Obed against an entire caravan. Her heart clenched with fear. Taleh slid off the bed, and walked past him to the door.

She stopped. "Please take care," she said softly, and walked out.

THE SUN WAS low in the sky when they first noticed the shimmer, like a cloud of dust on the horizon. Obed pointed, and Javan nodded. Obed had insisted they be up before the dawn. It was a wise decision. They had made good time.

"Yes, I see it, too, Obed."

"Will we catch them before dark, do you think?" Obed shielded his eyes from the sun's rays, and squinted again at the tell-tale sign.

"I cannot guess their speed." Javan's own eyes felt swollen. They had walked into the glare all day, after a restless night during which neither slept much. They had saved their water skins for drinking, despite the temptation to pour some over their heads, to wash off the dirt the wind delighted in throwing at them. Gilead and its lush stands of trees, its heavy dews, and grassy fields lay far behind. The ground here was dry, the plants under the camels' feet brittle enough to crackle and snap. Hills rolled in shallow abundance ahead and behind. Palm trees were more common than figs and olives.

Limestone poked its white head up everywhere, and lay in sharp chunks along their path. They had pushed the animals to greater speed, taking less care to the path. Even this late in the season, the sun was still warm. Javan knew they would need to find a well or even a cistern, both for their own sake and that of their mounts. But none had appeared all day.

Why would the traders take an entire caravan of camels, whose great appetite for water was legendary, on a forced trek through an area devoid of water? There must be a well soon.

The sun sank lower as they kept up their punishing pace. The dark shimmer grew nearer, and nearer still. In the long shadows of twilight, they finally saw an oasis, palm trees, muddy bank and waving rushes, and the caravan of Midianite traders.

And spears, bows, arrows, and shields.

The two men pulled their camels up, struggling to hold them as the smell of water tormented the animals. From the dancing shadows of the campfire, a man stepped forward.

"Why do you follow us?"

"You have something that belongs to me." Obed spoke quietly, making no move for his own weapons.

"And what would that be?" The man moved closer, his words taunting, his courage the spear and shield.

"My wife."

The man laughed, and tossed words over his shoulder to his companions. "Do we have a lost wife among our supplies?"

The men returned his laugh, bold and careless, but Javan had been watching closely. The spears that had flashed so threateningly as they rode up were held in unsteady hands, the bows were not pulled taut, and the shields tended to dip as arms trembled under the unaccustomed weight. He followed the direction of Obed's gaze, and knew that Obed saw as well. He longed to pull his own sword, for no one would miss his years of experience, but Obed gave the commands here.

False bravado faded under the steady regard. Javan knew the advantage for the moment was theirs. The traders' own camels had been hobbled for the night. They could not afford the time it would take to release them and mount.

Obed, moving slowly, pulled his bribe out of the sack. Javan knew what Obed was willing to trade for the life of his child, but even he felt the beauty of the worked gold, the glow of polished stones, ruby, topaz, onyx, amethyst, and jade. He had seen the necklace among Obed's booty from the spoils of Ammon. Beautiful in the sun, the necklace gave off an unearthly shimmer in the firelight.

"I believe you know the woman of which I speak." His voice was calm, without concern. He seemed to pay little attention to the necklace, letting it drip from one hand to the other and back. "Did she tell you she carries a child? Who will want a woman so burdened? It will be a long time before she is able to give full measure to her owner." The gold slid through his fingers, the stones swaying on the delicate chain. "How much did she pay you for her passage?"

Javan watched the greedy eyes follow Obed's movements. The men glanced at each other, and back to the wealth Obed flaunted before them. Tense moments passed, as the outcome hung poised on a knifeblade.

The spokesman gave a new laugh, hearty and welcoming. "We must be careful. Thieves lie in wait, and are not above telling pitiful tales to win sympathy and ease their way." None of the men moved to go for Merab, wherever she was hiding. Javan sat and waited. The Midianite trader continued to smile. "But now I can see you are a man of stature and means. One might wonder why a wife would leave such a happy home."

Obed would not let himself be drawn by flattery or taunts. He let the necklace slip down, catching it on one finger and letting the evening breeze play with it. The traders continued to watch, fairly drooling at the prize almost within their grasp.

Spears lowered, bows were flung down.

"We did take a young woman with us." The leader had given up. "She gave us silver, a pretty payment. What might this wife of yours look like?"

"Bring this woman out to me." Obed's voice grew quieter.

The trader shrugged. "What is one woman to me? This one would have made for an unhappy journey with her weeping and complaining."

Javan caught his smile in time. He could not have described Merab better himself.

They were able to follow Merab's progress from the back of the camp by her shrill cries." No! No! I will not go! I paid for transfer to Ammon, I will not go back!"

Obed's face might have been carved in stone. He held the necklace, still out of reach, while the men varied their attentions from the struggling woman to the reward. It was easy for Javan to see which one held more appeal.

When the men flung Merab to the ground at the feet of the camels, Javan could see her hands had been bound. He wondered until he saw two of the men rub at their faces. The flickering fire sparkled against dark lines glistening wet blood. Merab had obviously given a good account for herself first.

Obed looked down at her impassively, and then tossed the golden necklace to the spokesman. "You have made yourself a good bargain this night." He gave a tug on the reins and the camel reluctantly knelt. He slid off and walked over, ignoring her bonds. Javan felt Obed's ache as he stared at his wife in silence. Without saying a word, he lifted her to her feet and tossed her easily onto the camel's back, and then mounted himself behind her. She denounced him with ever more colorful curses, hurling abuse upon him with words, since her hands were denied her.

Javan finally spoke. "Our camels have need of a drink."

The men cheerfully moved aside to let them pass. Javan went first, while Obed urged his camel to rise. His arms trapped her as he held the reins on either side, holding her in place as the camel rocked upright.

"Have you a cloth?" Obed muttered to Javan. He fit the words between Merab's curses.

"I will find something."

Leah watched Taleh and wondered again, as she had done each of the past days, if she had done the right thing. It had worried her, the thought of Taleh alone with slave boys not much younger than she was, whose dispositions she did not know. So she had come, to wait with Taleh for the men's return.

Something was wrong. Taleh said nothing, but it was as obvious as sunrise that she was miserable, unhappy and afraid. She stared off into the distance and Leah caught tears in her eyes. She sighed, deep and aching sighs that trembled out of her lungs.

Leah did not want to be caught staring, so she looked away. Isaac was having a wonderful time in this sojourn at the farm, eating dirt, poking chubby fingers at the sheep through the fence, following ants as they scurried about. He looked up at her now from where he sat on his muddy backside, clapped his filthy hands, and chortled with glee at the sheer joy of being alive.

Leah envied him, immune from the cares of the adults.

Taleh turned from the lamb stew cooking over the open fire and smiled at Isaac. Leah saw beyond the smile to the sadness, and could bear it no longer. "Something is bothering you, Taleh. I cannot make you tell me what it is, but would it not be easier to bear if you had someone to help you?"

"I do not know what you mean."

Leah followed the direction of Taleh's gaze. Straight back to her son. Isaac had made his wobbly way to the fence around the sheepfold, empty now at midday. The sheep were in the near pasture, out of sight, but he was not fooled. He obviously knew they had to be close. He struggled without success to lift his baby legs high enough to get over the lowest rung of the fence, trying first one leg and then the other, and back again, but always falling short. His small, round hands clenched around the slender fence pole as though it were a lifeline.

Leah had stopped trying to keep him away from the sheepfold. It did not matter that they were bigger than he was. He was thrilled by them, going back again and again as though pulled by a string. It had been difficult getting him to sleep, with the constant sounds of sheep to remind him that they were just outside.

Leah looked back at Taleh, and finally understood. "Some day it will be your children who try to climb in with the sheep."

"No. I do not think so." Taleh's words were heavy with grief. "Javan was so angry with me when he left! I knew Merab wanted to run away but I said nothing. I thought I had convinced her to stay. I did not leave with her, I told Obed about his baby, but none of this is enough to banish my guilt. Javan despises me now. How long will he keep me when he returns?"

Leah did not know what to say. Dared she speak for Javan? Leah asked, "If Javan had wanted to be rid of you, why did he not bring you with him? By the time they catch the caravan, they will be nearly to the border of Ammon. How simple it would be to bring you with and exchange you for Merab. But he is gone, and you are still here. Does that tell you nothing?"

The first signs of hope lifted some of the weight from Taleh's drooping shoulders. "I had not thought of that." But the brightness quickly fled.

"Taleh?"

Taleh raised tortured eyes. "Javan has been trying to teach me about your god. He tells me your god is fair." She glanced toward the sky, as though she expected instant punishment for blasphemy. "So why is Merab pregnant, and not me? Merab does not even want her baby. I would be happy to give Javan a child. Where is the justice in that?"

"Taleh, I cannot answer why God allowed someone as unworthy as Merab to conceive. Perhaps the child is to be a gift for Obed. Who can know whether His hand is behind an event? But I do know that it is far too soon for you to be worried. If you had been married two years, or five, I would worry with you, and hurt with you."

"If it had been two years, Javan would have another wife."

Leah could think of nothing to say. Taleh spoke truth. Javan needed a family. If she proved unable to bear children, Javan undoubtedly would take another wife.

"It is much too early to worry." She could think of nothing better to say.

CHAPTER 22

JAVAN SAW THE WHITE FLASHES OF HIS LIMESTONE HOUSE PEEKING THROUGH the slender poplar and more sturdy oak trees, and wondered at the flutter that started around his heart. He could see the clearing, too, between the trees, and smell the smoke of the fire. He wanted to push the camel to greater speed, but the path was narrow, branches waited to catch him off his guard, and the camel was tired and thirsty and ill inclined to obey.

No smell of cooking food reached him, no stewing meat or boiling vegetables. A brief moment of worry assailed him. Taleh's robe flashed blue through the trees. He had left her in anger; he wanted to remove the hurt his doubt had caused.

Another robe flashed yellow as he moved between the trees, and he heard the squeal of a child. . Leah must be here to visit. It would be a good thing, except he wanted Taleh alone. There were things to be said that deserved privacy. The last tree passed, and he moved into the clearing around his house. The two women sat slightly away from the fire, their attention on each other. He urged the camel forward a step.

Taleh looked up, her face wavering between joy and hurt. He cursed himself for putting that there, for making her dread his return. Did he smile?

Should he hold out his arms? Four days was a long time to leave her to brood and worry.

The camel drew near the fire, and he reined it in, nudging it down. He rocked with its movement, and slid off, standing beside it. How silly they must look, he thought, two people belonging to each other and yet not knowing how to take the first steps back. He held out his arms, ignoring Leah's interested gaze, and waited.

Taleh looked at Javan's outstretched arms. One step, another, and then she ran to him. His strong arms closed around his wife, so sweet, so missed. Joy bubbled up, and Taleh loosed peals of laughter as he swung her around in circles.

"I was wrong to leave as I did. I should have known you would not follow Merab's path. Can you forgive me my harsh words?" Was it that easy for her to forgive?

It was. "I forgive you. The situation did not lend itself to trust."

He looked down into her warm black eyes, open and sincere. "Perhaps not, but I had no reason to *dis*trust. I could not think of a single thing you had done to mislead me in all the time we have known each other. I should have remembered that first." Javan bent down for a kiss, and forgot the eyes around him. She tasted of joy and relief. When he lifted his head, he vowed, "I will not make that mistake again."

Leah quietly went about picking up their bowls and cups, and gathering her belongings.

Javan's handpicked guard agreed to take the camel back to its owner in the village. Leah would ride with her son. Their guests were scarcely out of sight when Javan picked Taleh up in his arms and carried her into the house. He set her feet down on the floor, sobered, and said gravely, "I have missed you, wife. I thought of you during the day, and wondered if you would ever forgive me. I do not know if I could have borne it if you had rejected me."

"How could I reject you?" Taleh framed his face with her hands. "You are my husband."

"A thoughtless one, at times." Javan spoke softly.

"But not too proud to admit it, and set matters straight." Taleh smiled at him. She reached up and drew his head down, looking into his still-shadowed eyes. "I am well pleased with my husband. I would not trade you for a fortune in jewels."

Javan ran a finger gently down her cheek and smiled in return. "How could I ever have associated you with her in my mind? I must tell you what Obed has decided. Obed will keep her under guard until the baby is born. At that time, he will give her a certificate of divorce and return her to Ammon. The child will stay here."

Taleh shuddered. "I am sorry for Obed, for Merab. No one will be happy at the end of this matter."

"Obed will have his child safe."

"Yes. That is true. But the child will not have a mother." Taleh was quiet for a moment. "Perhaps in this case it is not such a terrible fate."

Javan drew her into his arms, settling her head on his shoulder. "Obed already loves it. He will be a very good father. Then, of course, some day he will remarry. The child will probably never know the difference."

A DEEP PAIN wrapped around Taleh's heart. She wondered if Merab would ever think of what she had lost. Or if it would matter. Would it be different to know her child lived, and called another 'mother?'

Obed would give her a certificate of divorce. How very final that was. It sounded so easy, a certificate of divorce. A piece of papyrus, perhaps a goatskin, with writing on it. Everyone here knew how to write. Where was the boundary in this land, what laws made the division between a wife kept and a wife discarded?

There was so much she did not know yet, so many rules to learn. She wanted a child with unreasoning desire. She wanted a place here, next to her husband, in his arms. She wanted to give him his family, to watch them grow. Each time they lay together, she prayed to whatever god would listen for a child. Her body had never been reliable, her monthly times never dependable. Her hopes had risen to the skies, and then crashed down when the bleeding finally came. It hurt unbearably, to have those days of excited hope, that perhaps this time the delay was for real. Each month so far, her prayers had not been heard.

She believed Javan would keep her now, because she had to believe. To find out that Obed planned to send Merab away struck a blow at her trembling heart which not even his arms around her could ease.

One week later, when Taleh accompanied Javan to the village, she heard that Obed had already decided to take another wife.

The woman was Leah.

CHAPTER 23

Taleh could not keep warm. The cold seemed to be waiting everywhere, sliding under the door, and rushing inside every time it was opened. Mischievous tendrils wrapped around her legs in the house, having crept around the rags stuffed between the slats of the lattices and joining the cold from the door. Whenever she ventured outside, rain the same temperature as the cold pelted her with sharp needles of wetness. She had even seen a few flakes of snow.

The cooking had to be done inside now. Javan had lifted the small wood coverings in each room in the stone floor. Fires were kept burning in the dirt hollows between the stone floor that the board squares had hidden. Roof doors could be lifted up to let the smoke out. Or such was supposed to happen, but the wind had other ideas, catching it and driving it back inside. The house was full of smoke. Taleh longed to fling the shutters open and let the cold do its worst just to smell air that did not make her want to retch.

She ached for the days when she cooked outside and watched the birds dance on the air, the sky so blue it hurt to look up. The sun seemed to have forgotten how to shine. The trees that bordered their fields drooped in the cold and wet, even the early blossoms hanging limp on the citrus trees.

Javan did not understand her feelings. He spent time outside each day, watching for the first shoots of the seeds he had planted, checking on the slaves in their dwellings, hovering over the sheep and goats, feeding his various animals. He would bustle in, bringing fresh air and cold with him, and Taleh would come to stand next to him, breathing the scent of outdoors that clung until the smoke found him and chased the freshness away. He always smiled indulgently, but he could not know how it was for her.

Her world's only color was gray. She had to drag herself out of bed each day, and battled bone-deep fatigue just to complete the necessary chores.

Then, one day as she cooked a stew of lamb and lentils, garlic and leeks, the nausea she had battled for days overwhelmed her. She barely made it out the door when her knees buckled and she vomited, horrible shudders, wrenching spasms and the taste of bile. Once started, she could not stop, but remained hunched over outside the doorway, retching and trembling.

Running footsteps penetrated her misery, and Javan was at her side. "I was with the animals, and I could hear you even there. Are you all right?"

"No, I am not all right!" What was wrong with his eyes? "Do I look all right?" Her stomach lurched again.

Javan lifted her to her feet, ignoring her moan. "You cannot possibly have anything left inside. I have seen how little you eat."

He carried her into the smoky house, but he left the door open. The sun chose that moment to peek out from behind the clouds, flashing through the open doorway, and Taleh was surprised to find she could still smile. Javan set her carefully on the divan, and her arms fell limply off on either side, brushing the floor. He crossed to their bedroom, and emerged with a blanket and a smug smile.

He tucked the blanket around her tightly. "I have opened the lattices. I will leave them open until the smoke is cleared and you can breathe." He still had that oddly pleased look on his face. "What were you doing that made you so ill?"

"I was cooking . . . My stew!" Taleh fought the heavy blanket and her own weakness to sit up, but Javan pushed her back down.

"I can see it. It has not burned. I will watch it for a moment but I must send someone for the midwife." He actually grinned.

"Mid . . ." Taleh's voice trailed off as realization dawned.

"I think you carry my child," Javan said softly and with pride. He leaned over and kissed her forehead tenderly.

Taleh's eyes filled with tears. *Please, let him be right,* she thought. A child. Her life could hold no greater joy than to give him a child. One child might be enough to secure her place.

Her eyes followed him as he went out the door to send a slave to the village. As soon as he was out of sight, strange fears rose up to haunt her: Merab, well into her confinement, shortly to lose her child and husband at one and the same time. Leah, the second wife, reminding Taleh that she, too, could be supplanted, or supplemented.

She would not permit Javan to do the same to her. But how could she prevent it? She could not share him. He was her heart. How could she ever live with only half a heart?

To Taleh's surprise, Old Sarah appeared at the doorway. The old woman greeted her with a distinctly female smile of conspiracy. "So what is this I hear? Do you have need of the services of a midwife?"

"You? You are the midwife?"

Sarah chuckled. "Of course. How else would news reach me so quickly?"

Another figure blocked the sunlight briefly, and Leah entered the room. She stood hesitantly just inside the door, waiting.

Taleh looked at her friend, and was swamped with guilt. Leah had done nothing against her. She had merely married the man who asked her, the man she had wanted in silence for months. Obed deserved better than Merab. Leah still had milk, the baby soon to be born needed a wet nurse, and Obed needed a wife.

It was not Leah's fault that she had become what Taleh could not endure – a second wife.

From the loneliness on Leah's face, she had missed Taleh as much as Taleh had missed her. Taleh held out a hand in appeal. "Please come sit by me. Tell me what is new in the village."

Leah smiled in relief. She sat down close. "There is nothing to report. The only thing new is your . . . condition."

Sarah interrupted. "There will be plenty of time to exchange gossip later. We do not know yet if Taleh is with child. Come to your bed now, and we will see what there is to be found."

Under Sarah's imperious eye, Taleh did what she was told. Frowning in concentration, Sarah pressed and felt and thought. *Please let it be,* Taleh prayed. Her teeth began to chatter. Her hand trembled, and Leah held it.

At Sarah's smile, Taleh knew what she would say.

"You are with child, several months. The winter is nearly over, and spring will be here. I know you are feeling sick, but you must eat. For now, lots of dried fruits and nuts. And lots of meat, even if your husband must cook it for you. Soon it will be warm enough to cook outdoors again, and you will feel better." She looked at the open window. "You need fresh air, you cannot continue to breathe this smoke. Wrap yourself in a blanket if you must, but you cannot continue to breathe this smoke. Drink plenty of water. Your cistern is full. Use it!"

Taleh smiled at her spate of instructions, and hoped she could remember them all. She was with child. It was a wonder.

Javan's child.

"When you need me," Sarah was saying, "you know where I am. Your husband can send someone for me. You are thin, but you have good hips." To Taleh's startled delight, Sarah came over and, leaning down, gave her a brief hug. As though ashamed of her emotions, she shuffled out quickly.

Leah put a gentle arm around her shoulder. Taleh turned to her, smiling as if she would never stop. "Now Javan will have to keep me, will he not?"

"Silly woman." Leah smiled back. "I thought you were over that. You know he will keep you."

Taleh knew her words would hurt, but she had to set matters straight. "I want him to keep *only* me." Pain flashed into Leah's eyes. Taleh regretted it, but this very thing had almost cost their friendship. If it was to continue to survive, they must clear this between them. "I do not know how to say this. That is why I stayed away. I do not know how it is for you, and I do not wish to hurt you, but I cannot share Javan."

How did she tell Leah what it was like for her? "Leah, you cannot know what it is to still be seen as the enemy. People watch me, and wait for me to make a mistake, to break a law. After Merab . . . well, it has only gotten worse. Any one of the women in the village would be accepted before me, instead of me. If Javan were to take another wife, I would have no place here at all. I am tolerated here only because I am his wife. For what other reason would they let me remain? Not even for your sake could I accept another wife." She tried to smile to take the sting out of her words, but she knew it was a poor attempt.

Leah's face held aching sadness. "I knew you felt like this. So many times I wanted to come here, to explain, but the time was not right. Only today, when I heard Javan had sent for a midwife, could I decide to come. Sarah is training me to take her place." She held Taleh's hand firmly. "Taleh, it is not what you think. Merab has no status at all in our . . . in his house. Surely you can see that she has forfeited her position. She lives as a . . . guest."

"I can hear someone saying that about me, some day," Taleh said bitterly.

"No! It is not at all the same. When Merab is gone, I will be his only wife, like you. Oh, please, Taleh, know that I did not do this to cause anyone pain. I only wanted to make Obed happy. I was overjoyed when he made his offer. I had watched him all that time, hoping no one would guess my secret. I saw more than you did, because I lived in the town. I saw him grow ever more miserable, and how hard he tried to hide it. Soon she will be gone, and the child will stay. I will be its mother, and I will love it. Can you not accept how important that is?"

"Yes," Taleh heard herself say. "Yes, I think I can understand. But know that I will never accept another woman in my house."

Leah actually laughed, a choked watery sound, but a laugh nonetheless. "I would never expect you to. Can we be friends again, at least?"

Taleh hugged her tightly. "Yes. And I have missed you. I can only hope that Obed has not given Javan any ideas with his marriage to you."

CHAPTER 24

THE WIND BLEW ACROSS THE FIELDS, LEAVING A FLEETING IMPRINT BEHIND. Tall stalks of wheat bent before it, and rose, strong, as it passed, only to bow before the next effort.

Taleh watched the slaves as they climbed into the trees and plucked off the ripe oranges, apricots, and the first of the early figs. The branches, too, swayed before the power of the wind, and the boys laughed in delight at the ride. At the base of each tree, large baskets too heavy for one man filled quickly with the succulent fruit. More baskets of the first harvest of nuts were stored in the underground pits Javan had worked hard to build. The harvest was abundant, and promised much fruit to dry and to sell.

But for now, there was fresh fruit to eat, and nuts to chew to give her strength. The barley harvest was finally done, and the wheat harvest was well under way. Javan spent much of his time in the fields with his slaves, swinging the heavy sickles, binding the stalks into bundles. He came home each night tired, thirsty, and hungry for the food Taleh worked on during the day. She made huge pots of stews, baked endless bread, and cooked birds on spits over the flame, but no matter how much food she made, it was never enough. She could hardly remember the time before the harvest.

Her oven was always hot. Each day she stood over it, piling grass around it and carrying hot coals from the fire in the long-handled fire-holder to start the burning. Inside the clay oven, the dough she had mixed the previous night baked. Her days fell into a pattern of countless cycles: arranging the small rolls of shaped bread on the clean stones, setting the heavy clay jar over them, piling it with grass, and letting the grass burn away, waiting until the jar was cool enough to remove, then beginning again. While the bread baked, she had meat to cook, vegetables to cut, water to carry from the cistern that fairly bulged from the abundant rains.

The work was hard, and her burden heavy. Whenever she felt tempted to complain, she would look up and see her husband swinging the heavy sickle, or carrying the prickly bundles to the threshing floor he had built on the hillside. She could hear the voices of the men urging the donkeys to pull the heavy wooden sled across the piles of wheat. Occasionally the wind would blow chaff past her face, making her cough.

How could she complain when she watched how hard her husband worked?

The baby within her grew large, and her skin itched and pulled as it stretched to make room. Their child was active, kicking and rolling inside her, making her straighten quickly as it shoved against its confinement. She tried to guess what the small lumps were as it poked and pushed. Was that a foot, or a knee, or an elbow? The sickness of the early days had faded, leaving her free to enjoy this precious new experience. She knew it had still more growing to do, and marveled. And worried. How much bigger could it get?

As she stirred the hot stew and wiped her wet brow, she felt someone come behind her. How strange it was, she smiled to herself, that she could feel him before he touched her, sense him before he said a word.

"I worry about you." Javan's warm, deep voice slid over her as his arms came around her swollen belly. He pressed gentle hands against the tight mound, holding them still to catch any movement inside.

Taleh sagged against him, soaking up his presence, knowing that the work called him and soon he would have to leave. She arched her neck to give his lips more room as they slid down, teasing. She had worried, as her body lost its shape, that he would no longer want to lie with her, no longer find her appealing.

Her worries were for nothing.

"I have thought of buying another slave, a woman to help you. I see you lift the oven, and I fear for you. You do too much, and you are so small." He rested his chin on the top of her head. "What did Sarah say when she was last here?"

"She said I am well. The baby is well." Taleh gathered her courage, and asked the question that nagged at her. "Have you heard anything about Merab? When is she to have her child?"

She felt Javan's heavy sigh at her back. "Why do you want to know? What purpose will it serve?"

She wished she could see Merab, but not to talk. She could think of nothing to say. She simply wanted a look. She wanted to compare her size with another woman's, to prepare herself for what was to come. Sarah had been to see her several times, and pronounced her in fine health. The reassurance was welcome. For the first time in many months, she found herself wishing her mother were there. In her place, she had Sarah, and occasionally Leah.

"I want to see how big her belly is." Javan's hands tightened on her womb.

He turned her around to face him. "I, too, wish this was over. I know I have kept you away from the village, but I did not want you to hear the stories women tell. It is best to hear from Sarah." He kissed her fiercely, deeply, leaving her limp and clinging to him around her over-sized belly, her fingers digging into his thick arms. When he eased his lips away, she stared up at him through hazy eyes. "I will take care of you, I promise. We will have a healthy child, and all will be well. Do you believe me?"

Of course she did, but he was not a woman, and did not know what dreams teased her, even tormented her, at night when she slept. Sometimes she would hold her baby in her arms, and other times . . . those dreams she would not remember, would not let herself remember.

With a quick final kiss, Javan took himself off again to his fields. Taleh's mind resisted her best efforts at control, sliding back to Merab. She wondered if she would find out about Merab's baby before the other woman was sent away, or if people would decide it best she know about it only after it was done. They all had no doubt decided it best she not know, lest she be contaminated with Merab's thinking.

What a long time it took to be trusted.

The stew bubbled thickly, and Taleh turned toward it, her mind as heavily burdened as her body.

The shout startled her. She jerked toward the path through the woods, to see one of the men she recognized from the village running toward her. He lurched the last few steps, and she feared for a moment that he had been injured. But when he reached her side, he showed no sign of blood. His deep panting breaths and ruddy, sweating face told her it was exertion that taxed him, not a wound.

She waited for him to catch a breath. He bent over, braced his hands on his knees, and coughed deeply several times. Then he raised his perspiring face and gasped out, "Merab . . . in the village . . . asking for you . . . Sarah . . . sent me . . ."

Taleh stared stupidly at him for a moment. *How strange,* was all she could think at first, *how strange that I was just thinking about her.* Her mind started to function. "Has something happened with the pregnancy? What is wrong?"

The man gave her a strange look, and spoke with unnecessary slowness. "Merab is having labor pains . . . Sarah is attending her . . . Merab has been asking for you." His breath calmed. "Sarah decided it would be good for her if you would come. I was sent to bring you to her."

Taleh's arms wrapped around her own belly. All the fears of childbirth she had ever had came to vivid life.

The man seemed to understand, for he reached out and touched her arm lightly. "I am certain all is well. Sarah is a very capable midwife. She delivered my wife of our own three children. In fact, she has delivered most of the children in the village."

"I must tell Javan." She had to go. Merab's worst trial lay ahead, for when the birthing was done, she would be sent away with empty arms. Whatever wrongs she planned to commit, she did not deserve to bring to birth alone, attended only by angry strangers.

She waved a slave boy over from the sheepfold where he was spreading straw. "Wash your hands and do not let the stew burn."

He looked at the heavy pot over the flame with trepidation.

"Just stir it," Taleh said.

He nodded uncertainly, and Taleh gave up the stew as lost.

She hurried inside the house. Moving as quickly as her weight allowed, she packed a small basket: food for the trip, a clean robe, and a blanket. When she stepped back outside, Javan stood next to the donkey, the saddle already in place. Without saying a word, he lifted her carefully into place on the smelly creature's back.

Taleh wrinkled her nose.

Javan saw, and chuckled. "I agree, but it is faster than walking."

"I know. But my stomach has only been quiet for a short time. I should hate to get sick again." She smiled. Javan pulled on the reins. The donkey lurched into movement.

A DEEP GROAN, unlike anything Taleh had ever heard before, vibrated through the house. The eerie sound sent chills along her arms. She looked wide-eyed at Javan.

"What am I supposed to do?"

"I think you should go see what you can do to help." He looked uncomfortable, as though he, too, wondered just why he was there.

Taleh turned back to the stairs that ran along the wall, leading up to the second floor. Another unearthly sound shivered through the quiet, spilling distress and pain. She forced herself to climb them, walking into the emptiness the sound's cessation left.

In the brightness of midday, sunlight streamed into the rooms Taleh passed. They were well-furnished: sturdy beds, robes hung on pegs imbedded into the walls, oil lamps resting on tables. One room looked to belong to a child, and Taleh guessed Isaac slept there. The rooms were four in all on this upper level, a large house for Obed to build so quickly.

As if he had known all along he would take another wife.

The awful sound came again, stopping Taleh in her stride. She knew it came from the last room, the dark one with the shutters closed so no light crept under the curtain.

Merab's prison?

What am I doing here, she wondered desperately. She had never even seen a birth before. What possible help could she be? She reached out for the wall, pressing her hand to the cool stone for support. Was the terrible moan the sound of birth? Would she, too, make that sound when her time came? What an awful thought it was. She shoved it aside.

Taleh looked at the curtain of striped wool that blocked the doorway. Taking one final breath, she shoved it aside. In the dimness, Merab lay on her side on the bed, her face flushed and sweating, her eyes tightly shut. Soft, panting gasps came with a staccato pattern. Her head rested on one hand. The other gripped the blanket draped over her waist with enough strength to leach the color from her knuckles.

Leah sat on the floor, her fair hair sticking to her forehead by her own perspiration, her eyes closed in exhaustion. Beneath her eyes, heavy shadows colored the thin skin, and tired lines marred her face. Dark wet circles showed under her arms.

Sarah sat on the bed next to Merab, wiping the laboring woman's forehead with a wet cloth. The old midwife looked better than Leah.

But then, Leah was pregnant.

Taleh stopped, frozen in place. Now Merab was truly supplanted.

Something made Sarah turn to look. She smiled, and Taleh saw the telltale signs of fatigue, the gray cast of her skin, the unkempt hair, the trembling lips. Sweat beaded on the old woman's forehead, and her eyes were tired.

Her voice, however, was not. "Good! You got here at last." She spoke sharply to Merab. "Taleh is here. You made her come all this way, now say what you have to say."

Merab only groaned.

Sarah looked back to Taleh. "Everything with the child is going as it should. The pains are coming on time. The mother, she is another story." Sarah did not seem to care that Merab lay beside her, moaning her pains into the heavy air. "Merab refuses to get on the birthing stool, she will not walk to speed the birth, she will not take water to keep her mouth from drying out. She refuses our every attempt to help. I believe she hopes to cheat Obed of his firstborn yet."

The old midwife's frustration became more obvious with every word. "But I will *not* let her play this foolish game. I *will* get this child out safely. Whose side are you on? Will you help us?"

Whose side are you on? A sense of hurt, betrayal from an unexpected source, pierced Taleh. She could not believe those words had come from Sarah. *Sarah.* She could not associate her with Merab's treachery, she could *not*! If she had not truly convinced her friends, how could she convince her enemies?

She looked at Leah.

"It is true," Leah told her, misreading the plea Taleh knew was in her eyes. Leah pulled herself to her feet. Her pregnancy was barely visible. No wonder Taleh had not seen it on their last visit. Had Leah kept it quiet, knowing it would be a knife in Taleh's heart?

She led Taleh aside a few steps. "Before you talk to her, I want you to know something. I want her child as much as she does not. I have watched it grow these past months. I have seen it move and kick. Do not let her destroy this baby." Her eyes held a fierce, possessive light. "That child is mine by virtue of love, and I will have it."

"She could not truly kill her child in birth? She could not do that. It is not even possible." The old sickness, the dread of seeing life and knowing it would soon be gone, pressed in on Taleh.

"I do not know. I have never seen it happen before. But I think she could try. I *have* seen babies and mothers die in birth. Would she be willing to take it that far? You might know that answer better than I."

"But what can I do?" Taleh wanted to turn and flee, anywhere, away from this oppressive burden.

Leah's gaze held unyielding sternness. "You can tell her your stand. You can try to reason with her. You know how they think. There must be something you can use."

"Reason with her? *Reason?* Leah, she has no reason left. She is filled with hatred, and there is no reason in hatred." Taleh did not understand Merab's mind, she had never understood the mind of her own people.

"Perhaps you are right. But she is also in labor, and her body has some say in this." Leah gave her a quick hug. "You must tell her what you think is best."

She stood in place after Leah let go. It all seemed unreal, incomprehensible. Her child kicked, reminding her what was at stake.

That kick also stiffened her resolve, and started a small flame of anger. So Merab thought even now to make her side against these people? She would try until the last moment to turn the villagers away? She would sacrifice Taleh's marriage, as well?

Taleh walked closer to the bed, her anger driving her steps. She knelt awkwardly beside the bed, her bulk robbing her of grace. Sarah patted her hand. "Good!" She rose stiffly, and left Taleh alone with Merab.

The anger kept rising. To hold it in, Taleh clenched her hands into her robe. Words pounded against her skull, words of fury and hurt, of insults she had borne that belonged to Merab alone, slights that included her which Merab's behavior spawned.

She looked down at Merab, and the words died. Merab's lips were tight with pain. Her young face had pulled taut from the strain her body endured. Sweat left its drops on every bit of visible skin, and dampened the hair that touched it. Her breath trembled as it sighed in and out.

The trauma of birth, seen up close, startled and frightened Taleh. Her anger disappeared, and she could not resurrect it. She could only stare at the woman who had almost been her friend.

The child within Merab pushed, and Taleh watched the lump grow and fade. A child was at stake, and she would not let Molech's reach win.

Her voice would only come as a whisper. "I am here, Merab. I had hoped to find you begging for a reprieve, to be allowed to stay and raise your child. I wanted you to change your mind. I have been hoping for that all these months. If you choose that, I will back you, I will plead with Obed on your behalf myself." Foolish dreams. Merab's already pursed lips seemed to harden.

She must be firm, Taleh reminded herself. She would not give in, not even to her sympathy. "I did not come to help you kill your child. Merab, do not think to make me choose between you and Javan, between Israel and Ammon. You will not like my choice."

She sensed movement nearby. Leah shuffled to the far side of the room. Sarah waited beside the bed. Neither gave her any assistance.

At last, Merab's green eyes looked into hers. "When this is done, if I live, come with me."

Again? "No."

"If you do not, the gods will hunt you down and punish you for your betrayal," she spat.

"They cannot reach me here," Taleh said with a confidence she did not entirely feel.

"You know nothing – OH!" Merab's voice ended in a shriek. Her attention turned inward. Her legs, held so close together, fell apart and she strained.

Sarah gave Taleh a gentle push aside. "It is what I hoped. She cannot fight this, her body will have its say." The midwife did not waste time on a smile, just moved to the bed.

Taleh stepped back, glad to get away from Merab's eyes and from the scent, the very pulse of pain that permeated the bed. Leah was at her side, carrying a strange short stool with thick legs, flat arm rests and a seat like a horse's hoof, with an opening in the center and no front to it. After Leah set it down near the bed, Taleh realized it was the birthing stool. She wanted time to examine it for her own turn, but there was too much to do.

The men must have been called in, for they both appeared. Merab did not fight them as they settled her on it and disappeared in a hurry. Sarah quickly stripped off Merab's robe.

Merab did not even notice she was naked. The birth had taken control, her reactions no longer belonged to her. Deep animal-like groans came from somewhere far inside her. Her hands gripped the arm rests, and she pressed her feet against the floor, shoving as though she meant to tip herself over.

But the chair had been built to withstand such treatment, its stubby legs splayed against her force.

Taleh watched in fascination as the birth progressed. The groans became screams, broken by rasping, throaty breaths and agonized whimpers. Sweat poured off Merab's body, and gleamed on her golden skin. The smell of her hard-working body hung heavy in the air.

At last, Sarah, sitting on the floor in front of Merab, crowed, "I see the head! Lots and lots of dark hair!"

Taleh did not even know she pushed into the crowded area. The sight was shocking, and wondrous. A head, a real live baby's head! emerged from inside Merab. In the background, Merab started to cry with the last effort, but Taleh could not look away. Obed's dark hair showed first, then tiny, scrunched eyes, a nose surely too small to be genuine, a mouth, open, emitting only gurgling noises, then a strange jumble of loose-joined parts as the body slid out faster than Taleh ever imagined.

A daughter!

The women vied for the best position, as Sarah deftly slipped a finger in the baby's mouth and scooped out mucus. The cord slowly lost its color, fading and shrinking, forcing the baby to try to breathe again.

And then a cry, strong and healthy, a new life announcing to the world it had arrived.

Sarah held it in hands suddenly young, waiting to sever its connection to the woman who did not care if it lived or died. At last, the clean knife had its turn, and the baby was free.

Sarah handed it, cord swaying, only a little blood dripping from the end, to its mother.

Leah cradled it close to her heart, and then lowered her robe as she put her daughter to her breast.

CHAPTER 25

SUMMER'S HEAT BAKED THE SOIL. ONLY THE LAST OF THE FRUIT TREES, THE figs, grapes and olives, were left still green and productive. The grains were long harvested, their precious yield carefully stored away. The ground suffered, as it did every summer, under the sun's oppression.

Taleh felt her time draw close. She drank water faithfully, under Sarah's constant reminders. It helped some to combat the hot days, made hotter by her body's strain. Her back ached always as it curved under the great mound of her belly. Her waist had become a distant memory. Her hands and feet were swollen and sore. She could not even see to put on her sandals. It was just as well, for her sandals no longer fit over her puffy feet. She had tried wearing Javan's sandals, but they slipped around, and the leather straps rubbed the bloated tissues. As she waddled through her daily chores, she felt the soil collect between her toes and on the soles of her bare feet. She had to content herself with soaking them in a big bowl of water to clean them. They only got washed properly when Javan did it for her. She could not bend down far enough to try.

There was not even room inside her for a deep breath.

But today she could handle these discomforts with grace. Today, Javan had promised her a trip to the village.

She tied the belt of her robe above her belly, and it settled into its familiar place just beneath her breasts. The day's warmth stuck the curls around her face to her forehead. She pulled the headband off, and tied it around the tumbled curls clinging to the back of her neck. As much as she loved having her hair grow back, it was hard to appreciate its length on hot days like this one.

Javan's deep voice rumbled to someone outside the house. Today would be theirs, and she intended to enjoy it, despite her large belly and swollen feet. While her mind skipped gaily to the door, her body moved more sedately. Javan smiled at her when she came outside. He did that a lot, but Taleh had seen the worry in his eyes when he thought she was not looking.

The camel sat in cud-chewing boredom behind her husband. He had sent someone to the village to collect it once again from its owner.

"I thought we were going to walk," Taleh muttered.

Javan folded his arms. "You are in no condition to walk the entire way to the village. I know you dislike the camel, Taleh, but I cannot carry you far if you grow tired."

She resisted the urge to stare at his massive arms. "I do not dislike the camel. I just . . . distrust him. He always acts as though my presence demeans him."

The deep chuckle she cherished and did not hear enough sent sweet chills along her spine. "He treats everyone the same way, even me."

She smiled into Javan's twinkling brown eyes. "Well, then, let us presume upon him."

As THEY RODE over the hill, Taleh's mouth dropped open. She gave a delighted shriek, and twisted to look up at her husband. "A caravan! A caravan, oh, Javan, you knew! Am I right? You knew all the time!"

He kissed her nose quickly, then turned her back around. "Yes, I knew. You missed the last caravan to come through. I wanted to surprise you, to make up for the other times." He took a deep breath. Taleh felt the strength of his muscular chest pressing against her back. "It seems every time the

Midianites have come through, something bad happened. I wanted to give you pleasant memories."

Her heart melted. He *must* love her. Would a man who did not love his wife show such thoughtfulness?

She would hope, and continue to love him. Some day he would find the words to tell her.

Some day. She would be patient.

This time there were no clouds to disturb her as they drew near to the impromptu marketplace. Even the sky was clear. Merab was no longer around. She had not been permitted to remain long after the birth. Obed had wasted no time putting her on the first Midianite caravan to come past, the caravan Taleh had not been allowed to visit.

Taleh had not been there to witness the event. Javan hurried her away shortly after Obed's daughter was born. But that did not keep the story from reaching Taleh. She gave an involuntary shudder, thinking about the rigid side of Obed she had never seen.

Javan slid off as the camel settled itself, and his hands closed firmly around her waist. He leaned close, holding her firmly, and scrutinized her face. "Do not look back. What is done is done."

He did that often, reading her mind.

He lifted her off the camel as though she weighed no more than when they first met. He turned to set her down, and she heard a muffled grunt. She giggled. "You have nothing to prove to me, husband. I already know what a strong man you are."

A dull red crept up his face, and she laughed. She raised herself onto her toes, and kissed him quickly on the cheek. "It is a wonderful gift, Javan. Thank you very much."

Javan smiled at her. Taleh's neck prickled with menace.

It was not from Javan. Ignoring the puzzled look on her husband's face, Taleh swiveled around. The crowd milled about, no one giving them more than a smothered grin. She could see no malice on any faces, the comfortably familiar faces of the villagers.

The feeling faded. She turned back to Javan.

"What is it?"

"I do not know. For a moment, I thought I felt . . . someone staring at me."

"What do you expect when you kiss me in public?" Javan's face held the smug look of a contented man.

But Taleh could not brush aside the menace that left a faint echo inside her.

"Taleh, there is nothing to make you afraid. Sarah told you to expect strange worries and fears, did she not?"

Taleh nodded hesitantly.

"You are pregnant, and near to giving birth. You must expect this, you know that. This is normal." He shook her gently, almost a caress.

She looked into his warm dark eyes, so confident and calm. Her worries eased away. Javan would take care of her. "You are right." She grasped the front of his tunic and tugged. "Let us see what is here."

Taleh found new pots, and a wooden bucket. Javan found a fine set of knives and some papyrus. Taleh discovered a bracelet of silver from Egypt that had a matching head wreath. Javan bargained for a leather-covered yoke for his donkeys. Taleh saw some citron seeds, and wistfully passed them by. Javan made an excuse, and went back to get them. His enjoyment in her pleasure came as a surprise. Taleh stopped to look at a finely woven wool blanket, just the size for a baby.

Their eyes met over its softness, and they nodded in unison.

It was a day for dreams, for happy smiles and warm laughter.

Javan tied their new possessions onto the leather straps holding the saddle blanket into place, and gave a tug. "I think they will be safe there. We should go home now. I see dark shadows beneath your eyes. It would not be good for you to become too tired."

Taleh did not want the day to end, but she felt the heaviness drag at her. "I enjoyed myself very much, Javan. Today has been all I could ask. I thank you."

"I am glad." He touched her face lightly. "Now, let us start back. I think you could fall asleep on the journey."

Taleh smiled. "I think you are right."

Birds twittered between the trees, flashes of browns and reds and yellows. In the underbrush, small creatures scuttled and crackled. It smelled of warm soil and musty wood, and camel. Taleh molded into Javan's arms, wrapping them around her belly and holding them in place. The baby shifted and stretched, and Javan kissed her hair. "We have a strong child."

"I think I will appreciate it more when he is out of me. Sometimes I do not enjoy his strength."

Javan shifted behind her. "Do you think it will be a son?"

Taleh mused in brief silence. "I must. Have you noticed I never say 'she,' only 'he?' I never thought about that until now." She had to ask. "What if it is a daughter?"

"I would love a daughter. We can always have a son another time."

Another time. Taleh smiled into the trees' lengthening shadows. Then the smile faded. What if he could not wait, if he took another wife, and she gave him his first son?

Taleh gave a brief prayer. Please, let this one be a boy.

They were almost halfway home when the warning prickle came back.

"Javan, stop! Quickly!"

He pulled the camel up. "What is wrong? Is it the baby?"

"No! Sh-h-h! I need to listen."

Birds again, the wind whispering through the trees, and tiny scrabbling sounds from the forest floor, but Taleh could hear nothing that sounded like a threat.

Javan waited patiently. He did not like this new oddity of Taleh's pregnancy. He liked even less how certain she was. The hair on his arms rose as he worried about her mind. Women did not go insane from pregnancy, did they?

Her behavior had been perfectly normal for her condition until they got to the caravan. What was it about them that always brought strange things into his wife's life? Had they placed a spell upon her?

He shook his head in disgust. Now *he* was thinking fantastic thoughts. A spell, indeed.

He urged the camel forward.

"Javan, wait!"

"There is nothing here, Taleh. There was nothing in the market, there is nothing here."

"But I felt something."

"It is the pregnancy, Taleh, nothing more. Surely you know I would do nothing to jeopardize either you or the child. I was a soldier for many years. I tell you, there is no danger. Did you see anything wrong at the market?"

"But –" Taleh began.

"No, wife. You must be reasonable about this. Did you see anything wrong at the market?"

"No." The word came out grudgingly.

Javan smiled. "Did you hear anything wrong just now?"

"No."

"Very well, then. Nothing is wrong. Now, relax. We will be home soon, and you can rest. Obviously we did too much for you today."

BUT THE PRICKLE was still there, all the way home.

Javan's words meant nothing this time, carried no reassurance, banished no fears. Taleh knew she was being followed.

Javan pulled the camel to a stop by the door. The camel knelt and he slipped off. Taleh missed his protection even as he reached for her. She bit her tongue to keep from bringing the subject up again.

There was no proof, nothing she could touch and say, *see, I was right*. It was just that tingle on the back of her neck as she had walked through the village, a shadow that was never there when she turned around. She, too, wanted to pass it off as a quirk of her pregnancy, but that would be a lie. Her pregnancy had its share of strange and new feelings, but this was not one of them.

She did not know what more to tell Javan, so she said nothing. How could she explain it better, what would she say? Javan was right when he said she knew everyone in the village. Which one would mean her harm? Their time of staring was long past. She might not be accepted yet, but she was acknowledged. No one stopped for a second look any more. Certainly no one cared enough to trail her as she moved around the village.

So who was it? She had to look away from Javan's steady gaze.

She was almost happy in this life of hers. Javan had become her reason for being, her very breath. She loved him with an intensity that terrified her. The feeling had grown from its tiny beginnings in their early days, until it consumed her. He had never said anything to her about how he felt, an omission that stole a bit of her joy.

She looked back as he led the camel away. Since she could not convince him, she would simply have to keep him within her sight at all times. He was her guardian. As long as he was nearby, she was safe. He had made the transition from soldier to farmer, but he did not completely leave the warrior behind. She saw it there still, in the alertness he could not stop, the quickness of his reactions, the strength of his body.

She wanted, needed his support, the comfort his presence gave her. She carried their child, and she would let nothing endanger that precious life.

There was danger now. It hung heavy in the air, it lurked in the shadows, hunkered among the trees.

And it left no evidence behind.

ONE DAY WENT past without incident, and another. She caught Javan giving her wary glances, but he made no comment. He did not understand her fear, she knew, could find no reason for it.

Three days and Taleh's dread grew. She had no proof, nothing even out of the ordinary, but she *knew* it was real.

Javan was not visible from the house. He wanted to expand his field, and was busily felling trees to make more room for crops. She followed his movements by the shivering trees as they trembled under his axe. She had not let herself cling to him and plead with him to stay close, no matter how badly she wanted to. She felt his frustration with her, his irritated confusion, and had stiffened her spine. Someone would be within view. If it had to be only one of the slaves, so be it. They would surely hear a scream for help.

She picked up the large wooden ladle from the long shelf and stepped back outside.

The sheepfold was empty. She turned in jerky circles, sweeping the area with a frenzied gaze. There was no one in sight, no sound, no thunk of an axe against wood, no slave boy puttering around the pens.

No protection.

Terror sent her cowering against the wall, gasping for air, afraid to stay outside, too panicked to go back inside. Arms wrapped tightly around her belly, swollen huge with Javan's child, she shivered and prayed, frantically searching the distance.

Javan, come into sight, someone please be there.

And one of the boys came from behind the sheep sheds. The fear vanished as quickly as it came.

How strange she must look. What would she say to Javan if he found her? It humiliated her, this odd behavior. She did not mistrust her instincts. She knew the threat existed.

The day was hot and sunny, the sky a sultry blue blanket. Burdened by both her awkward bulk and the heat, Taleh struggled to cook the meal. The fire under the heavy iron pot added its own oppression. Sweat trickled down her face. Her hair stuck to her neck. Even the child within was quiet.

She needed to add the vegetables to the stew. The meat was tender, ready for them. They sat, cut into neat pieces, on the table in the house – leeks, carrots, turnips, parsley. The boy was still in sight, carrying buckets of water from the cistern for the animals.

It would be perfectly safe. Just go inside, get the vegetables, and come back out.

She hurried. Everything was in the tightly woven basket of reeds, right where she remembered.

A footstep crunched behind her. Before she could turn around, a thick, hairy arm wrapped around her throat.

God, help me, she thought, and opened her mouth to scream.

A cloth was shoved inside. "Do as I say, and you will not be hurt," a deep voice growled in her ear.

She could not breathe! Ignoring his warning, she clawed with her fingernails at the arms that held her, a big arm with dark hair.

Her captor grabbed her hands and pulled them behind her. Taleh screamed against the gag, her cries for help trapped in her throat.

Rough rope scraped against her wrists as the man tied them together. She lost her balance and toppled. Cruel hands caught her and jerked her back upright.

Make noise! She had to make noise!

He held her by the wrists. He could be her balance. She lashed a leg toward the bench, ignoring the tearing pain in her shoulders. The bench scraped against the stone floor, but did not tip over. The man jerked her roughly away.

"Where is your cloak?"

The harsh voice rasped in her ear. Where had she heard it before? From the corner of her eye, she saw dark hair and high cheekbones. He moved and even that much was gone.

Who *was* he?

"Where is your cloak?" He pulled her arms up and muscles spasmed with the pain. Taleh choked against the gag. He stood still. Taleh could almost feel him thinking.

It terrified her.

"Come." The brutal hands jerked her again, this time toward the bedroom.

What she had felt until now paled before the horror that surged through her. She would die rather than submit.

Then the baby would die, too.

The man fought to hold her. Rope pulled skin off her wrists. A large leg swept her feet from under her, and she fell forward. Heavy hands pushed her face into the bed. The scent of rushes filled her nose.

"If you want to live, do *not* try to look." His breath was hot on her cheek. Cold chills raised bumps on her skin.

Her belly pinned her down. Without her hands, she could not rise. The man pulled her head back only long enough to tie something rolled thick over her eyes. Taleh heard him grab at a pile of robes that lay over the low chest. From the sound of his careless speed, he took whatever lay in easy reach. With rough hands, he pulled her back up by an arm and exited the room.

As he moved through the house with more haste than thought, he bumped heavily into the table. Taking her chance, Taleh pulled violently against his grip. Something ruffled softly to the floor, but he did not let go. She heard the small water jar tip, heard the first splashes fall on the floor.

But it was not enough. Taleh could not hear any sounds after they passed through the door. No one called out. No one waited to rescue her.

No shouts followed them around the back of the house and into the thin woods that grew close by.

He pushed and dragged her through the trees, into the thicker cover of the forest. Branches slapped her, roots tripped her. Pain lanced through her side as she fought to breathe. Her awkward steps slowed their flight. He took pity on her sightless fumbles and peeled the blindfold off, tearing out strands of hair as he did so. Always he stayed behind her, guiding her by tugs and pushes. Several sharp slaps taught her not to try to look back.

Finally he stopped. Taleh's last hope fled.

Two horses stood ready. He hoisted her clumsily onto one, and mounted his own with menacing skill. Taleh stared in horror at his back, feeling recognition tug lightly at her. She knew him from somewhere . . .

When he turned to grab the reins of her horse, Taleh screamed into the gag.

She looked into the face of Pelet.

CHAPTER 26

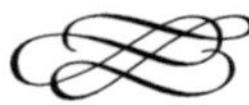

THE SLAVE RAN IN GREAT STRIDES ACROSS THE FIELD, HIS ARMS FLAILING THE air. Javan watched him come.

He did not like the feeling building within.

"Taleh! My lord, your wife . . . gone . . ."

Gone? On legs that could not move fast enough to keep pace with his fear, Javan ran from the field. The slave followed on his heels, exhausted but struggling gamely to keep up. All the others stopped what they were doing to watch

The stew bubbled the last of its moisture as he slowed for a look. He burst through the open door of their house, and stopped. He did not see her. He had no breath left to call her name.

His mind knew what his heart rejected. The house was empty of her presence. To another's eye, little seemed wrong, but Javan had lived with her too long to miss clues. A cloak flung upon the floor, a bench pulled awry, the jar of water dripping its last slow drops onto the stone.

He smelled her fear, faint on the air.

Taleh was gone. He walked with heavy feet across the room and picked up her cloak. Her scent wrapped around him, squeezing his terrified heart.

He prayed she would be warm enough until he could find her. Night would be here soon, and even this late in the summer, it would be cool.

Why had he not listened to her worries? Why had he been so quick to blame the pregnancy?

His hands were shaking, he noticed with a sense of shock.

Where was she now? Was she alive? Was she hurt?

Taleh – Taleh, come back to me. Taleh, be safe, Taleh, be brave. Taleh, hold on. I will find you.

He could not think. What had happened to his mind? Where did he start, to find her?

Had he ever told her what she meant to him? He could not remember saying the words.

Would he have time?

He turned to the breathless slave who had followed him. "What did you see?"

The boy's shoulders sagged, and his eyes were filled with shock and fear. "She had been here, cooking. I saw her go into the house. Then I saw a lamb stuck in the far fence, and I went over to get it free. When I was done, I turned to look again. She was not outside. I did not think anything of it, until later. I do not know how much time passed before I realized she would not leave the stew for so long. I heard nothing. When I decided to take a look, I did not find her. She was nowhere."

Javan barely absorbed his words. He could not be still, could not stand still, could not concentrate. He scanned the room for more clues. The cloak, the jar, the bench, - there must be something else, something they were missing.

Think! He had to think!

Taleh could not be ripped out of his life without leaving a hole so big everyone could see it.

He moved to the room where they slept, afraid to push aside the curtain. His legs trembled now, too. He held his breath as he shoved the divider aside.

No body met his eyes, no bloodstains, no death. He could be grateful for that much.

Where did he start? Images flashed through his mind: Taleh screaming, Taleh hungry, Taleh hurt.

Taleh dead.

He could not do this alone.

"WHAT DO YOU MEAN? What kind of story is this?" Obed stared at him over the leather he was cutting. The shutters had been thrown open to catch every bit of light and the lowering sun cast strange shadows. He squinted at Javan again, and waited.

"Taleh has been taken! I have the slaves starting the search, but I will need your help." Javan fought down the urge to grab Obed by his belt and drag him along. With every moment that passed, he could feel Taleh moving farther away. He found a fragment of calm somewhere inside. "She insisted for several days, ever since the last caravan came through, that someone was following her. I thought it was some strange effect of the pregnancy. But obviously, I was wrong!" The urgency burst past his fragile restraints. "Will you help me or not?"

"Of course, I will help you. You came with me to get Merab. It is the least I owe you. But, Javan, think – who would do this thing? I cannot seriously believe her family survived. We know her sister did not. If her father was in the army outside the city, none of them survived. No one in our village could mean harm to her. She is winning over even the hardest of hearts."

That came as a surprise to Javan. "She is?"

"Certainly. She is one of us, now." While he had been listening, Obed had tossed the last of his tools away, and shoved aside the leather pieces. With no wasted movements, he removed his leather apron and threw it toward a peg. "I am right behind you."

A crowd waited outside Obed's shop door. Javan stopped in surprise. Questions pelted him.

"What has happened?" "Is it true? Your wife has been kidnapped?" "Do you wish for assistance? I will be happy to help."

The concern of the crowd touched him. "Please, I must know. Has anyone heard of a plot against my wife?"

Heads shook all over the gathering. "No!" "I have heard nothing." "Who would want to harm her?" "Why would we wish her evil?"

Javan asked everyone's question. "But if no one here did this thing, who did?"

Saul worked his way to the front of the crowd. "Javan! Is it true? Taleh has been kidnapped?"

"Yes. It is true."

"God have mercy on me!" Saul tore at what was left of his hair. "I should have said something!"

"What?" Javan grasped his arms.

"It was when the Midianites were last here, when Obed sent his wife away. A man, a voice I did not know. He came into my shop, and asked if you lived here. He said he needed work, and wanted to work on a farm. He mentioned you by name. I thought little of it at the time. It did not occur to me that there should be no more displaced people. The Ammonites have been vanquished. So why is he not on his own land?"

"A good question." Javan thought hard, his mind finally having something to pursue. "Did he have an accent, a lisp, anything about his speech that you marked?"

Saul shook his head. "He sounded like an Israelite."

"He never mentioned my wife?"

"No, I do not think so. Only you." Saul held a hand up, his brows furrowed in thought. "There was something more. I cannot remember . . ."

Javan kept still, afraid any word would block the memory trying to surface.

"Yes! I remember now! He asked about Obed, by name. And when he turned to leave, something thumped against a table, something metal. I thought it an unusual sound, a sword perhaps."

Javan turned around and stared blankly at Obed. "Who would hate me so? He knew us both by name. What madness is this?"

Another time, Taleh's frightened face. In a single, blinding flash, he knew.

"Pelet! It is Pelet. It must be." Javan's tongue felt thick in his mouth. "Did you hear what Saul said? He mentioned both our names, and now my wife is missing. It is like before. Who else could it be?"

"Why would he wait so long?" Obed asked.

"I do not know. But Taleh has been so frightened. Who knows how a warning comes?"

THE DEEP PULLING BEGAN AGAIN. Taleh leaned on the horse's neck, holding the mane tightly, and braced herself to endure. Pelet had removed the gag and retied her hands in front when they were far from the village and no one could hear. She had to remind herself to breathe, to remain calm. It did not hurt yet, but she was very afraid it would, and soon.

Pelet continued to push them onward, taking her farther and farther from her home, from anything familiar to her. The land grew steeper, the trees they passed were thicker. She had not seen any signs of people, or cultivated land. There were no fruit trees in neat rows here, only some wild figs, and some cedar. Occasionally she heard the screech of wild animals, then low growling that stood the hair on her neck on end.

Yet there had to be people around somewhere, for they followed a path that showed someone had gone this way, but who, and when?

They stopped at a stream to fill the water skins that hung almost dry from his saddle, and to walk and water the horses. Taleh relieved herself then. They stopped once more to take care of their bodies' needs. The new sensations in her womb continued, but still without pain. She wished she remembered more of what Sarah had told her of birth. She wished she had paid more attention when Merab's daughter was born.

What would Pelet do if he found out she had labor pains? Would he help her? Or would he leave her beside the road?

No, not that. He had not come this far to abandon her now. He had spoken little, and Taleh could not fashion a single safe question. There were too many of them, and no right way to ask.

By now, Javan surely knew she was gone. What was he doing? Would he be able to follow their tracks? Pelet had made no effort to disguise their movements, or so it seemed to her inexperienced eyes. He was concerned only with speed.

They had pulled up for quick moments during the course of their day to allow him to look around. He never told her what he sought, nor did he allow her off her horse at those times. She had tried it once. It was not a mistake to make twice.

She struggled to hold in her panic as they moved onward, leaving her heart farther behind.

THE SUN LAY low on the horizon. The horses could no longer keep the pace. They tried valiantly, but it was no use. Pelet was forced to allow the animals to slow.

Taleh hid her relief. This was the first thing all day that had gone right, the first thing that gave her hope she could be rescued.

The pulling came again, suddenly sharper, taking her breath away. She did not even have time to gasp. She knew now, with absolute certainty, that there was no turning back.

Javan's child wanted to be born.

From deep within herself, Taleh found a well of strength. Javan would come. She would bear his child and keep it safe.

The tired horse slipped on a rock, and the tightening came again, too soon, too hard, wrapping around her swollen belly. For a second time, she could not breathe. Her fingers clenched in the horse's mane. Her shoulders sagged as she curled inward. *I will not fall off,* she said to herself, *I will not, I will not.*

After a frighteningly long time when she was certain Pelet would see and guess, it eased. She felt limp, and tired to her very bone. Every movement of the horse jarred, leaving echoes in her teeth. *I must be strong. I can endure this.*

Javan will come.

Pelet glanced over then, but she had herself under control. "Are you tired?"

Taleh longed to say yes, but she did not trust his eyes. She spoke before the tightness reached its peak and words would be impossible. "I can go a little farther."

"I think we are far enough for today. It is getting dark. I will look for a place to hide until I am ready."

Ready? For what?

They went on slowly, heading into the trees. The horses carefully picked their way through hanging branches, beneath twigs and around rocks and brush. The trees' covering added to the dimness, as twilight settled slowly. The pains came ever closer. Her hands were swollen against the binding around her wrists. Taleh did not know how much farther she could ride. She was grateful Pelet had not listened to her and kept going.

At last, through a haze of pain, she heard Pelet say, "We will camp here. There is a small stream, and no one will be able to find us easily."

She could not open her mouth to respond. If she tried, she surely would scream. It was trapped there, locked in her throat, fighting to get loose as the pain reached the apex. Her legs would not move, her hands could not let go of the mane tangled within her fingers' tight grasp. The only way off the horse was to fall, and she did not dare do that.

"Get down now."

The pain released its grip, fading slowly and leaving a hollow behind, a hole where the agony belonged and which it would soon fill again. Despite the early chill of evening, perspiration formed between her shoulder blades and in the space between her breasts.

Sarah, Javan, help me. What do I do now? She thought of their God, and begged a silent plea. *Help me save the babe. Help him find us. Please, Javan's God, please protect us.*

Pelet grabbed an arm and pulled. Taleh tilted toward him, and let go of the horse. Her leg slid over the horse's back under his relentless force.

The pain came again, wrenching her without warning. The scream came out limply, only a moan on an outrush of air, as her unprepared body absorbed this latest, too sudden convulsion.

"What is wrong? What is the matter? Are you sore? I cannot make allowances for you."

Her legs buckled when they touched the ground, and without his firm hold on her, she would have fallen.

"Stand a moment and then walk until all the stiffness eases." His voice held an odd kindness, the first she had heard all day. "Walk now."

"I cannot," she gasped.

He began walking, holding her tightly to his side. Taleh wanted to push him away, ill at the thought of his closeness, but her body clung to his support.

"See? Is that not better already?"

She turned her head to stare at him, oppressively near, smiling down at her.

"No, do not make me do all the work. You must walk with me. Now, move your legs."

"I can*not*!" The words ended in a shriek when the next pain twisted through her. She arched away from it, from him.

Pelet stared at her, not releasing his hold, disbelieving the evidence of his own eyes. "Are you having labor pains?" His face held shock.

"Yes." She could barely groan the word.

"You cannot be!"

She did not answer, absorbed within herself.

Pelet shook her viciously. Taleh wanted to scream from the agony in her legs and hips, in her womb, in her back and arms, but there was no room on her lungs for the effort.

Her legs buckled. She slipped through Pelet's hands like water. He grabbed at her, but it was as though, despite her bulk, there was nothing solid to hold on to. She landed on her hands and knees, one more pain piling on the others. The ground was damp. She felt the moisture clammy on her gown, seeping darkly through the robe. Torment piled upon itself, chilling her bones while the sweat beaded on her skin.

She wanted to pull away from it, but it was stronger than she was. Her travail held her unmoving, caught in sharp talons.

He knelt beside her, and pulled her head up by her hair. His face was blurred and dark. "What are you going to do to me?" She had to speak quickly, before the next pain could come.

"Things have not gone well for me. I saw your – Javan's – farm. He has not suffered this past year. He has not had to fight for everything, he was not attacked on his way home. He did not arrive at his village beaten and robbed, with barely enough to buy food. No! Fortune smiles on him. Well, you should have been mine. I spoke for you, did you know that? But everything comes easily to Javan. He did not have to struggle."

Taleh remembered those lonely first days, when Javan worked until he could sleep where he stood. Another wave of agony spun her thoughts away before she could speak.

"I was to have you. Twice, I tried. I spoke, then I took. Now he can pay. Either way, whatever he decides, he will have to pay. If he does not want you, perhaps he will pay for the child. But heed me well. He *will* pay. I will have compensation, one way or another."

What was he talking about? "Javan found me first. I will go with him. You cannot keep me –" The next pain cut off her words. Her arms gave way, and she fell onto the ground, rolling away from the racking misery, curling into herself for protection. Someone whimpered nearby, a pitiful sound against the still night.

A waterskin was shoved against her mouth, and she gagged. The scent of wet leather overwhelmed her. She gave in to the nausea, vomiting what little remained in her stomach. It burned her throat.

The pain gave way bit by bit, leaving her wet and dirty from the forest floor. The air was cool, and she began to shiver, despite the heat inside her body. She was both hot and cold, and her belly felt like ice.

"Can I please have my cloak?" Surely he would not deny her that.

Pelet moved toward the horses. She could no longer keep her eyes open. She heard his steps get dim, and then reappear. The cloak dropped heavily upon her where she lay on her side upon the moist ground.

Javan's scent filled her nostrils. The chill deep within eased, pushed aside by the memory of love. In his hurry to get her out of the house, Pelet must have grabbed Javan's cloak instead of her own. It comforted her now, wrapping her in warmth both inside and out.

Javan would come for her. There was no room in her mind for doubt. Pelet had gone mad with bitterness, or maybe he had been such all along and no one had noticed. Surely a madman could not outwit Javan. Her husband was wise, and careful, and still retained the skills of a warrior. He would be here soon.

She had to take care of their child, keep it alive and safe until he found them. She would not let Pelet harm the baby, would defend it with her very life if necessary.

The pains came in rhythm, closer now, and strong. She could not move without help, could not turn over, could not stand to walk to the bushes to relieve her bladder and bowels unless Pelet helped her. The aura of bitterness and revenge that emanated from him no longer bothered her. She needed assistance, and he was all she had.

Pelet stood impotently by, doing what she needed him to do, but otherwise lost. Whatever plans he had made were held in abeyance by the needs of Taleh's birthing.

He lit a fire for her, for she told him she was still cold. He removed the brush from their campsite to make a place for her to lie. He saved moss from the nearby trees to tuck inside the swaddling clothes. Taleh knew she would have to tear her robe into pieces to make them. It did not matter.

Nothing mattered now except the relentless course of the labor, and the wait for Javan.

CHAPTER 27

Obed and Javan stopped at the same moment, holding their camels in place. The night was quiet, except for the wind against the leaves, and the crickets and night bugs. A small animal scuffled through the woods nearby.

"Do you smell it?" Javan allowed himself to feel excitement for the first time.

"Yes. Fire. Green wood."

"It must be them. Who else could it be?"

Obed could think of many people it could be, but he, too, wanted to believe, so he said nothing.

Javan turned and sniffed the air, and turned again. "It is coming from that direction." He pointed into the woods.

"Are you sure?"

"Yes." Javan's teeth glinted in the faint glow of the moon. His smile held only menace. "She had better be alive. I will kill the man regardless."

Obed cut him off. "Javan, we have Law for this. Be careful of your speech."

Javan clenched his jaw to keep the rest of his hot words inside. Remember Taleh, he reminded himself. She was all that mattered.

The two men hobbled the camels' legs, and made their weapons ready.

With only their noses to guide them, they eased carefully through the dense woods. Pungent with rotting leaves, the tang of cedar and musk from the animals that made this area home, Javan only noticed the smoke that clung to the damp night air. Even in the dark, there was evidence someone else had gone this way, and recently. Broken limbs from bushes still bore fresh leaves. Whoever passed here, the leaves had not had a chance to dry.

To Javan's cautious ears, their movements made far too much noise. Every footstep sounded like the beat of a drum now. Even the pounding of his heart was too loud.

The scent of a campfire grew stronger. He motioned Obed to slow. Like shadows in the dark, they slid through the trees, finding their old skills again.

A faint glow showed a clearing in the trees. A man strode past the fire's light.

Pelet.

His instincts had been correct. But there was no time for self-congratulation. Javan watched in horror as Pelet paced back and forth like an animal in a pit. He saw no sign of Taleh. Killing rage swept over him. His hand clenched around his sword before logic cooled his mind. He wanted to shriek a battle cry, to leap forward, to put a knife into Pelet and force him to confess that he had done with her. Was she still alive? Where had he hidden her?

Instead, he forced himself to stay, to watch, to plan.

A soft moan shivered on the air. A woman's sound.

She lived!

A whisper, barely a sound. Obed's whisper, breath put to words, came. "I can see her! In the dark, beyond the flame. I think she is in childbirth."

Childbirth. "We must keep his attention away from her. He cannot fight us both and guard her, also. You guard my wife. Keep him away from her. I will do the rest."

Obed nodded. "Give me time to get to her before you move." He slipped away, fading into the cover of trees and dark.

Javan counted slowly, keeping his eyes on Pelet as he paced. How much time would Obed need? He still could not see his wife. If not for that one sound, he would not know she was near. She was birthing? He could not think of that.

A branch swayed across the camp, on the opposite side of the fire.

Pelet whirled around, even though he had made no sound. "Javan? Hiding like the thieving jackal that you are? Take care what you do, I have your wife!"

Javan said nothing, his silence goading Pelet.

"You thought you had her so safe!" The mocking voice polluted the air. "You are not too clever for me! I found her." Pelet paused, standing there, still. Javan could feel his waiting, hoping for a wrong move. "Perhaps I will keep her. I should. I deserve her."

Javan did not move, did not speak. Rage tore at him with bitter claws, but he held it at bay. He would not play into Pelet's hand.

"How much value do you put on your woman?" Pelet's sword was in his hand. Javan prayed Taleh stayed calm, that she had faith in him. He prayed he deserved that trust.

"You do not answer? Is she not worth a sheep? A goat? A camel? Truly, how much is she worth to you?"

Obed needed a distraction to get into place. Taleh needed to hear his voice. Javan rose. "Why Taleh? Why my woman? Why this long? I expected you to lay in wait for us on the trip here. That would have been a challenge worthy of your skills, taking both Obed and me. You could have had two women, all our animals, our seed for your fields, our slaves to add to your own. Why did you wait this long?"

"I was robbed on the way home after the wars. I had no time to come for Taleh." Pelet's sword came up. Behind him, Javan could see Obed in the shadows. He still had not seen what he truly wanted to see, his wife. And he could not look. Pelet was watching him too closely. Did Pelet really think Javan would come alone?

"You know I claimed her? Did Jephthah not tell you?" The sword was absolutely steady, the only movement on it the flickering of the fire. Pelet had not grown soft. "He offered me other women, my *pick*." He spat the word. "But I wanted *her*. She was my choice, from the very first. I almost had her that night. If I had not been stopped by Obed's men, we would have been long gone."

"Obed's men did not stop you. Taleh did not want to go. Now you think to steal her a second time?"

The sword shivered in the air. The man was not as calm as he wanted Javan to think. "You call it theft?" Pelet leaned forward, and laughed. "I have her now. Perhaps I could say she wanted to come, she was eager." He threw back his shoulders and stood proudly.

Javan jerked before he could stop it.

Pelet had not turned to check on Taleh. Javan could not plan his attack if he did not know where she was. Pelet went on, mockingly. "I am surprised at how quickly you came after her. She must be a prize. I had thought, after this much time with her, you would have had your fill. I heard rumors in the village as I waited. A wife sent back? Only they did not say which wife. Not yours, I see." Pelet shifted.

It was quiet on the other side of the fire. Obed had not moved. Javan wanted to start the battle. The cold night chilled his muscles. He would need to be loose to hold his own against Pelet. He took a step out from the shelter of the trees. A sword swing needed room.

"So you come for her. You track her through darkness." Pelet laughed, but it was strained.

"You knew I would come."

Pelet nodded, a bare bend of his head. "I hoped. You see, it is very simple. If you wanted her gone, perhaps you would pay me to take her. One Ammonite wife discarded, why not another? Or you would want her back, and pay me to return her. You see, I win every way." Pelet's voice was chillingly reasonable. "As I said, I was robbed on the way home after the wars. The thieves missed very little. You, no doubt, arrived to a great welcome. I had barely enough to repair my home. I had no time to come for Taleh." He gave a bitter snort of laughter. It was the only sign of emotion. Javan went cold at that calm voice. "Your cattle are healthy, your sheep are fertile. Your land is rich. You had so much. You could share. There were not even women in my village to choose from. And why should I? I had a woman claimed already. All I had to do was go get her."

Javan took another step.

"But I need gold, and I did not know where you hid it. Then my house burned. There was no more time. It was very simple. If you did not want her, I would ask money to keep her, you would pay me for release. I needed a wife, I did not care that she belonged to you first. And if you did want her back, you would pay handsomely. I would be gone before anyone would find me, but for you! You, always you!"

Pelet's eyes were black with hatred. "The child was a bonus. An instant heir for me, or more money if you wanted to keep it." He was poised on his feet. "You see? I win!"

The sword came so fast it split the air. Metal clanged. The ground was slippery. Swords flashed, the fire sliding down the blades, making the sound of vicious bells as they rang together again and again.

Suddenly Taleh was close behind Pelet, Javan saw her at last on the ground, Obed behind her in the thick brush. A sword came too close in Javan's distraction, the tip burning his skin as it rushed past, and Pelet's eyes gleamed with satisfaction.

Javan pretended retreat, anything to get the battle away from his wife, hoping Pelet would follow.

He did. How had he not seen Obed?

There was no time to think. The swords rang again and again. Javan's skin shivered with the vibrations from meeting Pelet's mighty swings. Pelet had forgotten nothing. Javan had to trust Obed to keep Taleh safe.

The battle went back and forth. The ground turned into mud as they churned it, and dug it up, feet cutting in for purchase. Javan stepped into the fire, and smelled the hair on his legs singe. He leapt aside and kept swinging. Sweat broke out.

Taleh moaned. Javan blocked his ears.

And then Pelet's foot slipped, his sword dipping down for one blink of time. Javan found his chance and drove home one last swing, all his strength in one blow. Pelet's sword cracked, but held Javan off for one instant. Javan saw a knife in his other hand just before Pelet tossed the broken sword aside. Javan dodged, felt the wind as the knife went past. It slammed into a tree, imbedding itself, and hummed, trembling like a live thing.

Pelet suddenly froze. He held his hands out to either side in surrender. Obed stood behind him, his sword against Pelet's back.

"You think you have won. I will plead my case before the village." There was evil in Pelet's grin. "You think I am beaten? I still have a chance. She will be mine yet."

Obed grabbed a hand, jerked it behind him and twisted it up. He was fresh, Pelet was tired. Pelet rose on his toes, and made himself settle back. He still grinned.

Javan grabbed the other hand. He stuck his sword in the ground, and pulled a rope from his belt. With Pelet bound, he knelt beside his wife, and watched her breathing in little pants, soft whimpers, and pitiful moans.

"Oh, wife, this is not how it was to be."

Her eyes opened, and his heart ached with joy as she smiled up at him. "I knew you would come. I knew you would find me."

"I will always find you, do not doubt it. You are mine."

Another spasm swept her away from him, and he could only watch helplessly as she endured.

"You must get her to Sarah," Obed said.

"How? How can I move her like this? What if I hurt her?" It was easy for Obed to speak so easily. It was not his wife at stake.

"Leah says first births are often long. If she tries to give birth here, what chance will either have? She needs Sarah."

Javan gave him a panicked look. "But the trip! Will she survive the trip?"

"She has survived labor pains in the company of Pelet and his madness. Women are stronger than we think. Better the journey with you than a birth here."

CHAPTER 28

JAVAN FORCED THE CAMEL AT FULL SPEED INTO THE SLEEPING VILLAGE. IT was much faster coming back than trying to follow hints of a trail, not knowing where it led. The sun was near enough to the horizon to take the edge off the darkness. Taleh twisted in his arms, fighting another pain. Sweat beaded on her skin, and soaked through her robe. He had wrapped her warmly in his cloak. He did not know if that was the right thing or not. Too hot or too cold, which was right?

He guided the camel around the curving streets, glad of the emptiness, for he could never pull the animal up in time to stop. Sarah's house appeared, and he hauled back on the reins with one hand while the other held desperately to his struggling wife. They stopped in front of Sarah's door. The camel folded its ungainly legs, and Javan wrestled himself and his precious burden off. His arms were full of his wife, so he kicked at the heavy door, and yelled for Sarah.

His frantic voice echoed down the quiet streets. "Sarah? It is Javan. I found her! Please let us in. We need your help!"

A lattice creaked open. "God be thanked, it is you!"

The lattice closed again, and Javan leaned against the wall for support.

His arms trembled from the strain of holding her for so long. Wrapped in her pain, Taleh stiffened in his arms, adding to his burden.

The door opened much too slowly to suit Javan. His feet dragged against the threshold as he stepped inside.

"Be careful! Do not trip." Sarah raised a sputtering oil lamp, its scent thick on the air. She held it close to Taleh, and Javan thought he heard her gasp. One wrinkled hand moved against Taleh's flushed cheek. "Poor dear child," she whispered. Then she became commanding. "Bring her into my room. It is on this floor." She led the way.

THE EARLY MEAL came and went. The village stirred into busy life. Someone brought word that Obed had arrived and delivered Pelet into the custody of the elders. The sun rose higher in the sky, the air warmed. Morning dragged by, while Javan walked outside and then back in, unable to decide what he should be doing. Whimpers and moans coming from Sarah's room sent chills down his spine. Every whimper stuck like a dagger in his heart. He ached at what she must be enduring. Had he hurt her by the awful journey to bring her here? He wanted to go and ask Sarah if this was normal, if she was well, if the child still lived within her, but he was more afraid of the answers, so he did not.

How long had it been, how much longer could it go? He had some idea of what went on, for he had held her during the journey and had seen her torn with pain, trying not to cry out.

Women died giving birth. Was not the history of his people filled with such stories?

She could not die. How could he live without her? How had this happened, that a young woman from Ammon of all places should take total possession of his heart? When had he started loving her? Why had he never told her? He needed to tell her now, needed her to hear it. He wanted his child to be born into that love, to feel its warmth sheltering him.

He held this new knowledge close, and paced the walls of Sarah's house, looking through the open door at the villagers outside while his heart was a wild tumult inside him, tangled with fear and hope.

Women sat on the ground along the house walls, waiting for word. Children played nearby so they, too, would hear when the baby was born. Javan did not remember ever seeing this happen. Did the women do this for every birth? He did not think so. So many coming to check on her, to see if she was well. So many who worried about her.

The months she had endured uncertainty, wondering if she would ever belong! He did not know now how she had done it. Where had she found the strength?

A scream tore through the house, and another. Javan froze in the doorway, the sun warm on his back.

He had to see her, be with her. Anything was better than this torture, this not knowing. He strode to the doorway, and thrust aside the curtain.

"Javan!" Sarah sounded surprised.

"How is she? Why did she scream?" His words came out in a whisper, strangled by the sight of his wife wet with sweat, pale with pain, thrashing on the bed. "God help us! Will she live?"

"Yes, I believe so. It is just taking a long time. You could help by bringing Leah. I know she is heavy with child herself now, but she is learning much about birthing, and the extra hands would be welcome."

"I will bring her right away." He would bring her even if he had to drag her over Obed's body.

THE MIDDAY MEAL CAME, but Javan could not bring himself to eat. He spent more time in the room where Taleh lay, but Leah and Sarah found his size a hindrance so they kept sending him back out. He could not stay away. Taleh still lived, a miracle which astounded him each time he went back into the room. To think women did this more than once, that they had child after child and survived it as often as they did!

A sudden flurry of activity from inside the room caught his attention. Leah bustled out, her womb leading the way. She grabbed the well-used birthing stool and tugged at it, unable to lift it around her own sizeable belly.

"Let me." Javan came over and picked it up. It gave him the perfect reason to be allowed back in, to see Taleh again. Leah held the heavy curtain aside.

Sarah had her arms around Taleh, holding her upright in the bed. His wife was soaked with sweat, her hair hung in wet ringlets all around her face. Her skin was blotched with red. Her glazed eyes stared in his direction. She did not seem to see him. He could see her hands tremble where they clutched at Sarah's robe.

"You *can* move your legs," the old woman was saying. "You can! I will help you." Then she saw Javan. "Put that close to the bed. It is time for the baby to be born."

Javan forgot to breathe for a moment. As he stood gaping at Sarah, he wondered that he had forgotten the purpose of this event, that this was not just an exercise in endurance. Their child was about to be born!

"Put it down here, Javan." Sarah grinned at him.

Grinned! If Sarah could find humor at a time like this, perhaps things were not as frightening as they seemed.

He set the birthing stool down close to his wife. "Please let me move her." He wanted to hold her, to feel her in his arms. He wanted to be the one she clung to in this, despite the capable assistants waiting for him to get out of the way.

Sarah moved aside. He slid his hands under Taleh's arms, feeling her belly press against him as he lifted her. He could feel it tighten as another pain struck her. Her legs folded, and only his strength held her up. Her nails dug into his arms, seeking a handhold, support for her tired body.

How much more of this was there?

He set her on the stool and let go reluctantly. Sarah helped pry Taleh's fingers off his arms. They left red marks. *I will bruise,* he thought with surprise.

Sarah placed Taleh's hands on the arms of the chair and they closed instantly. The tightening of her belly was visible. Javan watched, forgetting fear in fascination.

"It is time to get the baby out, Taleh." Sarah spoke sharply, talking through the haze of pain that clouded Taleh's mind.

"It hurts."

Javan winced at the first words he had heard Taleh speak since bringing her into Sarah's house.

"Yes, I know. You must push past the pain."

"I cannot." A tear slipped down Taleh's cheek, and Javan reached past the women's heads to catch it.

"Yes, Taleh, you can." Leah's voice was more gentle than Sarah's had been. "You must. The baby wants to come out now. You have to help him. Push!"

Taleh seemed to understand. She squeezed her eyes shut under the force of her effort. The guttural groan could hardly belong to her. Pain slithered up Javan's arms. When he looked down, he saw his hands clenched, as though he was straining with her.

SHADOWS STRETCHED LONG. The women waiting had gone home to prepare the evening meal, and the first coolness of evening settled down. Javan stared out the window into the street, watching people with disinterest. His attentions were on the room behind him. He had been ushered out, and ordered to eat something. Sarah claimed she could not hear over the rumblings of his stomach. He had chewed some dry bread, and drank a little wine to calm himself. It did not live up to its reputation.

To think he had believed when they placed Taleh on the birthing stool that it would soon be over!

At least Taleh responded when spoken to, at least she recognized him now. His heart leapt into his throat each time she met his eyes and he saw the awareness in her own.

A happy laugh rang through Sarah's house, and he gave a start.

Laughter!

And then the cry of a baby came.

His legs did not work. He could not remember how to walk.

He sagged against the wall, rubbing shaking hands across his face, and reminded himself to breathe.

Leah poked her head around the curtain. Her eyes sparkled with excitement. "Javan, you can come in now." She giggled, and Javan wondered what was so funny. "Come, Javan, do you want to see your child?"

When had Sarah's house gotten so large? The doorway with the curtain loomed like the entrance to a cave, and he was afraid to step inside.

But he did, and saw only his wife. Taleh lay on the rumpled bed, tired, sweaty, and glowing. Somehow the two women had managed to get her back onto the bed themselves. Dark circles ringed her eyes, her skin was still mottled and shiny with her body's moisture, her hair stuck in sweaty curls wherever it touched and her lips were trembling and pale.

There was a radiance about her, a contentment that went beneath the surface all the way to her heart. He knelt by the bed, and started to reach for her, only to stop. Did she still hurt? Where could he touch?

"I will not break," she whispered.

He drew her in then, needing to feel her breath on his neck, her arms around him. Her heart beat against his hands, and he cherished the feel of it. "I was so afraid," he whispered into her ear. There was so much more to tell her, but he did not want to say it with an audience. He pressed his lips to her damp forehead, tasting of Taleh and salt.

"I worried some, too." She pulled back slightly, and smiled.

He drank it in, committing the smile to memory.

"Javan, do you not want to see our child? We have a son!"

A son? They had a son?

"We have a boy," Taleh said in her soft voice. "Look at him. He is so beautiful, Javan. Our child is beautiful."

At Taleh's insistence, Javan stood and Sarah met him with the wiggling baby. She tugged Javan's outstretched arms this way and that, nodded approval, and carefully tucked the baby in. Javan drew the tiny morsel close. He felt awkward, his big muscles too hard for the soft baby skin it touched, his hands too calloused. But his son seemed not to mind, looking at him with blue eyes of a cast so dark they held promise of becoming the same color as his mother's. His black hair was hers, also, wrapped in wet bloody curls tight to the delicate bones of his little head.

He looked at the new life, and for the first time understood how people picked out features that belonged to either parent. He had always thought they were deluded, for how could such small, squashed things look like their full-grown counterparts? It was amazing, but the nose was Taleh's, a bit flatter but that was only to be expected. The mouth was his, a baby version of his firm lips. He had not seen his chin for years, but the little one he looked at reminded him of his before the whiskers grew. The eyebrows, too, were his own masculine line, fainter and thinner, but definitely his. No lashes were visible yet, but if the child had his mother's eyes, he expected the lashes would be hers also.

There were ten toes, and ten fingers, gripped into tight fists. Two slender legs, and two strong arms, and a strong heart, pounding under his hand with a reassuring beat.

His gaze went back to the face of his son, and the eyes that stared at him so unwaveringly, attentively. He felt he should say something, but his throat was so clogged with emotion that he feared no sound would come.

A silver drop fell on the baby's face, startling him into a fierce cry. Another fell, and Javan suddenly realized that he wept.

CHAPTER 29

"Bring in the prisoner." Eli stood to make the pronouncement, his voice deep and ominous.

Javan watched him closely, hoping for a sign, something that would give him ease. The other older men moving about close to the long benches by the city gate joined Eli in avoiding Javan's eye. He felt sweat trickle down his back. The sun had many hours to go before it reached its peak. Heat had nothing to do with it.

They had waited overnight to begin the trial, giving Javan time to rest with his wife and child from the birth. Worry had tormented him during the dark hours. He had kept his fears from her.

I will win, Pelet had said. He had been so confident. He had something planned.

A small crowd formed amid quiet whispers, the shuffling of feet, and a heavy, ponderous mood. No one was qualified to give testimony except Pelet, Obed and himself, but they gathered nonetheless. With much clearing of throats, the elders took their seats. A hush settled down. Here and there a baby fussed. Somewhere a donkey made its protest. Javan jumped at the echo of metal being dropped nearby.

The air was still, hot and humid in the last of summer. The smell of dust and warming bodies and the fragrant oil used to anoint the skin tickled Javan's nose. He rubbed away a sneeze.

The crowd waiting behind him shifted, and Javan registered the movement over the turmoil inside him. He turned.

Two large men from the village pushed Pelet forward harshly, overzealous in their new roles. They carried their swords as though uneasy at their weight, the scabbards slapping awkwardly against their legs, and Javan felt their embarrassment at being the center of all eyes. Their duties gave them unexpected prestige, however, and they reveled in it.

Pelet caught Javan's eye, and seemed to smirk. Javan turned his head away. As Pelet walked up close to the benches where the village elders sat, Javan watched them closely for reactions.

What decisions had they faced in the past fifteen, no – sixteen years now? Had they ever dealt with a crime like this one? Or had it been petty thievery, the loss of a bull, a goat or a tunic? Did they rule on inheritance, perhaps?

Such trivial matters! This one carried the sentence of death. The Law was very clear on kidnapping. She had not been sold or killed, but she had been found with him, and by two witnesses. Even without Taleh's testimony, for she had the required week's ban of recovery to endure before she dared come among the villagers, he and Obed were more than enough to prove the crime and demand the ultimate judgment.

Stoning was an ugly thing, but so was what he and his wife had just endured.

Could these men make the decision for death? Did they have the hardness inside?

Eli seemed again to be spokesman. He raised a hand to still the restless crowd. "Pelet, we give you the opportunity to explain your actions."

Pelet puffed out his chest, and Javan's anger simmered at his poise.

I will win. The words from the forest whispered through Javan's head. Pelet knew something, something he was positive would sway the village, some weapon that could tear Taleh from Javan's arms.

"Peace to all," he started. His voice was soothing, and self-assured. He showed no guilt or remorse, nor did he seem to need any. "I am glad for the chance to state the truth. You all welcome and accept Javan. He came here with a woman from Ammon, and presented her before all of you as his wife."

A trickle of dread touched Javan's spine.

"What he did not state, and what none of you know, is that he stole her from me!"

A gasp rose from the gathered crowd behind them. Javan did not dare turn around.

Pelet smiled at him. Hot words pounded against Javan's closed lips. He bit back his fury, and helplessly felt his color rise to match his anger.

The village elders watched, meeting his eyes with no expression in their own. They exchanged glances among themselves.

Eli spoke quietly. "Continue."

Pelet inclined his head graciously. "The woman you know as Javan's wife should have been mine. It is he who should be on trial this day, and not myself."

Javan tasted blood in his mouth.

Eli turned to him. "Have you anything to say?"

Javan nodded. "Ask Pelet why he believes Taleh belongs to him. By what right does he claim her?"

Pelet waited until Eli nodded, and spoke with his smooth voice, his careful words. "It happened in the last city. We, my men and I, were going through the houses, executing everyone we found. Those were Jephthah's instructions, and we obeyed."

The important name brought nods and murmurs of approval from the listeners. Yes, they seemed to be saying, he was only doing his duty.

Javan clenched his jaw. He, too, had obeyed Jephthah. He felt the stares of the crowd on his back.

Pelet raised his hand, just as Eli had, and the crowd quieted. "We had taken some captives from earlier cities, but none that I knew of that day. Javan and his men came from the hill. He had been destroying the altar there." His words were generous, even magnanimous. "They had not begun to search the city. I signaled him to take his men around the back side of the street to cut off an escape route."

Javan's eyebrows went up.

"My men and I were to take the houses, while he and his men handled the rest. To make sure he understood, I called out to him, to tell him what I needed him to do."

Javan blinked at the casual way Pelet made him a mere soldier, instead of an equal. 'What I needed him to do!' As though he answered to Pelet!

"He did not do as I directed." Pelet's voice was louder. "He took his men into the very houses I had chosen. He usurped my role. I asked Jephthah for permission that very day. I told him of her, that I had seen her, that I wished to claim her. Had Javan done as he was supposed to do, had he not usurped my duties, I would have come upon her first. I *did* ask Jephthah first. I challenge you to go to him. He lives not far away. Send a messenger and ask who spoke for her first!"

Javan could only stare at Pelet. He knew Pelet had spoken for a woman. Jephthah had told him that very thing. He tried to remember that first night, when Minnith lay burning and he stayed to talk to Jephthah after the meeting with the army's chiefs. Jephthah had told him he had given permission to several men, he remembered that. But which men? And had Jephthah known that Pelet asked for Taleh?

What happened now?

One gray head turned to Javan. "Surely you have something to say about this."

Javan hastily collected his thoughts. "I do. Pelet's memory differs slightly from my own. He did not wave me *around* those houses. He waved me *into* them. He may have asked Jephthah before me, I cannot say." He could use Jephthah, too. "However, I claimed her in front of my men when I first found her. My claim precedes his. I, too, have men who can be found to speak for me. He knows this. Why else would he steal her away? Did I sneak her into your city? Did I hide her? Or did I rather bring her openly?"

He let his words sink in.

A strong hand clasped his arm. He turned. Obed stood beside him, smiling encouragement.

"My lords, I have something to say as well."

The elders nodded as one, heads bobbing in perfect unison.

"You have not heard the entire story. Pelet left part of it out, part he does not want you to know. This is not the first time he has tried to steal the woman. Before we even got onto Israelite soil, Pelet tried to smuggle her out of the encampment. I know this, for I was the first to stop him."

"Indeed?" One of the other elders turned to Javan. "Is this so?"

"Yes, my lords." Why did he not think to mention it? It might help now. Or knowing Pelet felt his own claim so strong that he had tried once before to guarantee it might tip the scales to him, pushing them to right an error.

"There is more," Obed said. "I was there when Taleh was found yesterday. Pelet needs money to rebuild his home. He reasoned that Javan would pay either to get her back, or to send her away. He can no longer see right and wrong. This has nothing to do with any claim on Taleh. Do not let – "

One of the other men raised a hand and stopped Obed. Javan was relieved. He knew what Obed was about to say. It would not help to tell the village elders they were being fooled.

The man turned his attention to Javan. "I want to know – what was done to Pelet the first time this happened?"

Javan could guess what he thought. Pelet should have been stoned then. He remembered arguing the very issue to Jephthah. Yet, Pelet stood before them all, alive. *If his sin were so great, why had Jephthah not cut him down?* He could see that very question in their eyes.

Pelet had been so certain.

Javan's nails cut into his palms. He forced himself to unclench his hands. "He was not thrown out of the camp, if that is what you wonder. However, when the army separated and we all went home, as you see, Taleh left the camp with me." If it would help, he would plead. "My lords, I am the one who found her. I claimed her before anyone had a chance to see her. Ask her. Ask my men." He searched the judges' faces. No one nodded, no one smiled. Their eyes gave nothing away.

Who did they believe?

"You cannot know, or perhaps you do not remember, what war sounds like. There are screams all around, doors being smashed in, weapons clashing together, shouting, the roar of fire. I cannot deny without exception Pelet's claim that we entered houses assigned to him. I can only say I remember it differently." He did not see that it mattered now, but he managed not to say that. "Taleh has been registered as my wife. I saved the sheet with her virgin's blood. I can present it, but her virginity is not the question. Our first child has been born. All of you are witnesses that I followed the Law perfectly. You have seen."

He met each man's eyes down the bench. None looked away. Was that a good sign?

"She was found with him. Perhaps she wanted to go."

He did not see who asked the question. Maybe it had not come from the elders at all. Outrage seared his veins. "She had been bound! The marks still show on her wrists. I know my wife. She would never leave me. She was kidnapped! He –" Javan caught himself, and went on more calmly. "That man who stands before you stole her from my house, bound her, and dragged her off."

Eli cleared his throat. His tone was level, authoritative. "I understand she was not in fact bound when you found her. We all remember Merab, and what she did to get away. Why would you not think your wife could do the same thing?"

White spots blurred Javan's vision for a moment. He blinked, clearing away rage. They had to ask, he reminded himself. Yet his throat was tight. "Merab and Taleh are different as night is from day. You have all seen my wife, you have watched her work to learn our laws. I spent the winter teaching her our letters, and helping her start to read. Did Merab ever make that effort? Taleh is not Merab. She did not leave of her own will."

The men leaned toward each other, conferring in soft voices. The crowd waited with remarkable patience. Pelet stood where he was, and even with the armed guards at his side, even after Obed's testimony, even after Javan's plea, he looked undaunted.

JAVAN STARED at the elders still huddled together. Nothing gave him a clear view of the debate going on in hushed tones. They leaned together, gesturing into the circle formed by their benches. Fists pounded into open palms, arms swung wide, but the voices came only as murmurs.

How much longer? A two-fold decision, ownership or kidnapping. Did Pelet's accusations of first claims carry weight?

Swollen from heat and standing, his feet ached and chafed against the leather straps of his sandals. He looked around. The women had taken their children home for the midday meal, but a goodly number of people still remained.

Who minded the shops? Most of the shopkeepers and craftsmen stood nearby, or leaned against the walls of houses. Sweat glistened on their faces. Javan could feel it, tight and sticky, on his own. The sun glared down from its zenith, having eaten all the shade that might have offered some relief.

The village elders rose, and Javan stood rigid. They pushed the benches back against the stone wall.

With much shifting of robes and slow, ponderous movements, the older men took their places again. They turned to Eli, who got back to his feet. He faced Javan and Pelet where they stood to one side, close but not too close.

"Not just one, but two questions were brought before us. First of all, to whom does the woman Taleh belong? The second question depends on the answer to the first, namely, which man is guilty of kidnapping. If the woman rightfully belonged to Pelet, the charge of kidnapping would not apply. If to Javan, as the woman was found in Pelet's hand, on the testimony of two witnesses, the charge could stand."

The answer! What was the answer? They all knew the questions. Javan's heart pounded against the wall of his chest. His breath came in short, rasping pants.

"The Law permits a man to take a wife from the captives under conditions. We are all witnesses that Javan met these. Was he entitled to take her as wife? This we must leave to Jephthah's wisdom. He permitted the woman to leave the camp of the army under Javan's protection; therefore, we state before all onlookers today that the decision on the ownership of the woman Taleh was established before she came to our village."

Javan's knees buckled. Obed grabbed his shoulders and pulled him upright, then pounded his back with excitement. Javan found his legs again and locked them to hold himself tall.

She was his!

He rubbed a trembling hand across his face, and saw Obed's smile. He wanted to laugh, to shout his gladness to the heavens, to dance around the gathered men in rejoicing. Instead, he stood in his place, feeling the glow burning through his very veins, bursting from his heart to light up his eyes. Sentence was pronounced, but he did not hear.

A wild scream of rage and terror slammed cut through his dreams. He swung around and leapt away just as Pelet hurtled at him and lashed out with a sharp knife. Where did he get it? Javan braced for another attack.

Men lunged upon Pelet from all sides, burying him beneath thrashing bodies, flailing arms and legs.

A heavy hand thumped on his shoulder. He whirled, still battle-ready.

Obed looked at him calmly. "It is enough. Let the others deal with him. You have only a little time before the stoning. Someone else needs you now."

HER SON SQUIRMED beside her and Taleh came instantly alert. His every sound amazed her, his soft squeaks and funny sighs. She had slept little last night, whether from the distraction of her child or from the restlessness of her husband, she did not know.

Something was happening in the village. She could sense it. It hummed in the air, the strange quiet in the village, Sarah and Leah's whispers outside the doorway, Javan's odd absence.

She pushed her worries from her mind and cradled her baby, to have him turn immediately to the smell of milk. She would not let anything spoil her time with her child. His eagerness amazed her, how anxiously he searched for the nipple and how excited he was when he found it. She relaxed and watched her son nurse at her breast. The tugging feeling surprised and delighted her. How wondrous this all was, that she had grown a child within her, and that her body could nourish it even now. She counted fingers again, and toes. She traced the faint line of an eyebrow, and smiled at his scowl. How dare she interrupt a meal?

A laugh bubbled up. If only Javan were here to see this!

No. She would not worry. It was not good for her milk, Sarah had told her.

As though her thoughts had produced him, the curtain opened and Javan stepped inside.

His face was somber, but his steps were light. She stared at him, feasting her eyes on his face. He took another step inside the room, letting the curtain fall behind him, and stared back at her.

"Come, Javan. Come look!"

Javan bent close, a proud father, to share Taleh's amazement. She reached out and stroked a hand along his beard. Her thumb slid across his lips in their secret game, and he kissed it, knowing she expected him to.

Javan smiled at the babe in her arms, and sat down on the edge of the bed. His gaze moved over her face, an intensity in his eyes. "I must tell you what has happened."

Taleh watched his smile fade. A tightness gripped her heart. Her mouth dried up. Her arms tightened around her child. She wanted to push time back to the happy moment just past and hold it there, capture it like a bird and imprison it.

"Taleh, the village elders called a trial this morning. That is where I have been."

His son gave a frustrated squeak, interrupting him. He waited while Taleh worked the nipple from the tiny, grasping mouth. Javan slid his rough hands under the baby, easing the little bundle away with hands that looked much too large, turning him to the other breast. He said nothing until their child was happily at work.

"Taleh, the village elders found Pelet guilty of kidnapping. In this land, we have strict punishments for crimes. Kidnapping merits the death penalty. Pelet is being taken out of the village even now."

Taleh stared at him, wide-eyed.

"I have to go now, to help enforce the penalty." He paused. "Pelet will be stoned."

"You are going to stone him?" Taleh was aghast.

Javan frowned at her. "Taleh, you should want this. He deserves to die, and die he will. I do not want either of us to lie awake nights, worrying if he will come back. He knew the laws. He knew what he risked when he took you." He rested his hand on her cheek. "You could have died. My son could have died."

"Yes, I know. I wondered several times if it might end that way. But, Javan . . ." her voice trailed away. They would execute one of their own for her? How very strange it was, and how tragic, that a man of this country would die in place of her. "I do not want you to have to bear this for the rest of your life. I hardly expected another to die to avenge me." The past year's pain was still there. It would take time, she knew, for it to fade, but it would. Leah had told her about the villagers and how they waited for the birth.

Javan gave her a sharp look. "Taleh, we must live by law here. We must stand together, or we will be like . . . Ammon. Now, I must go. When I return, it will have been done. You are my wife, and I will keep you safe. Remember that, while I am gone. I will do whatever it takes to protect you." He pressed his lips to her forehead and whispered something, and then he left.

HAD HER EARS DECEIVED HER? He had not really said what she thought she heard, had he? She trembled so hard she feared the baby would wake, and carefully laid him down.

Could it be?

She stared at the light coming through the slats of the lattice. *Please*, she prayed to Javan's God, *please let it be true*. While the sun chased shadows across the floor, she heard his whisper echo in her mind.

She would have to banish the last fear that haunted her. She would take her happiness in her hand, and risk everything. Perhaps his God would deign to hear her, and grant her this most important request.

And then Javan was there, bringing in the scent of fields and freshly turned dirt and satisfaction. She could only gaze at him, wide-eyed and hopeful.

He smiled, and she truly saw something different in his smile. He crossed the room to sit on the bed where he had been not so very long before. She could not look away. He gently stroked the dark tumbled curls off her forehead, then pulled her into his arms and rested her head against his shoulder.

"Oh, wife." His voice vibrated with warmth that wrapped around her as surely as his arms. She leaned back to look at his eyes, dark and tender, and saw those whispered words there. "You have been so patient with me." An odd shyness lurked behind his words. "I have never told you this before. It does not come easily to me. And then you were gone, and I thought I would never have a chance to tell you. I looked for you, and the guilt tortured me."

He took a deep breath, as if to fortify himself. "Taleh, I love you. Not just for giving me a son, but for you yourself, for the joy you brought me, for teaching me to smile again. Even if you had been barren, I would still have loved you."

Tears filled Taleh's eyes, clogged her throat. To hear it out loud, to know those words she had wondered at. "Oh, Javan." Her words trembled, weak and inadequate. "I wanted to hear you say that for so very long. I have wanted to tell you myself. I love you, too. I rejoice that you found me. I am sorry I did not tell you long ago."

The moment had come. Her courage almost failed her. There would never be a better time. She soaked up the love shining from his eyes to give her courage. Only one thing remained to make her life complete.

Fear battled with need.

If she loved him, and she did – Oh! how she did – and if she trusted him – how could she doubt it? – there was no room for this one fear.

"Javan, if I asked you . . ." her courage failed.

He smiled with clear, glowing eyes, his emotion finally freed. "Ask. You know I will grant you anything in my power."

Such a promise! If she asked this of him, she knew she would deprive him of a right many men, not just in his land but in her own, took for granted. She did not know of any woman who had dared.

Take the chance, her heart urged.

She blurted it out, unable to wait for the proper phrase to come. "Will you never take another wife? I do not think I could endure it. Can you be happy with just me?"

JAVAN FELT STUNNED. The puzzle finally fell into place, the haunted look in her eyes that she thought she hid from him, the strange friction that troubled her friendship with Leah. How stupid he had been not to see, that she should have carried this worry for so long!

He set her away just a little, enough to hold her gaze while he still held her arms. "Taleh, you must never keep such things inside. I thought you knew I would not – but how could you? I tell you the truth, since the first moment I saw you, there has been no one else."

"No?"

He smiled at her whisper. "No one. There never will be. You say you ask for a boon. This is not a boon to me. I give you my promise freely, I swear to you by everything I hold sacred, you are all I will ever need."

HAD she thought only moments ago that her heart could hold no greater happiness? She felt it stretch, widening out, catching a joy that was bottomless, boundless, endless. Tossed by war, buffeted by death and strife, Taleh felt like a seed drifting at last onto safe ground. She nestled in his strong arms, cradled and protected by all she had ever dreamed, now come true.

Her home was here, in the warmth of Javan's love.

Read on for a preview
of
Days of the Judges, book 2

His Brother's Wife

Deuteronomy 25: 5,6
(An American Translation)

If there are brothers living at the same time, and one of them dies, leaving no son, the wife of the deceased must not be married to a stranger; her brother-in-law must go to her, and marry her, doing the duty of a brother-in-law to her; and the first son that she bears shall succeed to the name of the deceased brother, so that his name may not be blotted out of Israel.

CHAPTER 1

"You shall not covet your neighbor's house. You shall not covet your neighbor's wife, nor his male servant, nor his female servant, nor his ox, nor his donkey, nor anything that is your neighbor's."
Exodus 20:17

The land of Gilead, 1157 B.C.

"Levi?" Joshua leaned in the open door of Levi's house, and looked across the small eating room, the table where a lone plate holding remnants of the last meal still sat, drying in the summer heat. He called out his brother's name again. He heard something move inside, beyond the whitewashed wall holding shelves where more plates and cups and bowls were stacked neatly, the wall that separated the rest of the house. The sound had been far too light to belong to Levi. "Hannah?"

"Levi is not here." Hannah's voice, barely audible, came from the other room, but she did not appear. It was just as well. How could he face his brother with Hannah's gentle face fresh on his memory, her soft hair the color of the sand by the river, her eyes the rare green of spring leaves? She was all softness and delicacy, the top of her head coming no higher than his shoulder –

She was not his wife! An honorable man would not notice such things about a woman not his wife.

Another sound came, a soft squeak in Hannah's voice, a wince put to sound, a wet sniff, followed by – was that a gasp?

"Hannah? Is all well?" He fought down to urge to step inside.

He would be an honorable man. God had given him the strength so far. He would just have to redouble his prayers . . .

"You came quickly." Levi spoke from behind him.

Joshua spun around, hoping his guilt was not visible. A swath of dark hair fell across his eyes, and he pushed it back, a perfect excuse to cover his face for a brief instant. "I heard a sound from Hannah. I thought something might be wrong."

Levi scowled at him. How awful it would be if his brother had seen, and guessed. "She is my responsibility. You need not worry about her."

Despite his efforts, Joshua could not help the glance at the open door. "Did you want to go look in on her? I can wait."

"No." Levi added nothing more, just turned away from the door. His mouth lifted on one corner as he looked at the rope slung over Joshua's shoulder, and the wide leather strap crossing his chest, a brace for the heavy tools hanging down his back, tucked in the broad loops. "You are well equipped."

Joshua shrugged his shoulders and felt the weight of the tools shift. A wooden handle brushed his spine. Levi's request had come at a bad time, to walk all this way and sacrifice a day of his own work, but a debt was a debt. "Your slave said you needed some help. I brought whatever might be useful." His own work would have to be done again from the beginning, for the metal had hardened before it could be properly refined and poured into the mold, but his brother gave him few chances to balance the scales. If Levi were to ask for a month of hard labor, it would not begin to equal repayment.

So he would work today, and he would not complain.

How long would it be before he no longer felt the weight of the gift his brother had given him? Feeling as he did himself about the farm, how the worry pressed in daily, it was hard to understand how his brother could live there and be content.

"Good. I have some tools of my own waiting. Plan to work hard." Levi grasped Joshua's arm in belated welcome, and turned toward the woods, walking off with his large strides.

Joshua watched his brother for a moment as Levi's long steps ate up the ground, and had to brace himself for a day working on the land. How blessed he was at his end, the better end, of their bargain. He had escaped the chains of their land and gone on to another life, where every day brought challenges to his skill. Levi had never complained, and Joshua knew the land was good. He had seen the loads coming in on Levi's donkeys and Levi's wagons, the yield from the barley harvest, the wheat harvest, the olives, the fruits.

But to be tied to the land, a prisoner of the rains, controlled by the seasons and the sun!

Levi broadened the distance between them, not turning around, as if he assumed Joshua would fall into step. Joshua grasped the leather straps. "Huuh!" He barked with the sharp pull as he hoisted the weight more comfortably, and picked up his step toward the stand of trees behind which Levi was disappearing. The hot sun pierced through the fragile layer of leafy shade, dappling both their bodies with moving patches of light and dark.

Levi led the way through the trees into the meadow where they had played as children. This part of his parents' land was held in trust for his own use, or it had been until he turned it all over to Levi. He had forgotten this section.

But then, he had put most of the farm out of his mind the day he walked away to find his own life.

Levi turned around slowly, scanning the grassy field dappled with white limestone. "This is our work for today." He faced Joshua, the sun at his back, its golden rays lightening the pale brown of his hair. "We haul rock."

Joshua scanned the meadow, the limestone tips poking through the ground and dotting the field with white. The grasses had lost most of their green, but the occasional flower still held onto its petals, blue and purple and yellow. But the main color came from the limestone. "Planning on white-washing your house? Or are you patching mortar?"

"Looking to help me with that also, if I am?" Levi's light green-brown eyes crinkled with his smile, but the sparkle of earlier was missing, and he did not answer the question.

Perhaps he had overstepped his bounds, Joshua thought. Really, what Levi did with the house was no longer his concern and a man's house and all that went on inside it was sacred.

As was a man's wife. He stopped to wipe an arm over his forehead, wishing he could remove his sister-in-law from his mind as easily as the sweat wiped from his face. Levi surely knew all that went on with Hannah. If she had truly been hurt enough to gasp, Levi would know and would have gone in to check. And, Joshua scolded himself, he had no place in that house, and she had no place in his mind. He forced his attention back at the rock, a good way to vent his frustration. And heartache.

They collected the loose stones first, hauling the chunks in rope slings to ever-growing mounds around the grassy field for later. Then they turned to the stones that only poked their heads above the dirt. The sun cooked them as they worked. Their spades chopped at the hard summer soil as they found the edges of the rocks. The soft limestone that littered the meadow hugged the ground tightly, and let go only after much struggle. The piles of white rock grew as each newly released one was added. Joshua's shoulders chafed from the rope that scraped his skin through the robe each time he dug his feet in to pull.

"Why did you not do this during the rainy season?" he finally asked as they caught their breath before tackling another limestone chunk. He flopped down to catch his breath against yet another rock that was larger than they expected, the stone scraping the backs of his legs. His robe was filthy. He stood up, his legs protesting, peeled it over his head, and tossed it to one side, then tightened the knot of his loincloth.

"I did not need limestone then," was all Levi said, looking over the white stone's top from his position on the other side. His own robe was stiff with dirt and sweat. He squinted against the sun. "Are you helping, or are you going to beg off like an old man?"

"Who is calling whom an old man?" Joshua bared his teeth at his brother, groaned, and picked up the rope. "I think it will go beneath now." He shoved the end into a small gap at the bottom of the stone. Their fingers tangled as his brother caught the tip of the rope, then Levi pulled it out the other side.

The sun was low when Joshua finally raised a weary hand. "You have enough rock now, Levi, to begin whatever you wish. If I do not stop, I will not make it back home."

Levi nodded, tossed aside the spade he had been using to push dirt back into one of the deep holes they had dug, and flopped on the ground. "I agree."

They lay side by side, as they had done as children, and watched the fragile wisps of clouds drift past. Joshua did not feel like talking. Neither, it seemed, did Levi. Joshua rolled his head to glance at his brother. How different they were, Levi the older, a quieter, more content version of himself, even in coloring. Levi's light brown hair nearly matched Hannah's in fairness by the end of the planting and harvesting seasons after the sun's harshness, while his own features were so much darker, black hair, olive skin and his odd golden eyes, unmuted with the green of his brother's. Levi's hair was straight, while his own dark locks insisted on curling, and falling in his eyes at the most inconvenient times. Levi seemed happy with his roots in the soil, while Joshua had cut his ties to this land years ago. Levi was the sun, while he was the fierce fire of the kiln.

He sat up and looked around the meadow for his tool strap. It was in a jumbled heap of leather and metal a few cubits away. They had made good progress, but so much limestone still peeked out of the hard soil. He walked over and picked the belt up, arranging the straps and sliding the tools in their loops.

"I am going now, Levi. Send for me again if you need me." Levi merely nodded his head, hair rubbing along the dusty ground, and raised one hand in farewell. Joshua started back across the meadow, his legs tired and dragging. He would have to be careful tomorrow. Working around kilns with hot metal was not for the weary.

He stumbled, caught himself against a chunk of limestone almost as high as his chest, and looked down in reflex to see what tripped him. They had looked at the stone and ignored it, Levi ruling it too large to waste their time. Today was for removing the rocks they could, not for digging out stones the ground might not release. Yet the area around his feet was littered with chips of whitish stone. They matched the large rock beside him. He glanced over at his brother, still resting on the ground. Joshua could not tell if Levi's eyes were open, so he did not bother to call. His brother deserved a brief rest, for while Joshua could go back to the village, Levi had more work to do.

It might have been the chips littering the ground that teased his curiosity, kept him there instead of moving on. Joshua bent down to examine the limestone boulder. A hole left its shadow in the shady side of the rock, the small opening nearly hidden by the growth creeping up its sides. He reached inside, but the hole was small. Someone had been working on it, though, it was the only way the ground could be so littered. He supposed it could be a place to keep food cool as the shepherds watched their sheep. Levi had meant this forgotten meadow for a pasture, after all.

Joshua stepped back and measured the rock with his eyes. It was almost big enough for a grave in this land where bodies had to be buried quickly. There was no one dead, no one even ill who might need it soon, and the hole required much work before it could be put to such use. For now, it made a good place for a shepherd to store the day's repast.

Joshua shrugged, anxious to go to his own home, resettled his tools, and walked away.

CHAPTER 2

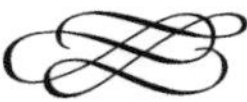

"You shall make judges and officers in all your gates . . . and they shall judge the people with righteous judgment."
Deuteronomy 16:18

HANNAH WATCHED THE MERCHANT COUNT THE FRESH-PICKED EARLY FIGS carefully in the basket. Her mouth watered as the sun-warmed scent reached her. She could almost taste them. Just one. . . But, no, she did not dare. Levi might be waiting for her, and he would never allow such a luxury. He would check the coins and ask for prices, and the numbers had to match. If even one fig were missing, he would know.

He always knew. Hannah suspected him of following her, but if he did so, she could never find him, no matter how quickly she turned to check.

"One more," the man muttered, and reached down into the pile. The scale in his hand swayed gently from side to side and found a balance.

The merchant had not met her eyes since the first startled look when she walked up.

Hannah pulled her long sleeve down and tried to hide the ugly wrappings she had managed to fasten around her aching arm. She struggled to ignore the heat as the sun beat down on her over-dressed body. The day was too hot for the robe and wrappings, but what choice did she have?

It had been three days since this last beating. She would not have come today, but her food supplies were low and she could not take the chance Levi would notice how boring his meals had become – and find her.

Maybe she would heal just enough to endure before that happened.

The merchant handed her back her purchase. He still did not meet her eyes. Hannah looked at the basket's handle, and willed her other arm, the one less injured, to move. It had been hard enough to hand the basket over empty. Such a small measure of figs to cause such pain. Her arm, her shoulder, her back, pain streaked like fire as she lifted the basket and its load over the seller's cart.

She had only begun her shopping. Hannah looked down at the basket and its little load of figs, and tried not to think how heavy it would be on the long walk home. She refused to cry. It helped nothing, and when she got back home, how would she explain her tears?

"Fresh lamb's meat," a voice pealed out. "Slaughtered this morning! Fresh!"

Hannah glanced over at the booming voice. A display of copper pans stopped her cold. The face that stared back at her, distorted and orange, had dark shadows around each eye. One was swollen almost shut. A large, ugly splotch puffed out one cheek.

She gasped. No wonder the fig seller had been so uneasy! If only she had known what she looked like before she came! Levi did not permit her to have mirrors in the house. It was hard to get a good look in the wavy image of a hammered copper pot anyway, so she had worked by touch alone, trying to arrange the headdress to cover the worst of the sore spots.

What a poor job she had done.

She lifted her sore arm, unburdened by the basket, awkwardly pulled her headdress further forward to hide her cheek, and glanced around at the crowd. No one was looking her way. A woman in a green robe busily checked the edges of a length of linen. Another counted something in her own basket. Children shrieked in play.

"You had your thumb on that scale!" The sudden shrill complaint, loud and directly at her elbow, startled Hannah into a jerk of surprise. White heat burned down her spine and around her ribs.

"Never! I run an honest business!" The anger coming from the stall made Hannah's wounded muscles tighten.

Hannah left the fruit display, and stepped toward the vegetables. Her legs were stiff, every movement forced and stilted. She had abandoned her bed in the fresh hay in the sheepfold yesterday because the friendly sheep poked their curious noses into bruises and bumped into her, piling new pain on old, nudging her aside as they sought their own comfort, so she had found another last night, under the empty sacks in Levi's own shed. Why he had not looked there yet surprised her, but she was grateful. She would have to find a different place tonight. Three days was a frighteningly long time to go without being caught. She watched for Levi each time she had to venture out to make another meal, peeking out from her hiding place, creeping carefully into the house only when she knew he would be far away.

Why Levi had not come inside the day Joshua had heard her still surprised her, but perhaps it was simply his brother's presence. Joshua had even called her name, and yet Levi had remained outside. He could have strode boldly into that room and pinched and twisted in all the places that would cause pain, all the while crooning the most loving of words for Joshua's listening ears, but he had not. She would not count on such mercy happening again.

Under the spreading awnings that drooped between their support poles at each seller's stall, huge woven baskets sat on wooden tiers, their tempting display sending fragrance into the air. The rich soil of the hills of Gilead produced abundantly: grains, fruits of all kinds, from the common figs, fig-mulberries and olives, to pomegranates, apricots and citron, and vegetables, carrots and beans, onions, peas, leeks and lentils. Her garden produced the common foods, but Levi always found a way to ask for what it did not grow, seeds he would not buy for her – radishes, cucumber, spinach, turnips and eggplant.

So many ways to punish.

Hannah stared at the rich display before her. She had wept and pleaded with God, made endless bargains for the child that would spare her Levi's abuse, but God had not heard her, or if he had, he had not answered, and she had no place else to turn.

She went to set the basket down carefully, trying not to bend. It slipped from her fingers and landed with a soft thump on the ground. She reached across the piles of vegetables for the spinach at the back of the tiers of produce, so far away. The basket at her feet teetered. She leaned down to catch it, too quickly.

"Ooo-oo!" The moan burst out.

No one noticed. Children still played and yelled and ran through the market. Metal clanged from the metalworker's cart. A donkey brayed. Laughter echoed around her. People called back and forth. The woman still complained about the merchant's cheating, attracting a small crowd.

It was a slow process filling the large basket one-handed with things she needed to please her husband. She hesitated over the garlic that scented the air. Should she get some, and add it to her own bowl of stew? Would that keep Levi away from her?

The urge for subtle revenge passed, squashed by the reminder of Levi and the power of his anger. When had she become this cringing creature? How many beatings had it taken?

How much longer could she endure?

Out of the corner of one eye, she saw Joshua, Levi's brother, tall and dark-haired, standing at another stall. She turned her head away quickly, praying he had not seen her. He was tall enough to see over the heads of most of the villagers, he could easily spot her. And if he came over for a friendly greeting and asked about her face, she could hardly tell him the truth, he would never believe it, and she did not feel up to lies. The fig seller had guessed without being told, she was certain of that, but Joshua? Never!

A hand touched her shoulder. Hannah went as still as death, afraid even to breathe.

"Hannah?"

A woman's voice. She took a breath, easing her burning lungs. The buzzing in her ears went quiet.

"Hannah? Is anything wrong?"

She forced a smile and turned. "Hello, Taleh."

Taleh's mouth dropped open in a silent gasp. "Oh, Hannah, this cannot continue." She reached out and touched a spot on Hannah's cheek. Even under her gentle fingers, it set up a throbbing. "Hannah, Javan can help you. He is one of the elders now. He can do something, speak to Levi, whatever will stop this. I thought abuse was not permitted in this land. Why do you say nothing?"

"No!" Hannah heard the fear in her own voice, and fought it back down. "No, please, Taleh, let it go. Please."

"But you should not have to live like this!"

"Has anyone in the market said anything?" Hannah tried to turn her head, but Taleh would not permit it. Her touch on Hannah's cheek was careful, but firm. "I look frightful. I did not realize."

"People *should* know, Hannah. Perhaps that would stop him." Gentle, mild Taleh's voice held a scorn that surprised Hannah. She took Hannah's hands and squeezed carefully, as if she feared the simplest touch would cause more pain. "Please let me say something to Javan. We can fix this, Hannah, we can. Javan can make him stop. Maybe all it will take is the warning that people know."

Misery dragged at Hannah. How could she feel so old, and be only twenty and six? Taleh had ten years more, and seemed younger. Was that what being cherished did, form a shield against time? *What will I look like in ten more years*, she wondered. "Please say nothing, Taleh. Please, for my sake. It will only get worse. Besides, it is my fault. If I could give him a child, all would be well." She tried another smile, but it trembled, so she let it fade.

"Is *that* what this is about?" Taleh's voice was dark with disgust and disbelief. She wiped away a tear Hannah had not even known was there. It left a cool trail. "If you are afraid, come to us. We will give you safe haven. I mean it." Firm words, a promise. "Come to us. We are closest."

Hannah dared not bring another into her own horrors. "No. Your children . . ." she started.

"Javan and I will take care of our children. He was a soldier, you know." Taleh let go of Hannah's hands and started to turn away, then changed her mind and turned back, raising her finger like a scolding mother. "If I see you like this one more time, Hannah, nothing will stop me from interfering. I never thought to see women treated so in this land. I thought I had left all that behind when Javan captured me. I do not intend to let your husband bring such fear into my life again. I will *make* Javan take action, and I will visit you, to keep watch at least, as often as the children will permit me to get away."

Such a tiny woman, so much determination. Hannah knew enough of Taleh's history to know she meant what she said. She had endured life among the depravity and brutality of neighboring Ammon, the death of her own family in war, a trek as prisoner across the desert, the initial distrust of this village, kidnapping – why should Levi frighten her?

A little of the aloneness faded before Taleh's quiet resolve. "Thank you."

Taleh's oldest daughter, a pretty girl of about ten with straight, midnight-black hair, the most recent baby clinging awkwardly around her neck and wailing, pulled at her mother's sleeve. "Mother, please take Saul back. He will not stop crying, and I want to go play with Tamar."

"Thank you, Jochabed. You were a big help." Taleh reached out to caress her daughter's cheek like she had done to Hannah, and plucked her baby away, smothering his sobs against her shoulder and crooning.

Anguish, deep and visceral, squeezed Hannah's heart tight as she watched what she had been denied. She turned away, but Taleh must have seen. She opened one arm and wrapped Hannah in a cautious hug. She said nothing, for what was there to say, but there was compassion in her gaze.

HANNAH CARRIED the heavy basket on her good arm away from the busy market, feeling the pain rip through her with every step. It would take longer than ever to make it back home, and the evening meal would be late.

She could not let herself think about it. She clenched her jaw and kept walking.

The edge of the village beckoned, the last of the whitewashed stone houses leaning against the thick rock walls that protected the inhabitants from the dangers outside. Above the walls, Hannah saw the grassy hill give way to the trees that framed the small town. She had almost made it outside. Just a little farther and she would be safely away from people, away from the threat of being bumped or jostled. Away from the threat that someone else would notice and ask questions, and she would have to come up with a believable lie.

Someone ran past her through the smaller west gate, likely from the lands outside the city, heedless of anything or anyone blocking the way, and shoved her in their frantic haste. Pain screamed through her. Above the agony that clamored within, Hannah noticed voices yelling and the sounds of anxious commotion. She leaned against the rough stone wall of the nearest house, shuddering as she tried to keep well out of the way of the crowd that bore down on the messenger.

The pain eased as she took careful breaths. A strange awareness grew. Fingers pointed at her, heads swiveled to look, and the crowd parted slowly, like the Red Sea in the days of Moses. At its center, she saw the runner, bent over as he gasped rasping breaths. An old man with thinning gray hair, who had clearly come a long way.

Then he straightened, and she looked into familiar faded brown eyes.

Halel, her husband's most trusted slave. Joshua stood by his side, his face a ghastly pallor. He looked in her direction, but Hannah did not think he even saw her.

"What is it?" Her voice scraped like rough gravel.

"Levi . . ." the slave only managed the one word. Hannah waited in numb stillness.

"Levi . . ." he tried again, "is dead."

ABOUT THE AUTHOR

ABOUT THE AUTHOR

Mary Ellen Boyd is a romance author whose passions are in Regency and most important to herself, Biblical fiction, although if the muse strikes, she will happily branch into other genres. Her special passion is building a fictional story around a factual account. She is always on the lookout for another tidbit that begs to become a novel.

She lives in the beautiful state of Minnesota (and yes, it does get hot there in the summer). She and her husband have been happily married since 1982, in May, the prettiest month of the year. They have one son, who is now married himself to his high school sweetheart.

To follow her and receive news of any upcoming releases, you can follow her here:

http://www.maryellenboyd.com/newsletter/

ALSO BY MARY ELLEN BOYD

His Brother's Wife

Warrior of the Heart

Days of the Judges box set

Regency books Available On Kindle and in paperback

Fortune's Flower

The Thief's Daughter

This Time Love

Made in United States
Orlando, FL
21 May 2024